ORGAN
HUNTERS

ORGAN
HUNTERS

Gordon Thomas

Chapmans

First published in Great Britain in 1994 by Chapmans
An imprint of Orion Books Ltd
Orion House, 5 Upper St Martin's Lane, London WC2H 9EA

A CIP catalogue record for this book is available from the British Library.

ISBN 1 85592 818 3

Typeset by Deltatype Ltd, Ellesmere Port, Cheshire
Printed by Clays Ltd, St Ives Plc

To
NICHOLAS and NATASHA
For making life what it is.

SPECIAL THANKS

The House of Chapmans
A new home has not diminished their loving care – especially
Julia Martin.

Caroline North
Once more for some superb catches.

Sean Carberry
Once more he played a role way beyond friendship.

Paul and Mary McGrath
Eagle-eyed as always – and for the fun of it.

Noel Walsh
No one is owed more.

Frank Dolan
For making so much possible.

Catherine Egan
She shared the darkness – and was the first to see the light.

Johnny Quirke
More, much more, than a name including, of course, Rachel's.

Mary Ellen Doyle
For achieving the impossible.

and Edith
Against all the odds she made sure this book became what it is.

1

The smell seemed to travel faster than the red of dawn colouring the dusky sky in this corner of the Indian subcontinent; the stench of poverty subsumed by something even more universal: human fear. It clung to the young woman, souring her body as she stumbled across the wasteland. Those who had spent the night here – the poorest of the poor – looked the other way, creating their own private spaces, wanting to be no part of what was about to happen on this moonscape of smoking fires and picked-over garbage; surrounded by more than stink, by hopelessness; they were the wretched who would never inherit the earth. As the woman passed, a man squatted carefully, placing his feet with the precision of a dancer, before relieving himself. Another cleaned his teeth vigorously with fingers dipped in a fetid puddle. Holy cows wandered across the ground, depositing unholy smells, adding to the powerful reek of human excrement and pollution.

A van stood parked at the edge of the wasteland. From it had emerged the two men who were now pursuing the woman. One carried a plastic box. Both wore green coveralls, the type medics use, and sneakers which squelched through the garbage. Their dark glasses marked them as city people. But it was their rubber gloves which were a final proof for the human vultures beginning to pick over the fresh garbage dumped during the night. The men reached the woman as she glanced desperately back.

'No!' she screamed, the first and last words those close enough heard her cry. They pretended not to hear.

One pursuer expertly strangled her with a looped wire, the other pulled open her shift. His companion took from the box a scalpel and cut into her chest cavity, then used surgical shears to rip through the ribcage. With the knife he snipped free her heart and placed it in a plastic bag in the box. From first to last the removal had taken no longer than one of the women tending her fire needed to quick-bake her morning bread.

She, along with all the wretched of the earth, had seen this happen before, many times. The woman had been sold by her family to a dealer in human organs, one of very many on the subcontinent. Her family needed his money to keep themselves alive a little longer. The dealer had sent the men to collect his part of the transaction.

Reaching the van, one of the men tossed a coin to a hovering scavenger, and drove off. The scavenger stripped off the woman's clothes before burying the body to fulfil his contract with the dealer.

The dealer had a client for the heart, a man on the far side of the world, a foreigner rich enough to bypass the lengthy waiting lists in his own land for a replacement organ. The dealer had negotiated through a woman he addressed only as Madam. He saw his respect had pleased her. Now she had arrived in Madras to finalise their transaction. But when he telephoned her hotel suite to say the heart was available, Madam informed him she had just received a call informing her that the man for whom it was intended had died. She sounded calm and totally in control. The dealer proffered brief condolences and went about the business of finding a new recipient for the organ.

In their weeks of negotiation he had created in his mind a picture of Madam. She would be tall and blonde, elegant and remote, with a *memsahib*'s liking for gin and cards. On all counts he was wrong about her appearance and habits. And doubtless he would have been astounded at her reaction to his call. After she put down the gold-plated telephone, she stood in the living room of her palace within the hotel palace, and cursed and screamed so loudly, so terribly, that the junior staff who stood and listened at the corridor door were too fearful to knock, and sent for the general manager. He used his pass key to enter. What he saw moved his dark, puckish face to tears. Such naked grief he had never witnessed in all his years as a hotelier.

Madam returned home still consumed by her loss, which had taken her to the very edge of madness. For months she lay in a private nursing home, while some of the very best doctors and nurses worked to heal her mind with a careful balance of drugs and psychotherapy. Gradually, she appeared to return to her former self.

On the day of her discharge, her chief psychiatrist reminded her again that to have loved so dearly was both noble and life-sustaining, and that the way to cherish those feelings was to perpetuate the memory of her loved one. Given the great fortune her lover had left her, there was almost nothing she could not do. The doctor had suggested she should endow a foundation, build an art museum, launch a charity; with her wealth the opportunities for philanthropy were endless. She must do something to constantly remind her of the only man on earth she had ever loved.

Later she realised, the doctor's well-meaning words finally dredged from deep within her subconscious, what she had always planned to do. After all those months of treatment she knew no one could possibly now match her strength and ruthlessness. And no drug nor therapist had been able to uncover her need to take revenge on a world which had cheated her of a life with the one man she had respected as her equal.

She had planned with the utmost care and stealth, always working through others, never revealing herself. To the world she was now one of its richest women. She had played the role for perfection, while using a portion of her new fortune to investigate all the ramifications of the traffic in human organs. She had discovered much that shocked, albeit brieflly. She asked herself questions she suspected others had already posed. Do the world's governments really want to keep the terminally ill alive? Or was there some hidden international agenda which paid only lip-service to prolonging life? The fate of ordinary sufferers, the million or so who at any given time need a replacement organ, did not concern her. Her interest lay only in a relatively small group. Through them, she would take her revenge. Once more she had moved with the greatest secrecy.

She had spent vast sums of money to create a network of companies and institutions so cleverly interlinked that only she knew all their intricacies. Sovereign, proud and expansionist, under her iron control, the conglomerate was as ruthlessly

11

acquisitive and exploitative as any mediaeval kingdom, as far-flung as the British empire had been once, as cohesive as the states of the American republic still were. The conglomerate maintained its own private security force, intelligence service, banks and airline. It had its own hospitals and even a worldwide network of fitness centres.

To all those it employed, her empire was known as the Organisation. She remained its first and only head and had chosen to be known by the same respectful title the Madras organ- broker had used. Madam.

With the Organisation up and running, Madam had set out to take her revenge on the inhabitants of the earth who spent more money on illegal drugs than they did on food, and yet had been unable to provide a drug or a replacement organ which could have saved her loved one.

First she had recruited her medical team and built them a clinic equal to none. Then she contacted the leaders of that other great growth industry – crime – and assured them that if they, or their associates, were in need of replacement organs, she could provide them. To make them understand how little she was asking in return, she told each of them that a billion dollars, measured in gold, was equal to the weight of a grown man. All she required each time was the equivalent of the weight of a man's heart, liver or kidney. It was an offer so eminently reasonable that they all accepted her terms.

And so, with everything in place, the harvesting had begun.

2

Standing in the motel bedroom doorway David Morton allowed the scene to go flat, finding a place in his mind for only all-important first impressions.

He'd briefly wondered if the cop beside him would come to understand the value of this. A couple of murmured questions had told him all he needed to know about the rookie: he was a week out of academy and, until now, had never seen someone dead.

That's what this stranger likes to do, thought the rookie, observe without being observed. Yet he wasn't a desk man, not with those eyes. There was something buried in them, a secret, like his accent. English? You couldn't tell. Everything about him spoke of self-protection. But one thing was sure: he wasn't a cop, or FBI, or even Agency – at least, not judging from those who had been guest speakers at the academy. There'd been a swagger about them, a challenge, a dare-me attitude. This stranger possessed only a troubling intensity. They hadn't said anything about that in the body-language course.

Out of the corner of his eye Morton saw the patrolman moisten his lips. The kid had been plunged right in at the deep end. A corpse that looked as if Hannibal Lecter had been feeling peckish. And the CIA as attendant pallbearers. No police academy taught you how to cope with that.

'Would have been worse if he had been a woman,' suggested the rookie.

Morton affected not to hear. He had no small-talk about corpses.

'Wonder how he ended up here?' went on the rookie, not discouraged by the lack of response.

Morton continued to preserve a dead silence.

'Who are you with?' asked the rookie with too much casualness.

'Whoever you like.'

'You mean mind my own business?' the rookie asked, colouring.

'Something like that.' Morton smiled his on-loan smile.

'Sorry. I didn't mean to pry.'

'It's OK.' He smiled again and gave that quick sideways look. The observer's glance that stays on you after it's turned away.

The patrolman had a football jock's build, all shoulders and no waist. In ten years he'd have run to fat unless he took care. It would take effort to do that. Just as it did to cope with the death which had occurred in this room. 'Ever seen anything as gross as this, sir?' asked the rookie, once more wetting his lips.

'Violent death is always gross,' Morton replied in a voice designed to discourage further questions.

He had done the same this past month in Bangkok, Mexico City and Delhi. He had gone to those places with no more than that indefinable *something* – even now he could not put a name to it – which had always driven him. In the past others had tried to formalise it into a methodology. They had called it 'creating situations', 'drawing fact out of darkness' and 'applying the art of informed conjecture'. It was all that, and more. At its simplest – and most complex –it was the right to violate all the rules of critical enquiry to reach the basic truth. To discover that the few known facts are designed to lead to some distant, unwritten goal. In this case it had been Bangkok, Mexico City and Delhi which had acted as the first stepping stones: what had happened there, and what he had learned since, had reinforced his initial suspicion, confirmed that action could not wait for certainty. Those first victims had established he was right to deal in the middle range of probability – that surmise, a willingness to make an imaginative leap, were as important as the known facts. Because all together they added up to that *something*. As usual, he had shared this with no one outside his trusted circle. Police in those cities tried to probe when he'd viewed other bodies which had undergone the same desecration. You almost expected it in places like that. But here, in Washington?

And it had happened to Ronald Stamp, who actually worked for

Hammer Force; in the end had worked for him. One of those life-is-strange coincidences? Or had Stamp used his vacation for a little private sleuthing? But he had been a desk man, one of the Prof's team. The Prof ran Psychological Assessment with a firm hand, and he'd have fired Stamp quicker than you could say psycho-profile if he'd ever suspected the researcher was stepping out of line.

The Prof had said that with Stamp you were still talking potential: *Lively mind. Can spot the uglies quicker than most. But his heart still leads. Another year he'd have been on the Top Desk. Drugs, arms, money-laundering. Could have handled one or all of them. But not yet. Such a waste, such a waste. Think this is connected, David?*

Exactly the same question had filled Morton's mind while he stood in the doorway of the motel room. Those other deaths had been similar. The same surgical skill involved; the same surprised looks on the victims' faces. Tenuous, maybe. But enough to confirm that once more he was right to deal in the realm of surmise. Speculation was a way of life. Others, he knew, were sometimes shocked by his seeming lack of precision; his readiness to resist the obvious: that the killings were the work of ritualists, or a demented serial killer with flesh-eating tendencies. Instead he knew the connection between the slaughters was different, even if he could not yet define who, exactly, was behind it. That, too, was a part of his *something*, to be comfortable with giving suspicion the same credibility as fact. That was a part of what he himself was, someone always ready to fill in the gaps, recreate the conversations no one had recorded, mesh what had happened with all the finer details of life – or, in Stamp's case, death. But all this he also kept to himself for the moment, not only out of a natural self-restraint, but because it was also a part of that *something*.

Now it posed one question in his mind.

How had Stamp ended up in a motel within walking distance of the White House, half a world away from his computer, dead and minus his kidneys?

Who needed them was easier to answer. The same person who required the heart ripped from a French paedophile in a Bangkok brothel, the liver of an Australian backpacker in that Mexico City flophouse, or the eyes of a respectable German tourist, taken while she was sightseeing in the grounds of a Hindu temple in Delhi; each killed by someone who understood enough anatomy to know how and where to cut.

Local law enforcement said the murders were committed by cultists with a hunger for the more bizarre forms of ritual killing. They had pointed out there were scores of sects in Asia and Central America for which eating human flesh was a requirement. He hadn't pressed the point. Those deaths were nothing to do with appeasing the gods of voodoo or offering sacrifices to Satan incarnate. Any more than was Stamp's.

Once more the rookie broke Morton's reverie. 'At the academy we had a seminar on grave robbery and mutilation of the dead. There's over a thousand such reportings a year. Our lecturer said not one has ever been proven. He should see this.'

Morton pretended to address the matter for the first time. 'He'd probably still tell you that policemen look for explanations which make sense, especially to juries.'

The rookie looked uneasily into the room. 'Who would do this?'

'Good question.'

'Any thoughts?'

'No.'

'You play it pretty close.'

'Yes,' Morton replied more firmly. The kid had been trained in checks and balances, where evidence was tagged, cross-referenced and secured in plastic bags. He'd wanted reassurance that this killing was part of that world. It wasn't.

Lester Finel's computers – Hammer Force had the very latest – had established that in the past six months there had been a hundred similar cases of stolen human organs. A Canadian in the Australian outback, with his heart and kidneys removed; police said dingos were responsible. a Dutchman in a mountain hut in Peru minus his liver; ritual killing, insisted the Lima Federals. The youngest victim was a six-year-old girl in Sarajevo; she lost everything. The organ thefts were spread across all five continents. He'd told Lester to subject every case to detailed analysis. The computer chief had cautioned that could take weeks, given that special programmes would have to be written to take into account each victim's tissue-matching capability and much else. He'd also explained that the number of cases would increase as his computers sifted and collated. Lester said they could be looking at a thousand, perhaps even more, victims.

Morton had known then that this was something evil almost beyond belief. There wasn't a transplant hospital without its waiting list. Someone had seen how to profit from that. Someone ready to take life and grant its extension to others wealthy or powerful enough to pay. A million dollars apiece for a new heart on demand would be a small price, with appropriate rates for other organs. Lester's figures showed organ-stealing was already a billion-dollar industry. As medical techniques continued to increase longevity, the demand would grow. Soon stolen organs would rival drug-running in profitability.

Morton glanced at the patrolman. The kid's throat was working as he stared fixedly into the bedroom. 'Go stand by the corridor window for a while,' Morton said, not unkindly.

'Thank you, sir.' The rookie smiled weakly as his stomach turned and walked to a window overlooking the interstate. How could this guy just stand there and not show anything? He shook his head at the enigmatic ways of the mortician he had decided Morton must be. Only someone used to death could remain so comfortable in its presence.

Morton continued to watch the men around the bed. When they paused in their work there were glimpses of Stamp's body. It was that which had made the kid queasy, leaving too much to his imagination. You coped by looking beyond the obvious. That way you never mistook the beat of the war drum in your ear. A killing like this would need back-up. Surgeons, immunologists and state-of-the-art transplant equipment, plus a totally secure medical facility, with skilled nursing staff. Someone who had put all that together had formed an unholy alliance between medicine and crime. Hippocrates joins the Underworld.

Chantal – Chantal Bouquet ran Hammer Force's Foreign Intelligence – had suggested a short-list. The Triads, as part of their burgeoning global network. Japan's organised crime syndicates: they, too, had the expertise. So did the Russian criminal fraternity, now rapidly expanding into the West. And, of course, the Mafia. He respected Chantal. But his own gut reaction told him none of them were responsible.

There was a new player on the block.

A renegade surgeon, perhaps? Enough of them around. But no surgeon alone would have the resources and contacts to run such an operation. It had to be someone rich and powerful enough to guarantee against failure and who knew the market requirements – who at a particular moment needed a replacement organ and could pay. Someone like that would move in the highest circles and know how to survive in those dangerous places, would be part consummate politician, part old-fashioned wheeler-dealer. Someone whose connections bridged the overt and covert worlds. A Jekyll by day, a Hyde at night.

Before he had come here, the Prof had suggested a number of possibilities: *We're looking at self-justification. For someone who believes it's all done for the best of motives. Like cutting down the rainforests because you believe it's important to provide more schoolbooks. Or someone who believes selling arms to that madman in Iraq, to all madmen anywhere, is fine, just fine, and only becomes a crime when they use them. Or someone who's become bored with venture capital and corporate raiding and wants a different buzz. That someone will say that procuring replacement organs by any means is fine, just fine, as long as they go to the right people. All those, for a start, who believe it's also fine, just fine, to chop down the rainforests. We're looking for someone with self-justification on a manic scale. A Hitler crossed with Stalin, with a touch of Saddam thrown in.*

But the Prof didn't have a name.

Whoever it was had to be stopped – fast. That Stamp was the latest victim only added to the urgency. Not in any emotional way – in his work there was no room for the heart to lead. Only a time to allow the adrenaline to surge, to make a snap judgement in all those places where the stakes are highest, where the gap between human strength and weakness was no more than a heartbeat; where it was kill or be killed. Or a time to stand perfectly still, breathing slowly and evenly, absorbing information with his eyes and nose. A time like now. When the heart still doesn't lead, you just pretend it does.

One of the men around the queen-sized bed glanced towards the doorway. Morton nodded to Bill Gates, the CIA's Director of Operations. Theirs was a bonding forged out of mutual respect and tempered by previous battle experience. But it was not quite time yet to rekindle the past.

He watched Gates wrinkle his nose before turning back to view the others around the bed. Even here in the doorway, death's own special odour was unmistakable, and by now six hours advanced.

That was the elapsed time since Bill had telephoned his office above the north, and less fashionable, shore of Lake Geneva. The building had once been the repository of Switzerland's gold reserves and now served as Hammer Force Headquarters. Afterwards, he'd pulled Stamp's file from Records. His parents were both dead from natural causes; he had no siblings. Stamp was single and in no steady relationship. In a week's time he would have been twenty-nine and had been with Psychological Assessment for almost three years. Previously he'd taught computer science at a Whitehall-sponsored think tank. He'd gone there on passing a Foreign Office selection board after coming down from Trinity College, Dublin with a First in History.

His last medical report had once more passed him physically fit. A note from Personnel showed he'd booked his holiday to the States three months previously, and had provided an itinerary. The usual procedure.

Morton had asked Anna Cruef to run a trace on Stamp. There was no one better at doing that. Anna worked for the Prof. Next he'd sent for Danny Nagier, his surveillance chief. Long ago, Danny had passed the hardest of all tests, loyalty – that special kind of loyalty which came from sometimes going against the book. He'd asked Danny if he had any ideas. Danny had sat for a long while before shaking his head. That was Danny; he never ventured an opinion unless he could support it with at least a couple of wire taps. That was good. Tommy was different: he was always ready to plunge and plunder possibilities. Perhaps it was because Danny's boy had so much to live up to. That was good, too. You needed that kind of balance when feeling your way towards the secret centre, blindfolded, knowing that the action could not be kept at bay for long. He'd told Danny to put together a team and to include Tommy.

The first orders given, Morton had driven round the lake to Geneva-Contrin Airport. He'd used the carphone to call Yoshi Kramer, catching the neurosurgeon between operations, and explaining he was going to Washington but still planned to be in Stockholm to see Yoshi collect this year's Nobel Prize for Medicine. His old and close friend had spent the last five years developing a surgical technique to successfully remove a cerebral embolism, a blood clot in an artery, in part of the human brain hitherto inaccessible. In its telegram, the Nobel Foundation had said the method had already saved the lives of thousands of stroke victims. Yoshi had sounded tired. Morton was one of the few who knew the reason. Three months ago Yoshi had walked down the corridor of the Geneva Medical Institute where he worked to the office of a colleague. An hour later the cardiologist confirmed what Yoshi already suspected. An excess of fat on the wall plaques had constricted the arteries supplying his heart muscles. He was a classic case of a heart attack waiting to happen. Yoshi had agreed to undergo surgery after Stockholm.

By the time Morton drove on to the tarmac, a flight plan had been cleared to Washington for Concorde. The aircraft was a flying battle headquarters and formed part of the deal which led to the creation of Hammer Force. Born out of intelligence failures in the Balkans, Middle East and South America to give advance warning of particularly horrific incidents, its midwife was a far-sighted United Nations Secretary-General who'd seen the need for an independent strike force. He'd persuaded the big seven world leaders to provide secret funds to create the Hard Attack Multinational Megaresponsibility Emergency Response Force. Morton had shortened it to Hammer Force.

His matchless record for the past twenty years in intelligence made him the only choice as its Operations Director. He had asked, and been granted, unchallenged say on targets and how they were dealt with. There was also an unwritten understanding he had full and immediate access to presidents and prime ministers – to anyone – with no questions asked. He reported to the Secretary-General only on a strict need-to-know basis.

Out of the corner of his eye he saw the rookie was back. 'Feel better?'

'Yes, sir.'

'Get your watch commander to let you stand in at an autopsy or two. That way you'll get a proper distance and respect for death,' Morton advised quietly.

The patrolman nodded. Once more that sideways glance. Only now the mortician looked more like a boxer, chin tucked a little lower as he waited for the bell.

On the flight to Dulles International he'd studied the reports faxed from Washington. A floor maid had found Stamp and run screaming to the motel manager. He'd phoned the local precinct. They'd sent a couple of uniformed officers who had promptly called Homicide. The two-man detective team had found in Stamp's suitcase pointers to his holiday activities. The stub of a Disney World three-day pass; another for the NASA facility in Houston. A used ticket from a helicopter ride over the Grand Canyon. Hotel bills showing a single-room occupancy. And an almost used-up book of tickets for Keep-U-Trim. Stamp had visited one of its health clubs in each city on his itinerary. His airline ticket showed he'd arrived in Washington only a few hours before he was killed. The detectives' interest in his murder had ceased when they found Stamp's Hammer Force ID. The card bore the overprinted logo in pale blue lettering, UNITED NATIONS, and the signature of the Secretary-General. The FBI's preliminary search of the room had turned up nothing further. Whatever other investigations the agency had planned came to an abrupt halt once the CIA declared its interest.

Clearing the decks was Morton's first priority. A crime like this drew all kinds of people out of the woodwork. The last thing he needed was some hotshot from Public Health claiming this was his investigation. Shut it down now, Bill, he'd said from the Concorde's onboard communications centre. Bill had reminded his Director that the CIA was the only US federal agency mandated to work with Hammer Force.

Gates had arranged to bring his own team here to do the necessary forensic preliminaries. Stamp lay on an autopsy sheet, waxy and shrivelled from the loss of blood from the hole in his loins through which his kidneys had been removed.

Morton walked over to the bed.

'David, let me introduce you,' Gates said. His manners had always been exemplary for an operational encounter.

The two men on his left were technicians collecting body samples. The wiry little man with a permanently indignant expression on his right was the Agency's forensic photographer. They both nodded, then continued labelling their specimen pots and rolls of film.

Gates turned to the last in the group, a middle-aged man with a thin black moustache wearing a perfectly tailored three-piece suit protected by a plastic apron. 'This is Dr Sternway, our pathologist.'

Dr Sternway's head was bent over Stamp's abdomen, inspecting it with a headset and lamp. 'Good afternoon, Herr Colonel Morton.' His pale face was now close to Morton's.

'Good to see you this side of the wall, Herr Professor,' Morton said, matching the pathologist's formality.

For years the pathologist had provided Langley with details about the medical condition of former East Germany's Communist rulers. He was among the first of its assets the CIA had retrieved after the collapse of the Berlin Wall.

'It is fine to be here, Herr Colonel.' Dr Sternway's tenure at George Washington University had done nothing to loosen his Prussian rigidity. Nor had anglicising his name from the German – Sternwullerweg.

'You find anything?' Morton asked.

The pathologist switched off the headset before he spoke. '*Ja* –of course. The removal was professionally done with a scalpel, and retractors to keep free the opening.'

Morton looked at Stamp's body with its large crescent-shaped cut. 'Was he still alive?' he finally asked.

'*Ja* – yes, almost certainly. The volume of blood loss points to that.'

In places the skin was turning reddish-brown. The staining came after the heart stopped pumping and bodily fluids settled into the lower parts of Stamp's body.

'Was he unconscious when it happened, Herr Professor?'

The pathologist bowed his shoulders. 'If you are asking me if the incision killed him the answer is almost certainly not, Herr Colonel.'

'Then what did?'

The heaviness in Dr Sternway's voice was more pronounced when he next spoke. 'There is no sign of strangulation, axyphasia of any kind, let alone a gunshot wound.'

Dr Sternway had finished speaking, but Morton continued to listen. Finally he turned to Gates. 'Was he naked when the maid found him?'

'Yes. Lying on the bed, face up, spewing blood.'

22

Morton glanced at the ceiling. There were fresh-looking spots. Stamp must have bled like a stuck pig. 'What about puncture marks?' he asked Dr Sternway.

'I've checked the entire body,' replied the pathologist. He used a hand encased in a thin rubber flesh-coloured glove to indicate the headset.

'How about the back of his head?'

Dr Sternway's eyes were fixed on Morton.

'What are you looking for?' Gates asked Morton.

Inside himself Morton continued to be watchful. 'An insect bite, something like that, Bill.'

Dr Sternway's face had developed a second skin, even paler. '*Ja* – OK. I look again, but first you help me.'

Between them they manoeuvred Stamp on to his stomach. Dr Sternway switched on his lamp and brought his face close to the back of Stamp's neck. The silence in the room was total. Morton glanced towards the door. The rookie was gone. In his place stood a woman patrol officer, chewing gum and looking professionally bored. She raised a hand and made a circle with her index finger and thumb. He turned back to the bed.

Finally Dr Sternway straightened, the muscles around the jaw taut. 'It looks like a mosquito bite, Herr Colonel. Where the spinal cord joins the brain stem there is a puncture so small I almost missed it. Even now, under magnification, it is no bigger than a pinhead.'

'So he got bit by a mosquito,' murmured one of the technicians, not quite under his breath.

'Not the mosquito season,' Morton said equably.

Gates laughed lightly and nodded his head.

Morton glanced at the doctor's bag on the carpet, and when he spoke Dr Sternway had to lean closer to catch his words. 'You got anything to test the sugar level, Herr Professor?'

'Sugar? *Ja* – of course.' Dr Sternway rummaged in his bag and produced a standard diabetes test kit. He placed it on the bedside table. 'Help me roll him on his back.' he said. He was no longer bemused, not quite able to keep the excitement out of his voice.

When Stamp was repositioned, Dr Sternway broke the seal on a surgical swab, removed the small spatula and inserted it into the open wound, then placed the blood-coated swab in the kit's tester.

He started the timer. A minute later it pinged. He looked at the read-out on the tester's tiny screen. 'His sugar level is twenty times above normal. More than enough to give him a heart attack. Did you know or just suspect, Herr Colonel?' He was transfixed with admiration.

'A little of both,' confessed Morton. He had asked for the same test to be performed in Bangkok, Mexico and Delhi. Each time the result had been the same. He glanced towards the open door of the bathroom. The curtain was neatly tied back and a paper strip was fixed across the cover of the toilet seat. Stamp had been too far gone to urinate, let alone take a shower.

He turned to Dr Sternway. 'Would I be correct in saying he was probably conscious when his killer came into the room?'

The pathologist nodded. '*Ja.* Such a hypothesis is reasonable.'

The technicians exchanged puzzled little smiles.

'You have a theory about how this was managed, Herr Colonel?'

Morton looked at Gates, who gave an almost imperceptible nod. They were all sufficiently cleared. Morton spoke quickly, as if he were racing his words against the clock. 'Stamp was shot with a sugar fléchette bomblet, not much bigger than a microdot. The weapon could have been concealed inside a rolled-up newspaper or a walking stick. Almost anything you care to mention. Stamp probably felt no more effect than with a gnat bite. But soon his mouth would have tasted like a glucose factory was working overtime. His clothes would have irritated his skin and he would have felt increasingly dehydrated.

'The Chinese are credited with inventing the bomblet. Their secret service gave it to Saddam Hussein's security people to deal with some of his post-Gulf War enemies. We think they used it to kill a leading Iraqi dissident in London and a Kuwaiti diplomat in Canberra. I say "think" because the one great advantage of the fléchette is that it leaves no trace. The bomblet instantly dissolves on the victim's skin.'

Even when he had finished, the silence continued.

'If Baghdad's starting to play dirty pool again, we'll kick ass – hard.' When he finally spoke, Gates' voice showed his tension for the first time.

Morton smiled. 'For sure. But our data bank shows the Chinese have now supplied half a dozen other countries with this weapon. A couple in Africa, the others in Central and South America. It's part of Beijing's drive to win friends. But I'm sure China or its surrogates are not involved, at least not in organ-stealing.' He told them about the other identical killings.

Afterwards, Dr Sternway broke the silence. 'Romer. Herr Doktor Gustav Romer. He was working on such a concept for the Stasi in their research complex near Dresden.'

The technicians and the photographer looked at each other with a collective: 'Never heard of the guy. Never heard of his research complex. And isn't Dresden that place they make all the fancy china?'

Gates enlightened them. 'Romer was killed in an air crash in Ecuador three years ago. Animals had pretty well eaten everything when the recue team finally got to the scene. My people there identified Romer by his briefcase.'

'Anything in it?' Morton asked.

Gates shrugged. 'A lot of promising leads that went nowhere.'

The photographer nodded. 'I remember that briefcase. We weren't told who it belonged to. But as I remember, there was some film stock supposed to be the latest infrared the Stasi were using. It turned out to be stuff the KGB had rejected.'

Morton turned to Dr Sternway. 'Tell me about Romer.'

The pathologist removed his headset. 'One day they will make a lighter frame,' he said, carefully placing it in his bag. When he straightened he addressed Morton's question. 'Romer was the best immunologist the Stasi had. There is nothing more to say. Only that he was the very best, Herr Colonel.'

'What was Romer doing in Ecuador, Herr Professor?'

Dr Sternway shook his head. 'Who knows?'

There was a time to push. Now was not it. Time to wind things down, Morton decided.

'You finished here?' Gates asked Dr Sternway.

'I would like to do a full autopsy, Herr Gates.'

Gates looked at Morton. 'Your call.'

'Go ahead, Bill.' But he doubted whether forensically ripping apart Stamp would produce anything new.

The two technicians unrolled a body bag and began to manoeuvre Stamp inside.

Morton walked over to the dresser. Laid out on top were Stamp's wallet, passport, Hammer Force ID, airline ticket and, in a separate little pile, the evidence of his holiday travels. Morton picked up the book of coupons for Keep-U-Trim. The stubs bore the address of each health club Stamp had visited. The last one, still unused, was here in Washington, on Dupont Circle. Clubs like that would be expensive, probably at the very limit of Stamp's budget, judging from how he had spent the rest of his vacation. Was that why he had stayed in a place like this, saving his money to pump iron in very clearly upmarket surrounds? Vanity came in all forms.

After a moment he slipped the book of coupons into his pocket.

3

In the living room of an apartment near Washington's Union Station, Klaus Klinger changed his appearance back to normal.

First he removed the wire-framed spectacles with their useless clear glass, then the pepper-and-salt wig, and next the cotton wadding in his cheeks and nostrils which made his aquiline face appear pudgy and left a furry taste in his mouth. Then he took off the shoes whose cleverly concealed elevators had added a couple of inches to his real height, five-seven. He unbuttoned his shirt and finally removed the custom-made rubber foam shape which had given his body the appearance of someone run to middle-age fat. Stripped to his vest and shorts, Klinger looked every inch a superbly fit thirty-five-year-old. Beneath his own lank fair hair were hollowed cheeks and, as men of his calling often have, steady eyes and a hangman's smile.

He dumped the items of disguise in the refuse bag left by the Disposer, and walked over to the dining table, where he had placed the briefcase. He unclasped the fastening and took out the set of surgical knives and retractors and the latex gloves he had worn while removing the kidneys. The steel and rubber were stained with the man's dried blood. He placed the instruments in the bag.

He'd been in a hurry to leave the motel, driven by the memory of how close he'd come to discovery in that whorehouse in Bangkok. The surgeon's saw had been unexpectedly loud. Only fast talking and a fistful of baht notes had appeased the curiosity of the rent-boy in the room next to the Frenchman's.

Reaching into the briefcase he ran a finger around the lid of the container containing the kidneys, checking for seepage. They were in a solution that would ensure they remained healthy, and therefore transplantable, for the next twenty-four hours. He had no interest in the chemical properties of the liquid, only that it allowed him a comfortable margin between removal and delivery. He could get back to the island from anywhere in the world inside a day. On the lid of the container was a bold stencilled label in red:

Dangerous Pathogen Sample
Open only in Contagion Laboratory
at
Center for Disease Control
Atlanta, GA.

Satisfied there was no leak, Klinger closed the briefcase with the same care he would have shown if Herr Doktor Romer had actually been here. Thankfully the Medical Director's fury at the slightest lapse in operational procedure was matched by his generosity to those who pleased him. Klinger smiled and, since he had no sense of humour, there was something truly evil about his smile. The Herr Doktor had once said he was evil, adding that that was all to the good. He had accepted that in the same way he had once accepted his reputation in Kommando One; in his two years with the elitist Stasi unit he had killed more enemies of the former German Democratic Republic than any other member.

Yet whenever he looked into the face of the Herr Doktor, he felt a chill colder than the grave itself. It wasn't just his physical appearance, shocking though that was. Or the way that, even when he allowed you physically close, there was a separation which went beyond distance, as if he was constantly flagging and cross-referencing in some secret annexe in his head, yet never taking his mind's eye off you, not for a moment. There was only one person more forbidding. Madam.

He'd once briefly glimpsed her on the closed-circuit television in the Herr Doktor's office. Eyes hidden by dark wraparound glasses and a wide-brimmed hat which left her face in shadow, there had been no way to tell Madam's age or nationality. The few words she had spoken had been in English with an Italian-flavoured voice. But he wasn't very good with accents. And Madam had suddenly broken off, as if sensing his presence. The Herr Doktor had quickly waved him out. Afterwards, though it could not have been his way of apologising, for he never did, the Herr Doktor had explained that Madam was a very private person, implying that everything had been done in the greatest secrecy. She had arranged the recruiting of the surgeons and their assistants and the nurses; the state-of-the-art equipment and laboratories; transportation. *Her real genius, Klinger, is she is able to place the right people in the right place.* Perhaps the Herr Doktor needed at times to confide a little to escape his inner self. And listening, hearing the edge to the Herr Doktor's voice, he had wondered if he had touched a nerve.

A soft breeze billowed the living-room drapes as the air-conditioning came on. He drew the curtains, though the window looked on to a blank wall, then took the refuse bag to the kitchen and pushed it through the flap of the laundry chute. The Disposer would be waiting in the basement.

The Organisation owned the entire building, and others like it across the country. Real estate was one of its many fronts. Klinger didn't know them all. Except pharmaceuticals was one, a chain of health clubs another. And, of course, aircraft leasing. He looked at his watch. The charter freighter would now be three hours out of New York's Kennedy Airport.

In his work, timing was all. It had allowed him to arrive at Washington National just as the flight from O'Hare parked at its gate. Yet it gave him sufficient leeway to buy a souvenir poster in one of the concourse gift shops and place it in its protective cardboard tube, then go to the airport men's room and insert the fléchette gun into the tube. He had also allowed enough time to memorise the face on the photograph faxed from the Chicago Keep-U-Trim. The print showed Stamp working out with weights. The Organisation's Targeter had made a small X-mark over the kidneys. Even without the photograph, he would have recognised Stamp. You could always tell an Englishman in a crowd, and this one walked as if his Queen still ruled over an Empire. The rest was routine. The bomblet struck Stamp in the back of the neck as he entered the taxi. His only reaction had been a shake of the head as if to ward off further gnats. Klinger had followed him to the motel and hovered around in the check-in long enough to learn Stamp's room number. By then Stamp was already looking sweaty and pale-faced.

29

Once more timing had come into its own. A full hour in the motel's coffee shop, a guest with time to pass, reading a magazine. The only other occupant had been an employee, the barman, judging by his uniform, eating an early dinner. When the man left, he'd gone up to Stamp's room and knocked. He'd waited, counting under his breath. After twenty – timing again – he'd inserted a plastic strip between lock and jamb. The strip was an old Stasi standby which never failed. The door clicked open. Stamp was naked on the bed, not quite unconscious.

The final timings had followed a prescribed order. Five seconds to wait inside the door and check the room. No one else. Go to the bed. Remove the surgeon's kit from the briefcase. Position Stamp. Thirty seconds. Then cut fast and deep, the way the Herr Doktor had shown. Stand clear until the spume of blood subsided. Another minute. Then snip out the kidneys and place them in the container. Two minutes. Stamp's moaning had accompanied the entire procedure. He'd learned to ignore such distractions. Four minutes after entering the room, he had been back in the corridor, leaving Stamp still twitching on the bed. Though he was certain no one saw him leave the motel, he'd paid off the cab a couple of blocks from the apartment and walked the rest of the way. He had returned here ninety-five minutes after leaving. Par for the course.

From the kitchen Klinger went to the bathroom and showered, rubbing vigorously to remove the last of the gum which had held the wig in place. Towelling off, he went to the bedroom. The Disposer had already laid out a neat blue suit for the next stage of his journey. Earlier had been work, this was routine; but he still dressed to a timetable.

He returned to the bathroom and changed the colour of his blue eyes to brown with contact lenses. Next he removed an old-fashioned cut-throat razor from the wall cabinet. Draping a towel around his neck, he nicked his left cheek with the sharp blade. Blood trickled down the skin. Leaning closer to the cabinet's mirror, he carefully made a zigzag cut a couple of inches long. The blood ran freely. He held the towel to the wound, pressing hard to staunch the flow. When he removed the towel the cut looked livid. From the cabinet he removed a bottle of surgical spirit and began to dab the skin. The pain made his eyes smart but the astringent sealed the wound. Once more he carefully inspected his handiwork in the mirror. He had made the cut in the same place before. Each time the skin had healed perfectly.

Everyone who had been in the motel would soon be on a most-wanted police computer. But even if anyone remembered him it would be as a greying, overweight, middle-aged man with no distinguishing marks like a scar.

He checked the contents of the wallet which had been left in the suit pocket. A shuttle ticket to New York; a well-used American passport in the same name as the ID card which identified him as a medical technician with the Center for Disease Control.

Still adhering to his timetable, Klinger left the apartment carrying the briefcase containing Stamp's kidneys.

Three hours later, after an uneventful journey, Klinger arrived at Kennedy Airport and walked the short distance from the domestic arrivals building to the international departures wing. The Global Transporter counter was at the end of the long line of airline desks. Unlike the adjoining busy Royal Air Maroc check-in, Global Transporter had no one waiting to be ticketed. An airline poster showed a TriStar in flight, the setting sun bathing the fuselage in a tropical red and burnishing the intertwined 'GT' logo on the aircraft's tail. The Organisation owned five TriStars.

Klinger took a longer and more studied look at the girl standing behind the counter. Her scarlet uniform enhanced the bloom of youth upon her skin. She was tall, and even the ridiculous pillbox hat did nothing to detract from her thick sun-gilded blonde hair, twisted into a braid at the nape of her neck. A Polak, he was certain.

Before going on a mission he always eschewed sex. It made it that much more enjoyable afterwards. Part of his pleasure would be to make no attempt to flirt with the woman; foreplay had never been his forte. He thrust his ticket at her. She smiled and said nothing. He handed over the briefcase and watched while she tagged it as crew baggage, then went to the departure door and presented his passport. The immigration officer nodded him through.

Klinger walked the length of the concourse to the gate shown on-screen for the Global Transporter flight. The Polak was waiting at the cabin door of the TriStar. She gave him another smile and led the way on board.

31

He saw that the briefcase was securely stowed in the rack. The woman tossed her hat on top of the flight bags before locking the cabin door and using a hand-mike to inform the flight deck they were ready for departure. Her accent made him wince. A Polak with a magnificent body and a voice from the Steppes. She turned to him. 'A drink?'

'Later.'

She smiled, such a radiant lovely smile. 'Come,' she said.

He followed her down the cabin. Behind the galley were the two crew bunks and the bulkhead which divided off the cargo area. He watched the woman close the curtains shielding the sleeping area from the galley.

'Come,' she said again, a formal precision to her voice. She hoisted her skirt around her hips as she lay on a bunk. She wore no panties.

'Come,' she said again, even more urgently, fondling him, eyes alight.

He obeyed with a savagery which made her whimper, then scream. And the more she cried out, the more savage he became. It was part of her job to ensure that a harvester found release after the tension of an assignment.

Then her cries were drowned by the even louder sound of the TriStar's engines running up to full power for the long flight to Nicaragua.

4

On the balcony overlooking the beach at Malibu the pianist worked his way through his repertoire of standards. He always played them in the order Madam had requested. Making his way to the balcony, he had heard the guests speculating on where she had come from this time, how long she would be staying and where she would go next.

And, of course, on her business interests.

'My broker tells me she's taking a bold position on gilts.'

'I see that new commodities company of hers was showing a ten-point hike on this afternoon's Dow.'

'She's pulling out of the London market, so my lawyer says. She's worried about creeping Socialism.'

'I hear she's told her shipping people to move back into tankers now that the PLO and Israel are in bed together.'

'You hear about the couple of banks she's just bought in Manila?'

And, of course, about her toyboy.

'He's English. Rough end of the market, though you could never tell now that she's fitted him out. My broker in London says's he's the hottest dick in town.'

'How would your broker know that?'

'You don't know my broker.'

Laughter all round.

And, of course, on her latest local surprise.

'Anybody any idea why she's handed over Santa Chiara to that fancy charity, what's its name?'

'Drug Rehab.'

'Yeah, that's it. Whatever. But why give them Santa Chiara? That could affect land prices.'

'Hardly. She owns all the land around the place. And how many mansions does she need, for Chrissake?'

'OK. But why does she want to stuff Santa Chiara full of foreign junkies?'

'That's Madam.'

Everyone had nodded as if that was eminently the most sensible explanation.

A moment ago the pianist had glimpsed her at the bedroom window. Rumours about what went on there were legion. If only half were true, she was a real ball-breaker. Not that you'd ever tell from looking at her; her demeanour would make a nun seem positively raunchy.

Around the pool the three bars were busy but only the hungry were beginning to hover at the buffet tables. The guests were a cross-section of the privileged of southern California: politicians, lawyers, movie actors, the power-brokers of a dozen professions. Mostly new money and often gauche with it. But even the crassest of them would dare not mention in front of their hostess the source of her own incontestably far greater wealth. That would be a social kiss of death, a reminder of the other woman who had shared the life of the late Elmer Crayton.

The pianist had heard them talking about him in their well-bred voices.

'I figure Elmer taught Madam all she knows so he could perpetuate himself.'

'You think so? I figure she would have made it anyway. Look at the way she saw off Elmer's wife. Now you saw her, next you didn't.'

'Fact is, Elmer needed them both for different reasons.'

'Absolutely. The wife to cook and collect art, Madam to screw him and check the balance sheets.'

'Lucky him.'

'Lucky them. They both came out well in the end.'

'Especially Madam. I hear she's putting half a million into platinum. My accountant thinks I should get in now while it's still trading low . . .'

The pianist knew that while waiting for Madam they would go on speculating about what she did with all her money. How many private planes did she need? At the last count she had three,

34

including the customised 747 which had flown her to California. Or yachts – she already possessed more boats than some countries had ships in their navy. But that still left billions. What did she do with them all? But Madam had made privacy an absolute.

He began to play the last number on her list, the cue for guests to expect her arrival momentarily. When he finished he stood to acknowledge the polite applause. Then, like everyone else, he turned towards the white marble staircase that swept down from the house to the pool area.

French doors leading to the upper patio opened and she emerged. She walked to the top of the steps and paused. New applause, louder and more sustained than for the pianist, swept the pool area. Clapping himself, he smiled cynically. No one knew how to brown-nose better than these folk.

Madam stood silent and still, her customary way of acknowledging their customary greeting.

The glow from the lanterns in the orange and lemon trees for the moment cast her face in shadow. Her neck was concealed by a chiffon scarf; expertly applied make-up gave her face a smooth, wrinkle-free appearance. A long-sleeved smock and pantaloons tucked into calf-length boots cleverly hid her figure. She looked as authentically ageless Californian as any of the women studying her. She could see the envy in their eyes and the glances of appraisal from the men. Her own eyes were hidden from them by dark glasses.

The patio doors closed and Pierre, whom she had selected as her escort for the evening, came and stood not quite beside her, but a half-step behind. It was her way of reminding him of his position, and also a way of reminding herself that no one could ever replace what she had lost.

'Can you see him?' She spoke without turning her head, her eyes continuing to scan faces. In the dusk it was hard to make out those on the far side of the pool area.

'I'm not sure. But that man over by the buffet table looks like a German banker,' Pierre suggested quickly.

She sighed. 'That's the state governor. And he's from a long line of French wine-growers.'

Not that she could entirely blame Pierre. Dieter Vogel had only recently been made the new President of the German Bundesbank,

35

the first East German to achieve the single most important office in the entire financial world. His appointment was seen as a determination on the part of the unified Germany to put the recent past to rest, and to use his expertise to establish itself as the pre-eminent financier in rebuilding the old Soviet empire. She knew that many of her guests were concerned about this. She was not. She had seen Vogel's appointment as another opportunity, one which would undoubtedly require careful nurturing but which ultimately would be of immense benefit to the Organisation. When she had heard the banker was giving the keynote address at the World Bank's annual symposium in Los Angeles on how to restructure Communism's debt, she had flown here and invited him to be her guest of honour at this party. Pierre had hand-delivered the invitation to Vogel's hotel suite.

'You are sure his aide said Vogel had no prior engagement he couldn't break?' she asked.

'Yes.'

'Then find out where he is,' she commanded. This had never happened before, a snub like this. Behind her she sensed Pierre's hesitation. 'Why are you waiting?' she demanded sharply.

'You'll need an escort down there, someone to head off the bores.'

'Tell Dirk to come here. You just go and find out where Vogel is.'

He said he would. He gave her a look that suggested he was a tiny bit hurt to be treated like this.

The pianist saw the knowing looks among the still-applauding guests. Madam's tiffs with her toyboys were celebrated. Moments later another handsome young man appeared to take his place a half-step behind her. Even down to the gold sash replacing his tuxedo's cummerbund Dirk was a physical replica of Pierre.

'You know what to do, Dirk?' she asked. This was his first outing.

'Absolutely.'

'Try not to use that word. It makes you sound a little too English for some of my guests.'

'Sorry, Madam.'

Glancing towards the balcony she began to descend the staircase, followed by Dirk. The pianist swung into an upbeat version of a Neapolitan love song, ending with a resounding scale as she stepped on to the pool area. He would not play again until it was time for her to signal she was leaving.

She allowed Dirk to steer her from one group to another. After reintroductions, she listened attentively, smiling occasionally, and sipped the mineral water she always drank. Once, when Dirk reached to take a second cocktail from a passing waiter, her swift glance was enough to change his mind.

She had a word for everyone: 'Christie's are putting up a couple of good pieces next week, Marcel.' This was to a short, sallow-skinned man. He smiled a predator's smile.

'I don't think you should board Giles in England, Emma. The education system over there is bursting at the seams.' This to a middle-aged woman encrusted in jewels yet still managing to look dowdy. She nodded gratefully.

'Thanks for that tip about Irish bottled water, John. It's certainly better than the French produce. Must be the bogs.' This to a tall, barrel-chested man with a film director's ponytail. He smiled, glad to have been of service.

She spoke about the weather in Europe, the depressed tuna-fish market in the Pacific, the signs of recovery in Japan, a new kind of ginseng just on the Beijing market. And, of course, the rainforests, bankruptcies, the prospect of next year's Dublin Horse Show, and of an absolutely splendid parador in the Basque country. She spoke about everything. Except herself.

It was dark by the time she reached the far end of the pool area. In the distance the lights of Santa Monica and Manhattan Beach sparkled. In the sky the nightly rush out of LAX was easing. She glanced back towards the guests; she knew they had sensed her mood, even though they could not know the reason. She had intended Dieter Vogel's presence to be a surprise, the way in the past she had astonished them with Ronald Reagan, one of the English Royals, or that memorable occasion when Gorbachev had come here. Someone would surely have told Vogel that he risked more than social disgrace by standing her up, that her connections were legendary? That there was no one better at bringing together the movers and shakers of the financial and political worlds?

Her gaze turned to the house. She had designed this place for that very purpose, giving it the appearance of a doge's villa, somewhere where deals could be brokered without distraction. Through the ground-floor windows she could glimpse the wide arches dividing one area from another, and the tapestries hanging on otherwise stark white walls.

'Damn him,' she said viciously, almost under her breath.

Dirk responded in the only way known to his profession. 'The man's a turd.'

'How observant you are.'

In the living room she could see Pierre on the phone, gesticulating. He was good at that; it went with his Latino temperament in bed. But she had shown him that there she was his match, the equal of any in her stable. She frowned. Suddenly Pierre put down the telephone and ran from the room. A moment later he emerged on the upper patio and, hardly breaking stride, bounded down the staircase and began to cut a path through the guests.

On the balcony the pianist watched. This *was* unexpected drama. He settled himself at the keyboard. Pierre reached Madam, his face flushed from running.

'Never do that again,' she said, her voice stone. 'My guests don't like to see staff run. It suggests matters are not under control.' She was standing with her forearm against her chest, as if she was already prepared to ward off a blow.

'I'm sorry. But I wanted you to know as quickly as possible. Vogel has had a collapse.'

'With what?' She managed her most glacial smile, as if she had been asked to invest in the Mexican economy.

'It's a heart attack. Nothing too serious . . .'

The smile had switched to its most patronising: a no to Mexico. 'Is that your diagnosis?' Her head remained angled as she continued to watch the guests around the pool.

'It was what I could make out from his aide,' Pierre said uneasily. For a fleeting moment something ugly had crossed her face, as if a mask had slipped.

'Is he a doctor?'

'No.'

'I see. Do you have a doctor's report?'

'No.'

'Where is Vogel now?'

'He's insisted on being flown home at once. The Bundesbank

hired a medical plane. It's the one they used to bring back the President to Washington when he was taken sick on his Russian tour last year.'

She nodded, her eyes still on the guests. Given what Vogel was trying to achieve, he'd want to be as close as possible to the bank; in Frankfurt he'd be able to turn his hospital suite into an office. 'Did the aide say how it happened?' she asked.

'Vogel was actually dressing to come here when he had this sudden pain in his arm and chest. He was able to call for help.'

'So he didn't become unconscious?' More guests were staring at her, realising something had happened. She smiled quickly towards them and turned to Pierre. 'Call my pilot. Tell him I want to leave at once.'

'Shall I tell him to file a flight plan for Frankfurt?'

'To Stockholm,' she said firmly. 'Have you forgotten? It's Nobel Prize time.'

Once more Pierre saw that look cross her face.

'Use your mobile.' She nodded to the bulge in his jacket. 'There's a darling boy.'

Pierre went to a corner of the pool area to use the phone as she walked briskly towards the staircase, murmuring her goodbyes and urging everyone to continue to enjoy themselves. Behind came Dirk, politely heading off any guest who tried to engage her in further conversation. At the foot of the staircase she nodded to the pianist. He began to play.

Climbing the stairs, she continued to think, the way Elmer had taught her to do. *Always cut to the chase, my companion for life*, he would say as she struggled to master an investment portfolio. *The more complicated it is, the simpler the solution if you strip everything to the bottom line.*

Vogel's heart attack had not been serious enough to stop him being flown home. And on the journey he would have the best doctors and medical facilities. Nevertheless, if he were to die, it would definitely set back all the plans she had carefully laid. Almost certainly his replacement would not be so potentially malleable. A man with Vogel's background – and weakness – came only too rarely. Her staff had researched him with their usual thoroughness and had spent considerable sums of money on acquiring the evidence. The negatives were now in her bedroom

39

safe. Vogel was still alive and she had the evidence now to control him. That was her bottom line.

She reached the patio doors and turned to Dirk. 'Go back and amuse the guests. I won't need you on this trip.'

The pianist saw the doors close firmly behind her and her crestfallen escort turn and walk slowly back down the staircase.

In the living room she went over to the telephone console on a Renaissance side table and dialled a number. When the voice answered in Stockholm she spoke briefly. 'I want you to arrange for me to see Dr Yoshi Kramer.' She replaced the receiver. As a Nobel laureate, the neurosurgeon was about to join the élite of medicine. He would know what she needed to know, and he would never suspect why she was asking. Once she had the answers, she could arrange the next step. And there would still be time. Gustav had said the critical period after any heart attack was the next twelve hours. If Vogel survived that long he would, being the man he was, begin to plan his life ahead. Then would be the time to approach him about getting a new heart. With the memory of how close to death he had come still fresh in his mind, he would be grateful. *Always remember the bottom line. You just remember that, my companion for life, and you'll have no problems.*

She walked over to the Reubens, the only decoration on the otherwise plain white walls, removed the painting and opened the wall safe. From inside she withdrew the envelope containing the negatives and the set of prints made from them. She had studied them many times, but each time was like the first in the revulsion the photographs still evoked. How could anyone obtain pleasure from doing that to a child?

At the time of Elmer's death she had been two months pregnant with his child. The shock of his death had brought on a miscarriage. She replaced the prints in the envelope and tucked it in her luggage. As she did so the bedside telephone rang.

'Your appointment with Dr Kramer is confirmed. It will be immediately after the Nobel Prize ceremonies, Madam,' said Count Olaf Lindeman, the Director of the Nobel Foundation in Stockholm.

5

A couple of blocks away from the flashing strobe lights of the police cars, Morton saw the pick-up truck parked where it was meant to be, outside the building housing the Keep-U-Trim health club on Dupont Circle. Crime-scene ribbon blocked off all access to the Washington intersection and cops were diverting traffic off Massachusetts. From the police radio under the dashboard of the unmarked government car came continuous cross-talk, confirming that the bomb alert he'd asked for had created mid-morning chaos in the area.

'I'll lose more than my pension if this ever gets out,' growled Gates after he'd flashed his ID at another traffic cop. 'I'll be lucky to avoid a spell in the slammer.'

Morton gave his on-loan smile. Bill had a weakness for expressions past their sell-by date. 'It was the only way to make it look good, Bill. Any other kind of emergency wouldn't give us acceptable access. No one would expect the CIA to be interested in a fire or a burst water main. This way our involvement looks authentic.'

Gates grunted.

'Anyone ask awkward questions?'

Gates shrugged. 'Some. You know how it is.'

Morton knew. In operational matters there was always someone who needed to know more than he should. 'Looks like they did a good job with the truck.'

'Should have. It's costing enough,' Gates replied in a voice that suggested he wasn't really worried about the cost.

They continued to watch the scene beyond the crime tape. The Agency's Technical Services division had removed every vestige of original identification from the truck and fitted false California number plates. Thirty minutes ago one of Gates' agents had parked the vehicle on Dupont. Fifteen minutes later another field man had used a payphone in the concourse on Union Station to call police headquarters. He'd spoken with an authentic Irish accent and used the correct codeword.

The result had been satisfactory. Uniformed police and firemen were everywhere. A SWAT team was being deployed on the rooftops overlooking Dupont. Two white-painted vans were parked on the edge of the circle. Emblazoned on their sides were the words BOMB SQUAD. Inside the crime-scene ribbon those grey-suited figures with out-to-lunch eyes had to be FBI. It was authentic, for sure.

'In the old days we'd have used burglars,' Gates sighed, parking the car between a couple of police cruisers.

'And look where that led to, Bill – Watergate.'

Gates suddenly grinned.

'But they weren't our burglars. Strictly second division.'

The Bomb Squad team in white coveralls were manhandling out of a van a creepy-crawly, a radio-guided robot. Its distinctive mechanised arm would be used to detonate a controlled explosion. Another coveralled man had his eyes to the viewfinder of an infrared sensor, searching for the explosives. A colleague was doing the same on the far side of the truck. Morton could see the tension on their faces as they spoke quietly into their lip-mikes. As if in empathy he quickly brushed the back of his hand across his own chin. 'Let's sit for a moment longer, Bill,' he murmured as Gates moved to open his door.

Gates slumped in his seat. These past twenty-four hours Morton had worked from an office adjoining his own at Langley. He had never known anyone who could accomplish so much in such a short time. After David set up a radio link with the Concorde parked in a corner of Dulles International, the aircraft's communications centre had routed information to and from Hammer Force Headquarters. He'd used it to conduct briefings, give a stream of orders and receive progress reports which produced further orders.

Watching, Morton continued to mentally run down his checklist. In Geneva, Danny, Chantal, Lester and the Prof were pooling their considerable resources. Tommy had flown to Florida to begin backtracking on Stamp's every known holiday move. Anna was in London, going through the researcher's previous career. Lester's programmers were trawling for names. After Dr Sternway's autopsy had produced nothing new of value, Stamp's body had been coffined and flown home to England for burial.

Gates finally glanced at his watch. 'Better get going. The Technical Service boys set a limited-time fuse on their fire-cracker in case someone decided to get too close.'

Morton continued to watch the Bomb Squad team. 'What about those sensors?'

'All they'll identify is the shape. At that distance it'll look like all the others those guys are trained to spot.'

Morton reached into the back seat for the silvered metal suitcase that he'd ordered to be delivered from Concorde.

'They've located the charge,' said Gates quietly.

The operative on the far side of the truck was speaking urgently into his lip-mike. His colleague had moved side on to the truck, directing his sensor towards the cab.

'Technical Services placed it under the drive shaft where you'd expect a Paddy bomb-maker to stick it,' Gates murmured.

Behind the crime-scene ribbon Morton saw that their arrival had triggered sudden interest among the FBI agents.

'We've got ten minutes,' Gates said.

Hefting the suitcase, Morton followed him out of the car as one of the FBI agents emerged from behind the ribbon. Morton clocked the shoulder holster, worn high under the left armpit.

'Harris. Agent-in-charge.' He thrust his ID under Gates' nose. 'What's Langley's interest in this?'

Gates ignored the card and shrugged. 'Same as yours, I should imagine. Or have you cornered the market in dealing with terrorism?'

Harris thrust his card back into his jacket and glanced at Morton. 'Who are you?' he asked in the same tense voice.

'He's with me, Harris,' Gates said equably. 'The only other thing you need to know is that he outranks us both. Remember that, otherwise you'll be back on the border.'

Morton continued to study the agent. Harris's breath smelled of something cooked in garlic washed down with vodka. He'd also earned a name for being short-tempered. One day he'd made the

43

mistake of shooting a DEA contact. Harris had been given an hour to get out of Mexico.

'I hear they've got long memories down there,' Morton said pleasantly, shaking his head as if it was all a bit of a mystery.

Harris's jaw worked. Then he turned and stalked back under the ribbon.

'Some people need a mouthwash,' Gates said, loudly enough for Harris to hear.

Morton took in all the familiar movements. More police cars, trucks and ambulances were arriving. Two of the Bomb Squad were priming the creepy-crawly. The sensor men had retreated from the truck.

'Reminds me of Belfast,' Gates grunted.

'Except the sun's shining. And no one gets killed here.' Morton always played his best cards obliquely.

'You're right about the sun. I spent a whole August in Armagh. It rained every day. Makes you wonder what the Brits want with a place like that.'

If Morton knew, he didn't say.

A tall, chesty uniformed police captain was using a bullhorn to order back the people pressing against the ribbon. Which of them worked for Keep-U-Trim? Together he and Gates ducked under the ribbon with the same quick, economical movements and walked over to the Bomb Squad. Morton noticed their hands. Long, almost feminine fingers. You needed them to feel for a contact wire. He'd learned that in Armagh.

Gates showed his ID card to the squad leader. 'We've got to get into the building, Chief. The guys who left this may have also left a clue inside. Give us a clear ten minutes.'

'No problem. But I can't speak for what's in the truck. It could blow any minute. Or it could be timed to go off in evening rush hour. No way of knowing.' The Chief's voice was serene and composed. He had the manners of a first-generation immigrant. Polish, Hungarian, you couldn't really tell any more. Except for the politeness: mittel-European.

'Understood,' Morton said. He disliked playing games with a good man.

Glancing one more time at the pick-up truck across the street, he led Gates into the building.

Keep-U-Trim was on the second floor. Access was through a pair of frosted-glass swing doors on which was painted the health club's name and its logo, Apollo encircled in a garland of leaves. Beneath, in the same gold-leaf scroll lettering, was the slogan: 'We Guarantee to Keep You Trim'.

The reception area was small and plush. A deep-pile red carpet led to an antique desk on which was a telephone console and appointments ledger bound in rococo leather. An inkwell and pen completed the impression of elegance and affluence.

Morton lifted the well's lid; the pot was empty. He rubbed a finger over the pen. Plated.

'All show and no substance,' grunted Gates, pointing to the diplomas on the wall. 'From campuses where they give basic exercise fancy names.'

Morton flicked through the ledger. The place was fully booked seven days a week, from early morning until late evening. Many were regulars. He glanced towards the framed price list discreetly positioned behind the receptionist's gilt-framed chair. At these prices, Keep-U-Trim had the kind of clientele who probably never worried about money.

'Recognise anyone, Bill?' he asked, pushing the ledger towards Gates.

Gates ran a finger down the names and shook his head.

To the left of the desk was a frosted-glass door on which were the gold-lettered words 'Fitness Center'. On the right was an identical door which bore, in the same gold script, 'Medical and Administration'.

Gates nodded towards the door to the left. 'I'll go check. Maybe I'll spot something to beef up the new health spa our esteemed Director insisted on installing now we don't get much practice keeping fit going in and out of Mother Russia.'

Morton knew the Agency's can-do mentality had waned after its mission to roll back Communism ended. Men like Bill were the last of the great mavericks of Langley, always prepared to face the consequences of finding themselves up a creek without a paddle. Bill didn't care what he did as long as the job got done.

Gates went to the Fitness Center while Morton opened the other door. Beyond was a short corridor with several unmarked doors.

Behind the first was a superbly equipped examination suite. A smock lay on the floor beside a pair of men's shoes; a jacket and tie still hung on a wall peg. Morton walked over to a desk along one wall. A nurse – or whoever – had been working on the man's medical report when the alarm sounded. He glanced over the paperwork.

The form identified Joseph Butterfield as a native of Sydney and the Third Secretary at the Australian Embassy in Washington. His marital status was given as bachelor. His age next birthday was stated to be twenty-nine.

Butterfield was being asked the kind of questions you found on an insurance proposal. The diplomat seemed to be in the peak physical condition you'd expect from a non-smoker, a moderate drinker and someone who said he ran a mile every morning. In a section marked 'Reason for Enrolment' was the note: 'Client is a newcomer to the city who has found in the past a health club offers good social opportunity'.

Morton turned over the form. The reverse side contained the outline of a male human body and boxes, each with the name of an organ printed underneath. The boxes were empty. Replacing the report exactly as he'd found it, he left the suite.

The next room was a secretary's cubbyhole, its shelves stacked with stationery supplies. Morton opened the door to another room. Storage. The air was filled with the smell of rubbing alcohol and embrocation. There were drums of the stuff on the floor. Racks of towels and laundered smocks lined the walls. At the end of the corridor was a door marked 'Director'. He opened it.

The curtains were drawn to mute the daylight. A coat-tree stood in a corner of the office. The remainder of the room was mostly filled with a large desk on which stood a VDU terminal, its screen glowing but empty, and a Honeywell against a wall. Behind the desk was a high-backed, heavily padded leather executive chair. The indentions suggested its occupant was a large person. The office walls were panelled in a light wood and unadorned. On a low table a coffee-maker steamed on its electrical hob. Morton sniffed. Brazilian. The best.

Beside the table was a filing cabinet, its doors open, as if someone had either been removing or returning the small pile of computer discs on the desk when the bomb alert interrupted matters.

Morton placed his suitcase beside the VDU screen. From a pocket he fished out a metal probe and inserted it into the first of two holes on either side of the case's handle. He gave the probe two turns to the right, each time waiting for the click, then three more to the left. He repeated the process with the second hole. From inside the case came a faint hissing sound as the protective airlock was released. He lifted the lid.

- The case contained the disc-transporter developed by Hammer Force's Research Division. A dozen experts in electronics had worked on nothing else for the past year. The cost had made Finance wince.

Morton pulled up the stubby aerial from the black bakelite surface. Then he tapped numbers onto the transporter's keyboard, watching them appear digitally on the adjoining screen. A moment later, visual confirmation flashed that the transporter was now pulse-linked to a receiver in Concorde. A technician on board would automatically have established a similar link with Lester's computer room in Geneva.

Morton picked up the first of the discs and inserted it into the maw of the terminal. The screen announced he should follow the displayed instructions on how to proceed. He did so and the screen began to fill with names and addresses in fashionable Washington suburbs. Clients, for sure.

Extracting the disc, Morton placed it on the transporter's turntable, similar to one in a domestic compact-disc player. He lowered the metal hood over the turntable and pressed a button on the keyboard. Fifteen seconds later the transporter's screen confirmed the transmission was complete.

Morton inserted a second disc into the maw. Another list. People? Clients? Staff? Or even places? No way of telling. Just a jumble of letters, like airline baggage tags. But he didn't recognise any.

He sampled two more discs. Both contained further lists of letters that also had no intelligible meaning. He transmitted them. Lester's code-breakers, he suspected, were going to have a field day.

Why would a health club go to such elaborate lengths to hide information? He could understand a need for discretion. People could be touchy about having to work off their extra pounds. But this kind of hi-tech security was normally associated with corporations working in ultra-sensitive areas like defence or the space industry. Why would a fancy health club behave like it was a subcontractor to NASA?

He shoved the last disc into the maw. A word appeared on-screen: 'Password'. He tapped in the command 'Display the password'. The screen ignored the instruction. He ordered the terminal to bypass the demand. The screen repeated 'Password'. He tried every computer trick he knew. Each time his fingers stopped tapping, the word returned.

Morton glanced at his watch. Seven minutes had gone since he'd entered the building. No time left to pit his wits against the computer. He removed the disc and placed it on the turntable so that its contents could begin their electronic journey to Geneva.

Morton walked to the cabinet and began to riffle through the shelves of files. Client billings and paid invoices, Keep-U-Trim was an accountant's dream of what paradise must be; everything in date order and in its right place. More names and dates, like those on the discs, written in ballpoint pen. Membership? Subscription reminders? Stop guessing. Take now, think later.

He completed the first shelf and turned to the next. And the next. Still more of the same. Methodically, he placed the papers back in their rightful places and moved on. The same name and title was on copies of all outgoing correspondence: Karl-Wolf Thrung, Director. There had been a Karl-Wolf Thrung in the last Olympic team the East Germans had fielded. A weightlifter. Sent home for taking a banned drug stimulant. Afterwards Thrung was supposed to have gone to Central America. There had been something about his becoming personal trainer to one of the drug barons.

On the bottom shelf Morton found it.

Right at the back was a file stuffed full of body outlines. Boxes for hearts, livers, kidneys and eyes. Each marked with the same neat cross. He turned over the forms. All the relevant personal data on the reverse side had been whitened out with corrector fluid. Why do that and keep the forms? Why not just dump them? Supposing you were going to do that when the alarm went?

From the corridor came the sound of footsteps. Gates came into the office. 'Some set-up,' he said appreciatively. 'There has to be a million bucks of fitness hardware back there. They've got machines to tone up muscles where you never knew you had them. Plus aromatherapy, diathermy and just about anything needed to make you look and feel good.' He paused, squinting at the file. 'Manna?'

'Take a look.' Morton handed him the folder.

Gates thumbed through the file, his frown deepening. 'Makes no sense,' he said at last.

'Unless they are unwilling donors,' Morton said quietly.

Gates took a deep breath and exhaled slowly, giving an anguished grin. 'That's a quantum leap, David! There's got to be forty, fifty forms here. There's no way that many people in this city have been killed for their organs.'

Morton sounded as if he was making another attempt to clear the high bar. 'Maybe they are killed elsewhere. Or maybe they are recipients. We may know more if my people can remove that corrector fluid to see what's written underneath.'

Gates was shaking his head. 'We've never had much luck doing that. Each time the solvent's dissolved the writing. Technical Services tried—'

Whatever Technical Services had attempted was lost in the sound of an explosion.

'Right on the button!' Gates yelled. 'Let's get the hell out of here before the smoke clears.'

Morton shoved the file into the suitcase and locked it by reversing the process he'd used to open the transporter. Pausing only to ensure that the computer discs were exactly as he had found them, he hurried after Gates.

Technical Services had laid on a glorified Fourth of July explosion that would look spectacular but would do no more than leave the truck a burned-out wreck that the FBI would spend days fruitlessly examining.

But how long would it be before Thrung discovered the missing file?

6

Six miles above the earth the cardiologist in charge of the medical team on board the flying hospital smiled reassuringly at his patient. 'All your vital signs are stable. You've had a lucky escape, Mr Vogel.'

It was a dolphin's smile, carefully put together from all the other smiles he had observed in his masters before he became his own. Smiling was the one certain way he knew to hide his contempt for those who could afford his fees.

'So I will be fine?'

'Of course.' Another smile, like a star pleased with his performance. How was I, schmuck?

The banker shifted in the full-sized hospital bed bolted to the floor of the aircraft fuselage. The cabin was brightly lit and smelled of chemicals. Surgical trolleys and drip stands were positioned around the bed. The range of more sophisticated diagnostic and maintenance equipment included an intra-aortic balloon pump and a heart monitor which displayed its information in the continuously moving form of a city skyline. Another screen showed Vogel's heart as a pulsating muscle in three-dimension.

'Then I would like to make a phone call,' he said, trying to sit up.

The cardiologist gently but with sufficient firmness pushed Vogel back on his pillow. 'Take it easy, Mr Vogel. Any sudden move like that and you'll send all this equipment into overdrive.' He made a show of checking the electrodes on Vogel's chest and studying the heart monitor. The trace was steady. But he wasn't being paid to play hunky-dory. It was riot-act time. 'Just remember, Mr Vogel, that while the heart is a surprisingly primitive and resilient muscle, you have to show it a little respect.

You haven't done so for a long time. Forty cigarettes and a bottle of wine a day is no way to treat your heart. That's why it suddenly said, enough.'

'I only want to make one call,' said Vogel. He had to tell Frau Sauermann to have Finkle transfer those billions of dollars to Moscow. His deputy was a nervous Berliner at the best of times. He'd want to be reassured – like this damned American doctor was trying to do to him.

'Why don't you relax and enjoy the flight, Mr Vogel?'

'I'm trying to.'

'Terrific.' Another dolphin smile. 'Vogel. That's bird in German, isn't it?'

'Yes.'

'Terrific.'

And more of the same. Bedside small-talk at a thousand bucks an hour. After this little trip he'd be able to buy another condo. God in Heaven was kind.

Vogel closed his eyes. Calling Finkle would be an opportunity to check on his own electronic mailbox, to see if there had been a follow-up call to the one he suspected had precipitated his heart attack. That call had come only hours before he flew to Los Angeles. The caller had been a voice from the past, Boris Kransky, once the senior KGB officer in East Germany and now of no fixed employment. In those days they'd been dependent on each other, not out of any sense of loyalty to the regime, for that had become passé, but from a mutual need to survive beyond it. That Kransky had obtained his unlisted direct-line telephone number at the Bundesbank was no real surprise; he had always been a careful and methodical man. It was what he had said that was shattering. The negatives – the compromising, career-wrecking negatives – had not been destroyed by the Stasi, as he had been promised. Instead they had come on to the market and been bought as swiftly as they had appeared. The purchaser was almost certainly a front man. Kransky had said he was willing to find out who the front represented – for a price. Times were hard, etcetera, etcetera. It had been like negotiations with the Poles. In the end they'd settled on a million US dollars for the return of the negatives. Ten per cent now, balance on delivery to Kransky's numbered Swiss account. He'd had it for years, he'd explained.

'Just one call,' Vogel pleaded, something he had not done for a long time.

The cardiologist shook his head. 'Remember, Mr Vogel, your people know what's happened. They want you to know there are no problems at the bank. So no one expects you to be making any calls. Even if they did, I wouldn't allow it. My job is to get you back home alive. So just relax.'

'I wish you would stop telling me to relax.'

The cardiologist laughed pleasantly. 'I'm going to give you something to help you to sleep. It's important that you do. Your heart's taken a bit of a beating. The remarkable thing is that despite your lifestyle, you're still in good physical shape. Otherwise you probably wouldn't have made it.'

He turned to the nurse holding a steel bowl containing a syringe and ampoule. He removed the sheath from the needle and drew off the contents of the vial.

'Am I going to . . . "make it"?' Sometimes Americans could be very imprecise in their language.

The cardiologist's eyes once more made a show of studying the heart monitor. 'Of course, Mr Vogel.'

He waited while the nurse rubbed surgical spirit into Vogel's upper arm and then injected the liquid into a muscle. 'When you wake up you'll be in Frankfurt,' promised the cardiologist. 'And feeling a lot better.'

He remained looking down at Vogel while the banker's eyes began to droop. Moments later Vogel was asleep. The nurse looked questioningly at the doctor. 'His lab tests didn't look too promising.'

'I know it. But what do you tell someone who's having this kind of money spent on him? That we're just keeping him ticking over until he gets a new heart?'

'And will he get one?'

The cardiologist gave another pleasant smile. 'Thankfully that's not my problem. In our system enough money can still somehow buy what you want. But in Europe there's a real shortage of all kinds of organs, hearts most of all. So he's going to have a problem finding a donor.'

In the communications centre of the Concorde parked at Dulles

International, one of the technicians informed the CCO that the hospital plane had passed overhead. A little later another technician noted that a privately owned 747 had entered Washington airspace, bound for Stockholm. Logging all such flights was routine and the details were fed into the on-board computer.

Shortly afterwards the CCO received a call from Morton to say that he was on his way to the airport and requesting the flight crew to clear an immediate departure.

7

Dr Gustav Romer listened to the rain on the verandah's tin roof. Once more the storm had risen in mid-afternoon off the close-by peaks of Costa Rica and swept across Lake Nicaragua to reach the island that was part of the Solentiname Archipelago. As scenically beautiful as its name, the archipelago was among the most remote places on earth. Towering majestically above the lake was Mount Masaya; the volcano had been dormant for over a century. Dr Romer continued to sit motionless in his wheelchair, hand resting on the control box he had designed to give his ruined body its place in the world.

Physically he was here, and it was mid-afternoon, three o'clock precisely, the hour when the rain always came. Mentally, it was still sixty minutes ago, when he had been alone in the living room leading off the verandah, leaning back in his chair, eyes closed, face towards the ceiling, listening to the concert on the tape. Then had come the polite knock on the door and the clinic messenger had entered, delivered and was gone, with that nervous smile that suggested he would have dearly loved to know what was in the telefax inside the sealed envelope.

After reading the message, Dr Romer crumpled it into a pocket and pressed shut his eyes. It had taken a supreme effort to go on listening to the music and close out the urgent questions over what had happened in Washington. When the music stopped, he had wheeled himself out here to listen to the almost as loud beat of the rain.

The darkened sky produced only sufficient light to outline his tinted glasses. The rest of him was in vague outline: the curiously shaped skull, the scrawny neck and the truncated body which left him legless at both knees. His head had made childhood a misery and, in adult years, had become a focus of psychological conjecture. When he became powerful enough, he had sent for his Stasi file. Its evaluation was remarkably close to his own self-assessment. A person born with such a visible abnormality developed his abilities in isolation, becoming suspicious, resentful and hostile. Such personality distortion was well suited to high-risk pioneering research.

The rest of the file had been equally unsurprising, describing in laborious detail how, having entered the field when immunology was in transition, he immediately saw what could be done with the new drugs, and how his readiness to use them experimentally on prisoners had brought him to the notice of the service.

The rain was falling straight, undisturbed by wind, the great drops exploding on the ground. Normally at a time like this he felt he was being reborn, and that the ache would not return to his body. It would, of course; that was part of the price he had paid when he had finally taken his leave of the Stasi, flying out of East Berlin on that long journey to Ecuador. He had felt nothing, certainly no sense of betrayal.

Every stage had been researched and double-checked; Madam had said it would not matter what it cost, just as long as he vanished without trace from all those searching eyes of his old masters, and probably others as well. They'd check and check again. Nothing must be left for them, for anyone, to say other than that Gustav Romer, hero of the state, honorary member of the Soviet Academy of Sciences and of the Chinese Medical Association, had died a tragic death in the prime of life. Leaving his Stasi briefcase at the scene of his 'death', he had to admit, was a stroke of genius on her part. It had contained just enough to satisfy curiosity.

Until an hour ago he had not for a moment given serious thought to the idea that the world might not accept he was dead. Since then his mind had been filled with nothing else. It had taken more than iron will to remind himself that the greater part of his life, those first fifty-three years, was still officially buried, and only he could disinter it when he needed to wander in the private kingdom of recall. Then he could adjust matters accordingly, play back everything at his own speed, not like the past hour, when the film had constantly threatened to race off the screen. To stop that happening required supreme effort, a constant reminder that he was schooled in rote, analysis, logic, and that he must stop this dangerous speculating. The rain helped; it eased the physical pain that had been a constant companion since Ecuador. Hearing what Klinger had to say would also help. He would be here soon. Until then he would enjoy the temporary relief the rain brought, and stop thinking about what the message had said. There was still no proof. He must not make a drama out of his unspoken fears. Enjoy the rain. And take satisfaction from what had been achieved.

Before choosing this island he had inspected all the others in the archipelago. Some were completely covered with tight forest rising straight out of the water. Others were too small or too populated. When he had finally made his selection, the few score fisher families had been resettled elsewhere and he paid the new regime in Managua, as corrupt as all its predecessors, their exorbitant asking price for the island's name to be removed from all existing records and the sea around it declared a *zona militaire*. Signs were posted offshore warning that trespassers would be shot.

Earth-moving equipment had cleared the jungle to build the *finca*, the clinic, staff housing and a runway. The very latest security system had then been installed. The only glitch no one had been able to solve was that the afternoon rainstorm temporarily affected the system's capability. Then members of Kommando One not on assignment patrolled the island in their jeeps.

A swathe of jungle separated the medical facilities and the *finca* from the staff quarters at the southern end. The nurses and doctors lived in villas around their multi-purpose recreational facilities. The airstrip adjoined the staff area.

Madam had said the money had been well spent at the end of her inspection trip. She had never returned to the island. He suspected she disliked its howler monkeys and parakeets and, above all, this daily downpour.

The drumming on the roof was easing. Soon the sun would emerge. Other people recharged themselves through its rays; for him the sun was too painful on his many skin grafts. Nor had he once in his adult life taken a day's holiday. The very idea of such time-wasting was repugnant to him.

Driving himself was how he had come to the cutting edge of medicine. And when the Stasi had given him an open-ended

56

budget to create new weapons to destroy without trace the body's immune system, he had seen it as a means to an end – not the end. As a welcome and respected visitor to the secret research centres around Beijing, he had learned about the sugar fléchette bomblet the chemists of the Chinese Secret Service had developed. Back in Dresden he'd begun to adapt the discovery for the agents of Kommando One. Klinger had visited his laboratory to discuss the best delivery system. The man's enthusiasm had been almost childlike. Later, when he realised the whole edifice of Soviet Communism was doomed, he'd included Klinger and his colleagues when preparing the plans which finally brought them all here.

The rain had ceased. Dr Romer pressed a button on the control box and the wheelchair hummed to life. Air filled its skirt, lifting the chair clear of the wooden deck. He pressed another button and glided to the edge of the verandah so that the water dripping from the roof fell close to his face.

He had designed the chair in those long months of recovery after the crash. Its electric motor was so powerful it could propel him over all but the roughest ground. Madam had paid for it. Just as she had paid the pilot to deliberately force-land in one of Ecuador's more inaccessible jungles and for the execution squad to shoot him and the other flight crew, together with the remaining passengers, before setting fire to the wreckage.

He still remembered little of what followed. Certainly not the moment when he had been pulled from the plane, leaving both his legs behind. He had remembered almost nothing of that long journey north to the clinic in Managua, except a vague impression of one of the guerrillas constantly injecting him, and the pain was still unbearable. All he remembered of his escort was that they were very quiet, very professional and that none of them said goodbye after they delivered him to the clinic. There, he had finally slept. Only later had he learned he had been in a drugged sleep for weeks. When he finally awoke, his legs were stumps already fitted with their leather pads.

He had spent a year at the clinic. Madam had visited him several times and they had finalised their business arrangements. She would provide the funding, he the expertise. The profit would be divided equally. He had never questioned her motives for doing all this, and she had never offered her reasons. He suspected they both wanted it this way.

The rain had stopped. The clinic buildings were once more visible. They were a magnificent sight, an architectural blending of wood, glass and metal surrounded by barbered lawns, fountains and a curved driveway. When the building costs had reached $200,000,000, he had informed Madam. She had said to continue to spend what it took. Now there was not a private hospital like it in the whole world; inside its walls was the very best equipment from America, Japan and Europe. The fees were commensurate with such clinical excellence.

In one of the recovery suites, Mr Suto – it was an inviolate rule that patients were always referred to formally – should be coming round now. Thinking about Mr Suto for the moment kept at bay other, darker thoughts in what should have been the most perfect part of the day, when the rain stopped and the golden evening light bathed everything until, with a sudden plunge, the sun dropped beneath the horizon and left everything in darkness. It was a magical moment which for his northern blood had never lost its strangeness, as if suddenly the whole world had stood poised and then disappeared into an abyss. But now the enjoyable primitive terror of the Nicaraguan sunset was threatened by this other matter. To keep it away a little longer, until Klinger arrived he thought more about Mr Suto.

The Japanese patient had arrived six days ago from Tokyo, having transferred to the Organisation's bank account US $600,000 to cover half the cost of his kidney replacement surgery. When he was cleared to fly home, Mr Suto would transfer the balance to the account with Credit Suisse in Geneva. It was an arrangement on which only one patient had so far reneged.

A Mogadishu gang lord had contracted to receive a new liver. On the day of his scheduled departure home, his final cheque for $750,000 had not been honoured. Madam had said that in such a matter firm action must be taken; something like that could set a bad example. A member of Kommando One had gone to the man's room and suffocated the gang lord, a technique guaranteeing that no damage was done to the relevant organs.

In the operating room where the man had received his new liver, the organ was once more removed, together with his heart, kidneys and eyes. These were placed in the organ bank for future use, and the corpse fed to the piranha in the pond. He did not expect such a problem with Mr Suto. The Japanese were very punctilious about honouring a contract.

New drugs and improved tissue-typing techniques had made an operation like Mr Suto's, once a miracle of modern medicine, a matter of routine. But it also created a need to constantly replenish the supply of organs. In the past month there had been a run on hearts. There was now only one left in storage. More would have to be found. The same applied to eyes and that still most difficult of organs to transplant, a lung. At present there was only a single lung maintained on the life-support system he had devised for the purpose, waiting for a patient prepared to pay $3,000,000.

Madam had laid down the criteria for who would be treated. Upper-echelon criminals, dictators, terrorists. All those who for any number of reasons were unable or unwilling to obtain a transplant by conventional means. Madam had said a typical candidate was the godfather of one of New York's most powerful Mafia families who had died of a ruptured heart because he feared going into hospital would give his rivals the opportunity to kill him. He could have come here under guaranteed total security. Now not a week passed without a face from some country's most-wanted list arriving.

From the jungle came the renewed screaming of the howler monkeys swinging through the rain-soaked foliage. The noise always reminded him of drunken singing in a *bierkeller*. He sighed, partly because the storm was over but mostly because the image prompted familiar thoughts that would try to lead him back to that moment when he had first read the telefax from Thrung. He was part of Dr Romer's past.

A couple of nurses had emerged from the clinic's reception and were following a path to the staff quarters. Klinger was striding up the pathway. He stopped by the nurses and the sound of laughter carried clearly; he could be quite a charmer. Romer's hands stiffened as if to ready himself for the inevitable. After a final joke, Klinger continued on past the clinic and the laboratory complex. Beyond was the bunker where the fléchette guns and sugar bomblets were stockpiled. Then came the organ bank, the first of two squat, windowless buildings past which Klinger was striding. The other was the mortuary. Nearby was the pond.

'Good evening, Herr Doktor,' Klinger said, Stepping on to the balcony. 'You enjoyed the rain?' He flashed his mirthless smile.

'Probably not as much as you did the flight from New York.' Klinger could not possibly yet know what had happened in Washington.

Klinger stood for a moment in awkward silence. You could never tell the mood behind the Herr Doktor's glasses. But his training said something was, if not exactly wrong, then not quite right. 'The Polak made it pass very quickly.' The flight crew would have filed their reports.

'Come, we will have a drink and you can tell me about your trip, Klinger.'

Dr Romer spun the chair and led the way into the *finca*'s main living room. The walls and ceiling were done in beige tones, the floor covered with a natural-fibre carpeting which only emphasised the heaviness of the furniture. Dark woods, rich upholstery; everything seemed all the more from a bygone age set against the monitors mounted on a wall to provide constantly changing images from the security cameras around the island.

Klinger glanced at a screen showing a jeep bouncing along a track. Kessler had drawn the northern end of the island to patrol during the storm. Despite his slicker he'd quickly have been soaked.

Dr Romer motioned him to an armchair before propelling himself to a drinks cabinet. 'A new Moselle,' he said, removing a wine bottle from an ice bucket. Wolfgang Kreuse, the undisputed head of the Frankfurt underworld, had sent fifty cases as a personal thank you for his new replacement colon.

Klinger watched his host fill both glasses equally. Such perfect manners somehow made the Herr Doktor more forbidding. Dr Romer pulled a small tray from the arm rest. Placing both glasses on the tray he glided across to Klinger. 'Please,' he said, extending a glass. 'First your verdict on the wine – then your report.'

Klinger sniffed and sipped. 'Light, yet fruity and a good bouquet.' He watched Dr Romer raise his glass and sniff. How could he possibly smell anything with such a reconstructed nose?

'You are right, Klinger,' Dr Romer said, sipping. 'Truly

excellent.' He carefully put down his glass on the tray. 'Now, tell me everything. From the time you left here to the moment you flew from New York.'

Klinger had already marshalled his thoughts, and experience had taught him that an even-paced recital was required. The Herr Doktor disliked emotion of any kind.

For the next hour Dr Romer sat silent and still while Klinger spoke. When he finished, Klinger did not relax. The Herr Doktor always had questions. But this silence was more unnerving than discovering that, after all, you had overlooked a detail.

'Is there something wrong?' Klinger finally asked, not quite able to conceal the unease in his voice.

'Something is indeed wrong, Klinger. Very seriously wrong,' Dr Romer said at last, maintaining a careful watch over Klinger. He had no idea. He had told him the truth. And the Disposer had performed his duties with his usual efficiency. Which made what Thrung had reported all the more troubling.

'May I know what has happened, Herr Doktor?'

From a pocket Dr Romer fished out a piece of paper. 'Thrung says there was a bomb scare right outside our building. But he doesn't think it was a proper bomb.'

Loud and clear Klinger heard the call to duty. 'It could have been a dud, Herr Doktor. Or an inept bomber. I can think of a dozen reasons.' Then, with just the right amount of malice: 'Thrung is not an expert on such matters.'

'No, he is not,' Dr Romer agreed gravely. His voice had a way of producing silence. 'There is more, Klinger. Thrung also says that shortly before the explosion two men entered the building. One had a suitcase.'

Klinger gave a kind of slurred grunt which managed to suggest indifference, irritation and a touch of disbelief at the same time. 'A suitcase? What is the importance of that, Herr Doktor? People go around with suitcases all the time in Washington.'

'Thrung says it looked like a very heavy suitcase for its size. It could have contained a detonator or some kind of special equipment.'

'I take it he has searched the building?'

'Yes. And found nothing.'

'Then there is nothing to worry about, Herr Doktor. Providing

Thrung had done his job properly.' The malice was a little stronger.

Perhaps to focus his mind while it was tearing him in so many directions, or perhaps he had found the message so troubling, Dr Romer ignored what normally he would have regarded as stupidity on Klinger's part. 'Thrung sent a good physical description of both men. One we will need to check with our computers. But the other matches someone you should remember.'

Klinger tensed, the call to duty trumpet-loud. The Herr Doktor's eyes were fixed upon him. Yet when he delivered the sensational words, they were in a deadening monotone that seemed to barely escape his lips. 'Thrung's description fits very well the one we used to call Der Teufel Kolonel—'

'*Morton!*' Klinger said with such force that the last of the wine shook in his glass.

'Then you remember him. Colonel David Morton. The Devil personified. Remember how his file categorised him? "Most Dangerous". No one else had that category. You remember that?'

And a lot more. The Herr Doktor was examining him, frowning through his tinted glasses, peering at him from a few inches away. Klinger gathered himself and shook his head. 'Thrung could be wrong.'

Dr Romer nodded as if he was almost pleased. 'Of course, of course, Klinger. And even if he is not, we don't know what Morton was doing there, who he was with, what they were both doing. You are right. We don't know, because Thrung hasn't told us.' He leaned forward in his wheelchair. 'You will return to Washington and find out what else Thrung can tell us. Do everything you have to do. And as quickly as possible. Then report to me.'

'Yes, Herr Doktor.'

As Klinger moved to stand up, Dr Romer waved him down. 'Please, finish your wine first. You have time enough. Morton won't run away.'

He didn't want to be alone just yet, with only those dangerous thoughts for companionship. And when you were never quite certain if you were making the right decision in not sharing all this with Madam.

8

The northern daylight had faded a little earlier this day, leaving a chill in the air. It had been there when Sonja Crayton had stepped from her Lear jet and walked to the limousine waiting on the tarmac at Stockholm's Arlanda Airport. Forty minutes later the cold briefly penetrated her fur coat as she quickly crossed the pavement into the apartment on Sturegaten.

Nils had been waiting, Swedishly pale and resolute. She had given him a key to the apartment as part of her mysterious shedding of shame. He had led her immediately to the bedroom, *her* bedroom. Their first lovemaking had been almost silent, until a sigh of surrender escaped her, so faint that it could have come from the distant tundra. When he started to cry out in release, she placed a hand over his mouth and he bit it, leaving teeth marks on her fore and middle fingers. After a while she mounted him again and this time the bed shook with the force of someone who needed to satisfy her sexual obsession. Afterwards he lay intently beside her, saying nothing. Then, when he began to caress her once more, she left the bed on the pretext of fixing them a drink; despite her months of abstinence, she had still found no satisfaction.

She had handed him his glass, smiling disarmingly when he moved to make room for her in the bed. Instead she stood at the tall window and, despite the warmth of the room, felt the first hint of premature winter. Soon the wind would howl and the mist swirl in from Lake Mälaren and, finally, would come snow, obliterating everything except memory.

Studying herself in the window's reflection, she thought again, *I loved you. I loved you, but you betrayed all I believed in, trusted in, ever wanted, then and forever.* Very much in the past tense.

That was the most painful part of all, having to admit that the past was still here and present.

This was the first home she had made for Elmer. She had furnished it with the finest antique leather and the dark green carpeting he had liked. The library was designed to hold the investment journals which had been almost his only reading. In a dozen ways she had expressed her love for him. That was why she had felt, and still did, his betrayal all the more. It had been here, on a day like this, that he had first brought *her*.

Even now she could not bring herself to speak her name. She was either 'Elmer's whore' or, when she was absolutely forced to acknowledge her presence, 'Madam'. Both were always delivered with the same withering contempt.

From the bed, Nils was calling tenderly.

'Wait,' she called, her voice loud and non-sensual, watching the shadow of her face against the darkening sky. She had stood exactly here that night Elmer had told her, walking slowly up and down their bedroom, his hands, pale and delicate, emphasising his words with occasional little movements. She had seen him like that so many times, concluding some deal, trying not to sound impatient, as men become at sixty when they begin to realise there is only so much time left to make all the deals they still must. And he *had* been making a deal.

She was still reeling from his first revelation of betrayal, and the shock had been so great as to choke off her voice, leaving only a feeling that her heart had burst, which would explain the tightening band across her chest, when he had continued, in that quiet, even tone, to explain how it would be from now on. He would divide his time between them both. Financially he guaranteed she would not suffer, nor would there be any public humiliations, no suddden, unexpected encounters.

Behind her, the ormolu clock chimed the hour. He had given it to her on their first wedding anniversary. Six anniversaries later, when he finished setting out his conditions, her first instinct had been to blame herself. *I loved you, but didn't show it enough. I never understood what matters to you.* Blaming herself had made it possible to accept his terms of severance and continuance.

Her lawyers told her she could have extracted far better terms. But she had clung to the hope that one day he would return.

Instead, eight months later, he had come here, paler than usual, and told her he wanted a divorce; that he intended to start a family, to produce the heir to the Crayton fortune their own marriage had failed to do. He had made it sound like the next step of the deal she had already agreed.

She knew the fault this time truly lay with her; her gynaecologist had told her she was one of those rare cases even the latest artificial insemination techniques could not help. But when she had refused to grant him a divorce he had looked at her calmly, and had spoken in that voice that he always used when settling a deal. Very well, his new companion would still bear his child.

Companion. That was the final betrayal. He had once called her that. *My companion in life*, he would introduce her to his business friends. Elmer's whore had stolen her title as well.

It was after that last visit of Elmer's that she had started to use the apartment as a form of revenge, bringing to the bed she had once shared with him a succession of men, some she barely knew. One had been here on the night Elmer had died on the other side of the world six years ago. The doctor who called had gently explained that there was no heart available for the transplant which could have saved him. She had given a long, low laugh that must have continued to astonish him long after she had rung off.

'You'll catch cold standing there,' Nils called out. 'And people can see you.'

'I'm not cold. And no one can see me.' Her breath was beginning to steam up the windowpanes. Across the park, from the lake, a ship's siren lowed. Overhead, a plane was climbing out of Arlanda.

The taste of the schnapps was suddenly like gunmetal in her mouth, the way it had tasted after she had visited her gynaecologist in Paris. That had been three months after Elmer's last visit. She had dressed for the doctor's appointment in sensible clothes for a sensible precaution; she always had herself checked once a year. After the gynaecologist examined her, he referred her to a colleague in the building. She had known immediately that something must be wrong because this specialist had seen her immediately. After he finished, she caught his glance and he had come to the point at once. Her cancer was already too far advanced for surgery. Nor would chemotherapy or irradiation halt its progress for very long. All he could promise was that hers was a type of carcinoma which, almost to the very end, would show none of the usual outward physical manifestations: no weight loss, no hair fall-out, no grey pallor. Faced with the evidence of her own mortality, she had asked one question. How long did she have? He had said a year at the most. That had been six months ago. Yet even now the signs of impending death were minimal, giving her body only a slimness not there since her youth. Her skin and hair remained healthy. She did not look like a woman who would not see her forty-fifth birthday.

Sonja turned at last from the window and walked back to the bed, picking out the bottle from the bucket of ice. 'Another drink, my precious?' she asked.

'Too much already,' Nils murmured.

She smiled. For a Swede he had a low tolerance of alcohol. It must make his job difficult at times like this. Nils was the Assistant Director of the Nobel Foundation; the run-up to the awards was an endless round of eating and drinking for the Foundation staff. She was still smiling, still mysteriously out of rhythm with him. He wanted more sex; she needed information. To know more about the call he had mentioned when she phoned from the airport to say she had arrived. That Elmer's whore would attend the Nobel ceremonies was not unexpected; she came every year. It was the only occasion they were ever in the same place. That she should have called Olaf was something else. Sonja began to refill her glass and asked Nils what Elmer's whore had wanted with Count Lindeman.

'An appointment with this year's winner of the prize for Medicine.'

'Yoshi Kramer, the neurosurgeon?' She let out the low peal of laughter that is the signature-tune of the not quite sober.

'The very same. She wanted to see him before the ceremonies. Impossible, of course. The best the Director could do was a brief meeting afterwards. Our winners . . . are very much . . . in demand . . .' Nils' voice trailed off and he closed his eyes. In moments he was snoring gently.

She gave another soft laugh and drank her schnapps. The more she drank, the more her sodden nerves begged for the un-consciousness she could not provide them with. But now she

66

forced herself not to reach for the bottle one more time. Once she started, she would not stop, for days. And she needed to be sober at the reception for the Nobel laureates, not to be humiliated in public before Elmer's whore. That would be worse than death itself. And yet she had come to long for that as well. Sonja gave another crazed little laugh. *What is happening to me?*

A hundred miles out of Shannon, the 747 received in swift succession two encrypted messages. When the machine installed behind the flight deck decoded them, it sealed them in envelopes which were delivered into a basket. A bell announced their arrival. The aircraft's Chief Steward immediately removed the envelopes. Though, as usual, they bore no name, he knew they were for the eyes of only one person on board. Madam.

The steward walked down the aircraft's softly lit central aisle. Tall and handsome, he wore the same scarlet uniform as the waiters in Malibu. At first he had felt faintly ridiculous dressed like this, but the pay more than compensated. Reaching the master bedroom suite he knocked and entered. Inside, the sitting room was empty, the sound of the engines no more than a murmur. Not even Air Force One, the President's plane, on which he had served, had better soundproofing. He crossed to the closed door of the bedroom and popped the envelopes through its letterbox. Then he pressed an ear to the door. No sound came from beyond. The steward turned and left.

The soft thud of the envelopes falling on the carpet awoke her. As usual she had slept naked on top of the large bed. She arose and collected the envelopes and returned to sit on the edge of the bed before opening them. The first message contained brief details of the explosion in Washington. The other said that Dieter Vogel had survived his journey to Frankfurt. She crumpled up this one and concentrated on the first message.

Suddenly Madam heard her own breathing, and felt her nipples hardening. The first scent of danger always aroused her. It was the only thing that could do so now. Impulsively she began to touch herself, to encourage and then satisfy the aching urgency in her groin. *This* was all she had left. She began to move in rhythm with the ache, moaning. *This is all I have left!*

9

Shortly after Concorde crossed the French coast on the return flight from Washington, the CCO turned to Morton and sighed. 'Bitburg insists he has to speak to you.'

Walter Bitburg was Hammer Force's Administrator. Morton straightened in his high-backed leather chair in the aircraft's communications centre. Only his eyes showed his exhaustion. During the flight he had concentrated on the material faxed to him.

Lester's programmers had discovered that Keep-U-Trim had clubs in London, Paris, Berlin and Rome. One was about to open in Sydney, another in Tokyo. Danny had reported that his team was in place, his voice falsely relaxed, the way it always was just before the bell. Johnny Quirke's boffins in Technical Services had started to replicate fléchette bomblets and a variety of delivery systems. Everybody would be pressed to match the energy with which Johnny went about his business. Programmers were writing programmes, analysts, analysing. In a score of different offices, each with a different view of Lake Geneva, the espiocrats of Hammer Force had begun to march to a single drum beat. From here, 40,000 feet above Rouen at this moment, the sound was a promise of more to come. The only disappointment had been Chantal reporting that neither Anna nor Tommy had yet turned up anything in Stamp's background. That also happened.

In between this otherwise impressive flow of information, the Prof had faxed a profile of Romer, prefacing it with the warning that it was mostly drawn from old Stasi files, and was desperately short on personal detail, not even a hint of Romer enjoying himself in what had passed for Dresden's fleshpots. 'So sorry, can't offer you more for the moment,' the Prof had scribbled, in that hand which suggested he always wrote in the shadows. This further unspoken promise of more to come had also cheered Morton.

'Bitburg's champing at the bit,' the CCO said.

'Put him on,' Morton's tone displayed neither impatience nor irritation. He turned to the screen angled into his desk top. A moment later Bitburg's face appeared from the transmission suite in Hammer Force Headquarters.

'Are you there, David? Can you hear me?'

Morton watched Bitburg bring his face closer to the suite's camera. His eyes were grey, like everything else about him – suit, hair and expression. And above all his voice. Even on a summer's day, he sounded wintry.

'I hear and see you ten-ten, Walter. How can I help?'

Morton saw Bitburg purse his lips. 'The costings for Stamp's funeral.'

'What about them?' Morton finally asked. The silence between them had more than distance. It signified something wider and deeper.

Bitburg's voice was dry and precise. 'Stamp's contract of employment is quite clear. He was only entitled to full funeral cover if he died on duty. As he was on vacation the cost of flying home his body must come out of his estate.'

Only Walter would use a word like that. 'Stamp was a researcher. He didn't have a private income.'

Bitburg gave a twitch of his head that Morton had seen him do before, like a warthog about to charge. 'Nevertheless, the transportation costs must be deducted from what Stamp has in the pension fund, David. There is enough to cover the air-freight charge. All we are liable for is the actual cost of burial. And even then there's a question of why he couldn't have been cremated in America. We allow this and we set a precedent that will lead God knows where, you mark my words.'

Morton marked them as the lights in the transmission suite caught Bitburg's glasses. You needed Walter to negotiate a refit for Concorde or cost out the latest computers for Lester. But not to trample over your own dead.

'Stamp didn't want to be cremated in America or anywhere else. He wanted to be buried beside his parents, Walter.'

'I still don't see . . .'

Morton suddenly felt tired – tired and wasted. He wanted an end to this nonsense. 'Pay everything out of the emergency fund.'

Bitburg's eyes began to carom. 'No precedent.' Delivered in a winning-hand voice.

'Do what I say, Walter.'

The head twitch was the warthog retreating, the voice from the very depths of winter. 'I'll need your written authorisation, David.'

'You'll have it.'

'I regard this as an exception to the rule.' The voice was grey with defeat.

'In my business there are no rules except one. We look after our own. And Stamp was one of ours.'

Morton punched a button on the desk's keyboard. Bitburg's face instantly vanished from the screen. Morton calmed his inner fury by listening to the technicians fine-tuning their scanners. Those who worked here kidded each other they would be the first to hear about Doomsday.

As Concorde entered Paris airspace, the CCO said Danny was on a secure-relay circuit. If Danny was direct-dialling Concorde from his desk console, it had to be urgent. Morton picked up the handset on his own desk. 'What's up, Danny?' Beyond the cabin window were ridges of clouds.

Danny spoke with the brevity of someone who had had to listen to too many useless intercepts. 'Wolfgang Kreuse has been shot while in bed with his latest rent-boy. The kid took the full impact. Kreuse is just about alive but he's been calling for a priest. When they got him to hospital, the doctors discovered he'd had a transplant. A replacement colon. They'd never seen one before. At that point Mueller decided to take over.'

Hans-Dieter Mueller was Operations Chief of Germany's formidable security service, the BND, and one of the few Morton trusted in Europe's mish-mash of law enforcement agencies. 'What's Hans-Dieter saying?' Morton asked in a voice that was suddenly smiling.

'He thinks you should drop in. He's already cleared a revised flight plan,' Danny replied in a matching voice.

'What do we have on Kreuse?'

Danny was answering before Morton had finished. 'It'll be on

70

your fax machine in a moment. But don't hold your breath. There's nothing on his transplant. Mueller thinks that might have been done when Kreuse dropped out of sight for a few weeks. He was supposed to have gone for a cruise around the Caribbean. Lester's people are checking, but there's been something like a million people cruising down there since then.'

The smile in Morton's voice was even broader. 'But they weren't all looking for new colons, Danny. Oh, and on Kreuse's request for a priest, tell the hospital it's been looked after.'

'Will do,' Danny shouted gleefully.

By the time German air traffic control gave Concorde priority clearance into Frankfurt Rhein-Main, Morton had read the material Danny had faxed. Kreuse had swum in all sorts of murky waters, but there was no clue to the port in which he had obtained his colon transplant.

As the aircraft swooped earthward, nose cone angled down, the sun casting a huge delta shadow over the ground, Lester came on line. After they'd drawn a blank with Europe's transplant centres, his best hackers had tapped into the North American organ banks. No Kreuse. Same in Japan. Same everywhere. Lester had asked the Prof to call Yoshi, who said he'd never heard of anyone having his plumbing replaced on that scale.

'The Prof says, given that, we can rule out the Caribbean. Surgically, down there they're very much still at the basic kidney transplant stage. We're running out of places to look.'

'Have everyone keep at it, Lester. Kreuse had his operation somewhere.'

Morton broke the connection, pushed back his chair and strode to the cabin between the communications centre and the flight deck. The small compartment was known as the wardrobe. He was still inside when Concorde touched down and ground control directed it to the high-security area reserved for VIP flights.

When Morton walked down the aircraft steps he wore a clergyman's grey suit and walked with the slow, purposeful movements of someone who had spent a lifetime going between altar and pulpit.

Mueller was waiting at the foot of the steps. Nearby was a 747 with bold red crosses on its white fuselage and wings. 'Good to see you, Hans-Dieter.'

'You too, David.' Mueller's voice was soft for such a physically big man, as if he had spent a lifetime being patiently conciliatory.

Morton nodded towards the hospital plane. 'How is Vogel?'

Mueller grimaced. 'He's ordered extra phones and a fax for his room. Talk about dying on the job!'

'You know bankers.'

Mueller agreed he knew bankers then looked curiously at Morton. 'I assume you're not dressed like this for my benefit.'

'Not unless you wish me to pray for your soul.' Morton could not have sounded more saintly, as if a spiritual peace now filled him.

'Kreuse is still alive,' Mueller said, leading the way to a Mercedes parked nearby. Its uniformed woman driver snapped a salute and opened the rear door at the same time. After making sure Mueller and Morton were comfortably seated, she walked stiff-backed around the car to the driver's seat.

Mueller murmured. 'She's been with me for a year and still behaves like a robot.'

'Why not change her?'

'The next one could be worse. And she also makes very good tea. At my age that's important.' He smiled at Morton, who smiled back. 'Kreuse's transplant, I take it, is your prime interest?'

'Yes.' As the car left the airport he explained why.

Half an hour later they drove through the gates of the private clinic. A cobbled driveway led to a triangular pediment supported by a row of plaster pillars. Armed policemen stood before the entrance. After Mueller showed his ID, one led them to the surgical floor. A doctor was waiting outside the Intensive Care Unit. He had heavy eyelids and a white coat that rustled from too much starching. He glanced at Morton, frowning.

'How is he?' Mueller asked.

'There's no hope. But we go on trying,' replied the doctor.

'Naturally, naturally,' Mueller said, matching Morton's tone.

In silence they passed through a set of doors. Beyond was a sterile, windowless area, with a central horseshoe-shaped desk. A monitoring system enabled the two nurses to observe the vital functions of each patient. Wolfgang Kreuse occupied a cubicle to the left.

'I think it would be better if only one of you . . .' the doctor murmured.

'Naturally, naturally,' Mueller said once more.

He remained in the doorway while the doctor led Morton over to a cubicle. Kreuse was the focus of continuous medical activity. Morton briefly wondered what drove doctors. Or made someone like Kreuse believe he could still make his peace with God.

'Wait a minute, please,' the doctor said, going into the cubicle.

Morton studied the equipment around the bed, machines which clinked and pinged, providing confirmation for the medical team that all was not yet lost. But even as he watched, he sensed their actions growing quicker, the commands from the senior doctor becoming more urgent as the blips on the heart monitor became erratic. One of the nurses increased the flow of fluid from the bottle on the drip stand beside the bed. Another checked the electrodes attached to Kreuse's chest.

Morton's escort whispered to the others, who glanced quickly at him, then drew back from the bed. He walked forward slowly, careful to avoid the cables on the floor and a red-painted trolley, its lower shelf filled with equipment and supplies. He sensed their frustration; it was part of that familiar reluctance to admit defeat. Morton looked down at Kreuse.

'He's almost gone,' the doctor murmured.

Morton stared at the screen. The blips were slower and weaker. He turned to the doctor. 'Please, I need to be alone with him.'

The doctor joined Mueller and the others, talking quietly among themselves, watching the still figure on the bed. Morton guessed that deep down, they all knew they were looking at their own ultimate fate.

He bent his head towards Kreuse. 'Can you hear me?'

Kreuse's throat moved but no sound passed his lips. Morton bent closer, his voice even lower. 'It is important you tell the truth now, Herr Kreuse.' Morton glanced at the monitor. The blips were moving erratically. 'Where was your transplant performed?' Their faces were almost touching. For a moment Morton saw something flicker in Kreuse's eyes. Then they closed. 'A name, Herr Kreuse. Just a name.'

The merest sound crossed Kreuse's lips.

'Romer. Have you ever heard of Gustav Romer?'

Kreuse's eyes flickered open.

'Just nod if you have.'

Kreuse gave a faint, strangled sound. 'N . . .'

Morton's ear brushed against Kreuse's parched lips. Kreuse made another, even weaker sound. The blips on the monitor were even more irregular. A red light flashed above the screen. The medical team were back around the bed as a straight, unbroken line traversed the monitor. The light no longer flashed.

'I hope you sent him happy to wherever he's going,' said the doctor.

'I didn't get a chance to find out,' murmured Morton, turning away as a nurse gently pressed closed Kreuse's eyes.

Had Kreuse had been trying to say he didn't know Gustav Romer? Or something else?

10

Though it was barely ten o'clock, they had the restaurant to themselves; Madam had forgotten how early the Swedes dined. A moment ago the couple across the room had risen from their candlelit table, silent as worshippers in church.

'I need more than half an hour with Dr Kramer,' she said, dabbing her mouth with her napkin.

'It's simply not possible, Madam.' Count Olaf Lindeman sighed. 'Even as Director of the Nobel Foundation I am still bound by the timetable. Without it, the Awards ceremonies would disintegrate into chaos. As it is, every year it gets harder to control.'

He could see the maître d' hovering by the service door, smiling his passionless restaurateur's smile. He had already been tipped handsomely for the prime booth at the top of the room. The first time he had dined here with Madam a similar tip had secured the same table.

He moved a bony hand towards the pot the waiter had left. 'More coffee?'

She shook her head. 'But I will have a cigarillo.'

He produced the small silver case from an inside pocket, extracted a slim Cuban cigar, lit one with a match, then passed it to her, at the same time stopping the approaching waiter with a quick shake of his head. He would not be denied his pleasure. He watched her smoke in silence.

This was the first of their private rituals she had taught him. The other was to address her only as Madam. He had managed to give the word its own special caress. Meeting her had been like an Indian summer – and though it had come late, it had come in the end. He had thought, then, that he had not waited for no purpose, nor for nothing kept faith with the memory of Ilse. His wife had been dead for ten years when he met Madam, and he had told himself that had been the start of a new dawn, with its own special sound and colour of pure joy. He knew he was still an incurable romantic and, though in his sixtieth year, he was still prepared to wait for Madam to accept his proposal of marriage. So he had promised himself, as we promise ourselves anything in love. Since then he had hardly heard from her; a birthday and Christmas gift, no more. That had made the pleasure of her phone call from Malibu all the greater, even if, as usual, she had wanted something from him. But it was a small price to pay for an evening of her company. Clearly she was disappointed not to have more time with Dr Kramer.

'I've missed you,' he said, closing the case and putting it back in his pocket.

'I've missed you, too.' She watched the waiter smiling the smile which all servants hope will imprint their faces on the forgetful minds of clients. She looked across the table. 'Tell me the truth, Olaf. Did you really try? I mean, really, *really* try?'

'I promise.'

'And you mean there is absolutely no way for you to extend my time with Dr Kramer?'

'I only wish there were,' he sighed.

He watched her shoulders slip. Impatience? Resignation? He couldn't tell. There was so much about her he didn't know. So much he wanted to discover.

Madam continued to study him. He had an old man's way of behaving, as if he inhabited each day as it came. The very idea of sharing her bed with him made her want to be sick. His emaciated body with its flabby paunch and dead white skin disgusted her. And in the morning she would have to endure his unshaven chin when he planted his first new-day kiss on her lips. She would not only feel his scratchy stubble, but also smell his stale breath and see those rheumy eyes staring at her, and his hair, carefully brushed now to its best advantage, would be an unkempt grey. For a moment she wanted to close her eyes and ears, so that she did not have to look across the table and listen to his tremulous voice. But long ago she had learned to hide her feelings.

Madam reached to touch his hand. 'Are you sure you can't change the timetable, my dear Olaf? I need you so much to do that for me.' She did not easily sound like a woman who needed his help.

He sighed again. 'I only wish I could.'

Her eyes remained upon him. In the candlelight it was hard for him to see what she was thinking. She had looked like this when he had proposed. That had been after Crayton died, and he had judged sufficient time had passed for her to come to terms with her grief. Sitting across from her then, in silence, like now, he had felt like an unsure schoolboy.

'Naturally, I am disappointed, Olaf,' she said after too long. 'And surprised as well. I had thought that I meant enough to you for you to do at least this much. Clearly not.'

'No, no. You do mean a great deal to me. A great, great deal. Please believe me.'

'When you sound like that, I want to.'

'Anything else, Madam, I would do, and gladly. But to change the Nobel schedule is impossible. Not even His Majesty could do that.' He smiled weakly. 'Not even God Himself.'

He fell silent. He had a feeling she was coming to a decision.

'Very well, Olaf. If you cannot, you cannot. That is your decision to make, and you have made it. I am disappointed, not least to see a side of you I had not expected. I do not like intransigence in anybody, especially in a man. It suggests a less than generous spirit. That I do not care for.'

'Madam, please!' he implored. 'You know I would do anything in my power to please you. Only this is not in my gift.'

She straightened and seemed to regroup. She ground out the remnants of the cigarillo and pushed the ashtray to one side of the damask cloth. 'I assume you were able to make sure Nils told her? That much at least could not affect your schedule.'

'Yes, yes, of course.' He nodded, eager to redeem himself in her eyes. 'I told him to do exactly as you asked. Mrs Crayton will know by now you are having a private meeting with Dr Kramer.'

He saw something come and go in Madam's eyes and before she spoke he regretted his choice of words. 'I have told you before, Olaf, that I do not care for you to use her name in that way.' She spoke as if this was a pain they shared.

'Please forgive me for being so insensitive.' For a moment he had forgotten how deep-seated was the hatred between the two women; that they would both be guests at the Nobel ceremonies would need the most careful handling.

Madam had a specially cold smile for forgiveness. 'It's all right. Did Dr Kramer ask why I wanted to see him?'

'No. But he was very happy to meet you.' She couldn't possibly know he hadn't even consulted Dr Kramer about the appointment, simply scheduling the half-hour into his already crowded schedule.

'How is he?' She saw the relief in his face. How very Swedish Olaf was, always ready to seek the safe ground, play the humble servant.

'Dr Kramer's fine. Very much looking forward to everything, of course.'

She gave him a different kind of smile. 'Of course. So am I.' She glanced towards the long-case clock by the cashier's booth. 'It's late. It's been a long day. And I still have work to do.'

'I don't know how you do it, travelling like this. All those companies to keep track of, all those charities. It's just, well, just quite wonderful the way you do it all.'

'It's my work.' It was all she had ever told him about what she did.

The maître d' was hovering. Fresh coffee? A liqueur? She shook her head and looked across the table. 'Thank you for a wonderful dinner, Olaf.' The most believable lies were always told face to face. She pushed back her chair and the process of departure began.

Outside, his driver was waiting with the car. In the back, she sat apart from him, staring impassively out of the window as they sped through the deserted streets of the Old Town. Without saying anything she kept him at arm's length. When the car stopped outside her house, she kissed him chastely on the cheek before quickly closing the door behind her. His eyes followed her across the pavement. There was an animal magnetism in the way she moved and watching her he again felt the full, aching loneliness of his own life. He would do anything to make her a part of it.

At the front door of the house the Organisation owned, she turned and looked back towards the car. His face was pressed close to the window. Such an old fool and clumsy with his affections.

78

She waved once and unlocked the door. Replacing the key in her purse, her fingers touched the message about the Washington bombing. Before going to dinner she had made a number of telephone calls on the matter from the small and completely secure communications room in the basement of the building. Now it was time to make another.

Stepping out of the side door of the Australian Embassy, Joseph Butterfield, the Third Secretary, hit his rhythm as soon as he passed the bored-looking patrolman the Washington police department provided as token security for the legation.

Joe ran easily, on his heels, each stride frugal in expended energy, his feet hardly leaving the sidewalk. His shirt and shorts were faded and he wore a pair of sturdy outback boots, the kind he would need in the mountains. In a few days he'd fly to Seattle and put behind him for a whole week his desk chores. He hadn't realised how tedious a junior diplomatic post in the American capital could be.

Socially life was not much better. So far the claims he'd heard about Washington had turned out to be wildly overstated. He hadn't received a surfeit of party invitations. The few lunches and dinners he'd hosted were strictly business. Women, for all their reputation back home, hadn't actually strewn his path. The instructor at Keep-U-Trim he'd tried to date had said some other time, even though she'd said approvingly that he had the build of a runner: heavily muscled legs and thighs, the rest of his body scoured of fat.

After the bombing, the Ambassador had placed the club out of bounds for all staff, and he'd had to call and cancel his sessions. Rather than tell the instructor the truth, that the Ambassador hadn't forgotten his days in Beirut, he'd used his forthcoming vacation as an excuse. She'd asked where he was going and he'd told her, trying to prolong the conversation by giving her his detailed itinerary. He'd ended by asking if she'd like to come along. She'd laughed and said maybe next time.

Trickles of sweat began to dampen his back and chest and dripped from his forehead into his eyes, making them smart. He brushed them with the back of his hand and looked up at the sun. Noon: a good time for running. Few people to get in the way and destroy his rhythm.

A few blocks further on, a couple of kids began to run behind him, their knees high in a parody of his smooth running action. He glanced over his shoulder at them and grinned. There was something about the lone runner that always invited mockery. Was it because his repeated inexorable stride rippled the daily pattern of the lives of those it passed? Or was it simply that the runner had to be challenged? Maybe one day these kids would come to understand that every runner was making a personal statement with every stride. I run. That is what makes me different from you.

He could feel his rhythm settling as the muscles, idle from the long morning at his desk, began to absorb oxygen from the enriched blood coursing through his body. He increased his pace slightly. He could hear the kids puffing and then the noise faded as they dropped away. Hardly breaking stride, he crossed another intersection, moving through the traffic with practised ease. After this the mountains would be a delight.

It is an article of faith in the United States Department of State that every incoming Secretary will choose a part of the globe where he can leave his personal mark on American foreign policy. For Henry Kissinger it was China. Alexander Haig had chosen the Middle East. Casper Weinberger, Europe. For the newly elected Wallace Armstrong, it was Central America.

In part the reason was because his own father, when Secretary, had tried, and failed, to expand American influence in the region. His successors had fared no better. For each of them their failure had centred on Nicaragua, then, as now, still the most infamous Central American republic. With its pivotal position on the isthmus, it had remained at the heart of the region's political instability.

Secretary Armstrong believed he knew the answer to the problem and was ready to confront it. He glanced across his desk at the aide he had summoned after a morning of uninterrupted cogitation. The man was poised, notepad open. The Secretary cleared his throat and spoke. 'Memo to the President. Copies to the Secretary of Defense, Chairman of the Joint Chiefs of Staff, Director, Central Intelligence. The usual Bigot List distribution.'

He paused. Before he had come into office, he had not known of the list's existence. Now he used its most restricted and secure status as a way of reaching key members in the administration with an assurance his voice conveyed as he resumed. 'Nicaragua remains our greatest problem in the region. The effects of the Contra War, which became a fatal obsession with President Reagan, are still felt. We are not trusted, let alone liked, because the Reagan administration supported the wrong side, the Contras. There is a fear in Nicaragua that we would make the same mistake next time.

'Therefore I am proposing a radical new approach. We will display a total hands-off policy towards Nicaragua – and be seen to do so. All external surveillance of that country, both by satellite and on the ground, will cease forthwith. The CIA will reduce its presence in Nicaragua to the absolute minimum. It will launch no further operations there, and will cease all those currently in force.'

He asked the aide to read back what he had dictated. When this had been done, Secretary Armstrong continued: 'At the same time, under State's guidance, the Treasury will begin to prepare a financial programme which will provide Nicaragua with sufficient funding to become totally self-sufficient. In short, we will do everything possible to make Nicaragua and this country bond together. I am totally confident we then will see a transformation of our present status in the region.'

Secretary Armstrong stopped. He had always been a one-page memo man. Without even having to ask, he knew he had managed to achieve that again.

Darkness came with its usual swiftness while Dr Romer sat before the communications monitor in the *finca*. The reflection from the screen revealed the room to be handsomely appointed; walled with leather-bound books and its centrepiece an eighteenth-century desk, it was a lonely man's sanctum. Not even a framed snapshot offered a link with Dr Romer's past.

As Madam paused on-screen to take another sip from her water glass, he could see through the window the lights of the clinic. A green glow came from the OR skylights; the surgeons were operating late again. A moment ago the emergency generator had cut in to boost the electricity supply from the mainland. The generator's dull thumping was almost lost in the natural sounds of the night, the endless dusk-to-dawn chorus of cicadas.

He turned back to the camera above the screen. Madam's image was being relayed over a satellite geopositioned over the north Atlantic. It was one of three the Organisation owned, providing a totally secure global communications network. Earlier he had listened in total silence to her account of events in Washington.

Putting down her glass, she returned to the matter. 'It really was most unfortunate your people selected a donor who worked for Hammer Force, Gustav. Could this be a single unhappy lapse or are your people getting careless?'

He had not asked how she had discovered this information. Such matters were never discussed between them. 'There was no way to discover beforehand who he was, Madam.'

'We need to change that. In future the instructors must obtain more background for the selection forms. Tell them it is the little things that always matter. Not just who someone works for, but where they go on holiday. Who do they socialise with? Do they go to church? Catholic or Protestant? You can tell a lot from that. The size of their family. How many cars? Where any children go to school. They need to ask as many questions as they need. I just don't want this to happen again, Gustav.'

There was no apparent threat in her words, no quickening of the flow. But Dr Romer stiffened, partly because he had never become used to her familiarity – no one had called him Gustav since his mother died – and from something else as well. She was coming close to intruding on his own area of responsibility.

'I believe you are unduly concerned, Madam.' There was no apology in his response.

'We should both be concerned with anything, however small, remote or trivial, which can pose a threat to the Organisation. A dead Hammer Force employee comes very much into that category, Gustav.' She still sounded unruffled.

'I agree entirely, Madam,' Dr Romer said, the sourness mingling with defensiveness. He waited, but she made no response.

In the basement communication room in Stockholm she stared fixedly at his face on the monitor. When she had chosen him she knew he was someone who would sell his talents to the highest bidder. But once she had bought him, he remained totally committed and loyal. It helped that he had no moral or political allegiances. Someone like Gustav was unique, but he could also be naïve. From the very beginning, she had warned him there would be attempts to infiltrate the Organisation, and had told him to take every possible precaution to stop that happening. Now this.

'I want to talk some more about Morton,' she said at last.

He nodded. She had already touched on Morton.

'There is no proof, Madam.'

'But let us assume it could be him. Do we know why he is in Washington?'

'No. But it will be checked.'

'Good. We need to also know how long he was there.'

'Of course.'

He saw her shift on the screen. 'There is a great deal we need to know before you can be so certain that his visit to our building is not connected to the death of his man.'

'Stamp never visited the Washington facility, Madam. Only those in Chicago, Los Angeles and Houston. And there are no indications of any enquiries being made in any of them. It may well be that Morton is engaged on another matter, perhaps related to this bombing. There have been several such incidents in the past months.'

'Anything which takes him into our building is, I repeat, a threat to the entire Organisation, Gustav! I don't want to labour this, but clearly after what's happened, you can't say our security is infallible. If Morton even comes close, you will have a problem. You should understand this better than anybody. After all, it was to make sure he didn't that I went to so much trouble to arrange your death.'

For the first time an edge of impatience had entered her voice. Instinctively Dr Romer's eyes scanned the bank of security screens. They reassured him. He spoke calmly and with just sufficient irritation to show he should not have to deliver his reminder. 'We have now harvested almost a thousand organs, and so far no suspicion has been directed at us, despite the investigation of scores of police forces. Even if Morton does become involved, where will he begin to look? Our harvesting is so widespread, the enormity of his task would simply be beyond him.'

Once again Madam sat in her bedroom, considering and

weighing. Elmer had warned her about the danger of creating bogeymen prematurely. And indeed, everything she had learned elsewhere was being confirmed by Gustav Romer. Perhaps Morton's presence in the building was a coincidence – if it even was Morton. But she had to be sure. 'Who have you sent to Washington to investigate?'

'Klinger.'

'Good.' Klinger was born to terrorise. He would find out all there was to know. 'Until Klinger reports, I think you should suspend all further organ harvesting.'

Dr Romer needed a moment to believe his ears. 'That's impossible!'

'Why?' She gave a surprised smile.

'Why? I will tell you precisely why, Madam!' He leaned forward, the reflection from the screen giving his face a ghostly hue. 'We have contracts to fulfil. Deposits have been paid by patients who, medically, cannot wait for their transplants. And our organ bank is in urgent need of replenishing. If we do not do so, we will have to cancel operations and make refunds. Financially, of course, that will not seriously affect us, but the damage to our credibility in the long term could be incalculable. We have established our unique position in the market by offering a guaranteed, no-delay service. Because we provide such a service we have been able to continue increasing our fees. I had envisaged another fifteen per cent shortly. To do that it will be essential to maintain a continuous supply of organs. Morton – no one – must be allowed to interfere.'

In the silence he glanced towards the window. The moon was rising behind Mount Masaya. The effects of the afternoon downpour were all but gone and his body had once more begun to torment him.

'You're very persuasive, Gustav,' she said softly. An early lesson of Elmer's had been to always be ready to recognise when you have made a mistake. 'Tell me, how many hearts have you left?'

'One.'

She looked directly into the screen. 'If you're that low, then you're right to be concerned.' She paused before putting her next question. 'Do you have a client for that heart?'

'Yes. Vishinsky.'

She nodded. Igor Vishinsky was Moscow's leading drug baron. If he died there would always be someone to replace him who would continue to pay part of his profits to the Organisation. 'Refund his deposit,' she ordered.

Dr Romer stared at the screen. 'Do you have another client?' he asked.

'When I do, you will be the first to know.' There was no need to tell him yet about Dieter Vogel. 'Very well, Gustav. Continue to harvest. But you must also maintain a very careful lookout for Morton. Whatever is necessary, you have my authority to do it. Goodbye.'

After the screen cleared Dr Romer wheeled himself to the window. He stared out into the night, watching the moon grow. It was a full moon, orange-coloured and angry-looking. A hunter's moon.

11

Ninety minutes after leaving Kreuse's bedside, Morton drove
north along Lake Geneva. The last shards of sun flamed on the
white-capped peaks of the Alps. Even for this time of year the
snow up there was unusually heavy. He drove carefully, not only
because of the black ice but because it was the way he did
everything, as if in another life he'd spent his time challenging the
elements. Beside him on the passenger seat was the file he had
taken from Thrung's office.

On the flight from Frankfurt he had telephoned the man
affectionately known throughout Hammer Force as Humpty
Dumpty, because of his physical shape, and given him a fair imitation
of Kreuse's dying sounds. He had asked Humpty Dumpty to try to
have them deciphered. Humpty Dumpty ran Voice Analysis.
Afterwards, Morton had changed out of his clerical garb and slept
deeply on one of the crew bunks behind the flight deck.

A car overtook him as he turned off the lakeshore drive on to a
road that ended, half a mile later, before tall solid iron gates set in
massive concrete pillars. A high stone wall, capped with razor
wire, extended on either side into the trees. Thick foliage rose
behind the wall. There was a smell of resin from the firs.

Morton pressed a button on the dashboard and the gates swung
silently inwards. He drove through the entrance, waited for the
gates to close, then continued. The small monitor under the dash
showed a steady signal. The infra-red cameras hidden in the trees
had identified the car. If there had been a bomb in it or under the
chassis, they would also have detected it.

Beyond the curve in the drive was the training school where he
lectured once a week, other duties permitting. His subject was the

changing role of terrorism; an endless topic. Those invited to listen had already distinguished themselves with the SAS, Delta Force or one of the European fast-response units. But still only a handful graduated. That demanded something only he ultimately judged. Each time he asked himself one question. Would he trust that person with his own life, no matter what the circumstances? That test never failed.

The main headquarters building came into view. Stone-faced and solid like a fortress, the former gold repository had narrow windows and an imposing arched entrance reached by a wide fieldstone esplanade of broad steps. Morton had never altered his opinion that the Swiss certainly knew how to store their spare gold in style. Parking the car, he picked up the file and stepped on to the gravel drive.

Around the side of the building, where the Communications department was housed, Danny Nagier appeared. Losing an eye while planting a bug had done nothing to reduce his skills. He had served with Morton longer than anyone else in Hammer Force, in all those places where alleys have no names and death comes in multiple forms. Danny toted a metal toolbox and was fingering his eye-patch, the way he did when pleased.

'When we go' – he spoke without preamble when still yards away – 'we'll have a couple of new gizmos.'

'So you solved the glitches?' Danny had said it could take weeks.

Danny grinned. 'Double shifts always concentrate the mind. Now we have a pocket-sized scanner that eliminates all mush. Hail, sandstorm, a force-ten gale. It'll still give you ten-ten sound over a quarter-mile. At a hundred yards it'll pick out a sigh in a rainstorm, guaranteed.'

'We'll also have a flying camera no bigger than a parrot. Whole thing's stealth-painted, and hard put to detect even at a few feet. The real fun part was to link images to the scanner. It means we can now see and hear in the field as never before.'

Morton's mind was already on the most practical step. 'I still don't know where we're going to use them.'

Danny squinted at him. 'I hear Frankfurt was a no-no.'

Morton told him what had happened with Kreuse. Then he opened the file to show Danny the Keep-U-Trim forms and the data covered with corrector fluid.

87

'Let me take this to Chapman,' Danny said. 'If anyone can lift that stuff, he can.'

John Chapman was the training school's expert on solvents and forgery. Taking the file, Danny glanced towards the school. 'One of the Russkies was banging on about the likes of Kreuse the other day. He reckons in five years, they'll all be dinosaurs, replaced by the crime czars of Moscow.'

Morton asked, 'How're our Russians doing?'

They were the visible tip of the new co-operation between Russia and the West on security matters. They were being trained as instructors for their new security service, which had replaced the KGB.

'Keen enough. But they don't yet have all the technical skills. That's going to take another year or two.' Danny shifted his grip on the box. 'Walter was over there this morning, talking to the instructors. He seemed to have this idea that if they lowered the standards a little we could get a bigger pass rate.' Danny had spoken with that special tone soldiers use when explaining the behaviour of civilians.

'The day we start cutting back on anything is the day they'll have my resignation.' The coldness in Morton's voice was more intimidating than anger. 'Where's Walter?'

'Gone to Brussels for that seminar the EC is hosting on computers. Like all late converts, he's becoming something of an apostle for Honeywell and Apple. But he plans to be in Stockholm when Yoshi picks up his prize. Walter wouldn't miss basking in all that reflected glory!'

Morton grunted. 'I'll talk to him then. Meantime remind everyone over at the school that if they have to reject the entire intake it's better than someone failing in the field.'

Morton strode into the main building. Beyond the front door was a marble-floored hall the size of a small ballroom, leading to a magnificent mahogany-balustraded staircase. It was all Morton had retained from the original furnishings. As he closed the door a group of shooters in black coveralls and berets and rubber-soled, calf-length boots emerged from their ground-floor wing, the immense hall echoing with their footsteps. With them were Sean Carberry and Johnny Quirke. Both wore the denims favoured by most department heads. The two Irishmen were chunky, muscular men in the prime of life.

Carberry had represented his country at the United Nations; few had known then that his skills as a fixer were matched by those with a gun. Quirke had been one of the best legal minds at the Dublin Bar until he took early retirement to concentrate on his first love: inventions. Morton had come across him at a trade fair looking for finance. After spending an afternoon talking serious money, Quirke accepted that joining Technical Services was the only way to satisfy his passion. On the day Carberry took over Covert Action, Quirke had assumed control of an eclectic group of boffins.

'You're just in time, David,' Carberry called from across the hall. 'We're off to see if Johnny's whizzkids have come up with the weapon that was used to kill Stamp.'

Quirke carried a canvas bag in one hand and a tin box in the other. He grinned at Morton. 'Come and see. If nothing else, it'll help you convince Bitburg at the next budget meeting we're not actually tossing money out of the window.'

Carberry rolled his eyes. 'He was in with me earlier, wanting to cut the ratio of live ammunition to dummy rounds during practice sessions. I told him I wasn't running a fairground.'

The tone reflected two professionals making professional complaints. Walter always got like this around budget time.

In a group they walked down the stone steps to the basement area and passed the vaults housing Records and Personnel. Beyond, the smelting room had been converted into a simulator where a Tomcat fighter cockpit was used to test recruits. A short corridor led to a door on which was a stencilled notice: 'Mike's Place'. Bitburg had objected to the poorly formed lettering. Morton had reminded him that Mike had not been hired for his penmanship.

The cavernous area where the ingots had been cooled was the size of a football pitch and contained the work of some of Hollywood's best designers. They had assumed the man who employed them was a European film producer, a role Danny had played to perfection. Their drawings and designs, which he had brought back from Los Angeles, had been built into the sets which filled the area. An urban residential street, complete with church, shops and school; a shanty town; a jungle setting. Against one wall was a realistic rock face festooned with pitons and abseil ropes. The opposite wall was faced with an office block whose windows were scorched. A control-booth panel could produce a realistic sandstorm, blizzard, flash flood, the sounds of raging torrents or a street riot. Every six months all field personnel came down here to sharpen their skills under the watchful eye of Mike.

From inside the booth emerged a figure in fatigues who had to stoop to get through the door. 'Hi, boss, I didn't expect to see you. You're not due for your work-out for another month.'

Morton waved. 'Just passing through, Mike.'

He'd found Mike at the tail-end of the Gulf War. When Saddam's Republican Guards had cornered Mike, he'd killed an entire platoon of them before driving off with their tank. In this group of tall men he topped everyone except Morton.

Mike turned to Carberry. 'So what do you want?' he asked.

'The works,' Carberry said cheerfully.

Mike wrinkled his nose and seemed mysteriously pleased.

'We need to test these under worst-scenario conditions,' added Quirke, beginning to take from his bag a variety of weapons: pistols, blowpipes and dart-guns. He turned to Morton. 'Any of these could have been the type which killed Stamp.'

After handing out the weapons to some of the shooters Quirke opened the tin box and held a pellet-sized object between his fingers towards Morton. 'We've made up the bomblets from a butter and resin mixture that should dissolve at the same speed as the real thing. Not having an actual fléchette to work with, it's been a little more hit-and-miss than usual.'

'Never known that to worry you before, Johnny,' Carberry said through his smile.

'You watch it now, Sean. One day we'll come up with something that'll drive you out of business!'

'Gentlemen. If you're ready, let's get this show on the road,' Mike said. Badinage had never been his strong point.

Quirke quickly distributed the pellets and delivered a reminder to the shooters on how to use their weapons. 'Remember, your weapons are all compressed-air operated. You'll have to get close before firing.'

Morton turned to a man holding a blow-gun. 'I'd like to try

that.' The shooter handed over the weapon and joined those who would act as targets.

Mike addressed them. 'Right you lot, usual rules. Once hit, you call out. Then come straight back here.' After they left for the various stage sets, Mike turned to Morton. 'Any preference, boss?'

'I'll take the jungle,' Morton said.

Mike nodded and walked back to the control booth, trailed by Quirke and Carberry, as Morton and the shooters headed for the stage sets.

Entering the jungle, Morton felt its cloying humidity begin to stifle everything. Long ago he'd learned the rules for places like this. There was a simplicity about them, of falling back ultimately on his own resources, which went to the very core of who and what he was. He held the blow-gun in one hand, the pellet in the other. His feet moved lightly over the mulch. From time to time he stopped, listening to the noise. He'd spent hours with Mike choosing the right sound tapes to play over concealed speakers. As he moved deeper into the damp, gloomy foliage, he forgot that the sounds were manufactured and that the putrid stench came from aerosols. He forgot everything. Once more his mind and body had come to point, fused into a single entity.

The target was good. Not by so much as a footfall did he betray himself. From above came the screech of monkeys. Morton looked up. The leaves were still again. Out of the corner of his eye he glimpsed movement, ahead and to his right.

Crouched double, Morton ran with extraordinary quiet and speed to where he'd spotted the target. The man had gone. He moved on, pausing to listen, then moving again. The ground was soggy here. He stooped. No footprints. Morton retreated. Then he saw him, to his left this time. The man was disappearing into one of the many warrens that festooned the place, going as fast as a jack rabbit. Morton raced to catch him emerging at the far end. He crouched behind the stump of a tree, blowpipe poised at his lips, hand ready to insert the pellet. There was no sign of the target. He must have taken one of the side passages in the warren. Morton rose to his feet and once more began to search.

Suddenly he spotted the man, standing facing him yards away. In one movement he brought the blowpipe to his lips, popped in the pellet and puffed. The pellet exploded against the man's neck.

'Bad luck, sir,' called out a voice from behind him.

Morton whirled, realising he had fired at one of Mike's cleverly positioned mirrors.

Together they walked off the set.

For the next hour Morton isolated himself in the sphere. The chamber was housed in a room immediately behind Mike's Place. Made from steel, it resembled a giant golf ball. The shape had been deliberately chosen by its Japanese inventors. They had wanted to remind its target buyers – the high-fliers of the business world – that the sphere was designed to regenerate them both physically and mentally. At first Morton had been sceptical it could achieve all claimed for it. But after a trial run, he had immediately seen its benefits.

Stripping completely naked in the changing room adjoining the chamber, he showered and, still wet, entered the airlock which led to the circular door in the side of the sphere. Closing the door behind him, he lay on the couch and slipped on a harness attached to it, then a headset and goggles. He was immediately plunged into total silence and darkness. He felt the couch gently tilt and he was lowered into a tank of water. Its temperature was carefully controlled to remain at a pleasant constant. A dozen different salts had been mixed with the water to create its buoyancy.

Suspended in the harness, he floated between oblivion and eternity. Gradually, his mind emptied until there was a stage when he felt incapable of thought. Then, just as gradually, he began to think again. As he floated, the possibilities became that much clearer, and he became comfortable with the idea that things which should not be true should be treated as the truth. Then, once more, he began to think about Gustav Romer.

12

When Dr Markus Gruber, the private clinic's Chief Physician, knocked and entered Dieter Vogel's room, the banker lowered a dictaphone, not bothering to hide his irritation. Used fax paper littered the bed's coverlet. The television screen in the corner was tuned to the Bundesbank's closed-circuit channel. As well as medical monitoring equipment, a fax machine and a multi-line telephone console stood on a bedside trolley.

'I see you're keeping yourself busy, Herr Vogel.'

Dr Gruber was a compact man in his middle years, though his exact age was hard to tell, for everything about him suggested a well-kept secret. Even when he spoke there was no emphasis on his words. 'All you need is your secretary,' he added.

'She's come and gone twice today to pick up my tapes,' Vogel said briskly. 'And I hope you have come to tell me when I can leave here.'

Dr Gruber ignored the invitation. 'How are you feeling?'

'Fine. The rest has done me good. But I'm sure it wasn't as serious an attack as we all thought.'

'As a heart attack, no.'

'So when do I leave? Being here is somewhat isolating. There is a good deal happening that needs my personal attention.'

Frau Sauermann had said there had been no calls to his private electronic letterbox. That was worrying. Kransky had promised to report by now; perhaps he was waiting for him to come out of hospital.

'Of course there must be,' murmured Dr Gruber, announcing another change of direction by peering at the heart monitor. 'I see the newspapers are speculating on your next moves in the financial markets.'

Vogel almost managed the right throwaway tone. 'You know the story about the legless man who tried to teach running? He knew the theory but couldn't put it into practice. That's the trouble with the media. All tell, no show. Pundits on crutches.'

'Pundits and crutches. I like that.' Dr Gruber leaned against a wall and folded his arms. 'Pundits and crutches. I like that very much.'

'Do you like what you see on the monitor?' asked Vogel, trying to sound light.

Dr Gruber allowed his dark eyes to dwell on his patient. The voice of the Bundes Chancellor had been insistent. *Tell him the truth. He'll decide what to do – for himself and this country.* A politician's response. But the subtext was clear; you only had to read the financial pages to grasp that. Germany's monetary stability, now that the country had finally emerged from recession, was delicately poised to become once more the financial power-house not only of western Europe, but also in the East, and beyond. It would all largely depend on decisions taken by his impatient and important patient. The timing really could not be better.

'What did the American cardiologist tell you on the plane?' Dr Gruber asked, unfolding his arms and coming to stand at the foot of the bed.

Vogel frowned. 'He seemed to be more used to dealing with children. You know the Americans.'

Dr Gruber neither confirmed nor denied that he did.

'Did he give you any idea of your life expectancy?'

Vogel's frown deepened. 'He said I had nothing to worry about. But my life expectancy? No, he said nothing about that. Why do you ask?'

On every such occasion there was always a moment to introduce the set speech. That it was always the same speech, yet always appeared spontaneous, was to the credit of Dr Gruber. 'No one is immortal, Herr Vogel. But some of us are more mortal than others. Usually we do not know we are until the very last moment. Sometimes not even then. We die in our sleep, unaware. We die, the lucky ones, in passionate embrace. But they die without knowing something was wrong. The lucky ones are given a warning. You, Herr Vogel, are one of the lucky ones.'

'What are you saying, man?' he demanded with a boldness he in no way felt.

Dr Gruber gave him a smile that suggested he didn't understand the need for the question. 'You need a new heart, Herr Vogel.'

The set speech delivered, the stage direction called for silence from the set speech-giver. He watched Vogel withdraw into himself, his eyes growing dull and expressionless.

Vogel closed his eyes and he was back in that room in Wilhelmstrasse in East Berlin, in that grey anonymous building where the Stasi maintained its internal security department. It was late afternoon when the flunkey had shown him into the Chief's office. He had been irritated to have been summoned here, having had to break off a deal with the Poles, and had said so. The Chief had said the matter would not take long – it was just a question of watching a film. The flunkey had drawn the curtains and switched on the video-player.

After a moment, when he had realised what he was watching, he had sat with his hands buried in his face, speaking through splayed fingers, trying to offer an explanation. The chief had leaned forward and placed a restraining hand on him. 'Just watch the screen, Vogel.' And he had done so, watched every last frame showing the growing unease in the child's eyes turn to terror as he stepped from behind the camera, and first penetrated her, then casually reached for a cushion and smothered the little girl to death.

When the screening was over the chief had given a quick, outwardly disinterested shrug. 'I understand she was a gipsy. Bulgarian. There have also been Russians, Czechs, Croats, Poles, even a Russian child. God knows how you brought her from Moscow. We have all the videos. You can see them if you like, but they are much the same. But then, I am sure you know that.'

'What do you want?'

'Let's try to look at this more sensibly. It's not a question of us wanting and you getting nothing in return. Let's see this as a partnership . . .' The Chief had smiled dangerously in kinship.

Under the Chief's direction he had distanced himself from the official focus of Finance Ministry policy to become the one banker both Moscow and the West trusted. Much of what he had learned surprised him; all of it he passed on to the Chief. In return, he had supplied Vogel with children.

Vogel opened his eyes, feeling the panic take hold of him, the way it had threatened to do so in the closing months of the regime, before he had confessed everything to Kransky. The Russian promised to make enquiries and when they next met again Kransky had been reassuring: the Stasi had destroyed the negatives. What a fool he had been to believe that! Someone from his past intended to blackmail him, threatening to ruin all he had achieved in his new life. It couldn't be the Stasi chief. He was dead. But who?

Not knowing if Kransky had managed to find out – and what was being asked for the return of the negatives – was almost as frightening as not knowing what Gruber was driving at. 'What do you mean, a new heart?' Vogel finally asked.

'I am speaking of a transplant.' Dr Gruber spoke gently.

Vogel stared, slack-mouthed, deprived of orientation. Had he gone deaf? Lost his mind? What was Gruber saying? A transplant? How long did a new heart take to adjust to? He could be here for weeks. Maybe even months! What about Kransky then? What about those negatives? What about his whole future? 'Why is this necessary?' he asked.

Dr Gruber picked up a sheet of fax paper from the coverlet, glancing at the columns of figures. Billions of Deutschmarks into tens of billions of Russian roubles.

'Can I use this to draw on?' The voice was a conciliatory murmur. First the bad news, now the good.

'Yes.' Finkle would have a file copy of the transfer to Moscow.

Using the progress chart as a support, Dr Gruber began to sketch. When he finished he explained his crude drawing of a heart. 'The main arteries to your heart have become clogged with all the residue in your bloodstream. Cigarette smoke, alcohol, all the fatty foods you enjoy—'

'The American told me all that!' Vogel interrupted roughly.

Dr Gruber appeared not to hear. 'The rate of blood flow to your heart is poor. But it is not just the arteries. Your heart muscle itself is worn out. You are a classic case for a transplant.'

'I would like a second opinion,' Vogel said.

Dr Gruber's gaze remained steady. 'I have already obtained two. From Professor Latham in London and Dr Morell in New York. They are the best in our field. I faxed them computer-enhanced images of your heart. They agreed with my diagnosis.'

'And your prognosis?'

Dr Gruber glanced professionally at his patient. Vogel looked like a bookworm who took care of his body. 'You are still young and, apart from your heart, in good physical condition. Normally, I would say four or five years. But in your case I can be more optimistic. I would think it reasonable for you to expect at least ten years from your new heart, perhaps more.'

The membrane lifted from Vogel's eyes. 'Very well. How soon can you perform this transplant?'

The doctor looked at Vogel. The man was like steel. Devoid of fear, devoid of any emotion once he had made a decision.

'Ideally, now. But we probably need a month to find a replacement heart. At the best of times there is a shortage of donors. For some reason, no one quite knows why, in the past year or so it has become chronic in Europe. The number of donor-card carriers has dropped. Relatives don't like to grant permission to remove organs from loved ones. Old superstitions die hard.'

'Spare me the details, Doctor. Where can I get a heart? Money is no problem. The bank will pay.'

The doctor nodded gravely. 'I've already been so informed. But it is not a question of money – only availability. I've already put out a call to all the donor organisations in Europe and Britain.'

'What about the rest of the world?'

'We're searching there, too. But the shortage is universal. Try to be patient. We have a little time.'

Vogel gave a small, humourless grunt. 'And you want me to spend it here? Waiting while you and your staff hope the phone will ring? Is that it?'

Dr Gruber crumpled up his drawing and replaced the clipboard before answering. 'Ideally, of course, it would be best if you could remain here, Herr Vogel. But then, as I have been told by the Chancellor, and as you have so clearly shown, you are no ordinary patient.'

'So?' Vogel looked at him like a predator poised to strike.

'In your case my clinical judgement is that the risk would be the same if you remained here or if you were to continue to lead your normal life while waiting for your new heart. I believe you are one of the rare people who would actually benefit from doing that.'

The predatory look had gone from Vogel's eyes. A ghost of a smile twitched at the corner of Dr Gruber's mouth. 'What I propose is this. We continue our every effort to search for a heart. In the meantime you can leave here and continue with your duties. I shall naturally keep you closely informed of our progress.'

Vogel reached for a piece of fax paper and wrote quickly, then thrust the paper at Dr Gruber. 'Here is a number you can always reach me on, day or night.'

Dr Gruber slipped the paper into a pocket of his long white coat.

'When can I go?' demanded Vogel.

'You driver is waiting downstairs,' Dr Gruber said, with no change in the inflection of his voice.

He left the room to make the first of two important telephone calls. After the good news, it was once more the turn of the bad for Dieter Vogel. But then, after all, he was only mortal, and decidedly so.

13

Morton took the elevator from Mike's Place to the second floor. Emerging into the corridor he faced a solid steel door on which was stencilled the words 'Computer Room'. He inserted his colour-coded plastic card into a wall slot and the door slid silently open. His was the only card programmed to open all such doors in the building.

The coolness of the computer room enveloped him. Lester Finel maintained it at a constant air temperature of 55 degrees Fahrenheit. He insisted that the humid-free atmosphere, as dry as his beloved Mojave Desert, was as essential as his decision to use only deaf mutes as programmers. At the best of times Lester disliked idle chatter.

That had impressed Morton as much as Finel's background when he'd hired him. At Honeywell Lester had virtually rewritten the lexicon for using computers in intelligence-gathering and cryptanalysis. He watched Lester rise from his desk at the far end of the open-plan area. A sinewy man in his early forties and prematurely grey, he wore one of his bold checked jackets and golfer's plaid trousers. Weaving his way past the work stations, his left hand maintained a curious motion. It had taken Morton a little while to figure out that it mimicked a revolving spool of tape.

'Hi, Dave.' No one except Finel called Morton that.

'How's it going, Lester?'

Waving his non-revolving hand at the room, Finel continued in his relaxed Californian drawl. 'Problem. Whoever coded those discs knew their business. We thought it was Umbra-related. But could be Solsus-gupy.'

Morton had decided Lester's speech pattern was either from

99

listening to computer-speak or using sign language with his staff. 'Weren't Umbra and Solsus-gupy the old KGB access programmes?' he asked.

'Correct, Dave. Later Stasi adapted them. Problem. They merged them into Magda.'

The Magda communications system had been the most secure within the Soviet empire. Lester had led a team into East Germany the day after Berlin became one city. They had combed through every Stasi command centre and found evidence of Magda's existence, but no clue as to how the system was accessed.

Lester continued to explain as he led the way through the computer room. 'We've tried Ruff, Zarf and Byeman. Each time, zilch.'

They paused to watch a print-out discharge into a wire basket beside an operator. The woman glanced at it, shrugged and turned back to her electronic console.

'So what's your gut tell you, Lester?' It had come down to that in the past.

The computer chief pursed his lips. 'Could be medical. Problem. We've several million medi-code systems on file. And that's only the bigger hospitals and clinics. Add the smaller ones and you're looking at close to twenty million. We're working through them, but it could take weeks.'

They stopped beside a laser printer producing hard copy. Finel glanced at the print-out. 'Keep-U-Trim clients in Washington. Boringly respectable, Dave.'

Morton nodded. He'd let Bill know. No point in his people chasing moonbeams. As they moved on Morton asked, 'What about that password?'

Finel grinned. 'I get to work on that. Figure rewriting Meditale is the only way past the blocker.'

Lester had harnessed pure mathematics to create Meditale. To rewrite the system under such intense pressures was a challenge to test to the limit even his formidable intellect.

'How long do you need?' Morton asked.

'Another couple of days. It's like sand yachting in a Mojava force-ten. You've got to spot the wind change a couple of turns ahead. Problem. I still don't know what language I'm trying to crack. My gut says it's Romantic. Spanish, Italian or French. Overlaying Basque will narrow it down. Soon know. Hopefully.'

'Crank it up to max revs, Lester. On this one everyone has to go the extra mile.'

Morton strode past the programmers writing software to identify possible links between the victims of organ thefts. He could see they were still some way short of finding any.

On the floor above, he emerged from the elevator into a central corridor. Halfway along, he pushed open a heavily padded door marked 'Voice Analysis'. Several of the original offices had been converted into a communal work area. Sound proofed listening booths lined the walls and workbenches covered most of the floor space. They were littered wtih tape-decks, oscilloscopes, editing machines and equipment with flickering dials and coloured lights whose functions Morton still had no clear idea about. But Humpty Dumpty insisted that every twitching needle or pulsing beam was an integral part of the mysterious world he ruled over from his heavily padded chair at one bench.

Physically Humpty Dumpty looked like the nursery-rhyme character, a human egg with a wrinkled forehead. For twenty years he had held the post of Professor of Synthesised Speech at MIT; he'd jumped at the chance to come here and see his theories put into practice.

He motioned to Morton while continuing to spin from one spool to another the recording he had made of Morton's impression of Wolfgang Kreuse's dying sounds. In the booths his staff were playing other copies at various speeds and pitches. Humpty Dumpty draped his headset around his fleshy neck and wheezed noisily.

'That 'N' of Kreuse's. We've allowed for the level of tension in your voice to be different from his. The consensus here is that Kreuse wasn't saying *nein* – no – when you asked your question. We've pulled up everything we have on deathbed sounds. Most of it's Soviet-sourced, though there are a couple of Chinese recordings and some stuff out of South Africa. It's surprising how alike people sound when they're about to die.' Humpty Dumpty always gave you more than you needed.

Morton's eyes strayed over the work area, where men in

headsets sat bowed in front of dials and the wavy green lines of sonic grids and scanners. He turned back to Humpty Dumpty. 'So if Kreuse didn't say "no", what was he trying to say?'

The chief of Voice Analysis completed rewinding the tape and waved a hand to a couch surrounded by stand-mikes. 'It could help us if you can recreate exactly what happened when you spoke to Kreuse.'

'No problem,' Morton replied.

Humpty Dumpty beckoned to one of his staff, then led Morton to the couch. The technician joined them, moving with the casual sanctity of someone about to rob a poor box.

'Sam will act the part of Kreuse,' Humpty Dumpty explained.

Morton positioned Sam on the couch and rehearsed him on exactly what had been said at Kreuse's hospital bedside. Humpty Dumpty posed his head at different angles until he was satisfied. 'Sounds good to me,' he said, waddling back to his bench. He put on headphones, plugged into a recorder and set tape rolling. He nodded at Morton.

'Can you hear me?' Morton began in the same low voice in which he had spoken to Kreuse. After Sam nodded, he brought his face closer to the technician's. 'Where was your transplant performed?' When Sam closed his eyes, Morton continued. 'A name, Herr Kreuse. Just a name.' He paused once more. 'Romer. Have you ever heard of Gustav Romer?' Morton waited a moment. 'Just nod if you have.'

Sam gave a strangled sound. 'N . . .'

'Stop!' Humpty Dumpty called. 'Did Kreuse give a clear "N" or did it begin to slur off?'

'It was clear. Only the rest of the word fell away,' Morton replied.

'Can you remember if it was an "N" as in "nuts" or as in "nobody"?'

'More like in "nuts".'

Humpty Dumpty nodded. 'A hard "N". Right, continue.'

Morton's ear brushed against Sam's lips. He gave the same indistinguishable response Kreuse had made. Morton straightened and looked questioningly at Humpty Dumpty.

'Definitely something to work on here.' It was the closest Humpty Dumpty ever came to promising a result.

Leaving Voice Analysis Morton walked to the end of the corridor. Beyond an unmarked door was the area of Hammer Force Chantal Bouquet had made her own. As he entered the door of her office, she waved him to an armchair. He'd brought Chantal into Foreign Intelligence after she'd shown her worth in places like Bosnia and Iran. She had just passed her fortieth birthday knowing a great deal more than most women ever knew about fear and evil.

None of this outwardly showed. Her immense poise made her seem taller than her actual height, five-eight. She wore her thick reddish-brown hair so that it framed her oval face. When she was angry Morton had seen her eyes narrow and turn a darker brown. Mostly they remained wide-spread and appraising, as they were now. 'Socialising?' she asked. Her smile did not quite diffuse the merest edge to the word.

'I wish.' Morton spread his hands in deprecation.

She looked at him for a long, silent moment and then admonished him gently. 'You can push yourself too hard.'

'It goes with the job. Same as for you.'

She sensed his sudden wariness and moved to reassure him. 'Sorry. I didn't mean to sound mother hen.'

He smiled quickly. 'It's OK. And you weren't. It's just . . . well, this whole Stamp business . . .' He watched her consult her notepad. When she spoke her voice was businesslike.

'I've just had Tommy on the phone. He's been to the Keep-U-Trims in Houston, Los Angeles and Chicago. He says the facilities are superb. He also managed to get a look at their appointment books. Nothing to show Stamp ever made one.'

'Where's Tommy now?' he asked.

'On his way to Washington. He's taken the same flight Stamp did, and arranged to book into the same motel room. First he's going to see Gates.'

'And Anna?' Morton asked.

Chantel glanced at her pad. 'She's turned up not so much as a blemish in Stamp's background. She's also checked out the new Keep-U-Trim in London. A ringer for those Tommy visited.' Chantel leaned back in her chair. 'You really think they're tied into this?'

Morton gave her a regretful smile. 'You're sounding like Walter.'

'God forbid.'

'For sure.'

She looked at him, troubled. 'The problem is that we've got a lot of leads, but we're still not sure of their status. The police keep on insisting its ritual-crime-related. So do all the experts we've spoken to. So far I've come up with nothing that can shake their belief.'

Morton walked to the window. Through the trees he could see the roof of the training school and beyond, the first lights coming on around Lake Geneva. Despite the warmth of the room he felt cold. For a moment he had imagined he could actually see the evil that had ripped out Stamp's kidneys and the organs of all the others. He turned back to Chantel. 'When Anna gets back I want her to start checking advertisements for nurses to work in transplant centres. We'll focus on one. Places like that operate their own network. There'll be interfacing, contact, the usual. Anna's job will be to monitor.'

Chantal made a note. Morton ran a hand down his cheek, a tired man's gesture.

In spite of herself, Chantal returned to her earlier concern. 'You need some sleep, David.'

'Right now I need to talk to the Prof.' He saw the hurt in her eyes despite her self-control. He hadn't meant to sound brusque. But whatever Chantal hoped could happen between them had never got started. Since Carina he had avoided all emotional entanglements. Loving her had been like opening a little-used drawer. Carina had been killed with a sudden violence which had closed that drawer forever. 'I'll snatch a few hours when I get to Stockholm,' he said, more gently.

She searched his face for a fleeting moment longer. 'Take care, David.'

'You too.'

There was a note of sudden exasperation in her voice. 'When you see Bitburg, tell him I'm seriously over his limit with what I'm spending on this one. But he'd better not try to cut my budget for next quarter. Otherwise he can have my job.'

'I'll tell him. And nobody's going to have your job,' Morton promised.

Minutes later the elevator deposited him on the top floor. Once more he faced another steel door. He spoke firmly into a voice box set in the wall. 'Quince.' The Prof used colours for his own security system to make Psychological Assessment impregnable to all but a few. After the door slid silently open and closed, Morton adjusted his eyes to the low-level lighting. The Prof abhorred bright surrounds.

Every desk in the large open-plan room was occupied by a man and woman, either reading or working on a VDU screen. No one looked up. A sepulchre-like quiet blanketed the area. The Prof detested noise. A new researcher sat at Stamp's desk. The Prof didn't believe in ever leaving a vacancy for Bitburg to make permanent.

Morton sensed the mood of expectancy as he walked past the specialists whose skills embraced the whole arena of how to create or deflect psychological pressures. Nowhere had Stamp's death left its mark more than here. At the far end of the room he opened the outer door, then the baize-covered divider and finally the inner door to the Prof's office.

The darkened office was lit by a single spot, focused to fall precisely upon the white-faced figure in cardigan and baggy trousers who lay motionless on an old-fashioned consulting couch against one wall. In repose the Prof looked anywhere between a frail sixty and seventy. In appearance no one could be more deceptive.

'Come in, come in, David. I heard you were making your rounds. Always a good idea to work your way to the fountain head, so to speak.'

Morton smiled. The murmured words were a reminder that the Prof was simply the best in his field. A Freudian with a killer's instinct.

'Now then, find a seat and let's see. Yes, yes, let's see.'

The Prof had a weakness for verbal repetition. It went with his other eccentricities: dressing like a fogey, working in a cultivated shambles, lying on his couch for lengthy periods, and, as he did now, cracking his finger joints when he spoke. But Morton had warmed immediately to his plain language and short way with psychobabble.

'Move those journals off the chair by the wall, David. Make yourself comfortable.'

When Morton had done so, the Prof resumed. 'Tell me what's been happening. I know about Lester's struggle with those discs. Don't let them assume an inflated importance. But this matter of Kreuse and Romer. I've been thinking a great deal. Yes, yes, a great deal.'

'Is there a link?'

'There's always a link, David. It's a question of seeing it.'

The Prof stared unblinkingly at Morton and then delivered a response that, as usual, was devoid of caveat. 'Kreuse was the world's first total colon transplant. Romer the best immunologist the Stasi had. Kreuse dropped out of sight in the Caribbean. Romer died, geographically speaking, more or less in the same area.'

With a sudden effortless movement the Prof rose from the couch, vigour flowing into his face. He continued to expound as he paced the room. 'What exactly was Romer doing in Ecuador? Nobody goes there for a vacation. Did the Stasi send him? Unusual, highly unusual. Romer was in their upper echelon. Someone like that doesn't go slumming in the Third World.'

Coming here always concentrated Morton's mind. 'He could have been on his way somewhere else when his plane crashed. The Stasi had begun operating in Peru and Brazil just before the end.'

The Prof stopped and stared at him, then resumed pacing. 'Let's tease this out a little more, David. Just a little more. Romer's body was never found. I know, I know, it's supposed to have been eaten. But the key word is "supposed". And was all of it devoured? Every last tooth and finger? Our people can do wonders with a single cavity or thumb smudge. The CIA, too. But there was nothing to work on. Nothing at all.'

The Prof paused by a bookshelf and pulled out a volume. He quickly riffled to the page he wanted and looked at Morton. 'This is Ashwood on predatory behaviour. A hundred years on, there's nothing better.' The Prof glanced at the text. 'This is what he says: "Predators, however hungry, always leave something behind to identify their victims."'

'There. Think of that.' The Prof closed the book and placed it back on the shelf.

It was like playing chess, Morton thought. He delivered his next blocking move. 'If your theory is right, Prof, and the Stasi discovered Romer was jumping ship, they could have put a bomb on the plane. That was very much their style. And it would logically explain why there was nothing left for anyone to identify.'

The Prof stopped in front of Morton. 'And Romer's briefcase? Wouldn't a bomb have destroyed that? Instead, there was just enough in the case to make the CIA happy. By the time Langley realised it didn't amount to much, the trail was cold. No point then in going back to check. No point at all. Someone like Romer would have anticipated that. Look at his psycho-profile. That man's mastery of lateral thinking is clear. So very clear.'

Morton nodded. The business with the briefcase had nagged at him. Now he put into words his unspoken doubt. 'Are you saying Romer is alive, Prof?'

'Why not? It's possible. Very possible.'

They looked at each other for a long, silent moment. It was Morton who spoke for them both. 'Then maybe what Kreuse was trying to tell me was a place name? Where he had his transplant?'

The Prof pursed his lips. 'You can discount all the obvious ones, David. You're looking for somewhere beginning with "N" that's out of the way – and certainly not where you'd expect to find a clinic. Not at all where you'd expect to find one.'

'I'll get Library working,' Morton said, walking towards the door. By the time he reached the outer office the Prof would be back on his couch.

As he crossed the open-plan work area, one of the operatives looked up and beckoned. Morton walked over.

'This came in while you were with the Prof,' murmured the operative.

On the screen was a news agency report that the body of the former KGB Chief in East Germany, Boris Kransky, had been found in a hotel room in Amsterdam. A Dutch police spokesman said Kransky had suffered a heart attack. There was no indication of what he had been doing in the city.

Picking up a phone, Morton asked the switchboard to connect him to the Police Commissioner in Amsterdam. When the Commissioner was on the line, Morton explained why he was calling. The Commissioner asked him to wait. He was soon back to report that Kransky's body had been cremated.

Morton thanked him and hung up. Now, more than ever, he needed to speak to Anna.

14

Close to midday Lindeman sat in the cushioned rear seat of the limousine the Swedish Foreign Ministry had provided to bring the Nobel Prize-winners from Arlanda to the city. Twice already this morning he and Nils, together with Marta Hamsum, an attractive translator from the Ministry, had made the journey to and from the airport to welcome this year's laureates for Literature and Physics. Now they all awaited and arrival of Dr Yoshi Kramer, the winner of the Nobel Prize for Medicine.

He discreetly checked his smile in the rear-view mirror. It was the Smile of Most Welcome he had perfected over many years: it blended graciousness with a careful measure of respect, for long ago he had learned that laureates could be arrogant to the point of shocking if they felt less than properly appreciated. This morning, for instance, it had needed very nimble work by Nils and himself to convince the Literature Prize-winner that all his books, every single page of them, were intimately known not only to them, but to everyone in Sweden.

Thankfully, the Ministry's briefing indicated that Dr Yoshi Kramer was blessedly free of such conceit. Yet, now he was only moments away from their meeting, the question of Madam's appointment with the laureate loomed large. After he had escorted her home, he had told the chauffeur to drive him back to the Foundation. There, after a considerable amount of juggling, he had after all done what he had told Madam was impossible: extended her time with Dr Kramer to a full hour.

He planned to keep the news a secret from her until the last moment. Then, when she was still recovering from her surprise, and no doubt delight, he would deliver the little speech he had rehearsed in between his journeys to and from the airport.

I am not a wealthy man, he announced one more time in his head, but I can offer you an abundance of love and emotional security. I will honour and treasure you like no other woman has been. Still looking directly into her eyes, he would quote the words of his favourite poet. Wordsworth. 'There is a comfort in the strength of love, 'twill make a thing endurable.' Then, without undue pause, he would ask her to marry him. And, deep in his heart, he truly believed that this time she would accept. In doubling her time with Dr Kramer, she would see that he was strong and as resolute as she was herself.

The flight from Geneva had landed and halted before he motioned the liveried chauffeur to open the rear door. Nils and Marta were already on the tarmac. She was holding a magnificent bouquet of flowers; his assistant a leather-bound folder containing Dr Kramer's schedule. Giving Madam her precious extra time with Dr Kramer had meant reducing his time with distinguished colleagues from Sweden's leading medical institutes. He had decided not to tell Dr Kramer about the change of plan. Emerging from the warmth of the car, he put on his formal silk hat and adjusted the collar on his black overcoat before glancing quickly to check that his black shoes still gleamed in the cold, grey daylight. Watching the aircraft door open he turned to Marta. 'Dr Kramer speaks perfect English and I hear his Swedish is also excellent.'

'Not like our Physics laureate,' Nils said curtly. 'Most of the time I could not make out a word of what he was saying. When it comes to his acceptance speech I'm going to insist he makes it in his own language.'

Testing his Most Welcome Smile, Lindeman turned to Marta. 'Perhaps you could do the translation?'

'I would prefer not to, Director.' Marta replied tautly.

Lindeman raised an eyebrow. 'May I enquire why?'

'The man is a lecher. In his suite he tried to corner me twice in a few minutes.'

Lindeman sighed. Every year there was always one winner who suddenly discovered his testosterone level had increased after receiving the Foundation's congratulatory telegram. 'Most regrettable, of course. And I'll make sure you are kept well away from him, Marta. But try to see what happened as part of the privilege of being able to acquaint yourself with one of the geniuses of the world.'

Nils' voice was almost lost in the engine whine-down. 'And one created by us. Like many of the others our Physics Prize-winner was completely unknown before this. Now he will be able to command more in a week on the lecture circuit than many of those who voted for him earn a year.'

Lindeman gave a swift, elegant shake of the head. 'No, no, Nils, not so. Our Russian was a genius, all our winners were, before we formalised matters.' He had heard this argument before, many times, within the selection committee about a candidate's overall past contribution to his field. Yet in Dr Kramer's case the vote had been swift and unanimous; his discovery was one of the most worthy to be honoured.

He turned back to Marta. 'Dr Kramer will give you no such problems. Your own Ministry's confidential report describes him as a gentleman of the old school.'

Further conversation ended as a tall, rangy man in a loden topcoat emerged from the aircraft cabin. Behind him came a steward, carrying a suitcase. Nils turned and beckoned to the photographers.

'He's younger than his pictures,' murmured Nils.

'And better looking,' added Marta.

'Forward,' commanded Lindeman, his Most Welcome Smile at full stretch, his mind isolating the salient points from the special briefing only he had been given. Yoshi Michael Kramer belonged to that group of European surgeons who did not believe in theatrical attitudes or excessive sensitivity. Childless marriage ended ten years ago. A number of affairs, none significant. A workaholic with no real hobbies. At forty-two, their youngest laureate.

They had reached the foot of the steps, looking up, all smiling; Yoshi looking down, smiling. Another curtain on the theatre of welcome had risen.

Yoshi gave the photographers their first shots, waving, turning this way, then that, his hair stirred by the breeze, crinkling his eyes so that the camera wouldn't see the tiredness caused by the reduced flow of blood to his heart. Before landing he'd taken two more of the tablets that kept his arteries open. They were a Russian preparation he had come to swear by. Still smiling, he descended the steps.

Lindeman doffed his hat in greeting. 'Most welcome,' he said, shaking Yoshi's hand and introducing himself.

Yoshi accepted Marta's bouquet, shook hands with Nils and allowed himself to be shepherded towards the car, ignoring the photographers and concentrating on what his host was saying now they'd gone through the set-piece about a good flight, honoured to have you here, glad to be here, no, no, the pleasure is all ours.

'First we will take you to your hotel. Then you can rest. There is a cocktail party this evening, six to eight, followed by dinner for all the laureates with the Nobel committee. Tomorrow morning there is the first of two press conferences. One for the Swedish media; the other for the international press. In the afternoon there is the first dress rehearsal for the Awards ceremony . . .'

Yoshi smiled at Lindeman. The world was full of those who lived through others, who worried whether their hands were doing the right thing as they marched across the tarmac in a cocoon where time was more than a measure.

They reached the open door of the limousine. Lindeman motioned Yoshi to enter while Nils waved the cameramen away. Marta joined Yoshi on the back seat, taking the flowers from him and smiling prettily. The Count and the Assistant Director sat on the jump seats. The chauffeur shut the door and, by the time he had settled behind the wheel, Nils had closed the dividing glass partition. He turned to Yoshi and offered him the folder. It was leather-bound, like the menu in an expensive restaurant.

'Your schedule,' Nils murmured.

Yoshi glanced at the single foolscap page of laser print. Every waking moment between now and departure time after the Awards ceremony appeared to be given over to meetings, media interviews, lunches and dinners, even that tiresome American habit of taking breakfast with strangers. He closed the folder. 'Any way of cutting back on some of this, Count Lindeman?' he asked with a perfectly pleasant smile.

Lindeman's Most Welcome Smile paled to a mere brightness. 'Cut back? I'm not sure I understand.' His voice seemed to be coming from far away. 'There are so many people who would like to hear first-hand from you about how you made your discovery.' He stopped, not able to continue for the moment.

Nils was speaking. Months of preparation . . . everybody carefully vetted . . . many left out. Please try to understand . . .

'Is there a reason why you wish to reduce the schedule, Dr Kramer?' Lindeman asked.

Yoshi glanced out of the window. They were in open countryside and picking up speed. They had gone to a great deal of trouble, and he didn't want to disappoint them. But the matter had to be settled. 'I have a problem, Count Lindeman.'

Now everything seemed to be happening in slow motion. The old man closing his eyes. The tall, good-looking assistant looking as if he'd just lost at cards. The plump girl's hips, which a moment ago had rested against him, suddenly pulling away. Then, after an eternity, the old man's eyes were opening, and he was asking a question. 'What sort of . . . problem?'

Yoshi spoke calmly and quietly, the way he would impart news to one of his own patients. 'I have a heart condition. When I return home I'm to undergo surgery. A triple bypass. While I don't wish to do anything to ruin the party, I also don't want to be stupid enough to take on more than I can cope with.'

The Most Welcome expression switched to Most Genuine Concern, not so much a smile as a grimace of sympathy. 'I had no idea, Dr Kramer . . .'

'None of us had,' Nils revealed.

Marta continued to look merely stricken.

Yoshi tried to sound cheerful. 'Sorry to drop it on you like this. But it's best to be up-front about these things and I'd appreciate it if you made sure no one else gets to hear, Count Lindeman. Especially the press. I'll have enough of them when I go into hospital.'

'The press will have a field day,' Nils said in a voice that hinted he was an expert on such excesses.

'You have my assurance, Dr Kramer. No one will learn of this while you are in Stockholm. Now, let's see what can be done.' Never surprised by his own obedience, he reached for the folder. The others watched while he scanned the foolscap, then produced a gold fountain pen from an inside pocket and began to score out appointments. He checked his work one more time. Satisfied, he handed the folder back to Yoshi. 'I have cut your schedule to the absolute minimum, Dr Kramer. The very absolute minimum.'

'Thank you.' Yoshi skim-read the paper. It had indeed undergone drastic pruning. But one item not scored through caught his eyes. Immediately after the Awards ceremony, a sixty-minute slot was still blocked off. Against it was the notation: 'Private Meeting'.

'Who is this with?' he asked in a voice not quite as perfectly pleasant as before.

Count Lindeman told him: his rheumy eyes on Yoshi, his voice tremulous, his hand, now that it had completed all its hard work of crossing-out, shaking ever so slightly. The longer he spoke, the more a part of Yoshi wanted to lean forward and say, of course, of course, there are just some appointments you can't break. Instead the other part, the greater part, put the question: 'Why does she want to meet me?'

'In all honesty, I don't know, Dr Kramer. But Madam has never made such a request before. That is why I granted it this time.' He was staring in the back seat like a supplicant. Do this for me and you will make me the happiest man on earth.

Yoshi looked out of the window. They were entering the suburbs of Stockholm, as dreary as any other urban development. Why did she want a whole hour? He only gave that sort of time to a patient.

'It's only an hour,' coaxed Lindeman. 'And as you know, she is a very important patron of medicine . . .'

'I know.' Who didn't in the cut-throat world of medical politics and financing? He'd glimpsed her at one or two of the conferences he'd addressed. But they'd never come closer than that to meeting. And he'd never asked her for funding. Nor had he ever operated on one of her circle, at least as far as he knew. He could think of no reason why she wanted to see him. A consultation? A relative who needed one? From what he knew that was not her style. So why?

'Do you know what she wants?'

'Truly not.'

'Can you find out?'

'I'll try. But will you still see her?'

Yoshi was still staring out of the window when the limousine drove along one side of the Strommen Canal and drew up beside the magnificent entrance to the Grand Hotel.

'OK. An hour it is. No longer.' In the window reflection he saw the Count's relief. First in the way his face cleared, then in the decisive manner he reached for the door handle. The old boy was really very sweet, smiling like that. The Most Welcome was securely back in place.

It was late morning when Dr Gruber made the first telephone call from behind the closed door of his office. It was to the National Transplant Organ Bureau in Bonn. The government agency coordinated the availability of donors in the Federal Republic, and acted as the link with similar agencies throughout Europe and the United Kingdom.

'We no longer require a heart,' Dr Gruber informed the bureau's deputy director. 'My patient has changed his mind about having a transplant.' He was very conscious of the sweat that had formed in the palms of his hands. Now there was no turning back. But then, there hadn't been for some time.

He dialled the number he had been given to call in Stockholm and heard the faint click of a recorder at the other end. He informed the machine what he had done.

Feeling a need to move, he began to walk around the office, the way he had a year ago when a stranger had telephoned for an appointment. Stuhm, he said his name was. Herr Stuhm. Later the joke-name had fallen flat when he'd found out that *stuhm* was Yiddish for keeping quiet. But by then he was more securely bound to silence than a Mafia oath.

Herr Stuhm had turned out to be courtly and in his late fifties, and his proposition straightforward. He was authorised to offer DM10,000 a month consultancy fee on behalf of Globax, an American pharmaceutical company. Herr Stuhm had produced all the supporting paperwork and explained that Globax was a newcomer and very much on the cutting edge of research. It wanted an established figure to refer its clinical papers. Would he accept? He would. A couple of papers had arrived in due course and their claims did not seem exceptional.

Six months later Herr Stuhm had visited again, this time with Mr Selby, an American lawyer. Mr Selby had done all the talking.

There was a problem: one of the referred papers had turned out to be for a toxic drug. Fortunately no one had died, but Globax had paid substantial compensation. Mr Selby, as the company's legal representative, was there to say that his client now intended to sue the referee. He had been still in deep shock as Mr Selby, after a great deal of lawyer's circumlocutions and hesitations, said there could be a possible way out. It so happened he also represented another drug company, whose name he did not wish to mention; that company was about to buy out Globax. As part of the deal, Mr Selby could arrange for the purchasers to absorb the legal claim. All he needed to do was sign a liability declaration. He had signed.

Three months later had come a call to say that the other company, still unnamed, had decided not to go ahead. The caller had been a Mr Umboto, and he had certainly sounded Nigerian. He had never heard of Herr Stuhm or Mr Selby.

A week ago Mr Selby had called again. In between the dead silences he had been brutally frank. 'With the collapse of that deal, Gruber, the securities people have moved in. They're looking at all kinds of paperwork. Gruber, you could be up shit creek without a paddle if they come across your waiver.' Mr Selby had then explained how he could offer a new paddle. Listening, he'd had the sensation of being in a long, dark tunnel that led to a place of public execution. From far away he'd heard Selby's reassurance. 'It will be easy for you as a doctor, Gruber. You know Vogel needs a new heart. Just offer to get him one, go through the motions, then cancel out. Do that and you'll never be troubled again.'

Now that he had done so, he felt exhausted. He badly needed to take a short holiday. Once more Dr Gruber reached for the telephone.

Wheelchair whooshing softly down the concrete ramp behind the main clinic building, Dr Romer reached the heavy metal door marked 'No Admittance'. He pressed a button on the chair's control box to open the door. Beyond was a small, bare-walled hallway with a second, unmarked door. He waited for the outer door to close, then used the control box to access and entered the clinic's underground operations room. From here the Organisation controlled its various global activities.

It was here that, among much else, the operation to entrap Markus Gruber had been patiently masterminded: the setting up of Globax, the paperwork which had given plausibility to the shelf company and the role-planning by three members of the Organisation. From here had been issued the order to buy the highly incriminating videos of Dieter Vogel, and then the subsequent order to deal with the meddling former KGB officer, Kransky. These matters had been dealt with in between the constant flow of buy-and-sell orders, contracts, bills of lading, freight certificates and all the other paperwork which, as a matter of course, ensured the Organisation remained securely on the right paper-trails.

The size of a tennis court, the room's low ceiling and walls were lined with heavy flocking as an additional precaution against eavesdropping. The floor was made of a composition, designed to deaden sound. The dimmed red lighting never varied. Only the wall clocks indicated to the operatives whether it was day or night in all those parts of the world where the Organisation's writ ran.

In the middle of the room was a plotting table covered with a bas relief map of the world, with the island as its centre. Around the table were work stations continuously manned.

After pausing to adjust to the light, Dr Romer glanced about him. The station against the far wall handled Global Transporter. A master screen suspended above the work area showed that the fleet of cargo planes were all airborne. At adjoining stations operatives monitored the constant flow of information into their headsets from the industrial, chemical and other corporations the Organisation wholly owned. From a glance at the screen he could see that in a hundred countries, subsidiaries were trading normally. He propelled himself across to the plotting table.

One of the operatives wheeled back his cushioned chair to allow Dr Romer a clear view. The hundreds of Keep-U-Trim clubs dotted across the map were each represented by a tiny Apollo figure, each holding a flag. One flag was half raised over the club in Washington; another above the one in Munich. The half-raised position meant a harvesting in the offing.

'What is their current status?' he asked tonelessly.

The operative turned to his modem. 'Washington reports a good prospect. The target is shortly going on vacation. He is flying to Seattle, from where he plans to drive alone into the mountains, then walk. The recommendation is that that would be the best time for his harvest.'

Dr Romer studied the information on-screen. Washington was right. The medical assessment made the target one of the finest physical specimens for a long time. With careful work, it should be possible to harvest all the organs.

An hour later, from across the lake, came a muted rumbling, not unlike thunder. The sound did not, however, come from the sky, but from the bowels of the earth, and it passed quickly. Mount Masaya had finally awoken after a century of sleep. But it was such a gentle awakening that no one realised what had happened.

15

Before leaving the island Klinger gummed on a black hairpiece, moustache and a full beard which hid his razor cut. Coal-black contact lenses completed the transformation. A Costa Rican passport and the appropriate paperwork described him as a commodity broker on a business trip to Washington. From Dulles International he took a taxi to Dupont Circle. Going into the Keep-U-Trim building, he saw no evidence of the recent bomb blast.

'*Pura vida*,' he greeted Karl-Wolf Thrung in his office, using Central America's commonest catchphrase. 'Pure life.'

'I prefer you speak English,' Thrung said in a heavy Prussian accent.

'Gone native, have you?' Klinger asked without humour. He liked to set the tone from the outset.

'I understand everybody also speaks English on the island.'

'When were you there? I don't remember seeing you,' Klinger said, eyeing Thrung through an imaginary gunsight.

'I have never been there.'

'So how do you know how we speak down there?'

Thrung's shrug, whether intentionally or otherwise, suggested a certain femininity. 'So what is it that I can do for you, Klinger?'

Klinger did what he always did: he took his time. Thrung was taller than he'd thought, closer to seven than six feet; and heavier, too, probably tipping the scales at over 300 pounds, and all muscle beneath that tracksuit. And they certainly spent money on the staff in this place; that double-knit suit had to be worth $500 of anybody's money, with all that hand-stitching and the Apollo logo picked out in gold thread. Thrung's hands were like twin hams;

they went with his weightlifter's haircut, cut down to the scalp. And the tan looked permanent. He wasn't fooled. Those enlarged pores and sagging cheeks showed Thrung was over the top. His eyes were the real giveaway. They always were. They were the eyes of someone who, the further he was from his last snort, the more desperate he was for his next. A coke addict, from the broken skin around his nose. Well, well, Thrung; no wonder you haven't been to the island; we'd soon have spotted you.

'So, Thrung, tell me exactly about these two men you saw?'

Thrung did. When he finished, Klinger shook his head.

'Not very good descriptions, Thrung. You can do better than that.' The hard, even eyes held the first hint of threat.

'I was at the back of the crowd.'

'Still close enough to see.' Klinger had begun to pace the room, slowly, like a caged animal.

'I was a bit shocked.'

'Rubbish. Nothing had happened up to then. It must have been more like a carnival out there. These two men: tell me again, exactly what you saw.' Klinger paused by the window and looked down on the street, as if he already knew in his mind's eye what Thrung should have seen.

'They went into the building so quickly I didn't have much time.'

Klinger's eyes continued to appraise. 'Let's go over it again.'

And he did: again and again, and again, again. The questions came singly, in bursts, softly, spat out, whispered, shouted, accompanied by fearful curses and in the whispers of the confessional. They came from all distant parts of the room and in close-up, with Klinger leaning across the desk.

'The tall man – how old?'

'Your age.'

'Thirty? Thirty-five? Older? What?'

'Around thirty-five. Maybe a couple of years either way.'

'The second man?'

'Older.'

'By how much?'

'Ten years. Could be a few more. Four, five, no more.'

'How were they dressed?'

Thrung sourly confirmed the descriptions he had already given and Klinger listened intently for discrepancies. What they wore was not important; only Thrung's ability to change his story.

'How long were they inside the building?'

'Ten minutes. No more.'

'Were they inside when the explosion happened?'

'Yes.'

'Did they come out at once?'

'Yes.'

'Run out?'

'I think so.'

'*Think!*' Klinger screamed. 'Don't *think*! Remember!'

'No – they walked out. But quickly. Almost a run.'

'Panicked looking?'

'I've already told you. I couldn't see their faces properly. They were side-on to me.'

But Klinger appeared not to hear Thrung's protest.

'Same man carrying the suitcase?'

'Yes.'

'It look as heavy for him?'

'Yes.'

'Where did they go?'

'I told you, Klinger. I think they went to a car.'

'You *think*? Stop *thinking*! Just remember! What sort of car?'

'I couldn't see. The police were pushing us all back after the explosion. There was a lot of smoke.'

Klinger let a long silence pass during which he sighed and appeared to resign himself to the idea that Thrung was telling the truth.

'How big a bang was it?'

'Big.'

The humourless smile was back.

'Come on, come on, Thrung. Big like a firework? Big like dynamite? Big like *what*?'

'Big like a bomb.'

'How many bombs have you seen exploding?'

'None.'

'So how do you know what a big bomb blast sounds like?'

'I . . . I just guessed. Judged it from what I've seen on TV, the movies.'

121

'You been guessing about anything else, Thrung?' The smile had gone, the lips once more like razor cuts.

'No.'

'Don't ever guess, Thrung. Now, let's go back to those men . . .'

Finally Klinger called a halt. The height was right for Morton. But the rest didn't quite fit. And the other man could have been anybody. Yet he hadn't come all this way for nothing. There *was* something here. Just be patient.

But Thrung could add no more. Should he start now to invent? He had had enough of this bullying.

'I'm sorry, Klinger. I can't remember any more.'

And Klinger, for a moment, was too out of breath from his questions to disagree. But there was something here. Most definitely.

An hour later. The same questions. But the more Klinger asked them, the less certain Thrung had become. Just stick to the old Stasi techniques and he'd get there. Eventually.

'Why are you so interested in these people?' Thrung mumbled in a pause.

'The Organisation's wider interests are not your concern! The taller man, describe the way he walked. Any mannerisms, like cocking his head to one side, or using his hands to make a point.'

As Thrung once more tried to recall someone he had only seen briefly from the back of the crowd in Dupont Circle, he felt dampness forming in the fleshy crevices of his body. What made it worse was knowing that the bottle of best Peruvian Flake was only inches away in the desk drawer.

'Please, Klinger, I can't remember any more. And I have sent a full report.'

Klinger deliberately took his time producing the photocopy of the message Thrung had faxed to the island. 'You have left nothing out, Thrung?' he carefully increased the degree of menace.

'Of course not. For God's sake, Klinger!' But it was no longer resentment in Thrung's voice.

Klinger stared at him for a moment longer, then began to read. There are more ways to open up a chink than with a verbal battering-ram.

The dampness had spread to the small of Thrung's back when Klinger finally looked up. The questions took on a new choreography. Klinger was like a man possessed now, here, there and everywhere in the room.

'Is there anything else you need to tell me, Thrung?' Shouted from beside the Honeywell.

'Anything else? No. I've told you everything.'

'Are you absolutely certain? A whisper from beside the coffee table.

'Yes, of course.'

'How can you be so certain? I haven't asked you everything I want to ask.' Screamed from over by the window.

'Then just ask.'

'Don't tell me what to do, Thrung. Don't ever do that.' Advancing across the room.

Klinger leaned across the desk, with his blue, washed eyes, his mirthless smile, so unnaturally relaxed, his manner once again of such uncontrolled concern that for the first time Thrung was truly fearful. He knows about the file. He must know. That's why he is here. The words were loud in his head. And if he knows about that, he knows everything.

When the police had let him back into the building he had discovered the file was missing. Everything else was exactly as he'd left it when he evacuated the office: the computer discs were on the desk top and the filing-cabinet door ajar. Only the file had gone. He'd transferred its contents on to a disc, used corrector fluid to whiten out the data and returned the file to the cabinet, intending to burn it later. To access the disc he had created his own password: the weight poundage he had successfully lifted at the Olympics before his fall from grace. In all this he had violated the Organisation's rule that no employee must ever use information for his own profit. And Klinger knew!

He was here because he had somehow learned of his very personal and very private reason for doing so. Each name on those forms was someone who had received a successful organ transplant. He'd intended to blackmail them to fund his ever-more expensive drug need. His generous salary no longer covered the cost; he now required $5,000 a week. And $5,000 the week after. And for every week he could see into the future.

Back to the present.

'Why are you sweating, Thrung?'

'A summer cold.' Thrung shifted and his chair groaned in protest at such a foolish lie.

Klinger resumed his pacing, but his eyes now never leaving the tense, glowering figure behind the desk. Thrung's nervousness had to be more than needing a fix. Something had happened here. Klinger stopped before the desk. 'Show me exactly what you did just before the bomb alert.'

He saw the unease in Thrung's eyes come and go so quickly that a lesser-trained man would have missed it. Thrung had either done something stupid or he was holding back information. He glanced towards the closed filing cabinet. 'Was that open?'

Thrung nodded. 'I was working on files.'

'Show them to me.'

Thrung's chair gave another creak. 'Is this really necessary? I have a weights class in a few minutes.' It was amazing how easy the next lie came.

'Thrung, show me!'

Thrung lumbered over to the cabinet and brought the files to the desk. Klinger riffled through them. Invoices and follow-up letters, confirming orders for equipment. He glanced at the VDU screen. 'Were you using your computer before the bomb alert?'

Another flicker came and went in Thrung's eyes.

'No,' he said.

Klinger smiled at Thrung. He was lying. 'Your discs. Show me.'

Thrung waved a hand in protest. 'Please! They are confidential . . .'

'Nothing is confidential when it comes to the Organisation, Thrung. Show them to me.' He'd found the chink.

Thrung opened a drawer and pulled out several discs. Behind them was the bottle. He quickly closed the drawer and placed the discs on the desk top.

'What's on these?' Klinger demanded.

'Client records.' Thrung fed a disc into the computer's maw and pressed keys on his keyboard. Names and addresses began to appear on-screen. The other discs contained similar data.

Klinger turned from the screen. Why had Thrung been reluctant to show him? 'Are these the only discs you were working on?'

'Yes.'

'Show me all your discs.'

'I will need Herr Doktor Romer's permission.'

'He has given me full authority.'

Thrung felt perspiration trickling down his thighs.

'What are you trying to hide, Thrung?' The menace in Klinger's voice was suddenly a vibrant, living thing.

'Nothing, nothing at all.'

Moving with sudden and totally unexpected speed around the desk, Klinger opened the drawer. He pulled out the remaining discs and tossed them on the desk top. Then he brought out the bottle. He unscrewed the cap and dipped a finger in the white powder. He held up the finger to his mouth, allowing his tongue to dart out and taste the powder. The last of the colour had drained from Thrung's eyes. They looked like cod, packed in ice.

'So, Thrung, this is your little secret. An expensive taste. Now you had better tell me everything else.'

The office was filled with a mad silence as Klinger placed the bottle on the desk. 'What else has happened here, Thrung?' The choreography now called for a whisper to match his sculptured stillness. Nor had Thrung moved. He looked as if he was in shock. Klinger reached across the desk and deliberately wiped clean his finger against Thrung's sleeve.

'Will you tell me what else happened here?' he asked softly, his face very close to Thrung's. He could feel the fear emanating like a physical force. Klinger stepped back and almost idly backhanded Thrung across the face. He saw him flinch, knowing the blow had struck like cold rolled steel. 'Don't irritate me, Thrung. Will you just tell me what you have been up to?'

Thrung nodded, swallowing the fury which had begun to rise. In the old days he would have crushed any man who lifted a hand to him. But this was not the time for false heroics; this man had the look of someone who disposed of people the way men swatted insects. 'I will try to explain.'

'That's better now: just tell me everything. Quickly and carefully. And truthfully. I shall know if you are lying. And if you do, I shall be very angry. And you won't like that, Thrung, not at all. But if you tell me the absolute truth, I shall be reasonable.'

'What does that mean?' Thrung mumbled.

Klinger stepped away from the desk. Give a man a room enough to hang himself. 'I know what you have been up to, Thrung. So let's start with how you intended to pay for your habit.'

Thrung let out a noisy breath. He had had enough. 'All right. I will tell you the truth. . .'

He spoke quietly and with resolve, a part of his mind congratulating himself, how well he survived. The part that had been deafened by this screaming figure who had behaved with as much outrage as if he had personally suffered over what had happened.

When he had finished, Klinger looked at him with almost a sense of wonder. That he had ever thought up such an idea was incredible, but that he had actually hoped to get away with it showed a deeply disturbing contempt for the Organisation. Klinger kept his distance, almost as if there was something contagious about Thrung. He took a deep, cleansing breath and the deadly, debilitating dialogue continued between them.

'Where is the file now?'

'I burned it.' The answer had come at once.

'Why?'

'Because I wanted to remove temptation.'

'You want me to believe you worked out this plan and then didn't go through with it?'

'It's true.'

'When did you burn it?'

'Just before the bomb scare.'

'Where?'

'In the furnace in the basement.'

'Did anyone see you go there?'

'I don't know. I don't think so.'

'Are you still lying to me, Thrung?'

'No, Klinger, I'm not. Honest to God, I'm not.'

'Then why are you sweating like a pig?'

Thrung's eyes flickered to the bottle. 'Sometimes it's very difficult to think straight without . . .' his voice trailed off.

'Take your medicine.' It was the voice of a stretcher-bearer calling out to the dead on a battlefield.

Klinger watched dispassionately as Thrung tipped some of the cocaine on the back of his hand and drew the powder noisily up his nostrils. Then he came to a decision.

16

Morton spun the high-backed chair to face the window. Its
magnificent view of the Alps had decided him on choosing this
otherwise nondescript room at the rear of Hammer Force
Headquarters as his office. During the night fresh snow had fallen
above the tree-line. When this was over he would once more spend
a few days up there testing himself. From boyhood onwards he
had continued to discover in climbing the physical satisfaction of
having complete mastery over his body, of knowing the risk was
self-imposed and threatened no one but himself, and that each time
he extended himself to the extreme limits of muscular control.

Behind him he heard her sigh, the way she always did when
concentrating. After enjoying the distant snowscape a moment
longer, he turned back into the room.

Apart from his outsize desk and conference-type chairs, the
office was furnished with state-of-the-art communications equipment. One wall was completely covered with a computer-
controlled liquid-crystal display map of the world; the computer
allowed for endless permutations to be created from the keyboard
on his desk. At the moment various light systems gave the display a
surreal appearance.

She was still standing with her back to him, absorbing the
display. Even in repose there was a fluid grace about her. Tall and
slim, thighs and legs long, it wasn't hard to understand why men
admired her from this angle. When she turned, only her eyes
suggested why she was here. A dark luminous green, they
displayed a watchful intelligence in a face whose fine angles did not
quite come together to make a whole. She had studied at Oxford,
worked for MI5 and lectured at Sandhurst.

'Interesting,' Anna Cruef said. It was the first word she had spoken since delivering her report on her trip to London. There had been nothing further to add on Stamp or Keep-U-Trim than she had told Chantel. Afterwards Morton had asked her to study the map. 'Can you run the sequence through one more time?' Anna asked, turning back to the display.

He tapped keys and red dots appeared across the continents. Each dot represented a place where a victim had been murdered for his or her organs. Some crimes had been committed quite close together, especially in Asia and Central and South America; in Europe the dots were a considerable distance apart.

Anna stepped closer to the map. 'Can you show the dates they were stolen?'

Morton pressed more keys. He saw her frown in renewed concentration as she studied the revised display.

She knew he was watching her, the way she remembered her father doing. Her remembrance of him now was of a gruff but kindly man, someone who had tried to the very end to do his best in everything. And he had always been good to her, encouraging her to do whatever she wanted in life as long as she was happy. She knew that by the time her father died she was very like him: she had the same single-mindedness, his willingness to work long hours and never to be particularly demanding about what she wore or ate. Until David she had not met anyone like her father. She turned away from the display.

'Interesting,' she said again. 'Can you now put up the centres?' Her accent was muted London. She tilted her head once more to view the display on the slant.

A series of blue dots appeared. Each represented a hospital or clinic where transplant surgery was performed. She concentrated for a while longer, then turned to Morton. 'The curious thing about these crimes is that they all took place when conditions were far from ideal.'

He nodded for her to continue; it was good to have her confirmation.

'Take the weather for a start. Each organ theft happened at the wrong time of the year. Monsoons, sandstorms, high humidity. The worst possible conditions to remove an organ out in the open, even one as durable as a kidney, let alone transport it. And these crimes were committed not only outside sterile hospital conditions, but also often considerable distances from the nearest transplant centre.'

'We can rule out those places, Anna, as far as where the organs were taken for transplanting is concerned.'

When he had finished telling her what the Prof had said, she was frowning in rebuke at her reflection in the display, as if she should have thought of that.

Silence. Finally Anna resumed. 'Wherever this place is, David, it's got to have top-class facilities. She turned back to the map. 'Let's have a look at just the hearts and their dates.'

Once more Morton changed the display. When she tilted her head, the shadowed hollows crinkled with concentration beneath her eyes as they began to quicken. She turned away. 'Even more interesting. Hearts are generally no longer usable after ten hours. Given that time contraint, these needed to be flown to their destination. That means we are looking for an airport which is not too particular who flies in and out. Which pretty well excludes all the major ones. And, for that matter, all the big international carriers. We are probably looking for something no bigger than a basic airstrip, just large enough to handle a small jet. The kind which regularly airlifts drugs into the United States from Mexico. Pilots who could do that will have no compunction about dealing in human organs.'

Morton nodded. The Prof said Anna was living proof that the distance between two points was not always the shortest, but was often the most interesting. 'I'll buy the idea that we are looking for a small outfit. Lester's trying to get a handle on that now. But there are thousands of them. As far as your theory on airports goes, I'm not sure. Last year at Rome, Customs found a crate bound for Saudi with a couple of girls inside. It was pure luck one of them came round in time from the drugs they had been given. But if live humans are shipped out of what's now supposed to be a secure airport, what's to stop people flying organs in and out of just about any airport in the world?'

Anna smiled, transforming her face. 'Point taken. But as I've said, a heart needs to be ready for transplanting no longer than ten hours after it has been removed. Otherwise you run into rejection problems. Which means our centre is probably no more than eight

129

hours' flying time from where the heart was taken. Even then the time margin would be tight.'

Morton pressed another key. On the display appeared a maze of yellow lines, each bearing a number. 'The flight distances from each organ-theft site to the nearest airport. It gives us a lot of options.'

Anna studied the new display. 'I'm sorry. I should have thought of that.'

'I didn't,' Morton said through his smile. 'The computers did it for me.'

She turned back to the screen. 'Let's get the other organs back on.'

Morton did so. Dots representing the thefts of livers, lungs and eyes reappeared. Anna once more tilted her head and sighed. After a while she turned to Morton. 'Normally a liver in particular responds badly to being exposed to non-sterile conditions. And at the best of times it isn't much use for grafting when it's been out of a donor for more than three hours. Same with eyes. Lungs have a little longer span. Logically most of those stolen organs would have been useless for transplanting. You see where I'm going?'

He was ahead of her. 'Unless somebody's found a whole new way of transporting theirs or some new kind of storage system. A chemical, maybe. Something like that, Anna.'

A thirty-second silence.

'It's possible. A few years back there was talk the Russians had come up with some new way of prolonging the life of donor organs. It was in Yuri Andropov's time. Remember, he had a dicky heart? Whenever he travelled from Moscow, his doctors were supposed to have brought one along. They kept it transplant-able in some kind of preservative. Or so the story went.'

He'd have Chantal check. But so much of the secret research done in Soviet labs had been lost in the wave of fury which immediately followed the end of Soviet Communism. In their search for food, the mob had destroyed much that would have been valuable – and had often killed those scientists who had lived pampered lives under the old regime.

Anna walked over and sat in one of the chairs, crossing her legs at the ankles, once more sighing, lost in thought. When she spoke there was a new certainty in her voice. 'My bet is that our place is supplied by its own organ bank. The organs will be taken there, stored, and then used when they're needed for transplanting. It's not exactly a new idea. Remember what happened in Honduras a few years back?'

Morton remembered. Adjoining the country's main accident hospital, police had discovered an illegal organ bank. Surgeons at the hospital had allowed trauma victims to die, removed their organs and then sold them to wealthy foreigners.

'Thankfully, they hadn't got beyond a dozen kidneys and a couple of hearts. We're looking at something far bigger here, Anna.'

'Agreed.'

'An organisation. Planes, ground handling, security, men in the field to spot and cut, doctors to open and insert. Nurses to care. Intensive care and safely home. The whole shooting-match.'

The force with which Morton painted his portrait threw out of kilter the rhythm of their conversation so far.

'And patients,' added Anna.

'Patients who can't go anywhere else.'

'The magna cum laudes of the godfathers. Drug barons.'

'The very top. Money no object. Able to buy a heart from an hour's profits from drugs,' Morton said, feeling his throat tighten.

'But where do they go for their transplants?'

Morton kept going at full tilt. 'Not Europe. It's just too difficult to move in and out. One of the old Soviet republics? Maybe. But I don't think so. For one thing we'd have heard by now. For another, they don't have the medical back-up. Somewhere in the Middle East? Possible. But only a possibility. Asia you can rule out. Nobody in their right mind is going to go to an Indian clinic for a new heart. Same for Africa. Australia? Japan? No. Too far to have to come and go without questions.'

'China?'

'China's trying to play softball with the world right now. Having a transplant centre for the wicked is not going to win it any friends.'

'We rule out North America, right?'

'Right. Not because they wouldn't try it there. But the risk of discovery would be too great.'

'That only leaves South America, David.'

At last there was silence.

Morton studied the display. The thing about the map was that you got what you saw. Or didn't.

Anna gave another sigh. 'There are over twenty countries down there.'

'The place we're looking for is probably not on the map.'

'So where do I start looking, David?'

He stood up and walked from behind the desk. Her directness had always impressed him. It went with her courage. She followed him across the office back to the map.

Morton scanned the display. 'Transplant surgery is certainly the most stress-related of all medical care. Burn-out among staff must be considerable. So there has to be a high turnover. And it's going to be no different at the place we're looking for – probably even higher, given the need for total secrecy about what they're doing. People willing to work in a place like that are going to be drawn from the medical dungheap. Struck-off surgeons, solvent-sniffing anaesthetists, tissue-matching technicians sacked for being drunk on duty.'

'Or those in the old Soviet system who see a way off the scrapheap.'

It wasn't a question.

Finally, he did what he had always intended to do. He told Anna about Gustav Romer. He held nothing back, gave none of what he said a special emphasis. He spoke in almost a monotone, the way he always did when it was important to make sure the throb of the war drum was unmistakable. Afterwards, the silence was like that in church.

'But Romer wouldn't have had the money to have created something like this,' she said at last.

'For sure. But he must have found someone rich enough to pick up the tab, Anna,' Morton said in a voice which left no room for argument.

He had nothing – yet – to support his gut feeling. Nor could he have defined it: motive, conjecture, surmise and probability – the feeling was all this and more. All he knew was that it went to the very core of his endeavours to draw fact out of darkness. In the past others, especially Walter, had been shocked by his readiness to make imaginative leaps, to fill in the gaps which often remain obscured despite the closest surveillance. The same gut feeling told him Gustav Romer was alive and close to the centre of all this.

'So what do you want me to do?' she asked, turning from the map to face Morton.

He told her he wanted her to join the staff of a transplant hospital. 'It's been a while since I worked in an OR,' she murmured. It wasn't an objection.

'You don't forget something like that,' he said reassuringly. 'And once you're in, you should pick up enough to bring us closer to the place we're looking for. Transplant surgery is a pretty small field, and those who work in it will probably have heard something, even if they don't recognise its significance. That's going to be your job.'

Anna glanced at the map as Morton continued to explain. 'Given Romer's last-known sighting was Ecuador, ideally you need to be as near as possible to there.' He touched a spot on the Californian coast. 'The Gift of Life Transplant Center.'

'Any reason?'

'It's new, barely four years old. It's small and tucked away and very private.'

'That's settled, then,' she said matter-of-factly.

Morton turned and led the way back to the chairs. 'Once you're in, you're going to need an outside link. When Tommy is finished up in Washington, I'll send him. OK?'

There was only a fractional hesitation on her part. She hadn't worked with Tommy since Hong Kong. He'd had some emotional growing-up to do then – though it hadn't been all his fault. Perhaps she had unwittingly encouraged him to believe there could be more between than she wanted to give.

She nodded. 'Tommy'll be fine.'

Morton then briefed her fully about The Gift of Life Transplant Center. He told her all he knew, what he suspected and why he suspected it. There were gaps that they both instinctively realised could not be closed – not even by one of his imaginative leaps. But that, after all, they also knew, was why he was sending her.

17

In the clinic's medical conference room, Dr Romer addressed members of Kommando One. The dozen men sat impassively before him. Each was young, superbly fit and dressed in his chosen operational guise. Two wore business suits. A couple were in jeans and sweatshirts. One was dressed as a hiker, complete with knapsack. The rest were in the clothes of holidaymakers the world over.

'. . . and so, because there is a need to replenish our organ bank most urgently, you will, this time, be allowed to choose targets of opportunity, given that our health clubs have not produced sufficient suitable ones to meet our immediate requirements,' Dr Romer continued, in the butchered English of a language laboratory.

He paused, looking into each face. He saw with satisfaction that not one of these experienced killers could hold his gaze. 'But the rules of selection apply as before. In all cases, organs should only be taken from persons who show no discernible signs of physical illness. Their mental state is not important as we have not yet reached the point of being able to transplant a human brain.'

He waited for the dutiful smiles his little joke produced. 'As usual, choose a person no older than his mid-thirties. You will all surely remember past experience shows that organs harvested from older persons are not ideal for our purpose. Finally, if you have to choose a non-white, then select a Japanese or Chinese. Only as a very last resort should you harvest from an African or Asian.'

Once more he searched their faces, to make sure his words had been noted. 'There is one other matter which I wish you to be aware of. Some of you will have good cause to remember that in your former days, you encountered the intelligence agent who now works for the United Nations. The man who is known only as Morton.'

He told them what had happened in Washington, though not about Madam's call, and explained that he had sent Klinger to investigate. 'His preliminary report suggests it may not be Morton after all who went into our building there. But you must take no chances.'

'Do you have any idea why he might have taken an interest in this, Herr Doktor?' The question was from an operative who had the military manner of pursing his lips just before he spoke.

'No, Kessler. But it is not important; the important thing is to be aware.'

Heads nodded in unison. Dr Romer turned and propelled himself to the small table on which was a small pile of envelopes. Each bore the name of an operative. He picked up the top envelope.

'Kessler.'

Kessler walked forward and stood before Dr Romer. Standing, he looked shorter, with a pigeon chest and too dark to be a Silesian.

'You will go to Seattle, Kessler. Once you have completed your harvesting the Disposer there will make all the necessary arrangements.'

Dr Romer handed Kessler the envelope containing his travel documents, shook him by the hand and walked towards the door. The strange little ceremony had the formality of a graduation. At the door Kessler paused at a table to pick up a briefcase. It contained a fléchette gun and a supply of sugar pellets, together with a container to hold the organs.

Dr Romer called forward the next man. 'Engel. You will go to Sweden. In your case, your briefcase will be waiting there for you. With the Nobel ceremonies, the Swedes are being unusually vigilant with airport security.'

In minutes the others received their instructions and were gone. Only the hiker remained. When he came forward Dr Romer eyed him carefully. 'Friedrich, you are going to Bavaria. Your harvest is a special request. You will find everything you need to know in the envelope. Take the greatest care to make it look like a ritual murder. I believe they are now commonplace in the Fatherland, with all those foreigners.'

Friedrich nodded, picked up his briefcase and left the room. Watching him go, Dr Romer could only admire the way Madam had decided to deal with a potentially difficult situation.

Dyson Teeling, the United States Vice-Consul, and for the moment his country's ranking official in Nicaragua, watched the first squall of rain dash against the office window. The sound of the afternoon storm drowned the ticking of the antique ship's clock on the mantelpiece. Together with the shelf of leather-bound books and the desk-top portrait of his mother, the clock had accompanied him to all his postings. There had been five so far in the region. This had been the worst. The resentment towards the United States was a tangible thing: he could feel it in the stares of people, in the way they openly confronted him.

Yet that morning, he had signed the travel orders which had recalled the six political officers, the generic term by which CIA operatives worked under cover overseas. He'd seen the operatives off at the airport and when he'd returned here, there was a fax from State's Central America Desk announcing that a team of seismologists from the US Geological Survey would be arriving shortly to inspect the volcano and check the stresses on the earthquake fault. It was all part of Secretary Armstrong's damn-fool idea you could win the hearts and minds of these people. If he came here he would see the truth.

The rain stopped as punctually as it had started. Thirty minutes every afternoon. It was the one thing he could set his clock by in this damned country.

He walked over to the window. Clouds were drifting cross the summit of Mount Masaya. They somehow made the volcano appear even more lifeless.

18

Leading Tommy to the CIA's executive dining room on Langley's seventh floor, Gates apologised. 'The food doesn't qualify for a restaurant review.'

Neither would the corridor wall art attract much critical acclaim, Tommy thought. The principal merit of the paintings was probably their low cost.

'After airlines meals, it's got to be gourmet.' He had lived off little else while retracing Stamp's holiday route across America. Over-sauced in-flight meals had been interspersed with short snatches of sleep in seats never properly designed for that purpose.

Gates grinned. 'You should ask your dad or Morton about the time we spent going in and out of Kabul on Afghan Airlines. They served undercooked sheep's testicles in sour curd no matter what the time of day. In California they'd market that as the latest weight-loss diet Morton said.'

'You known the Colonel long, Mr Gates?'

'Call me Bill. About the only thing that hasn't changed around here is our informality.' Gates nodded. 'Yeah, I've known him longer than I care to remember. Your dad, too.' He glanced at Tommy. 'How old are you?'

'Twenty-nine.'

It was relatively hard to judge his age. His skin was smooth for a man and he was in excellent physical shape. Even on this trip he had still managed to jog three miles a day. The only outward evidence he would be thirty in a month's time was the beginning of saltiness at the temples. Gates had noted, approvingly, that Tommy had made no effort to tint out the premature grey. He had a friendly face and that rare quality in their business of making

137

people feel comfortable. He guessed that almost everyone liked Tommy Nagier.

'How long have you worked for Morton?'

'Three years. You couldn't have a better boss than the Colonel.' He still addressed the Colonel only by rank. It seemed natural to show such respect to someone who judged everyone by the if you weren't part of the answer, you were part of the problem.

'This is my first solo field trip. Do you still remember the feeling, Bill?'

Tommy had Danny's way of looking at you directly when he spoke. And that fine-boned build and deep-set eyes which spoke of a total absence of fear were further confirmation

'Absolutely. And each time is still a first trip. When I forget that, it'll be time to quit.'

Morton said pick them young and work them hard, and that way you got the best of everything. But the boy looked bushed.

'The Colonel's great at a time like this, when nothing's falling our way. The trouble is that Stamp's itinerary qualifies for the Boring Holiday of the Year award. Nobody even remembers him,' Tommy said.

'Same at the motel.'

'I'll still check it out. The Colonel wouldn't expect anything less.'

Gates steered them into the dining room, a tasteful blend of soft lighting, polished woods and muted wall and floor coverings. The club-like atmosphere was almost undisturbed; it would be another hour before the evening dinner rush. A waitress led them to a table by a window with an overview of partially wooded landscape. After they ordered the catch of the day and salads, Gates offered a second apology.

'We don't have a liquor licence. So it's Coke or Pepsi, Diet or Regular.'

'Water'll be fine,' Tommy said. He'd drunk his fill of carbonated drinks during those flights.

Gates ordered a Sprite and lit a cigarette. 'I used to try to quit every three months. Then I thought at my age, what's the point? If Big C's going to get me, he's probably already staked out his claim in my lungs.'

He exhaled and looked at Tommy. 'OK – business. Some

background first. Thrung's sponsors are Drug Rehab. Or, to give it its full title, the Drug Rehabilitation Foundation for the Promotion of an Addiction-Free World.' Gates sucked in smoke. 'Nancy Reagan's dream to end the drug problem produced a number of fancy-sounding outfits eager for federal funding and tax breaks for helping junkies. Some looked after only kids or pregnant women, or just old folks. Some dealt solely with white middle-class pill-poppers. Others with blacks or Hispanics. In San Francisco there was one foundation which handled only Chinese opium addicts. When Nancy Reagan left the White House, most of the foundations quietly folded their tents or moved on to the next worthy cause. AIDS. Famine in Africa. You know the sort of thing.'

Tommy nodded. 'Sure. But why did Drug Rehab stay?'

Gates flicked ash into the ashtray. 'It helps only non-Americans try to beat their dependency. Every year a quota come here on the understanding that they can work only as long as they remain off dope. Our junkies are supposed to learn from their example.' Gates had spoken with a conscious effort at self-restraint.

'I know how you feel. But where does Thrung fit into all this? Last I heard he was a personal trainer to a drug baron in Colombia.'

'Damn right. For a while he was. Then Drug Rehab picks him up and hides him in one of their halfway houses down there. They've got a number of family places where pill-poppers wait until they get permission to come here. In Thrung's case that was probably easy. A celebrity driven into very public disgrace ready to make his way back into society comes close to Drug Rehab's ideal profile. When he first came here they had him on all the talk shows. He came across as a real born-again. Afterwards, Drug Rehab found him the job with Keep-U-Trim. They've placed a number of such people in their health clubs. But Drug Rehab keeps itself very much out of the limelight. No publicity or lobbyists, nor any of the usual trappings of a pressure group. But on the letterhead they're gilt-edged.'

The waitress returned with their drinks. Tommy emptied his glass of water in a couple of swallows. Flying always made him dehydrated.

'I'll bring you a jug,' said the waitress.

Tommy watched her flounce away. Nice body. He turned back to Gates. 'How gilt-edged, Bill?'

'A former Secretary of State, a couple of ex-ambassadors, a retired president of a high-tech company in Silicon Valley, one of yesterday's hardball players on Wall Street. They meet once a month at the foundation's headquarters out in Malibu to rubber-stamp who's next to be brought here. The real selection work is done by a permanent staff.'

The waitress returned with the jug and refilled Tommy's glass. Nice smile, he thought.

'Be back in a minute with your food,' she promised, heading back to the kitchen.

'She's happily married,' Gates murmured.

'Just looking,' Tommy said cheerfully. 'When you stop, that's the time to worry.'

'Morton tell you that?'

'No, the Prof.'

Gates shook his head in wonder.

Tommy topped up his glass and asked, 'Is there a top dog in Drug Rehab?'

'More like a top bitch. Simone Montan.'

'Remind me who the lady is.'

Gates gave a little groan. 'If you'd been over forty you'd have known. She was for Elmer Crayton what Marion Davis was for Randolph Hearst.'

Tommy grinned. 'You mean Elmer Crayton, the millionaire? Him I remember.'

'Correction. Elmer Crayton the *billionaire*. Compared to him Howard Hughes died a pauper. Compared to anybody you name, even those desert sheikhs, Elmer Crayton walked away with the title of single richest man on earth every year for the last twenty years of his life. Even now no one really knows how much he left. The only certainty is that when he was alive, like the cliché says, Simone's whim was his to obey. When she wanted to be a Broadway star, he bought her a theatre. When she decided to go into the movies, a studio. It still didn't make her a star. Or win any brownie points with Mrs Elmer Crayton.'

'Who was she? His wife or mother?' Tommy asked.

'His wife.'

'I didn't know he was married.'

Gates blew out a spiral of smoke. 'Most people didn't. Once Simone came on the scene, Sonja Crayton more or less went into social purdah. Now that Elmer's dead, she's come out. A few months ago I met her at a White House dinner party.'

'What does she do?'

'Sonja's one of the great and good. Into all the right charities. Planes to Bosnia, blankets to the Sudan. Money for everybody. When she's not doling it out, she winters in Aspen and summers on Martha's Vineyard. She's one of the few who calls the Kennedys by their first names.'

'And Simone?'

'Charities, too, of course. But not obsessive, like Sonja. Elmer left Simone the business.'

'What's the business?'

'What isn't it?' Gates asked aggressively. 'Ships and planes. Railroads and banks. Warehousing and real estate. She's supposed to be a bigger landlord than the Vatican in Italy. And cable TV, radio and satellites. She owns more cellular phone companies than Ma Bell. And there isn't a trading floor where you won't find her people buying, long or short.'

'All sounds very respectable.'

'Oh, it is. Everybody's taken a peek at her set-up. Forbes, the Securities Commission, the Office of Fair Trading in London, the French Bourse. Nada. She pays her taxes and takes her profits. Like Murdoch. Except she clears more in a week than he does in a year.'

'That big?'

'That big, Tommy boy. That bloody big.'

'What's she do with it all?'

'Back full-circle. Charities. Has to keep up with Sonja in that area.'

'What are they like as people, Bill?'

Gates smiled. The boy had a no-frills way of asking. He liked that. 'Sonja's supposed to have been a real lady until Elmer dumped her. Since then she's gone sluttishly discreet. Booze and men. The men she still manages to mostly keep under wraps. The booze is beginning to show a little. She's also got cancer. The dogs on the street say she's probably got less than a year. But she certainly doesn't show it.'

'Her men – toyboys?'

'No. That's very much Simone's scene. She's got the reputation of being a real nut-breaker. She gets through her boys quicker than shit goes through a camel.'

'Glad I'm too old, Bill.'

'Me, too, Tommy boy. Me bloody too.'

The waitress interrupted Gates' discourse. The fish was almost hidden by a small mountain of french fries on each plate. They were thick cut, the way Tommy liked them. The salad glinted from its dressing of oil and vinegar. Tommy began to eat while Gates savoured a mouthful of smoke and resumed.

'God knows how, but when he was alive Crayton managed to keep them both happy. He bought Sonja a château in France and installed Simone in the Malibu mansion she's just given to Drug Rehab for its headquarters. In Elmer's day anywhere west of New York was Simone's territory. Europe was Sonja's. When he was alive, neither woman strayed on to each other's turf.'

Stubbing out his cigarette, Gates picked up a chip with his fingers and popped it into his mouth.

'And now?' Tommy speared a piece of fish on his fork.

Gates mixed his salad before answering. 'Same as before, pretending to each other neither exists. I hear when they do both turn up at the same function it's like something out of an old thirties movie – lots of glacial looks and nasty murmurs.'

Tommy began to eat his salad. 'Why did Simone give her mansion to Drug Rehab?'

Gates pushed his half-finished plate away. He had a smoker's appetite. 'Maybe a need to show the money Crayton left her had given her unsuspected depths of social responsibility. Maybe to cock one at Sonja. Hell, who knows?'

'Think she knows anything about Thrung?'

Gates lit a fresh cigarette. 'He'd never get on the bottom rung of her totem pole. Keeping people very much in their pecking order is one of the two things she has in common with Sonja. The other is that they've both become very science-oriented since Elmer died of a heart attack. And they both make a point of turning up for the Nobel Prize ceremonies.'

Tommy pushed aside his empty plate. 'This year the Colonel's going to be there,' he said.

'Of course – Yoshi. I'd forgotten.' Gates glanced at his watch. 'I've still got time to send him a telegram of congrats.'

He stood up. 'What's your plan for the morning?'

'Check out Thrung's Keep-U-Trim.'

'Nothing like legwork,' Gates said, flashing another pirate's smile.

19

Striding across the tarmac at Arlanda moments after Concorde had landed, Morton frowned when he saw Bitburg seated in the back of the limo. Then he remembered: this was the courtesy car the Foreign Office would have placed at Walter's disposal while in Sweden. Walter was never one to pass up a perk. The chauffeur saluted quickly as Morton handed him his suitcase and entered the car.

'Hullo, David.' Despite the warmth of the car's heating, Bitburg wore a grey winter overcoat and matching fur hat. He looked more than ever like a short-sighted squirrel.

As he settled into the cushioned seat, Morton asked: 'Have you seen Yoshi?' He'd tried to call him from Concorde, but the hotel switchboard said Dr Kramer had left strict instructions not to be disturbed. A year ago Yoshi's hotel suite would have been awash with people. It was another sign that the sooner he had surgery the better.

Bitburg shrugged off the question. 'I sent up a note to say I was here and he didn't even reply.'

'That doesn't sound like Yoshi.' He remembered all those times Yoshi had been unstinting in his help.

Bitburg smiled weakly. 'I'm glad to hear that, David.' He paused to watch the chauffeur settling himself behind the wheel. 'Anyway, I've something more important to discuss with you. The seminar I've just come from.'

Bitburg leaned forward and slid open the glass partition to speak to the driver. 'Grand Hotel. I have a meeting in an hour.' He closed the partition and eased himself back into his corner. 'If you don't give these people a time limit, they'll take all day, David.

You'd never think there was unemployment, the way people treat their jobs.'

Morton wondered if Bitburg's glasses were to protect his eyes from reality as well as to see better. 'You can ride people too hard, Walter.'

'Come now, David. That's what man-management is all about.'

'Is that what you call it, Walter?'

Bitburg didn't seem to notice the edge in Morton's voice.

'When I started, I worked six days a week, twelve hours a day. No overtime and Sundays, too, if the bank wanted it. That teaches you a lot, David. Not least about the value of money.'

At the airport exit Morton felt the car bump over the steel ramp which could be raised to form a barrier against a car bomber. The idea hadn't worked in Beirut; he doubted it would do so here. He gave Bitburg another sideways glance. 'I've been getting complaints. You're being tougher than usual with cut-backs for my people.'

'Our people, David. Never forget that. They're *our* people,' Bitburg said quickly. 'That's the ethos of Hammer Force. And who, exactly, has been complaining?'

Morton told him.

The grey silence matched the day. Bitburg cleared his throat; he suffered from year-round colds. 'Nobody likes to see their budgets cut, David. But part of my job is to take the financial overview. Where I can cut today makes us even more efficient tomorrow. That means we must have funds available to purchase new technology. At that seminar they had all kinds of stuff Nagier, Finel and Chantal Bouquet probably never knew existed.'

Morton sat perfectly still. 'Is this why you're here, Walter? To tell me you've ordered some new computers?'

'Well . . . yes.'

'Cancel whatever you've ordered.' Morton's voice was calm.

'What?' I can't do that. That would be highly embarrassing.'

'You don't order operational material, Walter. You don't do that. Ever. You don't do anything involved with *my* work, without first checking with *me*. And that includes the training school.'

'David, really—'

'Let me finish. A month ago I had Danny run his eye over all the stuff on offer at that seminar. In every case he said it wasn't worth the money. What he says is good enough for me. Always.'

Bitburg's eyes began to carom. 'I still think computers are the future. They remove the uncertainty. Help us think more clearly. Increase our efficiency—'

'If you want more fancy hardware for your department, fine. Only buy it out of *your* budget. Don't ask any of *my* people to cut back.'

Bitburg, shaken, sat sullen and mute. After a while he consulted his watch, then leaned forward and opened the partition. 'You have to go faster,' he rasped.

'You'll be there on time, sir,' assured the driver.

Bitburg slammed shut the divider and settled back in his corner. From inside his overcoat he produced a small notebook and then a pen. He studiously jotted something, then returned pen and pad out of sight. The silence stretched. Out of the corner of his eye he could see Morton staring impassively ahead.

This time Bitburg took longer than usual to clear his throat. 'David, I didn't mean to intrude into your area . . .'

'Fine. Just as long as we understand each other.'

The car had reached Stockholm's suburbs before Bitburg spoke again. 'How is your operation going, David?'

Morton turned full-face to him. Even with Walter he never harboured rancour. And the more he could make him understand it was the operations side of Hammer Force which drove everything else, the easier it would be for everyone. First he told Bitburg about Gustav Romer and then what everyone was doing to firm up the situation.

'Why Dresden?'

'That's where Romer had his research labs.'

Bitburg frowned. 'I thought all those places were closed down after unification?'

'They were. But there's no one better at picking over the charred bits than Chantal's people.'

Bitburg gave another throat-clearing. 'Before I left Geneva, I saw something from Nagier's office about Wolfgang Kreuse. I take it he has nothing to do with any of this?'

'He may well have.' Another problem with Walter was that his mind excluded him from the realm of surmise.

146

'But surely he was just a mobster? Big enough, no doubt, in Frankfurt, but only a small player on the global stage.'

'It's the same play, Walter. Just different settings. Act One in Frankfurt. Act Two in Washington. And Act Three anywhere you like. A big stage, lots of players. And the special effects make it hard to see at times. But we'll get there.'

'I see. And Kreuse?'

Morton told him in the same patient voice about Kreuse's colon replacement and how it had been obtained in no known transplant centre. Then he told him where he had sent Anna and how Tommy would be joining her in California once he had finished in Washington. He told Walter everything.

Bitburg forced another weak smile. 'You seem to be doing a good job.'

'They're all doing a good job.' He glanced out of the window. 'How long are you staying, Walter?'

Bitburg looked at his watch. He would be on time for his appointment with Count Lindeman. Arranging a meeting at such short notice was his forte. 'I'll probably stay on for a day or two after the official ceremonies. I'm hoping to see the King. Plus one or two in the upper echelon of government. It's all part of oiling the wheels.'

'For sure.' Walter was a master at shoring up his own future.

'Where are you staying, David?'

'I hadn't really thought about it.'

Bitburg made a small clucking sound. 'If only you had asked me before I could have got you a room at the Grand. Now I fear even my influence with the management could not secure that.'

'I'll see if Yoshi has a spare bed.'

'Certainly he will have the space. The Grand reserves its best suites for the Nobel laureates.' Bitburg peered at Morton. 'Have you stayed there before?'

'No.'

'Ah.' Bitburg gave a sigh of satisfaction. 'Then let me tell you about the place. There still isn't a hotel in Europe like it. It was built in 1874 when Ulysses S. Grant was President of the United States and Benjamin Disraeli was Prime Minister of England. The hotel was deliberately sited opposite the Royal Palace and has remained its equal ever since for food and service. For instance,

147

with really important guests, the doorman actually brings messages out to your car. I expect there will be one or two for me.' Bitburg smiled deprecatingly. 'The usual thing. Invitations to some cocktail party or other. I try to limit myself. There are just so many hangers-on nowadays, even for the Nobel ceremonies. Of course, you won't find them at the Grand. It seems to have managed to keep out the riff-raff . . .'

Bitburg was still pontificating when the limousine drew up before the impressive entrance to the hotel. A doorman wearing a long military overcoat that made him resemble a Russian cavalry officer walked quickly across the wooden boardwalk. He opened the rear door, fingers to the brim of his cap.

'Welcome to Sweden, Mr Morton. Dr Kramer has asked that you go directly to his suite. I'll have your baggage sent up.' The doorman turned to Bitburg and produced from his overcoat pocket an envelope. 'One message, sir.'

With a knowing smile at Morton, Bitburg tore open the envelope. He scanned the single sheet of paper from the Nobel Foundation. His appointment had been cancelled. No reason was given or a rescheduled date offered.

'Damn Lindeman,' Bitburg muttered, crumpling the envelope and shoving it into his overcoat pocket. By the time he had eased himself out of the car Morton was already entering the hotel's huge revolving doors.

In the main lobby, Morton paused to survey the scene. At this hour the reading room to his right was deserted apart from a couple admiring the showcase displays of perfumes and cut glass. Guests were coming and going through the towering doors leading to the Winter Gardens. Several groups waited by the elevators. An American was asking at the *portier*'s desk about shopping bargains. A handful of people were checking in at reception, several more settling their accounts at the adjoining cashier's window. Over by the news-stand, waiters were serving coffee. Beyond, the cocktail bar was half full.

'Can I help you, sir?' murmured a formally dressed figure at his elbow. 'I am the duty Assistant Manager.'

'Dr Kramer's suite.'

'Your name, sir?'

'Morton.'

'Ah, yes. Dr Kramer is expecting you.'

'Do you do this for all your guests?'

The Assistant Manager gave a professional smile. 'Usually only for our Nobel laureates. It's one of our ways of showing our pride in having them as guests.'

'How did your doorman know who I was?' Morton asked as they began to walk across the lobby towards the elevators.

The Assistant Manager gave another smile. 'Secrets of the trade, Mr Morton.'

Morton nodded. Maybe he'd ask Walter to brief him on these little mysteries.

At the elevator the Assistant Manager murmured in Morton's ear. 'Suite 215. It's one of our most desirable, looking directly across to the Royal Palace.'

Waiting until Morton had entered the elevator, the Assistant Manager pressed the button to close the door and watched the light on the wall panel showing the elevator begin its ascent. Then he walked purposefully over to one of the tables where an elegantly dressed woman sat alone, sipping coffee.

'He's arrived, Madam.'

She nodded and continued to watch the light on the panel showing the elevator's progress.

Half an hour later, his bag deposited in the suite's smaller bedroom, Morton sat in Yoshi's altogether grander bedroom. With its overstuffed armchairs, pillared arches, gilt wall mirrors and vases of heavily scented flowers, Yoshi had said it was a room made for seduction. It was the only time he had shown a glimpse of his old self.

The surgeon lay on the bed, propped up by pillows. He wore a red silk dressing gown and a pair of embroidered Finnish house shoes.

Morton could see his questions had visibly tired Yoshi. And the bottle on his bedside table was a further reminder of his condition. Uncapping the bottle, Yoshi once more shook out two tablets. He used his saliva to swallow them. 'An old homoeopathic trick that gets them into the system faster,' he explained, closing the bottle. Placing it back on the table, he continued: 'Funny thing, when I first heard one of the Russians at the Helsinki conference

149

describing their efficacy, I thought it was more Soviet medi-babble. I can only say that without the tablets, I probably wouldn't have had the energy to come here.'

He smiled wanly at Morton. 'Don't look so worried. I'm scheduled for surgery the day after I get back to Geneva. Next day I'll probably feel a new man – or so my doctors say. But you know doctors, always promising.'

'How do you feel about answering a few more questions?'

'No problem. These tablets give me a lift for an hour or two. So fire away.'

'Can I go back to that Helsinki conference? You said there were a number of Russian immunologists there.'

'Yes, three or four. Top-notchers. The Russians always send their best people to showcase conferences. Partly to show they are up there with the rest of the world, but mostly because their top talent have the brains to pick up anything new we are doing. It's a real game of cat-and-mouse. Sometimes we'll feed them titbits to try to trap them. Other times they throw out morsels to tempt us to open up. It can be a lot of fun.'

'I'm sure. But did any of those immunologists drop a hint that they or their colleagues had come up with a chemical agent which could extend the life of an organ once it was removed from a donor?'

Yoshi drummed a couple of fingers against his lower lip, the way he always did when thinking hard. 'Come to think of it now, there was. Not from the platform, of course. With the Russians it's still either feast or famine in the formal sessions. They'll boast like kids with a new toy about something like this blood-thinning drug, then keep absolutely silent when it comes to sharing something we all know about anyway.' He shifted on the small mound of pillows supporting him. 'Most of the really interesting titbits you hear are away from the conference hall. One night a few of us who had been attending a workshop that was as boring as only a South African could make it picked up one of the Russians who was hell-bent on having fun. We all went to dinner and on to a club. Everyone was feeling pretty relaxed and our Russian who, until then, had been casting an eye over the in-house whores, suddenly turned to us and began to talk about David White's cyclosporin.'

'Who is David White and what's cyclosporin?'

Yoshi shook his head in mock dismay. 'You'd never pass your finals, David. White is to immunology what Christiaan Barnard is to transplant surgery – or Neil Armstrong to the moon. They are all genuine firsts. In White's case it was his discovery of cyclosporin's selective effect on the body's immune system – specifically in targeting the T-helper cells.' Yoshi smiled quickly. 'I know, "What are the T-helpers?" Very simple, really. They are produced in the thymus gland. And all they do is what you do in your work. They act as the first line of defence. In their case it's for the body's own immune system. At the first sign it's under attack from alien forces, the T-helpers launch an all-out counter-assault. It's rather like each of us having our own personal Hammer Force on tap.'

Morton smiled. 'I think I get the idea.'

'OK. So there we were, well into the schnapps and beer, and toasts for scientists of the world to unite when, out of left field, our Russian lets out that he has gone way beyond White. He said that by modifying cyclosporin, he had created an agent that could actually keep an organ transplantable for weeks. Drunk though we were, we still had enough wit to put him through the inquisition. But just when we thought he was going to say more, his minder turned up and dragged him off. I never expected to see or hear of him again.'

'But you did?'

Yoshi nodded.

'Six months later. I was giving a lecture in Dresden and there he was, in the front row. He must have overcome running off his mouth that night because he was surrounded by the local medical hierarchy.'

'Did one of them have a head like a banana, Yoshi?'

Once again the surgeon shook his head in mock dismay. '*Nul points*, David. In our business we call that kind of head shape a dolichocephalic cranium. But yes, Banana Head was there. I only remember him because afterwards we had quite a discussion about how long antigens remain before the immune system destroys them. I gave one time. He insisted on another. You know me – even though it wasn't strictly my field, I kept arguing my corner. Afterwards I learned he was their leading immunologist.'

'Let me try to redeem myself, Yoshi. Was his name Gustav Romer?'

Yoshi did not bother to hide his surprise. 'Yes. How did you know?'

'That's what we call in my business never forgetting a banana head!'

After Morton had told him everything he knew about Romer, Yoshi began to drum his bottom lip.

'That could explain something I heard that didn't seem important at the time,' Yoshi said at last. 'Shortly after Romer was reported killed in Ecuador – it made a bit of a splash in the East German medical press – I was back in Dresden to address a follow-up conference. I can't remember exactly why, but White's work came up again and I asked if the Russian was around. I got some very funny looks and I was told his lab had been closed down. That used to happen all the time over there. Somebody would die or fall from grace and his work would go into limbo until someone came along who would take things over and claim it as his own. It was one of the peculiarities of their system. But as I was leaving Dresden, one of my hosts said that the Russian had done what a lot of people would like to do – jumped ship. That was just before the Berlin Wall came down and the brain drain on the other side was well underway. I assumed my host was looking for a way out, and I had just begun to tell him that I wasn't in that business, when he said he was quite happy to remain where he was, thank you very much, and that anyway he wouldn't want to go where the Russian had gone.'

'Did he say where that was, Yoshi?'

'Yes. Of all places, Nicaragua. God knows what he could do with his skill there. There isn't a half-decent hospital in the country, let alone the kind of research facilities that a top-flight scientist in any discipline would expect.'

'Do you remember the Russian's name?'

Yoshi drummed some more on his lip. 'Boris . . . most of us were on first-name terms only . . . it's the way it is at those conferences. It's bad form to say, "I thought your paper on brain traces was crap, Professor Big Deal." But it's OK to rubbish your peer if you call him by his first name. Let me try to think. At those German conferences we all had to wear name badges. I can see Boris's now . . .'

Yoshi was silent for a moment. 'Boris Suri . . .' He nodded. 'Boris Surikov. That's it! Professor Boris Surikov. He spoke German like a Russian. And he was built like a Siberian bear, with an appetite to match. You get the picture. A real peasant. But if he has figured out a way to keep organs viable long after the usual transplant limits, he has to be as savvy as they come.'

He stopped and looked curiously at Morton. 'You all right, David?'

Morton once more repeated the deathbed sound he had heard Wolfgang Kreuse make. 'Never felt better, Yoshi. I never felt better.'

Then he explained why.

20

Two hours out of Seattle Joe Butterfield was up in the high country. An hour later he pulled the rented camper off the road on to the old Indian trail indicated on the map.

The glory of early autumn was all around him. Joe devoured it all in bright-eyed anticipation, absorbing the colours of the earth and rocks, the differing shades of the first fall of leaves and, above all, taking in the sheer emptiness, so that his heart filled with the joy of a pilgrim setting foot on the promised land. This will be all mine for a whole week. To go where I like. To share with no one. Mine to run and roam at will. Life could not be better.

He climbed into the back of the hired camper, stripped to his vest and shorts and exchanged his loafers for sturdy boots. The camper would serve only as a base; at night he would sleep out under the stars, his knapsack as a pillow, a sleeping bag to keep him warm in the chill night air.

Stepping out of the camper he stood for a moment breathing in the air, glancing upwards at the blue sky, letting the sunlight warm his face. After Washington and the plane everything felt and tasted sweetness itself.

All those weeks of pounding the city pavements had made his thighs and calves rock-hard and his hamstrings stand out when he stretched his legs. After one final deep breath, he began to run along the trail, slowly at first, allowing the climbs and descents to bring into play the various groups of muscles until they were all once more in accord. Then, when he felt sufficiently loose, he increased his pace until his legs were pounding over the dirt, pumping pain through his body. It was the most wonderful feeling he had experienced for a long time.

He ran for several miles until the trail came to a fork. Here he paused, head lowered, hands on knees, listening to the blood pounding in his ears, knowing it was flushing oxygen through his body, purifying it. When he recovered, he sat on the ground and studied the distant mountains. Then he ran all the way back to the camper.

There was a car parked nearby. Leaning against the front wing was a young man. He knew him immediately. His cousins had turned parts of Washington into no-go areas, some only a block from the White House. But how had he found his way here? And why had he bothered to change out of his street rig into this half-decent suit, a lighter blue than his shoes? He'd recognised him, of course, because he held one hand respectfully by his side, the way his cousins always did when it was shakedown time. In the other hand he held the mandatory gun. Home-made, by the look of it, with that funny, bulbous nose. All this Joe saw at once with his eyes as his brain told him how to respond.

'Take it easy, fella. If it's money you're after, my wallet's in the camper.' Even as he spoke, he knew robbery was not the motive.

There were two ways to go. Turn and run, or charge and run. He had the speed for both. But in the moment when he was still coming to a decision it was already too late.

Kessler shot him.

There was a hiss, no louder than a sigh, from the gun's air-compressor mechanism, and the sugar fléchette bomblet entered Joe's open mouth with such force that it shattered his larynx. The sheer impact drove him back a pace. Then he collapsed to the ground. His oxygenated blood began to dissolve the sugar concentrate even quicker than usual.

For a moment they remained a tableau: Joe's right hand grasping at his throat, his left hand waving towards Kessler, as if begging for help; Kessler bending over him, as if about to do so, but keeping his gun hand just out of range. Then Kessler stepped back and watched impassively as Joe tried to lift himself. Little spasms shuddered through Joe's body, as if they were caused by those fireflies Kessler liked to catch on the island. Then Joe stopped moving.

Kessler reached down and touched his face. The skin was cool-hot and clammy like a fever. That would be the sugar completing its destructive work. Always wait a few minutes, the Herr Doktor had said, then check again.

Straightening, Kessler walked back to the car. On the passenger seat was the briefcase together with the second bag that had been left for him when he'd collected the car at Seattle Airport. The local Disposer had made these arrangements.

He removed his jacket, tie, shirt and pants and placed them neatly on the back seat. Lying there was a copy of the fax that had been in the bag, and which the Targeter had sent from Washington. All the organs had been given an X-mark, and the photograph was a good likeness, the face relaxed, with none of the surprise which had been there in the moment before he had fired. At least surprise was better than the abject terror and even hostility he'd seen in some of his victims. Why not accept he had a job to do and that there was nothing personal in what he did? And some of the places he had to go to: *mensch*, you'd have to be really dedicated to go to some of them. Not like here. These forests reminded him of home. For a moment longer Kessler stood in his undershorts and vest and admired the landscape with a satisfaction not unlike Joe had experienced.

From the bag he took out the coveralls and put them on. Carrying the briefcase he walked back to Joe. The blood trickling out of his mouth was a pink foam. A shot through the mouth usually produced that effect.

Kessler squatted on his haunches once more and touched the face. It felt cooler. He lifted an eyelid. The pupil was glassy. Satisfied, he went to the camper and opened its doors and looked inside. The bunk bed was still not made up. He placed the briefcase on the camper floor and pulled the block of foam rubber off the bunk. He walked back to the body and, without any great effort, carried it to the camper. Pausing only to get a better grip, he lifted the body inside and he placed it face up on the mattress. Once again he checked, both eyes this time. It didn't really matter, only that it made it easier to work knowing nothing unexpected could happen. There was no sign of life. He opened the briefcase and took out the latex gloves and worked them on to his hands, flexing his fingers the way a surgeon would. He reached into the briefcase and took out the bone-cutters and other equipment. He used a knife to cut away the vest and shorts. Apart from the boots the body was naked.

Kessler set to work.

An hour later, his coverall spattered with blood, he had finished. The container was filled with organs: heart, liver, kidneys, testes, stomach and a pair of lungs. He had removed the eyes last of all. He never liked to work with those sightless sockets staring at him.

Repacking the briefcase, he carried it to the car. From the trunk he took the plastic five-gallon drum of gasoline the Disposer had left there and returned to the camper. First he doused the body then poured the remainder over the furnishings. He left the drum inside and closed the camper door to stop the fumes vaporising too quickly.

Back at the car he quickly changed into his city clothes. Then he drove the car down the track on to the road proper. Leaving the engine running, he ran back to the camper, carrying the bag with the coverall and the Targeter's report. He tossed the bag inside. From his pocket he pulled out a lighter and, standing clear, tossed the flickering flame into the camper, and ran.

There was a dull roar and the camper exploded in flames.

21

From the apartment Klinger sent Dr Romer a second coded message on the fax machine in the master bedroom. His thorough search of the building had established that whatever was in the suitcase, it had not been left behind. Health club staff had confirmed noticing two men come and go.

Here the problem of confirming who they were began. An instructor insisted they were both of equal height. And young, no more than thirty, he said. No, older, definitely older, said another. She had an eye for a man's age. These were in their late forties. One dark-skinned, Spanish-looking; the other fair-haired. And the suitcase? Made of aluminium, the kind salesmen carry. No, the other had said, it was a Samsonite. He knew, because he had one like it. No, no, one of those zip-around bags frequent travellers use. And the pair had left with the FBI, definitely. No, with the Swat team, in their van. By car. The dark-haired guy with the droopy moustache was driving. No, no moustaches, but both had sideburns. A grey car. No, blue. She'd had a good look at them as they climbed in. Both wore blazer and flannels, very English-looking. No, business suits, like the FBI guys. Not a blue car, a green Chrysler, Maryland registration. The registration was definitely Baltimore. And the model had a sunshine roof. No, absolutely no sunshine roof. The tall man was driving. He wore wraparounds, like something out of the movies. Neither wore sunglasses. You'd have noticed something like that, given it was such a cloudy day. Both were of slim build, you know, like dancers. Oh, definitely bigger, and they looked as if they took care of themselves. The brown-haired guy had driven off by himself. The other one had walked, carrying his briefcase. But it could have been a holdall. And it could have been Morton, or just as easily, not.

Klinger ended by describing the business of the file and Thrung's drug-taking and asked for further instructions. He saw the request as a mere formality. The Herr Doktor always responded instantly when an employee broke the Organisation's rules: he had him killed.

Puzzled he had not yet received a response, Klinger went to the kitchen where the Disposer was busy with dinner preparations. He was small, dark and wiry, with a manner which suggested he sought the approval of no one. After Klinger explained his surprise, the Disposer spoke with self-conviction.

'You're missing the point, pal. Romer owes Thrung one. He was one of the squad who pulled the good doctor from that plane in Ecuador. The way I heard it, Romer would have died if Thrung hadn't been there. You can forgive a lot when someone's done that for you.'

'There was nothing in Thrung's file about that.' He disliked the Disposer's American arrogance, the way he flaunted his culinary skills, and his studied contempt. There was also something else, out there on the rim of his own consciousness, he could not yet identify about the Disposer, but which made him uneasy.

The Disposer gave a lopsided grin. 'Those kind of things often don't get put down on paper, Klinger. But working here, I get to hear a lot. Take it from me, this could be Romer's payback. He's very unpredictable like that. Just when you figure he's doing to do one thing, he surprises you by doing the opposite.'

He began to toss the vegetables into pots.

Klinger noted without comment there was something almost effeminate about the Disposer's movements. He asked: 'How do you know the Herr Doktor?'

The Disposer gave another slewed grin. 'I know a lot of people. But I don't talk about them. That's why I'm still here. Romer knows I won't run off at the mouth even when I've had a drink or two.' He picked up a couple of glasses and ambled over to the refrigerator. 'You want one?'

'No.'

The Disposer shrugged. He removed a half-empty bottle of

schnapps from the fridge, uncorked it and filled one of the glasses. 'Chef's perk,' he said, drinking.

'You drink much?'

The Disposer refilled the glass and placed the bottle on a counter. 'Hey, you sound like my mother. I drink what I need, pal.'

'I'm not your pal.'

'OK. You're not my pal. So what does that make us? Enemies? Lighten up, Klinger. Romer will let you know all in good time what he wants done with Thrung. But like I said, when you owe your life to someone, you don't bang-bang him because he made a stupid mistake.'

'You think stealing from the Organisation is only stupid?'

The Disposer drank. 'You want to debate ethics? Go find yourself an ethics teacher. I'm just a cook and garbage collector. But in your line ethics surely can't be a big factor, Klinger. I mean, you don't bang-bang someone and then run along to the confession box and say, sorry, Father, I popped off this fella, but I'd like to give you the ethical side of it. You can't do that, can you?'

'Be careful,' Klinger said in a careful voice.

'Now you definitely sound like my mother.' He swallowed, enjoying the familiar spread of warmth in his stomach.' Every man to his little pleasure. Or don't you have any, pal?'

The blood seethed to Klinger's cheeks. But anger was a weapon and now was not the time to use it. 'Do you know Thrung well?'

The Disposer shrugged and took two large steaks from a plate and placed them on a chopping block. 'He stayed here for a while.' He began to trim fat from the meat. 'He used to eat steak, twice a day.'

'What about his other habit?'

'Which one's that?' the Disposer asked over his shoulder.

'Cocaine.'

The Disposer stared at Klinger full-face. 'I don't know anything about that.'

Spoken too quickly, Klinger noted. From now on he would pay attention not only to what was said, but how it was said.

'He's been snorting for some time.'

'Who says?' Arrogantly.

'I do.'

'He tell you?'

'He showed me.'

'What do you mean, showed you?' Less arrogantly.

Klinger produced his mirthless smile. 'He showed me his supply. He has to get it from somebody.'

'Yeah?'

'I thought you could tell me from whom.'

'Sorry pal. You're knocking at the wrong door.'

The Disposer took the steaks over to the grill with the same too-quick movement.

Klinger came and stood close behind him. 'I think I'm knocking at the right door. I think I am.'

The Disposer turned and stared at him with his deep and passionate eyes in which the arrogance had begun to struggle with something else. 'Stop hassling me, Klinger.'

'Then tell me what I want to know.'

The Disposer picked up a saucepan and carried it to the hob before he spoke. 'You ask a lot of questions for someone who's supposed to be fully briefed, Klinger. Maybe your ticket's not punched in the right places.'

Bravado. Mixed with something else. More than unease. Fear.

'It's punched, right enough. I've got punch holes it's a crime to even whisper their name,' Klinger said softly, speaking less to the Disposer than to his own reflection in the window.

The Disposer carried another pot to the burner. 'Then why keep questioning me?' he demanded, reaching for the bottle.

Klinger grabbed his arm. 'You've had enough.'

'I'll drink when I damn well like—'

Klinger frog-marched the Disposer over to the sink, took the bottle and emptied away the contents.

The Disposer broke free of Klinger's grip. 'Get off my back! And get the hell out of my kitchen!'

Klinger slapped him across the face. It was less the impact of the blow than the surprise of it that sent the Disposer reeling against the sink. He massaged his cheek. Klinger kept his face hard as a fist. He had known this feeling before. In the past it had burst upon him with the brightness of a muzzle flash or sneaked up like dusk. But however it came, it changed everything. A secret, worn like a second skin, had suddenly split open. 'My ticket's punched well enough to have seen your file.'

161

'Screw you!'

Klinger smacked him again, a little harder. Tears came to the Disposer's eyes, not from physical pain, but humiliation. 'You're crazy, Klinger.' But the look on his face showed something had started to fester. 'I just introduced him to a dealer.'

'Just introduced,' Klinger echoed with contempt.

'Jesus, Klinger. The guy was desperate. He'd started snorting again as soon as he left Drug Rehab. I felt sorry for him. Can't you understand that? Can't you?'

'No,' said Klinger after an age. 'I can't.'

'Please, Klinger. Give me a break. If I hadn't helped Thrung, he would have gone some place else. And that could have compromised the Organisation.'

Then suddenly Klinger was on to him, in his own voice the hardness of undivided allegiance. Who was the dealer? Where did Thrung meet him? How long had this been going on? When he had finished, when the Disposer had told all he could, there was silence.

It remained until the Disposer looked away, unable any longer to stand there staring at a sphinx.

'Make sure my steak is medium rare,' Klinger ordered, finally walking from the kitchen, his voice still hostile and accusing.

In the master bedroom he opened the small safe in the back of the walk-in wardrobe. From the top shelf he removed a sealed bottle and a pair of latex gloves. He relocked the safe and carried the items to the desk and placed them beside the fax machine. Then he lay on the bed.

He looked at his watch. There was still another hour before Thrung was due to arrive. He closed his eyes. When he opened them again, he saw that the Disposer was staring at him from the doorway and the sight fired his anger quite powerfully.

'What do you want? You have remembered something else? Or have you come to lecture me on ethics?'

'Klinger, please. I didn't mean any harm . . .'

'Get out.'

The Disposer sighed and, closing the door behind him, was gone.

After a while Klinger checked the time again. He reached for the bedside phone, paused then drew back his hand. He'd keep that motel clerk waiting, he thought, the anger still coursing through him. When he finally rang he forced himself to be polite, keeping the questions on a tight rein. Afterwards he wrote down the name he had been given. It meant nothing to him. He fed the sheet of paper into the fax machine, dialled the number and, in his mind's eye, he could see it emerging in the Herr Doktor's office. When the transmission ended, he returned to the bed and lay down. From the street came the wail of a siren, then the sound of a police car hurtling somewhere. He closed his eyes. This time the high-pitched incoming signal of the fax machine opened them.

Klinger went to the desk. Emerging from the machine was a copy of his transmission; only now the name was double-ringed. Beneath, in that unmistakable scrawl, were the words: 'He works for Hammer Force.'

The paper in Klinger's hand remained perfectly still. Nerve-endings, which in most people became frayed at times of unpleasant surprises, in his case became unbending steel. You could have hooked him to a lie detector at that moment and received a reading as flat as a pond on a windless day.

Klinger looked at the name one more time, then tore up the paper, balled the pieces together and walked to the bathroom. He flushed the wad down the toilet.

'Nagier,' he murmured, repeating it in full as if to better implant the name in his memory. 'Tommy Nagier.'

The atmosphere in the clinic's corridor was filled with foreboding, a reminder to those standing round Dr Romer's wheelchair that he could instil fear without saying a word.

He had been visiting convalescing patients when the bleeper had alerted him, and had arrived here to see the medical emergency team standing in the corridor, defeat on their faces. One glance at their red-painted surgical trolley containing the essentials for resuscitation showed that everything had been tried. In both cases they said, there had been no warning; death was virtually instantaneous. He had asked if there had been an equipment failure; a fluctuation in the voltage could have affected the mechanical ventilators of the life-support systems. There had been no drop in power. He had asked essential questions about each patient's histology. There were no surprises. Yet in both cases the organ rejection had been sudden and total.

Since then he had remained silent, his eyes bright with concentration, his arms resting on the chair's controls, shirt cuffs visible in all their starched whiteness. His immaculately pressed trousers concealed a pair of artificial limbs fitted to his stumps. One leg was casually crossed over the other on the footrest. His socks were held in place by suspenders to ensure they did not slip to reveal the plastic limbs. The legs were painful to wear, and he only did so for visits to the clinic because he knew it was psychologically important for patients to see a whole body.

When he finally spoke again his eyes remained fixed on some point over the heads of the others and his voice contained no anger, which somehow made it more frightening.

'To lose one patient is regrettable. To lose two is not acceptable, especially when one of them is Mr Suto. I am sure you all agree with that,' he proposed, as if he had selected this one thought from the many which had presented themselves to his resourceful mind.

He lowered his gaze and looked into their faces, one at a time, as if seeking individual responsibility for what had happened. He saw only the signs of unease and concern and he was not displeased. When he continued, his voice became slower and more pronounced, as if he needed every word to illustrate a danger far beyond what had happened.

'Mr Suto's death could have an adverse effect on one of the very markets we are trying to develop, Japan. To have lost him at this time is a very real blow. To have lost Mr Gonzales only compounds to the situation. And both from relatively simple surgical procedures. Let me remind you that Mr Suto was the four hundred and first kidney transplant, while Mr Gonzales is our seventy-ninth patient to receive a new liver.'

He resumed staring at the invisible point over their heads as if he was formulating all those other thoughts, regimenting them into order before delivery, not as interesting theories, but as an irrefutable judgement.

'The death of Mr Gonzales is the less important. He had already lost much of his power-base in Spain before he came here. But Mr Suto was at the peak of his authority and, because he came here, half a dozen lesser Japanese gang lords have also contracted for transplants. How will they react once they learn Mr Suto is dead? Will they cancel? That could start a chain reaction with potentially disastrous repercussions. Word will certainly quickly reach Mr Fung in Hong Kong. Will he still come here for a heart? He has close ties to his Mafia colleagues in North America. Two of them are due to arrive shortly for similar surgery. Will they now come? Both have contacts in Europe and the old Soviet empire. There are clients there who have contracted for transplants. Will they still come? The potential for problems is very considerable. I need to know why we have lost these two patients.'

He looked at them as if wishing the world was not so complicated.

'*Chefarzt!*' Boris Surikov dug his hands into the pockets of the long white coat, his finger encountering the supply of popcorn he kept there.

'You have an explanation?' He had waited for as long as it took to be rude. There was something about Surikov's peasant ways that offended him.

'An explanation? Yes, probably. Of course, *Chefarzt!*' Surikov spoke rapidly, his German almost unintelligible through his broad Ukrainian accent.

Dr Romer cut him off. 'English, Surikov! How many times must I tell you to speak English so that we can all understand! If you need extra classes, I will arrange them.'

All non-English-speaking staff had to undergo a crash course in the language.

Surikov bared his horse teeth in apology. 'Sorry, *Chefarzt*. But it is, how you say, very simple really. Both these patients were given anti-inflammatory steroids too early—'

'Absolute tommyrot!' The interruption came from a tall man with the malign look of a scion of the English shires. He wore OR rig, with his mask draped around his neck. 'Absolutely bloody tommyrot!'

'Tommyrot?' asked Dr Romer, in the tone of someone who has long ago given up coming to terms with the vagaries of a foreign language. 'What is tommyrot, Dr Krill?'

The reply came at once. 'Tommyrot? Codswallop, balderdash, rubbish. Anything that has no basis at all. It covers all kinds of nonsenses. And it's perfect to illustrate what my friend has just said.'

Dr Steven Krill, transplant surgeon, alcoholic, divorcee, womaniser and self-appointed expert on the colloquial use of English, especially when it came to the insulting use of 'my friend', paused in case Dr Romer required further elucidation. He seemed disappointed when he did not.

'Kindly continue, Dr Krill.'

Dr Krill leaned his long, angular body forward so that he appeared to be bending towards the wheelchair and addressed it in that clipped tone which is the hallmark of the better English medical schools.

'Gladly. When I was operating at Harefield, it was standard procedure to give a patient an anti-inflammatory. As long as we watched the blood pressure and made sure the lipids didn't form too quickly, it worked very well.'

He turned his pale blue eyes on Surikov. 'Whatever caused these deaths had nothing to do with my post-operative procedures, my friend.'

'How can you be so sure?' There was no offence in the question.

'Because, Dr Romer,' Krill began, in a voice that seemed to be sharing a deep secret, 'of a number of incontestable factors. For a start both operations followed exactly the same procedures as all the others, right down to the last suture. Because both patients went through the post-operative procedures without any cause for concern. Because it was only when they were returned to their rooms that this happened. We might just as well start looking there than in my OR.'

In the renewed silence Dr Romer looked impassively at the surgeon. Steven Krill had once been spoken of in the same breath as the legendary Magdi Yacoub in pioneer transplant surgery – until that night he had been called to operate on a child. Krill had been drunk. The child died on the table. The trial was a medical cause célèbre. A year ago, when he had been released from prison, the Organisation had approached him to head up the clinic's surgical team.

Surikov's snort of derision broke the silence. 'When you were operating in Engand we had already discarded steroids!'

'Except in an emergency,' said Joseph West, the clinic's protein chemist. A small, solemn-faced man, West had held the same post at Berkeley until he was discovered manufacturing Ecstasy in his campus lab. He'd fled to Bolivia, where the Organisation had found him.

'But there was no emergency,' said Dr Romer.

'We still give an anti-inflammatory to avoid one,' said Krill, as if that settled the matter for him. 'We'd be better off looking elsewhere for our culprit.'

Dr Romer turned to a woman with a raked-back hairstyle and a broad Slav face. 'You followed the standard procedure when Mr Suto's replacement organ arrived?'

A flicker of annoyance crossed Helga Niemens' face. She ran the organ bank. 'Both the kidneys from Washington were washed in our solution containing azathioprone to reduce the B-cell activity. The liver for Gonzales had already been similarly treated.'

Dr Romer turned back to Surikov. 'What about the solution used during the transportation? Is it a new batch?'

The immunologist considered. 'It was the same as the one the field agents used to bring back the organs from Mexico and Delhi. There was no problem then, *Chefarzt*.'

'That was two months ago,' Dr Romer said sharply. 'I thought we understood that six weeks is the sensible limit?'

'The solution is, how you say, OK for two further weeks. Klinger was still inside the limit when he harvested in Washington.'

'I don't work to limits! I work well within them, Surikov! Destroy all remaining stock and prepare a new solution at once!'

In the renewed silence the sound of popcorn being crushed in the immunologist's pocket was unnaturally loud as a newcomer joined the group. Instinctively, the others shifted a little apart. The man had a face that hid its secrets like a trader in the souks.

Dr Krill turned to him. 'Afternoon, Weill. Not quite your scene this, my friend. Probably all mumbo-jumbo to you, I expect.'

'I get the general idea, Dr Krill.'

Moshe Weill was that rarity, a Mossad agent gone bad. No one, not even Dr Romer, knew exactly how the seeds for Weill's treachery were sown. When they surfaced, the results were awesomely spectacular. Weill had provided the means for a terrorist group to strike at the very centre of Tel Aviv. Even before their explosions created carnage, he had vanished. By the time Mossad realised the terrible truth, his trail was cold. It was only by sheer chance that the Organisation's head-hunters, on a recruiting mission in Brazil, found him. He had accepted the position as the island's chief of security.

'Weill, I need to talk to you,' Dr Romer said.

He spun the chair and led the way down the corridor. Pausing before a door at the end, he pressed a button on the chair's control box. The security lock clicked and the door opened. Dr Romer propelled himself into the room, followed by Weill.

Unlike his study in the *finca*, the office was starkly furnished: a desk, a chair on either side, bare walls, strip light, no window.

'Sit down,' Dr Romer said, spinning his chair to face Weill. He then explained what he wanted done, watching Weill's face. He had seen that look in others, in men who were scarred by something more than bullets or shrapnel. Like them, Weill had been trained in the art of killing with more than guns.

'It will be costly,' Weill said at last.

'That has never been a problem.'

There was a short silence before Weill explained how it would be done. And, in spite of his naturally loud voice, his face revealed nothing. When he finished, Dr Romer told him what to say in his fax to Klinger.

22

After Tommy checked in at the motel he went straight to the room Stamp had briefly occupied and searched it carefully. He learned nothing Gates' men had failed to discover.

For a while he stood at the sealed window; far below the lights of the unoccupied swimming pool give the water an eerie reflection. The sort of guests this place had would be busy trying to dial up company from Yellow Pages. But nothing in Stamp's background suggested he used hookers. Like most else about him, Stamp's personal habits remained as elusive as ever. Yet someone had walked into this room and cut out his kidneys. Walked in and out again, like a room-service waiter. Except there was no room service.

Tommy went to the door and examined the lock. You could pick it with a hairpin. The safety chain wasn't much better: one good shove and it would burst from its keeper. A place like this cut everything to the bone.

He stepped into the corridor, shutting the door behind him, then used the motel key to open it again. The lock made a loud clicking sound, the way cheap mass-produced locks always do. He closed the door, flopped down on the bed and reread a copy of the CIA report Gates had given him. It was a classic example of the old 24/24 rule in homicide investigation, that the last twenty-four hours in a victim's life and the first twenty-four hours after the body has been discovered are the critical times. There was plenty of evidence of investigative endeavour in the time after death, but the twenty-four-hour period before was a desert as far as hard information went. To even think of going back beyond that now would be pointless: witnesses would no longer remember;

evidence, if it existed, would have disappeared. The only certainty was that it had been one hell of a way for Stamp to go, having his blood caramelised to the point where his heart became a giant sugar lump.

What had Stamp felt, lying here? Sick as a parrot? With that amount of sugar concentrate rushing through his blood, no way he couldn't be. Scared at what was happening to him? Yet he hadn't called for a doctor. The phone on the bedside table had one of those panic buttons even places like this nowadays had to install as a sop to the soaring crime wave. But there was no record of Stamp using it. He'd just lain here, dying and waiting for Jack the Ripper to show up and do a little radical surgery. What sort of ghoul could do that? Had there been only one? Or one to hold down Stamp, the other to cut and slice? The report didn't say – maybe nobody wanted to speculate, not about something like this.

Yet that was what this business was often all about – waiting for the stop light in your head to switch to green.

Tommy shoved the papers back in his jacket pocket, walked back to the door and examined the area around the lock. He then rapidly worked the mechanism back and forth, holding his open hand immediately beneath the lock. Minute fragments dislodged from around the bolt began to settle on his palm. When no more fell, he went over to the desk, removed a sheet of motel notepaper from the imitation-leather folder and deposited the fragments on the paper.

He could almost understand why no one had done this: everybody must have assumed somebody else had. The FBI that the local police detectives had done so; the CIA that the FBI had checked the lock and found nothing. It happened when jurisprudence passed swiftly from one law enforcement agency to another.

From his suitcase he produced a small but powerful microscope and a box containing blank slides. Never go anywhere without your microscope, one of the instructors at training school had instilled. He tipped some of the fragments on to a slide, positioned it in place and placed his eye to the viewfinder. The enlarged fragments were plastic. Only the Stasi's Kommando One had continued using a plastic strip to gain entry to a room. Everyone else nowadays preferred one of the electron burgling devices to trigger a lock.

Tommy straightened. Dad had said Kommando One disappeared overnight as a unit. In the general excitement over what was happening in East Germany at the time, no one paid particular attention. Kommando One was just another bunch of state-sponsored thugs who would quickly wither without the support of their paymaster. So what had someone from Kommando One been doing here, breaking into Stamp's room and stealing his kidneys? A freelance trying to cash in on market demand? Or part of a team? Had Kommando One found a new employer?

He had a feeling of getting ahead of himself. He started to think of a dozen other explanations. None of them really made any sense. He stood for a while, remembering exactly what the instructor in Orientation had laid down for a situation like this. What are the unadmitted intentions? The unseen gaps? The interior monologues? The secret decisions? She'd ridiculed the right to ignore the basic response. When you don't know, *ask*. And go on asking until you do know.

He went to the phone and dialled Chantal's direct-line number in Geneva. Her voice-mailbox recording said she was not available. He left a call-back message. Then he packed away the microscope and slides, and locked the suitcase.

From a pocket he removed a vial containing colourless plastic bristles, the kind found in a cheap shaving brush. He shook several strands into his palm, pocketed the vial and left the room. In the corridor he locked the door behind him, moistened the bristles with spittle, carefully placed them across the door and jamb and walked to the elevator. Whatever else they had clung to, he doubted if the Stasi would have retained such an old-fashioned means of knowing if anyone had entered the room. But the Colonel said sometimes the old ways were still the best ones.

On the apartment's security monitor Klinger watched Thrung arrive in the lobby and enter the elevator. Punctual to the minute. The camera in the cage showed Thrung checking his appearance in the mirror panels. A third camera followed his progress down the hallway, a lumbering figure in a dark blue suit and a tie the width of a hand towel. When Klinger opened the apartment door, Thrung looked surprised.

'Herr Klinger. . . ?' This blond-haired, casually dressed man with a scar on his cheek bore no resemblance to the bearded figure who had bullied him in his office.

'Come in,' Klinger said. He closed the door and led the way to the living room. A moment later the Disposer emerged from the kitchen.

'Good to see you again, Karl-Wolf. I've got your favourite steak grilling. Meantime let me fix you a drink.'

The glance and the glance away said everything. They were conspiratorial and loving, both at once. And they said: watch this heterosexual.

The Disposer turned to Klinger. 'How about you?'

'Tonic water.'

As the Disposer went to the kitchen, Klinger motioned Thrung to one of the room's armchairs. 'Your cold still bothering you?'

There was a trace of powder inside Thrung's nostrils. He must have taken a snort on the way here to make him as relaxed as this, like a hippo in a mudbath.

'You have heard from Dr Romer?' Thrung asked.

Klinger ignored the question. 'How long you been taking coke?' he asked abruptly.

'I would prefer to discuss such matters directly with Dr Romer.' He felt calm, in control, no longer fearful.

'I've told you, Thrung. Be careful. Be very careful.'

'What do you want from me, Klinger?' Thrung leaned forward in his anger.

'I don't want anything.' Klinger's face had set into a rigid impassibility.

'Then why are you so unfriendly?'

'I pick my friends.' Klinger glanced towards the kitchen. 'You don't look so good, Thrung.'

'I feel fine.' Klinger was like a sore that never quite healed.

'The coke make you feel like that?'

'You sound like a Russian. You know that? Just like a Russian.'

'Are you trying to insult me?'

'No. But why are you playing this war of nerves?'

'Are you forgetting why you are here, Thrung? I ask the questions, remember. So tell me me about your dealer. Who is he?'

In the silence the Disposer arrived with their drinks, announced dinner would be served shortly, and returned to the kitchen.

Klinger sipped and watched him go. How the hell had he managed to hide it from the Herr Doktor? He turned back to Thrung. 'I asked you a question.'

Thrung's eyes moved back and forth. 'These are matters I will discuss with Dr Romer.'

'First you will discuss them with me.'

'You think I'm a fool, Klinger. I tell you, and then I have nothing to tell Dr Romer.' Thrung sat back. He had no intention of telling.

'When he hears the rest you will wish you had told me everything.'

Thrung's eyes focused again, not so much to see, but rather, like a piece of glass catching the sun, to burn. 'Stop pushing me, Klinger.'

'Stop pushing you?' Klinger shook his head as if Thrung's words were evidence of a grievous lapse. 'When was the first time, Thrung? Did he pay you, or did you pay him?'

'You're a character-swine, Klinger, a real character-swine.'

'You want me to hit you again, Thrung – really hit you this time?' Klinger asked with menace. 'Or is that what you like?'

From the bedroom came a pinging sound. Klinger put down his glass and stood up. 'Think about it, Thrung. I know all about you and your friend.' He nodded towards the kitchen. 'The Organisation doesn't like love nests, specially your kind.'

'Don't push me, Klinger, just don't push me,' Thrung whispered. He could feel the fear on his palms.

Reaching down, Klinger carefully took hold of Thrung's tie, and tightened the knot. But Thrung did not complain.

'I'll push you as hard as I need, Thrung. And then harder. You remember that, now.'

He released his grip on the tie, then continued to instruct Thrung how he should behave. 'Stop sounding like a jittery asshole, Thrung. Just think about what I've said. And when I come back you're going to tell me who else in the Organisation you've been screwing. Think of it as a question of loyalty. Think of it as anything you like, just as long as you tell me.'

Klinger strode towards the insistent sound from the bedroom. This had to be the Herr Doktor's response. He'd listen to what Thrung had to say, then kill them both.

Klinger reached the fax machine while the transmission was still being received. He began to frown. Beneath his name and that of the sender were only groups of numbers. Why was he getting a coded signal? And from Weill? He didn't normally involve himself in anything outside the island. He went to the safe and removed a code book. From the living room came the whisper of voices. They would be feeding each other's fears. He sat at the desk and laboriously began to transcribe the groups, his frown deepening as he worked. When he had finished he read the clear text back to make absolutely sure.

'*Mensch*,' he said, looking at the window, gazing at his own reflection in the night. Then once more: '*Mensch*.' Only Weill could have thought of this.

He glanced towards the door. There was silence in the other room, almost as if they already knew. He stood up, feeling his breath growing short, an involuntary hand making a fist in his belly. He always felt like that before action. He went to the bathroom, tore up both the encoded and decoded messages and flushed them down the toilet. He stared into the mirror. The scar on his cheek was healing. It would still serve his purpose. Emerging from the bathroom he found the Disposer hovering in the bedroom doorway.

'Dinner's on the table, Klinger.'

'Give mine to your friend,' Klinger said.

'Aren't you hungry?'

'I'm going out.'

The Disposer affected not to understand. 'Out? Now?'

Klinger glanced at him. 'I'll be back. But if I'm delayed, you and Thrung are to go to Dulles and pick up a Global flight that'll take you to the island. Give me until midnight. The Global flight's due in the early hours.'

The Disposer smiled. 'You see, I told you Romer owes Thrung one. Maybe your ticket's not properly punched after all, Klinger.'

Klinger looked at him wordlessly, then stuffed into his jacket pocket the pair of latex gloves and the sealed bottle he had removed from the safe and left the apartment.

In the clinic's operations room Dr Romer saw there had been dramatic improvement on the plotting table. Flags were raised in

Montreal, Vancouver and Seattle, above Singapore and Bangkok, over Barcelona and Munich. One stood proud and erect above Johannesburg. Each flag represented a successful harvesting by a Kommando One operative.

The shift chief, a fortyish woman in a loose smock, turned to Dr Romer. 'We now have five hearts and the same number of livers. We also have seven sets of kidneys. Seattle provided a complete harvest, and we're expecting it shortly. The local Disposer up there said everything went perfectly. He sent the Fixer out to the site, and he was able to confirm that the police are satisfied it was an accident.'

'Good.' He turned back to the map. There was no flag raised over Stockholm. 'Why hasn't Engel reported?'

The woman gave a light shrug. 'His flight was delayed out of Paris. Another of their air traffic go-slows. You know the French.'

He did. That was why he never employed them. 'Inform those on the waiting list to make their first payments and then prepare to travel here. Begin with Mr Fung. He has been waiting a long time.'

The woman began to tap instructions into her modem to tell the Triad leader in Hong Kong his new heart was ready for transplanting.

Dr Romer propelled himself over to the Global Transporter station. The operative looked up from his console.

'The Washington flight. You will inform the captain as follows.' Dr Romer began to dictate rapidly.

When the operative finished typing he moved aside for Dr Romer to read the screen.

'Good.' Leaving the operations room he paused at the top of the concrete ramp, and sniffed. There was a faint smell of sulphur in the air. Mount Masaya was clearing her throat.

23

From the living-room windows of Yoshi's suite in the Grand Hotel, Morton watched a white-painted excursion steamer drifting down the Strommen Canal towards the Royal Palace. In less than an hour he would be driven into its courtyard, Yoshi's guest at the King of Sweden's reception for the Nobel laureates. While Yoshi had slept, Morton had spent the afternoon on the phone. He'd disconnected the handset from the Grand's switchboard – though its efficient operators would have no inkling of this – and run the line to a metal box. No bigger than a biscuit tin, it contained a rhombic antenna, half a mile of coiled fibre-optic cable, and four dipoles. The box provided a secure line but the first calls had not been encouraging.

Chapman had failed to remove the corrector fluid and discover what was on the forms in Thrung's file. Lester had run into problems rewriting Meditale. His programmers had still not found a compatible language to decode the other discs. That was holding up writing a programme common to all the thefts of human organs. Chantal had reported that more such crimes had taken place in Canada, South Africa and the Far East; the local police were treating them as ritual-related. Danny's one success in Dresden was discovering that Romer had taken Spanish lessons before flying to Ecuador. Of the Stasi report into his fate Danny had found no trace. Yet they must have searched. Someone as important as Romer wouldn't just be allowed to vanish off their screens, missing, believed eaten by wild animals. They'd want to at least find a bone. But if they had, the news had either been hidden somewhere so secure that no one would find it, or more likely, had gone up in smoke in that night of the bonfires before the Wall had come down, Danny had said.

In some of the calls he had sensed that their urgency had become becalmed, the way he had so often at this stage. The important thing now was to empathise, to remind them all that stalemate was an essential part of the thrust forward.

Yoshi was awake, and reaching for the bottle on the bedside table, and behind the Royal Palace the spire of Ridderholm Church was disappearing into the dusk, when the small display panel on top of the box signalled an incoming call. It was Gates. An hour ago he'd asked Bill to see if the National Security Agency would organise satellite surveillance on Nicaragua. Bill hadn't sounded hopeful. Now his voice bristled with anger.

'It's a no-go, David. It's that sonofabitch over at State.'

'Armstrong?'

'Wallace Armstrong, the Second,' Gates confirmed. 'Our Secretary of State's living proof that a carbon copy is never as good as the original.'

The steamer had drifted out of sight before Morton spoke. 'What can you do, Bill, at your end?'

Gates' shout of disgust sounded loud in his ear. 'That's the damnest part – not a thing. Armstrong has told the Director we are to steer clear of Nicaragua. We've had to pull out everybody. It seems the Secretary is working on some glorious plan of his own to make them all like us again down there.'

'That's what politicians do, Bill. Create wonderful dreams,' Morton said in a voice no louder than a sigh.

'But it still knocks a big hole in your net. Without sat. surveillance you'll be operating with one hand tied behind your back. Not a good position.'

Not a good position, for sure. 'If Armstrong's trying to make a new start down there, then let him. Each to his own. We'll just find another way.'

In the bedroom Yoshi was starting to get dressed, moving slowly and carefully, as if he wanted to conserve his energy.

'I just know the clinic's there, Bill, I just know it in my gut,' Morton said, in a voice he would have used to recite an article of faith.

Gates accepted the hypothesis but needed to introduce a caveat. 'The problem is Nicaragua's one mother of a big country. As our own people found out.' He'd been a field officer then, working out of Managua with the Contras. 'Away from the Pacific coast, the place is still a nightmare. No maps worth speaking of. Transport a shambles. Lousy communications. It's quicker to walk than phone – except the roads are often impassable. Throw in the annual hurricanes and you get my drift. Not to forget the odd earthquake tremor the tourist ministry says is heavy traffic. Tourist ministry! Talk about optimists. You'd have to be crazy to even think of taking a vacation there. To the south you have Lake Nicaragua, where you can be eaten by freshwater sharks. East you have country that makes the Louisiana swamps positively inviting. The Caribbean coast is even rougher. North, it's the rain forests, like the Amazon used to be before the loggers moved in. Pretty well anywhere you look you could build a clinic and no one would know, David.'

A massive certainty entered Morton's voice. 'That's why Romer chose the place, Bill.'

In silence he watched Yoshi sitting in a chair and lacing his shoes. The exertion from bending had brought an unnatural flush to his cheeks.

'Maybe there is a way,' Gates said at last. 'The Geological Survey people are going down there to check out Mount Masaya. It's supposed to have started acting up again. Our Contra trackers used to call it *Boca del Infierno*, the mouth of hell. It certainly was the night I ran a search-and-destroy op up her slopes. There was supposed to have been a guerrilla camp halfway up. Suddenly old Masaya coughs and we all had to run – Sandinistas, Contras, my people all going like bats out of hell down the one track. By the time we sorted out who was who, the Sandinistas had made it into the Solentiname Islands. And as sure as hell we weren't going in there after them. That's a real wild place.'

Gates had spoken quickly, the way one often does when recalling something which would never be forgotten.

'When do the Survey people leave?' Morton asked.

'I think in a week or so. I can check. It's all part of Armstrong's crap about trying to convince the Nicaraguans they really should be buddy-buddy. Only thing they understand down there is how to spend our dollars.'

Apart from his iron-hard smile Morton gave no response. A decade on, the bitterness still lingered in Bill's voice over how the

178

Reagan administration had poured money into supporting the Contras; before they had lost all credibility with Washington over 60,000 lives had been sacrificed.

Morton waited the decent interval something like that demanded before proposing: 'I'd like to take the opportunity the Survey people provide.'

'You mean have somebody tag along?'

'Too risky. I'd like to have somebody go along as the front man. No need to tell the Survey People. What they don't know, they don't feel compromised over.'

'How about Tommy? I was impressed with him. A real chip off the old block.'

Morton explained he was sending Tommy to California, adding that he would tell Danny what Bill had said. Then, in the same relaxed voice, as if what he now proposed was the most sensible solution, he put forward another suggestion.

'How about you going, Bill? Armstrong or your Director won't know you've gone before you're back.'

'Me?' Gates gave a self-deprecating laugh. 'Most days I feel past my sell-by date for the field. I haven't really been out since Hong Kong. And that was a while back.'

He offered the reminder in a voice of shared knowledge. But Morton appeared not to have heard. 'I could sent Danny with you. He's got some new gizmos he's eager to try out. Nicaragua sounds an ideal place to do so.'

'I don't know, David.'

'Just think about it,' Morton suggested helpfully.

Once more there was silence on the line. Bill would be working it through down to the amount of Lomotil he'd need for diarrhoea, together with water purification tablets and a rehydration powder. And how he'd fit an extra roll of toilet paper into his luggage without giving up space for a spare clip of bullets.

'What's the bottom line here, time-wise, David? A week? Longer?'

'Time-wise?' Morton happily allowed himself to echo Gates' past-its-shelf-life choice of word. 'Oh, a few days. In and out.'

'Like Iraq?'

'Better. There'll be more cover this time.'

Gates' sigh sounded like a small bellows being expelled. 'Tell

179

Danny I'll meet him in San Francisco in a couple of days. I know someone out there who knows someone with the Survey people who can brief us so at least we'll sound like seismologists. But as far as the Agency goes, this trip never happened. This is strictly me on my jack.' He chuckled. 'You know what they say – after forty a man needs something to keep his nerves and intestines in peak condition. Look upon this as doing me a favour.'

They spoke for a little while longer about all the small fiddly points that always underpinned a covert action.

Afterwards Morton called Danny in Dresden. He finished briefing him as Yoshi walked into the room.

'You really feel up to this?' Morton asked solicitously.

'I've just taken two more tablets. I'll be fine,' promised Yoshi.

The government limousine sped towards the mediaeval island of the Old Town. Ahead, amid a blaze of lights, rose the massive edifice of the Royal Palace.

'The illuminations above the main entrance are to honour the laureates,' explained Marta Hamsum: 'To honour you, Dr Kramer. It really is so wonderful you could come tonight. There are so many people who want to meet you.'

She inspected him carefully for a moment longer from the jump seat opposite. She had insisted on sitting there to avoid crushing her evening gown. Then she began to brief them.

'First, the laureates will meet each other and the distinguished guests of the Foundation. The second stage will be the arrival of our Prime Minister and senior members of his government. They will meet you and the other winners in turn, Dr Kramer. Finally, the King and his entourage will arrive. For that there will be a receiving line.'

Making a little gesture of apology with her hand towards Morton, Marta continued. 'His Majesty will only have time to speak to the laureates. But while he is doing so, members of the Royal household will engage others in conversation. One last thing, Dr Kramer: unless the King offers his hand, you should make no attempt to shake it. And you may address him as Your Majesty or His Royal Highness. Either is acceptable.'

Her trained smile suddenly turned into a girlish giggle. 'Please, can I share something with you?'

'By all means,' Yoshi murmured.

'This is the first time I have been allowed to escort a laureate.'

'I'm honoured.' Yoshi was still smiling gallantly as the car drove into the main courtyard of the palace.

As they emerged, the guards sprang to attention. Under the blaze of floodlights, the pikes on their steel helmets gleamed, as did their black leather boots and the white epaulettes on their dark uniforms.

A resplendent court servant stepped forward and spoke in Swedish to Marta. She looked in surprise at Morton.

'There has been a call for you. From Germany. He left no name.'

The only person in Germany who would know where to find him at any given moment would be Hans-Dieter. 'May I use a phone?'

'Yes, of course.' She led the way across the uneven paving, up a short flight of stone steps and into the palace. An equerry in regimental regalia greeted them. Marta spoke quickly to the officer, who nodded.

'We will wait for you while you make your call,' Marta decided. She smiled at Yoshi. 'Perhaps you would like to know a little of the history of the building? It dates from the thirteenth century. But our Royal family only moved in about two hundred years ago. It is still the largest inhabited palace in the world, far bigger than Buckingham Palace, bigger even than the Apostolic Palace in the Vatican. But our King uses only thirty of the rooms for his private quarters . . .'

When the equerry had shown him into a nearby office and closed the door behind him Morton dialled Mueller's direct-line in Pullach.

'*Ja?*' snapped an impatient voice.

Morton told the owner of the voice who he was and he became respectful. 'Director Mueller wants you to know we have a murder he thinks will interest you. The victim is a heart specialist named Gruber. He was treating the President of our Bundesbank. Herr Vogel, it seems, was a candidate for a transplant.'

'Is there anything unusual about that?' But his tone went further. There's always something unusual when it happens to be the world's most powerful banker, it was saying.

'I don't know. I am not an expert in such matters, Herr Morton.' The voice paused as if to come back on track. 'Gruber decided to take a holiday. A few days at the Tegernsee . . . a wonderful spot. You know it, yes?'

'South of Munich. Close to the autobahn to Salzburg?' His good humour remained undimmed.

'Exactly so, Herr Morton. To be exact, it was not by the lake that Gruber was found, but on the Wallberg. That is the highest mountain in the area, yes? Gruber had been there before. He seemed to like to ski a little, though nobody saw him do so this time.'

'Where exactly was he killed?' His voice was like one soft tread following upon another.

The pedant spoke reprovingly. 'I was coming to that, Herr Morton. He was found in the lodge he had rented. There are several up there. It seems a local skier noticed a door left open when it shouldn't be, something like that, and went to investigate. He found Gruber with his chest open and all his organs removed. Not a pretty sight, yes?'

'No,' said Morton. It never was. 'Do you have any report that this was done professionally? By a doctor? Or someone medically trained?' For all his emphasis, he could have been enquiring about the piste conditions.

'By a doctor?' The voice had risen an octave. 'No. There is no such report. I am no expert in the matter, yes, but from what I understand, there is probably no way of telling who did it. Director Mueller is looking at all possibilities.'

'Where is he now?'

The pedant's throat-clearing reminded Morton of Walter.

'Tell him I'll be with him as soon as I can,' said Morton. He put down the phone. An hour more wouldn't make any difference; it hadn't when he'd crouched over those other bodies. He dialled the CCO and told him to file a flight plan to Munich, take-off in a couple of hours. That should give him time to make sure Yoshi was tucked up in bed for the night.

There was a knock on the door and Marta came into the room, her trained smile once more in place. 'Did you manage to make your call?'

'Yes, thank you.' Morton motioned for her to close the half-open door. After a moment's hesitation she did.

182

'Is there something wrong?' she asked.

'No, of course not. But you know about Dr Kramer's heart condition?' Morton asked.

'It's so sad for him, Mr Morton. And he's so young as well,' she said, like someone who has researched the whole question of sadness and youth in heart disorders. 'Was your call about that?'

'Not directly. But it's still connected.'

She nodded quickly.

He placed no undue emphasis on what he said. 'I had planned to stay with him tonight, just in case he needed anything. Unfortunately, I have to go away on business. I was wondering whether you would know someone who could remain with Dr Kramer until I return? I don't want an agency nurse or anything formal. That could alert the press, and the last thing Dr Kramer wants is publicity. It's probably not necessary, but I'd feel happier if there was someone on hand.'

'I'd be honoured to accept. That is, if you approve.'

Morton waited the length of time he had intended, then said he was very glad to accept.

'And Dr Kramer? Will he also approve?'

'I'm sure he will.'

'Then it's settled. I'll go home and collect a night bag, and wait for Dr Kramer in his suite.'

'Aren't you coming to the reception?'

Marta's trained smile was back. 'I fear I'm not important enough to be invited.'

After Hermann Engel, the Kommando One operative assigned by Dr Romer to Sweden, cleared landing formalities at Arlanda, he went to a payphone in the airport concourse and dialled a local number.

A recorded voice ordered him to dial a second number. He went to a second phone and did so, noting down the number's first digit after the new voice directed him to phone another number. In all he made three more calls, following the same precise sequence. He then went to the bar on the fourth floor of the concourse, ordered a beer and wrote down the digits in the order he had received them. He then rearranged them in a new sequence. Finishing his drink, he went to another payphone and dialled the sequence. This time the new voice gave him another number to call after he had gone to the baggage deposit on the ground floor and presented the claim docket which had been in the envelope Dr Romer had given him.

The clerk handed Engel a locked briefcase. He went to a nearby men's toilet, selected a cubicle and took a key from the envelope to open the briefcase. As well as a fléchette gun and a sachet of pellets, there was a set of surgical knives and retractors, a pair of latex gloves and a plastic container. On its lid was a boldly stencilled red label stating that the contents were a dangerous pathogen sample which should be opened only in a contagion laboratory at the Center for Disease Control in Atlanta, Georgia. The container contained only liquid.

Closing the briefcase, Engel went to yet another payphone. A new voice gave him a name and a brief physical description. Engel replaced the receiver and immediately redialled the number. The repeat action erased the recording.

Despite its robot-like quality, acquired from speaking through a synthesiser, he had recognised the voice. Madam's. But he had never heard of her chosen victim.

24

Tugging open one of the two towering wooden doors – this had become more and more of an effort since he had left the clinic – Dieter Vogel entered his inner sanctum in the headquarters of the Bundesbank. Only in the thickly carpeted hall which led to his office did he begin to relax after the jolting telephone call.

Until then the BND, like all the other German security agencies, was something he had only read about, or seen occasional references to on the nightly news. Their activities belonged to a world far removed from his own, he had told Mueller. The remark had produced a soft chuckle from the operations Chief. Then, without preamble, Mueller had said Gruber was dead, and then explained exactly how he had met his death. He had still been trying to absorb the truly shocking details when Mueller had asked what had seemed like a hundred questions, none of which had made any sense, and all of which seemed to be directed towards Gruber's private habits. Had he spoken about anything unusual? Sex? Unusual religious attitudes? The Devil, perhaps? The sort of things he might just casually have mentioned to a well-connected patient that he wouldn't to staff? Doctors sometimes liked to do that; liked to show a patient an unexpected side. There were any number of reasons why they did so, none of them important now. The important thing was if Gruber had said anything a little strange. Perhaps bizarre, even, looking back on it? The more Mueller had asked, the more bewildering it sounded. When he'd told Mueller Gruber had spoken of nothing except medical matters, there had been a sigh and the wind-up apologies. If you think of anything, call. Mueller had given a number. In Pullach, he'd added; always somebody there who would know where to reach him. Just call, any time. Only when he'd hung up had he realised he hadn't mentioned his transplant to Mueller. When he'd started to recover from the shock of the call, he knew why. It was the one way he could separate himself from Gruber's death. That belonged in another, very different world, one far removed from his own, where keeping a proper distance was second nature anyway. If you didn't, you became emotionally involved, the worst possible thing for a banker.

And so, on such a sensible reminder, his mind had started to calm and focus on the day ahead. Now, as he approached the soothing surrounds of his office, he continued to grow more calm. The bookcases on either side of the corridor crammed with investment journals and leather-bound finance reports, the oil paintings of former presidents, the muted atmosphere: this was his world, not that dreadful one Mueller had so graphically described.

Entering the outer office Vogel saw Monika Sauermann, his secretary, standing at a fax machine, her back to him.

'Good morning, Frau Sauermann.'

She turned quickly, dutifully. She was holding a piece of paper in her hand, frowning as she returned his greeting. 'I don't understand why somebody has faxed us this newspaper report, Herr President.'

He took the fax from her. The face of Boris Kransky stared out beneath the headline. Former KGB Chief in DDR found Dead in Amsterdam.

The matronly Frau Sauermann looked anxious. 'Herr President, are you all right?'

Somebody knew: about his connection with Kransky and the negatives, knew enough to send the report to his private fax, understood all about timing, about operating in the highly controlled environment of terror; knew the most terrifying of all fear was the one you create in yourself. Somebody knew all that.

'Herr President, is everything all right?' Frau Sauermann asked again, her anxiety deepening.

'Yes. Yes, of course.' He gathered himself. He couldn't stand here not saying anything. He had to say something. 'I'm fine now.'

He began to tell her about Mueller's call. Frau Sauermann's look of astonishment now joined and then, for the moment at least, replaced the concern on her matronly face. 'Incredible, absolutely incredible,' she breathed when he finished. 'Do you think this newspaper report is connected?'

'Connected?' How is that possible? Of course it's not connected! Unless you think Dr Gruber was a Russian spy!'

He glared at the fax machine, then around the office that until a while ago he had regarded as the safest place ever, even safer than his home. Now, suddenly, its security had been stolen from him, stolen by someone who *knew*. But who? And how? The full fury of his glare came to rest on Frau Sauermann.

'Your trouble is that you watch too much television! No – it's obvious. Somebody must have dialled our fax number by mistake. Surely that's happened before, Frau Sauermann?'

She looked at him, the hurt now flooding into her face. He had never shouted at her before, never once even raised his voice. She remembered what she had read about the banker personality in her favourite magazine. Perhaps such generalisations were true.

'Of course, Herr President, it must be a mistake.' She reached to take the fax back from him. 'Maybe there is a transmission number I can protest to.'

He waved her hand away. 'No! Leave it.' He glanced at the paper. 'It's some idiot who can't use a fax. The world is full of them.'

'Of course, of course,' she said in her soothing secretary's voice.

Briefly they both smiled, though not at each other.

'So, what else do you have to amuse me with?' he asked, determined to end this on a more pleasant note. 'A bomb threat? It's about time we had one of those, isn't it? Or has that lunatic in London phoned the switchboard again to say he's going to buy the bank?' His attempt at levity was spoiled by the too-questioning stare. 'So: what is it?'

She took a deep breath. 'There is something, Herr President. It's about what Dr Gruber's gone and done.'

Suddenly there was silence and all Vogel could hear was the thumping of his heart. Gruber? Done? What had he gone and done?

Frau Sauermann told him in the only way she knew, a secretary's way, summarising, without losing any of its import, the quite lengthy telephone call from the director of the central organ bank in Bonn, once she had established her position as the Herr President's most trusted aide.

'He tried to call you at home. Then on the carphone.'

'What's Gruber gone and done?' Vogel spoke with an unearthly composure.

'The director said he had received a telephone call from Dr Gruber to cancel the search for a donor heart for you, Herr President. Until he received a counter order personally signed by Dr Gruber, in his capacity as your physician, nothing could be done. I called the clinic at once and was informed Dr Gruber was on holiday. It seems he issued his cancellation order shortly before he left, before this terrible thing happened to him.'

'Why would he cancel it, Frau Sauermann?' he asked at last, his mind still half-deafened by the import of Frau Sauermann's words.

'I don't know, Herr President,' she replied in a faltering voice.

They looked at each other in silence, as if each waitied for the lead that would tell them how to go on.

'My God, what is happening?' Vogel whispered.

'I really don't know, Herr President.' Frau Sauermann was close to tears.

There was something in her voice and manner that said there was more. 'There was also a call on your private line a few minutes ago.' She began to fiddle with the wedding band on her widow's finger.

'Who was it?' he spoke kindly, as if to make up for his previous lapse. Sometimes a finance minister or the head of a central bank called to talk to him on some particularly sensitive matter.

'A woman.' Frau Sauermann paused and at first she thought he was smiling, but there was no laughter in his expression. She walked to her desk and picked up a message slip. 'She left this number. It's in Stockholm.'

He took the slip, frowning. He didn't recognise the number. He looked up. 'Did she leave a name?'

'No. But she said the matter was both urgent and personal.'

'Is that all she said?' The question had slipped out before he had time to modify its sharpness. He had not meant it as a challenge. The words had emerged by themselves, escaping from the chaos in his mind.

'Yes.' She felt his gaze and wondered whether he was aware of her inner withdrawal. What was happening here had nothing to do with banking. 'That's all she said. Were you expecting more?'

He did not answer, yet he did not avoid her question. He absorbed it. Then he laughed, quickly and not very pleasantly, the way he usually laughed when deciding upon action. 'Get her on the line,' he said, striding into his office.

Moments later there was a knock on the door, and Frau Sauermann put her head in. A look of bewilderment was on her face.

'The number I called referred me to a second. On it was a special message for you.' She glanced at her notepad, then read aloud: ' "Now that you are interested, I will come to see you. Madam." '

Bundesbank President Vogel once more did not trust himself to speak.

Count Lindeman explained that the *Vita Havet*, the White Sea Room, had once been used for court balls, as he manoeuvred Yoshi and Morton with effortless ease around the spacious salon furnished with valuable artefacts and the homely furnishings of previous Royal generations. He led them towards a group standing before one of the two huge open fireplaces.

'Between them they burn a ton of logs in an evening,' Lindeman murmured.

Only someone steeped in old-world correctness would have had a fact ready to fill a gap, Morton thought. Not that there had been any. Yoshi had been in sparkling form from the first introductions. Now there were more. A bishop, an industrialist and his wife, a blue-rinsed countess, a brace of English diplomats and their wives. They stood between a handsome divan and a marble-topped commode.

Catching Yoshi's eye, Count Lindeman smiled. 'We Swedes are really very earthy about the basics of life. The King's father swore this particular commode helped his piles.'

'Whatever it takes,' Yoshi said cheerfully. 'Perhaps if we were all a little more open, we wouldn't have so much stress in our lives and, for that matter, fewer strokes.'

The industrialist spoke from the depths of his self-importance. 'My view exactly. But then, we wouldn't have had the pleasure of your presence, Dr Kramer. Your discovery is truly a benefit to mankind.'

Murmurs of agreement came from the group. Yoshi made a

self-deprecating gesture. 'There's still a long way to go. All I've done is show the way for others to follow. But there are a lot of hurdles to clear before we can say we can totally predict and control the brain mechanism which causes a stroke.'

He pitched his smile above the stomachs that could take no more lipoid suction and into the pouched eyes which no amount of further tucking would restore. How many of these were potential victims?

The gaitered bishop peered over his bifocals. 'I am of an age I believe you call CVA-prone, so I would be most interested to know more.' He spoke with the manacled slowness of advancing years.

'CVA? I'm not sure my favourite magazine has explained that,' the Countess said with an awesome display of orthodontistry.

Everyone laughed with artificial brightness.

'We now call a stroke a cerebral-vascular accident, CVA for short, Countess. It's supposed to make it sound less scary on your case notes. My profession's good at labelling – and when two words can be used, one will never do.'

Yoshi waited for the new ripple of laughter to subside. 'But however many words we use, it still doesn't change the basic problem. A stroke just doesn't happen like that' – he clicked his fingers – 'any more than a heart attack does. They've both been a long time in the making, perhaps months, sometimes even years. And that's part of the problem. With strokes we still don't know how to spot one early enough. The time we usually get to know the blood flow is impaired is when the blockage is complete and' – another finger-click – 'a stroke.'

'Oh my God. No warning. How *absolutely* terrifying,' the Countess whispered in a strangled aside to her husband. 'At least with my hysterectomy I had some notice.'

Yoshi continued to address the bishop. 'We think – and again it's no more than an informed guess – that as you get older the walls of the brain vessels lose some of their elasticity. But at what age and what is the loss of elasticity? Your guess is as good as mine. All we can say with some confidence is that a great deal depends on which side of the brain has been affected by a stroke.'

'My *goodness*, you mean there is a good and a bad side?' asked one of the diplomats, in that classless accent that had recently become fashionable in the Foreign Office.

Yoshi's smile lost none of its brilliance. 'Just as there's a good and bad side in everything else, Ambassador. If you get a stroke which affects the right side of your brain, the chances are your speech won't be affected because it is the left brain which controls that.'

'I'm left-handed. What then?' asked the Ambassador's wife.

'A good question, madam,' Yoshi said, as if something had just refreshed his memory. 'We think – and again it's no more than a guess – that twenty per cent of left-handed people have speech centres in both halves of their brain. We don't know why this is, any more than we don't know why it is that about half of all left-handed people have their speech centres on the right. The fact is that we don't know a hell of a lot, except that the human brain is highly resilient and underused.

'Let me tell you a story. A couple of years back, I had a patient who had been shot through the head by his wife. In here – out here.' He pointed behind his ear and on top of his head. He smiled at the women, aware of the frisson of excitement. 'She was a bad shot. But when I opened her husband's head, I found the bullet had travelled through an area of the brain we don't use. Two days after surgery, he was able to leave the hospital. He didn't press charges against his wife – or, for that matter, pay my fee – but the last I heard they were idyllically happy.'

The Ambassador led the laughter. When it stopped Yoshi continued. 'There are large areas of the brain which have no obvious function, yet which take over when another part fails.'

Morton marvelled at the way Yoshi's face and body continued to undergo a mysterious change. The gaunt lines had been miraculously lifted from around his eyes and mouth. He stood, one hand comfortably holding a glass, using the other to emphasise a point, a contented smile settled on his face and his head slightly bowed in acceptance of his considerable performance.

Twice already Yoshi had given his set-piece to equally enthralled listeners in other parts of the salon. Yet he had once more made it sound refreshingly spontaneous.

'The truth is that something far more effective in dealing with a stroke is often good old-fashioned TLC.'

The second Ambassador's wife, with a double chin to go with her double-barrelled name, brayed: 'That my favourite magazine *does* know about – Tender Loving Care.'

Yoshi nodded happily. 'Absolutely right. All we surgeons can do if a stroke is caused by a haemorrhage is to try to remove the blood. Fact is most people, if they do recover, do so with TLC.'

'Like the actress Patricia Neal,' said the Countess. 'She was left paralysed and unconscious and, when she woke up, she was speechless after her stroke. But with the help of her husband she returned to complete normality.'

Yoshi turned to Lindeman. 'There should be a Prize for Human Fortitude.'

'A splendid idea. I'll suggest that to the committee, Dr Kramer,' Lindeman said.

Morton recognised the cue for them to move on.

Klinger stood in the entrance to the motel bar, adjusting his eyes to the gloom. The long, low-ceilinged room was tricked out like a mediaeval baronial hall. Plastic shields and crossed halberds hung on the stucco walls between machine-made tapestries and imitation mediaeval torches. Long, dark-stained tables filled the middle of the room; booths lined the walls. The bar itself had swivel seats, a full-length mirror and a row of display tankards which were too bright to be genuine pewter. The American appetite for kitsch never failed to astonish him; there was something in their national psyche which went wrong between design and delivery.

A table at the far end was occupied by a party who joshed anyone who happened to be coming to and from the restrooms. It reminded him of Octoberfest. In one of the booths a Hispanic woman with heavy thighs was talking to a man whose hands were exploring her taut leather skirt as they negotiated. This was something else about Americans which baffled him; they still bought sex without any thought for the long-term consequences.

The motel clerk had shown that; his greed for a few hundred more dollars had overridden everything. Once he'd handed over the cash, he had given him Nagier's physical description and details of when he had checked in and what he had done since. Klinger had listened to everything the clerk told him. There had been two calls from Geneva for Nagier. The clerk had smiled craftily and asked why someone who stayed in a flophouse like this was getting calls from Europe? Stamp, he'd added slyly, had also come from Geneva. He'd looked at the clerk dispassionately for a moment, thanked him for that added piece of information and slipped him another hundred-dollar bill. Afterwards, from a payphone in the lobby, he'd called the Fixer and said the clerk could be of no further use. Every city had a Fixer who handled such matters.

The whore and her client had agreed a price and were coming towards him. The man was pawing her halter; she was looking straight ahead. Even Thrung hadn't looked that stoned. After they'd passed he continued to scan the room. A couple in one of the booths were holding hands across the table; he looked old enough to be her father. A serious drinker sat in another booth. A waitress was bringing refills to the party. Those at other tables had the weary look of salesmen at the end of a bad day.

At the bar a man sat with his back to the room, talking to the bartender. You could always tell when a pro was staked out somewhere. This one had positioned himself so that the full-length mirror gave him a view of the room without him having to turn in his seat. He sat squarely, feet firmly planted on the floor and slightly separated, so that he could launch himself with maximum speed off the balls of his soles. His position also gave him a choice of cover: in beneath the bar flap and down behind the counter, or a dive under the nearest table. A real pro, Nagier.

Klinger walked to an empty booth. When he'd ordered a beer from the waitress, he pulled from a jacket pocket a cassette player and headset. A tape was already on the deck. He placed the player on the table, slipped the phones over his ears and pressed a button. When she returned with his drink, the waitress glanced at the player and smiled. 'What are you listening to?' she asked.

'Stravinsky.' He didn't bother to lift the headset from his ears.

'I'm into Johnny Cash,' she said, losing interest and walking away.

Klinger settled in a corner of the booth. The tiny parabolic mikes in the headset gave perfect reception. He had bought the set at a Radio Shack on the way to the motel. That was another thing about Americans; they all wanted to spy on each other, if the sales of this kind of cheap surveillance equipment were anything to go by. Maybe . . .

The voice in his headphones made him forget everything else.

'. . . only this one guy, sitting there over a coffee longer than anyone normally would. Figured he had to be either somebody waiting for a hooker, or maybe a deal that had fallen through. Anyway, there he was, reading, and it was the darned magazine that made me remember him. It didn't go with the man, know what I mean? Just didn't fit. The mag was all about the great open-air life. You know the kind. Lots of ads for dude ranches, a week on the trail, catch your own cow and we'll air-freight home the beef. That sort of crud. But this guy didn't look like that was his scene at all. Like he'd never stepped inside a park. And he was also too well dressed, pardon my saying so, knowing you are a guest and all that, for a place like this.'

'What did he look like?'

'Running to fat, late forties, maybe a few years more. Grey hair – not completely grey, more flecked, you know what I mean? I think you Europeans call it salt-and-pepper . . .'

'We do,' Tommy said, smiling.

He'd taken his time coaxing the only game in town, and he'd been playing it since the barman said he had been on his break in the coffee shop the evening Stamp died.

'That's a pretty good description,' Tommy said encouragingly. 'Remember anything else?'

'Lemme see. Yeah, he had these old-fashioned spectacles. You know the kind, wire-framed. At police academy, they called them Dr Crippen glasses.'

'You were a cop?' Tommy's surprise was genuine.

The barman grinned. 'Almost. Flunked my final exam. But it was good training for a place like this. Weekends, we get our share of drunks. It gets kinda heavy at times. That's when I bring out my baseball bat. It always seems to quieten things down.'

'I can imagine.' Tommy smiled again. 'Did he have any luggage?'

In the booth Klinger continued to listen hard.

'Lemme see. Yeah. A briefcase, kinda expensive-looking. The sort drug-company salesmen carry to make them look like doctors. Or a doctor used to carry before he gave up on housecalls. But this fella didn't look like a doctor. And he wasn't native American.'

'How could you tell?'

'The old academy training again. He just looked European.

194

Maybe British or German. The clothes more than anything. Europeans wear them differently. Know what I mean?'

'You tell the police any of this?'

'Naw. Nobody asked me. The one other thing I learned at academy is never volunteer anything. If you ain't asked, you don't say. You some sort of cop?'

'Sort of.'

'Figured so. Takes one to recognise one.'

Tommy glanced in the mirror. The party at the end of the room was breaking up. As they passed one of the booths, the fair-haired man he'd noticed sitting there had slid out and joined them as they made their way to the door. Even in the dim light his scar was noticeable.

25

Morton judged there were now close to a hundred people in the salon, with the arrival of the Prime Minister and other government ministers. Bitburg had come with them, escorted by a flunkey in yellow court knickerbockers. Since then Walter had flitted from group to group.

'He's in his element,' Yoshi murmured to Morton. 'If there was a Nobel Prize for discovering a new way up the colon, Walter would win bottoms-up!'

Bitburg was lost to their sight as Count Lindeman steered them into the presence of the Prime Minister and his entourage. Another round of hand-shaking was followed by the usual questions and Yoshi's well-prepared replies. Ten minutes later, they moved on from the ministerial party.

For a moment Lindeman's pale gaze wandered over the salon as he decided where else to navigate them.

'You're sure this is not too exhausting?' Morton asked Yoshi. He'd seen the tiredness come and go in Yoshi's eyes.

'With service like this? You've got to be kidding!'

While they were with the Prime Minister's group, another knickerbockered chamberlain had handed Yoshi a telegram. It was from Gates.

'I had no idea Bill was an Emily Brontë fan,' Yoshi said now. The telegram message spoke of the pulse beginning to throb and the brain beginning to think.

'It's from *The Prisoner*,' Morton reminded him. 'Just make sure you don't become one to your enthusiasm. You're working pretty hard for someone who's supposed to be taking it easy.'

'I'm having fun, David,' Yoshi reassured him. 'Really, I had no idea it was going to be like this.'

'Just let me know, OK, when you want to go?'

'Will do,' promised Yoshi cheerfully.

Between the assembly of heads, Morton glimpsed the woman he had noticed a moment ago. Then she had done what she was doing now: raised her finger and pursed her mouth at a passing waiter to ask for another drink. She laughed, a sudden shriek, above the conversation level. Heads turned, then looked away again. Morton saw Lindeman frown.

'Someone's also having a good time,' said Yoshi. 'Who is she, Count?'

'Mrs Elmer Crayton,' said Lindeman.

'Ah, I've heard of her. Another of the great givers. Where would we be without them?'

'Where indeed,' murmured Lindeman.

Sonja's voice once again rose above the noise level. 'Olaf! Is that Dr Kramer with you?'

'Would you like to meet her?' Lindeman asked. Morton had noticed the moment's hesitation.

'Why not?' grinned Yoshi.

The Count led them over to the group surrounding Sonja.

'Hello, Olaf. I thought you were avoiding me.'

'Not at all, not at all.' He smiled quickly, introducing Yoshi and Morton to the group. As they began to ply Yoshi with familiar questions, Lindeman took Sonja by the arm and led her a little apart from the others.

'Is Nils looking after you?' he asked quickly.

Morton caught the tautness in Lindeman's voice.

She allowed herself a pause. 'Perfectly. I told him to run along and look after the others. I really don't need a watchdog.'

Morton glimpsed her evasive smile and saw the others had carefully turned their backs, leaving Lindeman and Sonja in an isolated hemisphere.

'Of course you don't,' Lindeman said in the same undertone. 'It's only that I don't want you . . .'

'To get drunk!' she completed, her eyes bright and their pupils small. 'Really, Olaf! You are being a bore. Of course I won't do anything to embarrass you.'

Lindeman obliged himself to smile. 'I know that.'

'Then why have you told the waiters to avoid me?' Her voice had once again risen and her face was flushed.

'I've done no such thing.'

'Good!' She turned and beckoned to a liveried servant bearing a tray of champagne in silver goblets.

'Waiter!' she commanded in an explicit voice. 'A toast for our new laureate.'

Morton realised she was very close to being drunk. And, judging from the growing apprehension on his face, Lindeman sensed the same.

'Olaf! Stop looking at me like that!' she commanded. 'What's a party for except to have fun?'

'Of course, of course,' he said quickly. 'I was just thinking . . .'

She gave everyone a brittle smile. 'Not tonight, Olaf! Take a break from thinking. You know what the Japanese say? In the morning you will still be able to solve all your problems under the cherry trees! Except you don't have any cherry trees in this country, do you, Olaf?'

He smiled weakly. 'No.'

'No,' she said in delight, prolonging the vowel. 'No-o! Oh, Olaf, if only you could see your face!'

He was standing there, his eyes accusing, still fearful she was going to make a scene. And this tall, silent man beside him – why was he staring at her with professional interest?

'Are you another doctor?' she asked Morton.

'No. No, nothing like that.'

'Mr Morton works for the United Nations,' Lindeman said quickly.

She peered around the group, then back to Morton. 'Well, well, one of the world's civil servants. That's what my husband called everyone who worked for the United Nations. You remember Elmer saying that, don't you, Olaf?'

'Yes,' Lindeman managed another weak smile.

Encouraged, she addressed the whole group. 'My husband used to wonder how could anyone *not* want to work for the United Nations. All those delicious perks. No taxes and a gorgeous pension at the end of it all. They must get *thousands* of volunteers *every day* for such a wonderful life. Geneva for the winter, New

York in the spring. And in between anywhere else you choose. My husband used to wonder if he could volunteer for that.'

She turned her eyes on Morton. 'Did you volunteer, Mr Morton?'

'Something like that.'

'Something like *what*?'

If she expected a reply she had to make do with a smile that told her even less. Uncertain which way to go, but determined not to lose the initiative, Sonja fell back on an old standby. She raised her glass towards Yoshi. 'To your discovery. May it turn out to be the great medical breakthrough we all hope.'

Yoshi inclined his head. 'I can only hope.'

She drank more champagne and tilted her goblet in the direction of Lindeman, spilling some of her drink. 'How wonderful to have a laureate who is not full of his own infallibility. Not like that transplant surgeon. What was his name? Dickerson, something-or-other. Very English.'

'Benedict Dickson,' murdered Lindeman. 'Actually he was Canadian.'

She shrugged, setting the last of her champagne dancing. Once more she addressed the group. 'All I remember is that he was insufferable. He stood in this very room and told me that if my late husband had been his patient he would have transplanted a baboon's heart into him. Imagine that. My husband with a monkey's heart!'

She giggled and several of the listeners smiled in embarrassment.

'It might have worked, Mrs Crayton,' Yoshi gave her a cheerful smile.

'Most certainly it would not! For the simple reason I would not have permitted it. If God intended my husband to have a baboon's heart he would have given him one. That's the trouble with science. It becomes too focused towards something the Lord himself would not approve of – the immortality of man. That's why he laid down the three-score-and-ten yardstick. There is an inherent danger in this idea that we should be devising new means to extend the longevity. God, I am sure, never intended that. And if God wanted my husband to have a baboon's heart he would also have taught him to swing from the trees, instead of doing what he was good at. Making deals. And bedding another woman!'

She stopped and peered around her, daring anyone to challenge. This time there was only an embarrassed silence.

'Well, Dr Kramer, what do you say?' Sonja raised her goblet. 'A toast to God's mysterious ways?' She lowered her glass. 'I think not.'

Yoshi took a long time to answer. First he thought of the risk of prolonging the embarrassment, then he thought of all he had tried to achieve. 'I don't know what God thinks or wants, Mrs Crayton. All I know is that I am glad I have found a means to improve the quality of life for some people. I don't know if it would have helped your husband to live longer. But I do know that animal-into-human organ transplants will be the future. They are going to have to be, because they are the only way to overcome the shortage of human organs. The only certainty about that shortage is that it will get worse.'

He looked around; everyone was listening to his every word. 'Let me ask you a couple of questions. How many of you carry a donor card? How many of you have gifted your body to medical research?'

No one spoke. Not even Sonja. And certainly not Morton.

'Don't feel bad. Almost nobody does. It's the emotional thing that's all part of the classic example of society in general and medicine in particular: failing to come to terms with the legal and ethical ramifications of transplant surgery. The technology is there. One day, I am certain, we will be able to transplant a brain. But the will to transplant what we can, here and now, is not there. Instead organs are routinely buried in the ground or consigned to the flames of the crematorium because no one has the wisdom and courage, for that is what it takes, to cut through the constraints and make them freely available. Instead, we still go on accepting rules that owe more to ecclesiastical rather than legal jurisprudence. While most countries now have a form of anatomical gift act, it often barely provides sufficient cadavers for our medical schools. And it has done nothing at all to increase the supply of organs for transplanting. Nor is there anything on the horizon to suggest the wheel of change will turn any faster. Until it does, my profession will have no alternative but to look elsewhere. And the only place we can look is at animals.

'The emotional problems of doing that will probably get worse.

The animal rights activists will oppose the idea. They don't object to anyone eating a lamb's heart or liver with his bacon, but do object, often violently, when it comes to using those organs for a life-giving purpose. There will be religious objections. No Jew, for instance, will ever accept a pig's heart – even though it is now feasible to transplant one into a human. There will be objections from the insurance world. What is a person in actuarial terms who has been given an animal's heart? There will be objections from all sorts of quarters. But they must be faced head-on until we come to terms with the need to supply more human organs. The only encouraging thing is that science has always faced problems and overcome them. We can all start now by carrying a donor card and leaving our bodies to medical research – with the stipulation that all salvageable organs are available for transplant. At least we would have made a start.'

'Well spoken, sir.' The speaker was a tall man in an old-fashioned tuxedo.

'I'm sure we all echo that, Your Excellency,' Lindeman said, his gaze on Sonja, straight and unblinking, as if it could stop her eyes slipping towards a waiter.

'Personally, if it meant I could go on enjoying life for a little longer at my age, nothing would deter me from having a pig's heart – or a baboon's,' continued the Peruvian Ambassador.

'And well said, you! Essentially they are both pumps, like the human heart,' Yoshi explained.

Sonja turned to him. 'Do you think a monkey's heart will give you a monkey's morals, Dr Kramer?'

'As I understand it, apes are quite faithful, Mrs Crayton.' Yoshi's friendly smile remained unruffled.

'Then perhaps my husband should have had a baboon's heart after all!'

Lindeman saw an opening to interrupt. 'You make an interesting point. But Dr Kramer is a neurosurgeon, not a thoracic one. And I really don't think this is the best place for such a personal discussion about your husband.'

'Don't be so Swedish, Olaf! I'm sure Dr Kramer is not offended.' She peered archly over the rim of her goblet at Yoshi. 'You're not, are you?'

'Of course not,' Yoshi said.

There was nothing sadder than middle-age coquettishness, Morton thought; He saw Lindeman giving a quick surreptitious signal to Nils. His assistant responded with an equally swift nod from across the salon.

'Then let's drink to your Prize, Dr Kramer,' Sonja said. 'If only I had something to toast you with.' Her eyes began to search out a waiter. Lindeman gave a stiff little bow in her direction.

'There are still so many people for Dr Kramer to meet, madam.'

She stared at him for a moment, her mouth slack. Then her anger coursed over all of them like a red-hot tide. She felt its surge embrace her like an old friend, allowing it to take possession of her entirely, while she herself took comfort from knowing that the anger dulled the pain of her humiliation and cleared her mind and vision.

'Don't ever call me that. Don't you ever, ever do that again. Never. Ever. Do you hear me, Olaf? Never do that again! Never call me by that name!'

'Mrs Crayton, please,' implored Lindeman.

Sonja continued to rave. 'Did you hear me, Olaf? Did you hear what I said? Never call me that again. Never. Do you understand?' She spat out each word like an individual machine-gun bullet.

'Yes, of course.'

'Then . . . then . . .'

She looked at the others, into their stunned faces, into their cryptic, knowing silence. A haze separated her from them. Didn't they know she wasn't drunk, only furious? God, she should never have come, not to be humiliated like this. To be confused with *her*! She'd seen her a moment ago, on the far side of the salon, as if she was waiting for this moment of final humiliation. There was a sudden silence all around her.

People had begun to talk loudly, pretending nothing had happened, but still avoiding her gaze. Except the tall stranger. He was speaking to her so softly she could barely hear, even though he had moved to stand very close.

'It's always good to get things out of your system, Mrs Crayton. It's the quickest and best way to restore our self-respect.'

'Thank you, Mr Morton. I feel as big a fool as I must have sounded.'

'For sure. But just wind it down the best you can.'

Lindeman opened his hands towards Sonja, at once self-reproachful and penitent. 'Do forgive me, Mrs Crayton. At times I am so clumsy with my words. I apologise, please believe me, for my lapse.'

She smiled bravely. 'We all make mistakes, Olaf.'

'Mine was unforgivable,' he said abjectly.

'You're forgiven.' She looked at the others and from somewhere produced another smile. 'My husband used to say that spiritual and personal matters are best left to the clergy, the psychiatrists and the courts. I'm not sure which I'd prefer right now.'

She turned to Nils, who had arrived and was anxiously hovering at her elbow. 'I would like to meet some of the other winners.' She took him by the arm. 'And please find me another drink. Something soft.'

As Lindeman led Yoshi and Morton away in the opposite direction, he sighed. 'When Nobel invented the blasting cap, he didn't know there was something far more lethal: human jealousy. You've just seen one side of it. Now you're about to be exposed to the other.'

He quickly told them about the other woman in Elmer Crayton's life. A moment later he introduced them to Madam.

'You may leave us, Count Lindeman,' she said firmly.

For a moment he stood fussing nervously before backing away. Only then did Madam turn to Yoshi.

'I have followed your work in the journals for years. No surgeon has more deserved his recognition.'

Yoshi inclined his head. 'Is that why you want us to meet – to discuss my work? I can always send you my papers. They'll probably answer all your questions.'

She considered what he had said. 'I will be glad to read your papers. But I also hope you will keep our appointment.'

Morton thought it sounded like a command.

She turned and looked at him. 'Colonel Morton, I believe.'

'Good evening, Miss Montan.'

Morton saw something come and go in her eyes, as if something was threatening to come apart somewhere deep inside her. 'I haven't used that name for a long time, Colonel,' she said with a furious smile.

Morton shook his head, as if to say, you could always learn. 'I'm

203

curious about one thing. When you make a deal how do you sign your name?' he asked politely.

'I don't, as you charmingly put it, make deals, Colonel.' Her face was set in stone.

'Sorry. I seem to be treading—'

Whatever Morton felt he was treading on was interrupted by a loud voice from the centre of the room calling for attention. It was followed by a chamberlain rapping on the floor with his stave for the receiving line to form. Madam took her place between Yoshi and Morton.

Then, in the respectful silence, came a stricken cry, followed by the sound of high heels crossing the floor. Heads turned in shock as Sonja Crayton ran unsteadily fron the salon. A moment later Nils followed her.

Yoshi inhaled, struggling for composure. 'Poor woman.'

Morton glanced sideways at Madam. She continued to stare impassively ahead. His hands stiffened and he instinctively lowered his head as if the drum beat had become a smidgeon louder.

A moment later, the King of Sweden, followed by the princes and princesses of the Royal household, entered the salon.

Engel checked the Stockholm street map which had come with the rental car, then drove the length of Sturegatan, noting the park on his left. The leaves had gone, leaving the trees outlined grotesquely in the reflection of the streetlamps. The tall buildings on the opposite side were in darkness. He parked the car at the end of the street and walked back its length, checking the numbers. He found the address he was looking for. Satisfied, he returned to the car. On the seat beside him was his briefcase. Adjusting the driver's mirror to give him a clear view of any approaching traffic, he settled in his seat and waited. Despite the cold, he enjoyed working in such conditions. They reminded him of his own Silesia.

26

Tommy was the last customer to leave the motel bar; he had stayed on hoping the barman would recall something else. The man he'd described seeing was probably just another businessman fantasising about what life could be like.

And Stamp himself hadn't come into his bar. Indeed, most of the details the barman had heard about Stamp's death had been gleaned elsewhere. He'd turned down the barman's offer of a nightcap and headed for the door.

Crossing the empty lobby he saw the Hispanic hooker talking to the desk clerk. He looked up. 'There was a call for you. She left a message.'

Chantal wouldn't do that, Tommy thought as he walked over to the desk and took the slip from the clerk. The message was from Anna. She was in California and would call back in the morning. Tommy grinned and crumpled the paper. Typical of Anna not to leave a number or say where she was. The clerk was looking at him curiously.

'You look like you just got good news.'

'I think I did,' Tommy said. Having Anna on the case was always good news.

The hooker smiled at him mechanically. 'Wanna celebrate?'

'A good night's sleep will do me more good,' grinned Tommy, walking to the elevator. He pushed the button for his floor. He'd try Chantal one more time to tell her Stamp was killed by someone from Kommando One. He was getting like the Colonel when it came to applying informed conjecture. But the bottom line here was that Stamp's killer was a grade-one professional with an appetite for the gruesome. That put Kommando One in the frame.

The elevator door opened and Tommy stepped out. Stamp must have liked slumming to stay in a place like this. Or maybe he didn't care about personal comfort. He'd heard a lot of body-fit freaks enjoyed the spartan life because it made them feel more macho. Maybe Stamp had harboured secret aspirations to join Covert Action? The truth was he still had no real idea what had driven Stamp. Maybe it didn't matter; perhaps all that mattered was finding who had snatched his kidneys. And whoever had done that had come and gone along this very corridor.

Reaching the door of his room Tommy ran a finger along the jamb where he'd placed the brush-hair bristles. He felt his own hair rising on the nape of his neck. The hairs were gone. Stepping back a pace, he crouched and ran his hands over the carpet, picking up several bristles. He stood up and looked both ways along the corridor. Apart from the sound of a TV from a room a few doors along, nothing disturbed the silence. He rubbed the bristles between his fingers. There was no way some drunk had tried the wrong door. To dislodge the hairs, his door would have had to have been opened. He wished now he had his gun. But he'd left it in the concealed pocket built into his suitcase for that purpose; it saved a lot of trouble at Customs.

Tommy inserted the key in the lock and turned it gently. The click still sounded loud.

As soon as he opened the door, he realised that whoever had come here hadn't bothered to hide his work. The room lights were all on. The drawers of the bureau and closet yawned open, and Tommy's clothes were strewn on the floor, together with the other contents of his suitcase. The microscope must have been used to smash the slides. There was no sign of his gun.

Tommy surveyed the wreckage. Someone hadn't just broken in on the off-chance of finding a weapon; on the street, anyone who wanted one could buy without risk. And why trash everything? A thief would have taken the gun and microscope and high-tailed it. Yet if this was a professional job, it was an angry professional who had done this. It was as if he'd put someone's nose out of joint. Which meant someone knew who he was and why he was here.

He closed the door behind him. The door to the bathroom was shut, the way he had left it. He walked over and picked up the microscope. Glass from the slides crushed under his feet. He hefted the microscope in his hand and walked across to the bathroom. At the door he paused to listen. Nothing. The tingling in his nape was stronger, like it had been that day with Dad and the Colonel in Brighton. He'd been twelve at the time and the Colonel had taken him on a seafront fairground ride. During its high-speed whirl, the ride's mechanical arm had worked loose, leaving them swaying dangerously above the ground. But, taking his cue from the Colonel, he'd calmly waited to be winched to safety. Always play to your strengths, Dad had said afterwards. Tightening his grip on the microscope, he firmly pushed open the door and stepped back. As suddenly as it had started, the tingling stopped.

No one rushed him. The door was three-quarters ajar, enough to allow him to see the wall-mirror and the washbasin in its plastic surround. His toiletries and the motel's drinking glasses, wrapped in cellophane, were exactly as he had left them. The mirror's reflection of the toilet and bath, with its suspended shower and curtains, was cut off by the door. But he judged there was just enough space between its frame and the tub for someone to be waiting there.

Tommy lifted his leg and kicked hard at the door. It slammed back against the side of the bath.

He stood in the doorway, feeling slightly foolish. Whoever had been here would be well gone by now. But why not complete the trashing? Smash his toiletries? Break the drinking glasses? Leave the bathtaps running? Maybe even stuff the towels down the toilet? Whoever had vandalised the bedroom wouldn't have had a problem doing that. He stopped, becoming aware of the pressure on his bladder. That last beer had found its way down to join the others. He stepped towards the toilet and, before he unzipped, he reached to place the microscope on top of the cistern. He glanced in the mirror. He'd left the shower curtains drawn halfway. Now they were almost closed. Which meant—

Tommy whirled. Ducking to reduce his target area, he brought the microscope protectively up before his face.

The curtain ripped back. It was the man who'd followed the partygoers from the bar. Blond, blue-eyed and muscle-bound, like a slice of satanic beefcake, with that scar on his left cheek. He was wearing latex gloves and holding a knife in one hand. Long blade, steel handle. A Kommando One knife. What the hell was Latex

Gloves worried about, wearing those gloves? That he'd leave fingerprints? Or maybe he was on another kidney-snatching mission? Tommy arced the microscope away from his face. Kept his eyes on the knife. Rotated slowly on the balls of his feet. Kept arcing the microscope towards the hand gripping the knife. A real bone-stripper. Latex Gloves had one foot out of the bath. It was now or never. Tommy began to spin faster on the balls of his feet, like a discus thrower.

Klinger paused, astonished. When he had found the gun, he had decided not to use it; even in a place like this someone would wonder about a gunshot. Instead he'd dropped the gun in the cistern. The knife he always carried, but it was the gloves he was depending on.

Tommy's swing caught Klinger's knife hand at the wrist. He grunted and winced. Gleaming steel flew over Tommy's shoulder into the bedroom. Tommy brought the microscope back in a reverse swing, catching Klinger high on the other arm. The blow drew no more than a second grunt and wince. Tommy didn't try for a third hit. The microscope was about as effective against Latex Gloves as trying to topple a forest oak with a child's saw. He ran into the bedroom.

The blows had left Klinger breathless. His wrist had started to swell and his arm seemed to be on fire. Yet instead of pursuing his advantage, Nagier had retreated. That was good. In the bedroom, he would have more room to manoeuvre, to get close. One touch with either of his gloves on Nagier's skin would be sufficient. They were smeared with a nerve agent from the bottle he had removed from the apartment safe. The oily compound was designed to penetrate the pores and kill in seconds. He had used up about half the bottle, which he'd placed in his trouser pocket. He stepped out of the bath.

Tommy watched Latex Gloves emerge from the bathroom, moving slowly in a half-crouch, hands extended, not bothering to look for the knife. Tommy guessed it had skidded under the bed. But Latex Gloves looked as if he didn't need a knife. He merely looked as if he had completely recovered. Tommy backed into the centre of the room, the microscope swinging from one hand as he watched the savage anger in those eyes. And something else too – cunning and a cold intelligence struggling for mastery over the pain. So he had hurt Latex Gloves after all. He gripped the microscope more tightly, swaying on the balls of his feet, looking for an opening. Maybe he should try for the arm again, around the elbow.

Suddenly Klinger stopped, glancing about him, calculating. Then he lunged towards the bed and, in one movement, ripped off the bedding and hurled it over Tommy, the way a gladiator in a Roman arena used his net to ensnare an opponent.

Half smothered, Tommy dropped to the floor and dived sideways as Klinger hurled himself forward. Freeing himself, Tommy drove the microscope upwards. He heard Latex Gloves give an animal-like growl, and saw him drop a gloved hand between his legs. Klinger pulled his hand away just as quickly, and rolled across the carpet towards the door. Then, in one continuous movement he shoved his legs against the wall, arched his back and somersaulted upwards, landing on his feet to face Tommy. Once more he came forward, eyes burning.

Tommy backed towards the window. Latex Gloves wasn't even close to being beaten. His grip on the microscope was slippery with sweat. He tried to circle back to the centre of the room. Each time his move was blocked. As he once again began to rotate on the balls of his feet, he saw the look in Latex Gloves' eyes and broke off the attack, retreating another step. He knew they were matched in height and weight, but he wasn't going to risk getting close. There was something distinctly uninviting about those hands reaching out for him. He could smell the man's breath, sour and stale. His tongue ran over his own teeth and he noted, detachedly, that his mouth was dry. The crunch of glass was loud under his feet. But there wasn't a piece of slide big enough to use as a weapon.

He had to make it to the door. Or else find something else with which to defend himself.

Klinger sensed the advantage. Another few steps and he would have Nagier cornered, and his only way out would be through the window. But he'd have to break it first with the microscope. That would be the moment to leap forward and smear his face with a glove. His crotch felt as if it were on fire; someone who had done that to him deserved to die slowly. Maybe, after all, he should throw Nagier through the window. His lips bared.

Latex Gloves had a real psycho smile, Tommy thought. He felt his feet against the suitcase, and he almost lost his balance. Instead, he managed to turn it into a controlled fall. Dropping to the carpet, his fingers felt for the suitcase handle and, the moment they made contact, he swept the suitcase forward so that it struck Latex Gloves ankle-high with full force. Tommy saw the smile leave his lips.

As Klinger staggered and swayed, Tommy aimed another crotch shot with the microscope. Instead, he struck Latex Gloves on the thigh. There was the sound of splintering glass. Tommy began to tarantella across the floor, not bothering to wonder what he'd broken. Yet for the moment Latex Gloves wasn't concerned about him. Instead, he was pulling feverishly at his thigh. Tommy jumped to his feet, heading for the door. Behind him there was a sudden crash. Latex Gloves was sprawled on the carpet, his head at an unnatural angle. The room began to fill with the stench of his body waste.

Tommy walked backwards to the bed, his eyes watching for signs of life. There were none. He waited a few more minutes, then walked over to the body, crouching beside it. There was a small wet patch on Latex Gloves' trousers. He bent and sniffed. His eyes at once began to smart. Tommy jerked his face away. He looked at the gloves. The same faint oily smell. At training school they'd said the really lethal new nerve agents were those that smelled like car lubricant. Taking care to avoid the gloves and the patch on the thigh, he rifled Latex Gloves' pockets. In his wallet he found nothing except a wad of hundred-dollar bills. No ID, no personal material of any kind. Not even a driver's licence. From a hip pocket he extracted a small brown leather folder. He flipped it open and found himself staring at a colour photograph of Latex Gloves on a plasticised card. According to the card his name was Klaus Klinger. Almost as German as Schmidt. But there was no clue to who had issued the card.

Tommy straightened and slipped the card into his pocket. He badly needed to go to the toilet. Afterwards he looked at himself in the bathroom mirror. His face was chalk-white. He filled the basin with cold water and immersed his face. He checked again in the mirror, then repeated the process. Drying his face, he returned to sit on the bed, staring at Klinger's body. The instructor in chemical-biological warfare had said that, now the Russians had disposed of their arsenals, the chance of encountering a nerve agent was pretty remote – unless you happened to be working in Iraq. He must remember to tell the instructor to add at least one Washington motel to his list.

The bedside phone rang. It was Chantal. He told her what had happened.

'Are you OK?' she asked.

'I'll be fine. But you'd better tell the Colonel I think Klinger's from Kommando One.'

'And you'd better call Gates. You'll need local back-up,' she said briskly. 'And don't let anybody touch those gloves.'

'You can bet my life on that,' Tommy said fervently.

27

The departure of the King and the Royal entourage signalled the formal end of the reception for the Nobel laureates. But groups still congregated around the winners, allowing them to govern the conversations, with occasional interruptions for praise and questions.

Gracefully detaching himself from one of the gatherings, Yoshi turned to Morton. 'I've had my fill of being ogled. Let's get out of here and leave it to the other four to hold the floor.' He squinted at Morton. 'Ever wonder why Nobel only honoured five disciplines?'

'No. But I suspect I'm about to learn.' Morton said as he led them through the gathering.

'Damn right you are, David,' Yoshi said cheerfully. 'Nobel only awarded those fields which interested him. So: no Botany, Biology, Zoology or Psychology. And Freud never had a chance. The same with Architecture and Economics. Nobel was also tone deaf. So Pavarotti will never collect a Nobel Prize. Nor can any of our great living painters ever expect to see their canvases honoured, because Nobel thought art was boring. And he only introduced a Prize for Literature when he started to read seriously in his last years.'

'You're a mine of information, Yoshi.'

Yoshi gave a self-deprecating smile. 'All courtesy of a briefing paper Lindeman sent me. He's a strange man, isn't he? If you didn't know, you'd think he was an undertaker. But he's certainly a dab hand at the soft soap. Look at the way he lathers Madam.'

Immediately after the receiving line broke up, Lindeman had come over and retrieved Madam and, since then, had taken her from group to group, hovering beside her; then, when she moved on, staying protectively close. She was on the far side of the room now, once more being introduced by Lindeman to other guests.

'I don't think anybody has spoken to her like you did for a long time,' Yoshi said.

'She's probably too used to getting her own way,' Morton murmured.

'It's the old movie-star complex still in her. That's why she likes to be called Madam. Makes her feel like Garbo.'

'Is that it?' But Morton didn't seem disposed to challenge the idea.

In those few minutes before the line-up, he had sensed something more than mere power in her. Politicians and tycoons used that to judge everything by its meltdown weight. What she possessed was altogether something stronger and deeper, and far more disturbing. She was like someone who was no longer merely interested in multiplying her worldly assets, but who had embarked on something far more important to her, in which success depended totally on her own total self-control. Even her curtsy to the King had been no more than a swift dipping and rising, as if for all his temporal sovereignty over this land, he had no authority over her. As if no one had. And least of all that endearingly old-fashioned Count, who was clearly besotted with her, hanging on her every word. Morton once more caught her glance. He couldn't tell what she was thinking.

'She carries her age very well. But she's older than she looks. Maybe a good ten years older,' Yoshi murmured.

'That much?'

'Surgeon's instinct. And all that gravitas. Someone with that much has done a lot of living but can't get used to the idea of settling down. Probably all those early lovers.'

'Psychiatry missed out when you elected for surgery, Yoshi.'

'You think there's no psychology in my work? Think again, David!'

But Morton smiled disarmingly and continued to think about Madam.

She stood on the edge of the circle around this year's winner of the Physics Prize. No doubt the man was a brilliant chemist but he was also an absolute bore, with a dreadful habit of drawing further attention to his albino face by frequently dabbing at it with a handkerchief, though she hadn't seen a trace of perspiration dampen skin that reminded her of the underbelly of a slug. The laureate continued to discourse in his barely understood Slav accent on the need for science to resolve the world's famine by creating synthetic foods.

Behind her Lindeman murmured in her ear. 'Shall we move on? We can safely leave here now and there would still be time for a late dinner.'

She spoke coolly without turning her head. 'Not tonight. I have work to do.'

He tried not to show his disappointment. 'Perhaps lunch tomorrow then?'

'You mustn't monopolise me, Olaf.'

Lindeman stood defeated, following her gaze as she once more watched Yoshi and Morton cross the room.

'Did Colonel Morton know I would be here?' He was like a walking contradiction of one of her theories about people: someone who had achieved that much should be open to an approach.

'I don't think so. Why do you ask?'

'No reason, Olaf. He's an unusual man.' Yet she had sensed that he had made no effort to fill the dead space between them, as if he wanted to neither please nor impress her.

'So I gather. But he certainly has a strange job, being the world's policeman. There's something heroic and absurd about that, don't you think?'

Whatever she thought she kept to herself, preferring instead to state the obvious. 'He and Dr Kramer don't immediately strike you as having much in common,' she said.

'I understand that Dr Kramer has worked with him. Some sort of advisory capacity.' There had been something about that in the Foreign Ministry briefing.

It took Madam a while to reply and when she did, her response could have applied to anything or nothing of what had been previously spoken.

'Ah,' she said.

They were about halfway to the exit door when Yoshi said to Morton: 'I don't trust that woman. She's been watching you non-stop since the Royal line-up.'

'Well, now. You're sure she's not keeping an eye on you?'

'It's you, and you know it.'

Morton neither confirmed nor denied that he did. They both caught her glance this time in another of the salon's bevelled-glass mirrors.

'She's sly, David. I had a girlfriend like that once. She used to park up the street and watch me in her wing mirror. Madam looks the same type. That's another reason I don't trust her.'

'How many reasons are there, Yoshi?' Morton asked comfortably.

'Probably enough. But they all come back to the same one in the end. She's a medical groupie. Those I really don't trust.'

Her reflection had turned back to listen to what someone was saying.

It had been a long time since Morton had heard Yoshi, or anyone, use that word. They walked past a gathering around this year's winner of the Peace Prize. He had a falsetto voice he was using to full pitch to argue that it was better to keep peace than honour peace.

Yoshi continued in a slightly aggressive voice. 'You heard what Lindeman said about her being Crayton's mistress?'

'That hardly makes her a groupie, let alone a medical one, Yoshi.'

'I'll come to that in a minute, David. But I'm certain Crayton was just a stepping-stone for her. Now she has his money, she can do anything. And pretty well does. Except when it comes to my business. There's been a lot of talk about how she supports medical foundations. The fact is that she really gives very little, given that *Fortune* last month made her the world's richest woman, richer even than the Queen of England. On that basis, she could probably afford to run Medicare or get the National Health Service in Britain back on its feet. The fact is she gives no more that she has to, just enough to keep her ahead of Sonja Crayton in the handout stakes. And she does that because it keeps rubbing Mrs Crayton's nose in the dirt by reminding her that when husband Elmer was dying, she didn't shop around for a new heart for him. No sir, it was good old Madam. And she doesn't want my peers to forget that. Any more than she wants the profession to forget that there was Elmer, in the very hospital he had completely endowed, and not a heart to be found.'

'What did she do?'

Yoshi smiled reminiscently into one of the mirrors.

'Our ladyship flew all the way to India. Somebody had told her she could buy a new heart over there, off the peg, so to speak – or, more accurately, off one of the pegged-out. Pick one up with no questions asked. Somebody had told her half down, balance on delivery. Amazing what people will believe and do, even someone as savvy as her. It wouldn't have worked anyway. In those days there just wasn't the technology to keep a heart transplantable for even a short while. But off she went to deal with one of those organ-brokers. You still find them on most street corners over there. Kidneys, livers, hearts: you name it, they tell you they can provide one. What they don't add is that the organs will almost certainly be rejected by the host body because there's been no proper tissue-typing. Anyway, Crayton died when she was over there. From what I've heard she's never forgiven the world's transplant surgeons for not being able to help, which is probably about all she has in common with Sonja Crayton. That's why neither of them contributes to any of the recognised transplant centres.'

'Your gift for nosing around is remarkable, Yoshi.'

'Is that a job offer, David?' Yoshi asked cheerfully. 'Want some more? When I heard Madam wanted to see me, I made a few enquiries among my colleagues. A lot of them feel she uses her charity-giving just to stay close to the medical profession. Nobody really minds. After all, these days every cent's welcome, no matter what the reason for donating it. But in my book that makes Madam a medical groupie.'

Morton was smiling contentedly.

'Did I say something funny?'

'Not at all, Yoshi. Anything but.'

'Jesus, David. I wonder about you sometimes.'

Morton sometimes wondered if God was in His heaven. Now was not one of them. He glanced towards the door where Bitburg was standing with impatient courtesy, shifting his weight from one foot to another, listening to an equerry who was offering to show him over the public rooms of the palace.

'Thank you. But perhaps some other time,' Bitburg was saying as Morton and Yoshi arrived. The equerry gave a stiff little bow and withdrew.

'I've been inside more palaces than that young fellow's probably had Royal dinners,' Bitburg said pompously, looking at Morton. 'Well, David. I had no idea you knew His Majesty.'

'We met some time back,' Morton acknowledged in a voice designed to discourage further questions.

The King had been on a private visit to Ireland, staying in a country inn and fishing the Wicklow lakes. Morton had been attending a conference in Dublin to review European Community strategy against terrorism. Afterwards he'd hired a car, driven down the coast and stopped at Hunter's for dinner. He'd been mistaken for a member of the Royal party and placed in a private dining room. The King had been amused and invited Morton to remain. Walter would probably have tried to turn the brief encounter into a lifelong friendship.

'I see,' said Bitburg, speaking at last, looking intently past Morton, his eyes once more alert. 'Who is that woman?' he asked.

Morton glanced over his shoulder. Madam had detached herself from the group around the Chemistry Prize-winner once the laureate had begun to engage Lindeman in conversation.

'There you are, Dr Kramer,' she said, walking up.

Her stride was a man's stride, Morton thought, and yet there was still a femininity and provocation about her body. He wondered briefly if it was a residue of her days as an actress, the creation of clever publicists. No, he told himself, no one could have created this. The carapace had always been there.

Yoshi greeted her with a non-committal smile. Bitburg extended his hand. 'I don't believe we have met.'

Morton thought that Walter, when it came to a new face who could be important to him, was like a Pavlov dog, reacting by reflex.

Madam turned towards Bitburg, slowly, without interest. 'I don't believe we have.' She took Bitburg's hand briefly.

'Walter Bitburg. I'm with the United Nations,' he said.

'I see. How interesting.' She spoke with no interest. She turned to Morton. 'Do you work with Mr Bitburg?'

'Yes.'

'How interesting.' She glanced back to Bitburg. 'And what do you do?'

'I don't think I can discuss that . . .'

217

Morton saw something come and go in her eyes. He waited, but she did not pursue the matter.

Bitburg smiled. He'd remembered her face from magazine articles. He hadn't recognised her at once because it had been a while back since he'd seen her in print. 'I always looked forward to your plays and films,' he said. 'They were events.' He waited for her comment, but she said nothing.

'I had no idea, Walter, that you were a devotee of the stage and cinema,' murmured Yoshi.

Bitburg ignored him and continued to address Madam. 'I never understood why you retired.'

She looked at him coldly. 'An actress never retires. She is always awaiting the proper role.'

'And do you have one now?' Yoshi asked.

She looked at him for a moment: then, ignoring the question, she continued to address Bitburg. 'It is the creative writers who have retired. I simply grew tired of waiting for someone to produce a role that was really challenging. Men don't seem to write about women any more. And women have never written really worthwhile parts for women. But you will know that, Mr Bitburg, if you are a genuine devotee.'

'Of course,' he said, laughing uncertainly. 'You know, there really ought to be a retrospective of your work. It would give some purpose to those wretched festivals that are now the vogue all over Europe. I keep on being invited, and each time I hope it will be better than the last. but it never is.'

Madam inspected him. 'I never go to festivals,' she said flatly.

'I see. Well, yes, of course. Yes, of course . . .'

Bitburg's voice trailed off and they once more stood in silence.

'You really believe that?' Yoshi asked. 'About women not being able to write for women?'

This time she answered his question. 'I would not have said so if I didn't, Dr Kramer. It's rather like me asking if you believe in this procedure which has won you the Nobel Prize.'

'Touché.'

She nodded and almost smiled.

Bitburg tried again. 'I understand you are still very much involved with that drug rehabilitation centre in California.'

'Yes. Drug Rehab is very close to my heart.'

He beamed. 'Quite so. Then you must know my good friend, Cyrus B. Wannamaker?'

She looked at Bitburg with distaste. 'Of course. He's one of our regents.'

'He was a great loss to banking when he retired.'

She ignored Bitburg's remark.

Yoshi looked at Madam. 'Why has Drug Rehab found such a place in your affections?'

'Because it works by example.'

Once more Morton saw that look come and go in her eyes. She was not used to being questioned. 'How, exactly?' he asked her.

She told them. She had a way with words, Morton thought. Short and to the point. As she spoke Walter was nodding sagely. When she finished, he turned to her.

'No wonder Cyrus is on your board, Madam. And, if I remember rightly, so is Jonas Jackson.' He turned to Yoshi and Morton. 'He used to run Globoil.'

'How interesting,' Yoshi murmured.

Madam glanced dispassionately at him. 'I had no idea your gift for mimicry was so well developed, Dr Kramer.'

'It comes with the job,' Yoshi grinned.

'Can Drug Rehab really work in the long term?' Morton asked.

He saw her face concentrate and, with it, her femininity disappeared. For a moment she again had looked like stone. Then, from somewhere deep inside her, she gathered herself.

'In the two years the programme has been running, we have not had a single failure.'

'What happens when they leave Drug Rehab?' Morton asked.

'We find them work. We keep a careful eye on them. Drug Rehab means just that – drug rehabilitation in its widest possible form.'

'A wonderful concept,' breathed Bitburg. 'If only there were more like it.'

'Thank you, Mr Bitburg.' She glanced at her watch and turned to Yoshi. 'I look forward to our meeting, Dr Kramer.' She looked at the others. 'Good night, gentlemen.' She walked quickly from the salon.

'An amazing woman,' Bitburg said admiringly. 'A really amazing woman.'

Morton turned to Yoshi. 'I think it's time we were going. I have a plane to catch.'

Bitburg looked at him in surprise. 'I thought you were staying for the ceremonies?'

'Concorde will get me there and back by the morning.'

'Where are you going?'

'Now, Walter. You know better than to ask that kind of question,' Yoshi chided. 'It would be like you asking me what your chances were on the table.'

Smiling cheerfully at Bitburg, he led the way out of the salon. As Morton turned to follow, Lindeman arrived.

'Did Madam say where she was going?' he asked anxiously.

'Sorry, she didn't.'

Bitburg took the crestfallen Count by the arm. 'My dear Count, I've been meaning to talk to you. About our appointment . . .'

In the car taking them back to the Grand, Yoshi squinted at Morton. 'I don't want to sound like Walter, but what's all this about flying off into the night? I was quite looking forward to our bedside chat.'

Morton told him about Gruber. Yoshi shook his head in astonishment. Then, when Morton explained to him about Marta, Yoshi grinned. 'Maybe she can tell me a bedtime story.'

28

As soon as Fung had received the message a heart was available, the Triad leader had flown from Hong Kong to Managua Airport, from where he had been brought to the island in the clinic's Lear jet.

For the next few hours the preparation for his surgery had occupied him. He had understood little of what was done or told to him. To ask would be a sign of weakness; to everything he had nodded. Finally a nurse had shaven him from throat to crotch, delivering her standard reminder that when the hairs started to grow again, he would feel all kinds of pleasurable discomfort. She had then given him a pre-med.

Now, late morning, the door to his room opened once more.

Dr Romer parked the wheelchair beside the bed. Fung's translucent pallor confirmed the damage a lifetime of smoking had wreaked on his arteries, finally leading to cardiomyopathy, the degeneration of his actual heart muscle. Krill and his team were already in the operating room, preparing for the long surgery. But there was one last preliminary Dr Romer reserved for himself.

'Mr Fung. I am Dr Romer, the Medical Director, and there is a matter I will explain to you. The heart you are about to receive is from the body of a young man who was in superb physical condition.'

Fung nodded. Instinctively he bunched his fingers against his chest as Dr Romer continued.

'You are seventy years old now. You can expect your heart to last ten years. Longer, perhaps. But there is one matter you need to understand from the very beginning, even before you are fully conscious after your operation. Unlike your present heart, the transplanted one will have no direct nervous connection to your brain. This means your new heart can't be told to speed up or slow down to suit your activities. Instead it will beat away at its own spontaneous rate.'

Dr Romer reached forward and felt for Fung's wrist pulse. After a moment he withdrew his finger. 'Right now your brain, because of your pre-medication, has told your heart to slow down. But it would not be able to do so after your transplant. That would not normally be a problem while you are at rest, but the heart you are about to receive has been conditioned by its donor to beat only sixty to seventy times a minute. He was, as I say, a highly trained athlete, a runner over considerable distances, who had trained his heart to beat more slowly so as to conserve his energy. But now that his heart is to be yours, it will begin to gradually beat faster, because you do not have your donor's physical condition. Eventually your new heart will speed up to more than ninety beats a minute. To cope with that you will have to improve your general stamina and muscle power. You will be given exercises by our staff here which you will have to continue with for the rest of your life. So, as well as your body, you must train your mind to behave differently. If you can, your transplant will give you many years of new life.'

Dr Romer looked searchingly at Fung. He seemed to be embalmed in his own emotional permafrost.

'We Chinese are an inward people. We never show much,' Fung began. 'Foreigners express a great deal more. But I understand all you have said.'

'Then rest now. They will be here for you soon.'

As Dr Romer began to manoeuvre his chair towards the door, Fung stopped him. 'There is one matter, Dr Romer. I would like a new room.'

Dr Romer frowned. 'All patients' rooms are the same, Mr Fung.'

'But this one smells of bad eggs. For the Chinese that is a symbol of misfortune to come.'

Dr Romer smiled. 'It's not bad eggs.' He nodded towards the window. 'It's caused by sulphur, Mr Fung. You can't see it from here, but on the other side of the clinic is a volcano. From time to time, when the wind blows in the wrong direction, it carries the sulphur fumes. But there is absolutely no danger.'

As he turned and left the room, there was a clatter of rotor blades overhead. That would be the patient arriving for the kidney transplant from the Seattle harvesting which had also provided Fung's heart.

Dr Romer manoeuvred the wheelchair through the double doors into the recovery room. Already the first of the fifteen spaces was occupied. Mr Al-Daba, the richest of the Bekaa Valley drug barons, had just received a partial liver transplant. Now he lay on a gurney surrounded by monitors and gas and suction lines, completely naked except for the dressings which covered his surgical wound. Several intravenous bottles were clustered on top of their pole, dripping fluids into his body.

Another patient arrived. Dr Romer recognised the bulky figure of Isaac Cohn. For the past ten years he had been undisputed head of the Chicago Mafia, the first Jew to acquire supreme control of the city's underworld. He had received the first kidney from the Seattle harvesting.

A third gurney appeared, bearing Mr Bonetti from Rome. This was the Italian gang leader's second visit to the operating room – the heart he had received was displaying an irregularity.

Satisfied all was going well, Dr Romer withdrew.

Sonja became conscious behind her eyelids and she waited, motionless, while awareness gradually spread throughout her body. With it came painful recall. After Nils had brought her home, he'd undressed her before covering her with the duvet. Then sleep, merciful, forgiving sleep, had claimed her.

Opening an eye, she saw that the first dim, grey light of a new day was creeping through a chink in the curtains. Nils must have left the window open to give her more air. Watching the curtains bulge inwards like a half-filled sail, she continued to remember: fleeing from the salon, knowing every scandalised eye was on her; blundering into the Royal procession, the King's smile of stiff politeness as she rushed into the ladies' cloakroom – something she had eaten, she had told the attendant – once more fleeing; Nils making a desperate effort to hide his feelings, agreeing it had to be the gravadlax. Had she mentioned Elmer's whore? She couldn't remember.

The room was coming into focus, the light touching one piece of furniture, then another. The curtains billowed again; the wind gentle the way Nils had sounded when she had asked him to pour a drink to settle her stomach. He'd gone through the motions, and she'd fallen asleep before he finished.

She looked sideways. The bottle was on the bedside table. She couldn't read the label in the half-light, but the shape was familiar. Armagnac. She closed her eyes, feeling the first prickling of tears. No one would ever again refer to what happened, at least not in front of her. But behind her back, the word would spread, like the pain in her head. Even if they understood that her behaviour had been caused by Elmer's whore, it would only add spice to the gossip. Socially, she would be ruined.

She opened her eyes and sat up with effort, pushing aside the duvet, even though she felt cold. She hugged her knees, listening to the silence that was not quite complete, to the small, reassuring sounds: the distant hum of the refrigerator, the drip of a tap she must have forgotten to close properly, the ticking of the longcase clock in the hall. The curtains billowed once more. She pulled the duvet around her, listening to the ticking from the hall. Clock time is not like other time; a minute could seem like an hour, an hour forever. A drink would help it pass faster, warm her body, ease the pain in her head.

Reaching for the bottle, she stopped. There it was again – the sound which she now remembered had first broken into the dark remnants of troubled sleep: the creak of a tread on the staircase. There were two spots, the third tread from the bottom – the one that had awoken her – and this one, the fifth step from the top, that gave the same faint, almost inaudible, sound, muffled by the carpet and underlay.

She smiled. Nils had come back to see if she was awake. She had allowed him to share her privacy, a stranger; allowed him to see her at her most wretchedly vulnerable, and he had continued to behave with unreserved kindness.

Suddenly the curtains flapped more strongly, like the sails of a yacht turning into the wind. She kicked back the duvet and brushed aside the hair tangles in her eyes. She removed her slip, bra and panties, smiling again. She owed him that much. She could smell her own body. She went to the window and opened the curtains, allowing the breeze to cool her skin. She frowned.

224

Further up the street a car was parked. A resident would never have done that; each house had its underground garage. She turned as she heard a footstep outside the bedroom.

'Nils, come in,' she called out softly, turning towards the door. Engel entered.

He was still half-frozen from his long vigil in the car: he had not run the engine in case he disturbed people. He had not expected the staircase to creak so loudly. Not that it mattered. He could see her surprise was total. He closed the door behind him.

'Who are you?' In the half-light she could see he was carrying a briefcase. Had Nils sent her a doctor? But there was something in his other hand.

Engel put down the briefcase, keeping the gun steadily trained on her. She spoke with her lips so close together in fright that at first he didn't realise she was speaking at all.

'Don't hurt me. Please,' she begged in the same set-lipped whisper. 'Please don't hurt me.'

He walked over to her. 'Kneel.'

Sonja did so.

'Close your eyes.'

When she did, dark spots like little fishes swam in front of her eyes. She blinked and they sank to the bottom of the pool and re-emerged. She squeezed her eyes and the fish swam to the inside of her lids. There was a curious pressure in her left ear; something hard and cold was pressing against it.

Engel's shot perforated her eardrum. In Kommando One he had made this form of killing his speciality. Even as he stepped back, she collapsed to the carpet.

She could see his shoes, with their brightly polished toecaps, begin to fade. Everything was becoming dim. The walls had receded. She couldn't see the foot of the bed. She could see nothing. Feel nothing. Even the pain in her head, which a moment ago had been unbearable, was going. There was only a small light bobbing in the darkness inside her eyes. Then that, too, was gone.

Engel stooped to examine her. There was no outward sign of injury. The sugar concentrate had penetrated her brain with such force it would have cut off the supply of oxygen yet without damaging any of her harvestable organs.

He rose and reached for the briefcase. And stopped. A key was

225

turning in the front door. Voices. Men's voices. One he could handle; two could be a problem. Outside the window was a fire escape. He climbed down into a yard. The door to the garage was open. Moments later he was back in the street.

In the hallway, Lindeman hesitated. 'It's still very early,' he said, glancing at his watch.

'If she's asleep, we'll come back later,' Nils promised, leading the way upstairs. At the closed bedroom door, they paused.

'I really think we should come back,' Lindeman whispered. He was in no mood for this kind of adventure. Late into the night he'd called Madam's number, only to repeatedly encounter her answering machine. Then, when he had finally fallen asleep, she'd telephoned to say she would be unable to attend the remaining Nobel ceremonies. He had asked her what could be more important than a seat at the King's table and she had said, the President of the Bundesbank, and hung up. He'd lain awake, thinking how very difficult she was becoming, almost as difficult as Mrs Crayton. An hour ago he had phoned Nils to enquire about her, and somehow Nils had enveigled him into coming here.

'I'll just check,' Nils murmured, opening the door.

From the street came the sound of a car driving quickly away. Then Nils was running across the bedroom floor.

'Oh my God, oh my God!' he kept repeating, kneeling beside Sonja's body.

'A heart attack,' Lindeman said, joining him. 'Look at her lips. When they're blue like that, it's always a heart attack.' He went over to the bedside phone to call an ambulance.

The Global Transporter TriStar had taken off from Dulles International two hours before. Now, at a cruising height of 39,000 feet and a ground speed of 500 knots, it was bound for Madrid, its first stop on a flight scheduled to end in Tokyo.

Six hundred miles off the eastern seaboard of the United States, the aircraft lost all radio contact with Atlantic air control.

Two preset charges detonated the 300 kilos of semtex carefully packed around the bodies of Suto and Gonzales in their coffins.

The crew, Thrung and the Disposer died instantly.

Moshe Weill had chosen the point of detonation where the Atlantic is at its deepest. Ships in the area reported a fireball, not unlike a small meteorite, entering the earth's atmosphere and breaking up. The fragments which rained from the sky were no bigger than the dust particles which sometimes accompanied such phenomena.

29

As the police helicopter banked, Morton saw the Salzburg autobahn lit by another flash of lightning. The helicopter had been waiting at Munich Airport to take Morton to the Wallberg. Its progress across the night sky of southern Bavaria was punctuated by electrical discharges and ear-numbing thunder. The same cauldron of furious weather had earlier accompanied Concorde as it flew south from Stockholm.

During the flight Morton had dealt with the aftermath of Klinger's death. Satisfied that Tommy was unharmed, though still a little shaken, he'd told him to continue and join Anna in California. Bill's toxicologists had identified the solution on Klinger's gloves as one of the Sarin derivatives. Lester had established that Klinger had been Kommando One's star turn. Then Bill was back with the news that Klinger's shoes bore a Managua label. After they'd agreed what was to be done about that, he'd told Bill what he wanted done with Klinger's body.

Morton felt his stomach once more rise in his throat as the cockpit floor seemed to drop from beneath his feet, and he had a snap impression of the pilot struggling with the controls. Then another shock-wave threatened to tear his harness free of the floor bolts. Apart from a tornado, Morton knew of nothing more formidable than a full-blown electrical storm.

The autobahn to Austria vanished from view as the helicopter banked and headed for the Tegernsee. The Wallberg was on the far side of the lake, the highest peak in the area.

Morton glanced at the pilot. No emotion there, just a quiet intensity as he concentrated totally on the job in hand. Morton knew the feeling; he'd flown a chopper like this out of Iraq in a sandstorm almost as bad.

'Ten more minutes,' yelled the pilot in Morton's headset.

'Understood,' Morton acknowledged into his lip-mike. He was sitting behind and to one side of the pilot.

'The air currents are even more unpredictable over the Tegernsee.' The pilot made a quick seesaw gesture with his hand.

A farmboy's hand in charge of a few million Deutschmarks of high technology. And he had one bad habit for someone flying in a storm like this: his need, from time to time, to touch some part of the cockpit as if to reassure himself everything was still there.

Though he couldn't see them, Morton knew the mountains would now be close. The last time he'd been down there was the night he'd brought out a couple of Armenians trying to sell off part of the old Soviet nuclear arsenal stored in warehouses and bunkers on the steppes of Eastern Europe. It was a crime waiting to happen, and what surprised him was how close the pair had come to pulling it off. They'd rented a ski lodge to finalise their deal, and he and Danny had walked in on what looked like a garage sale, with weaponry neatly laid out on the floor and the Armenians promising the Iraqi arms procurer that other items were readily available. It was only a question of what he could afford, the Armenians had told the Iraqi.

Was that how Romer also ran things? So much for a heart, more for a liver, less for a kidney? What about eyes? Undoubtedly more expensive would be a replacement lung. Did you pay twice as much for a pair? And what price a colon? In the end, it must also come down to what someone could afford. But how did Romer's patients come to him? Word of mouth, or—

The cockpit was once more brilliantly lit. The pilot's left hand was grasping a spar. Skin and metal were fused together in an arc of sparks. The pilot's head snapped back against his headrest, then sagged forward at an unnatural angle. The cockpit began to fill with the sickening smell of singed flesh. Morton knew that if the lightning hadn't killed him, the pilot must be dead from a broken neck.

He managed to free himself from his harness and stagger forward. The rotors began to scream. He unbuckled the body and dragged it clear. Another purple flash etched his retinas while he grabbed the yoke and manoeuvred himself into the pilot's seat. The helicopter was starting to yaw back and forth. A searing flash. Cannonade. Flash. Cannonade. Flash. It was like a crazed symphony. He could feel the chopper going into a stall. He pulled back the yoke. It was like a living thing in his hands, jerking, pulling away from him, threatening to come out of its mounting. The whole chopper was vibrating.

Below, the darkness was broken by pinpricks of light. The first of the small villages and towns around the Tegernsee. The lights vanished as the rotors sliced into another clotted thickness of black cloud. The rev and altitude counters were windmilling on the panel before him. He pulled harder on the yoke. The vibrations increased. His mouth felt as if a dentist's drill was running amok on his teeth. Another crabbing bolt of light seared through the darkness. The shock-wave sounded as if it had detonated inside the cockpit.

He used all his strength to pull the yoke hard against his body. The chopper tilted even more alarmingly towards the waters of the Tegernesee. The pinpricks were closer. The lake seem even blacker.

A fusillade rattled against the windscreen. Hailstones. Millions of frozen droplets smashed against the perspex, the airframe, the engine cowl, hammered the entire helicopter like sustained volleys of gunfire. The wipers couldn't cope; ice began to build up on the windscreen. God only knew what it was doing to the rotors. Was that why the rev counter had slowed its demented spinning?

The chopper's nose was coming up! The rate-of-climb gauge was no longer threatening to spin through the glass. And rain was doing what the wipers couldn't, sluicing away the ice. But the lake was closer now, the lights around it brighter.

Climb! When you're in trouble – climb. When he hadn't yelled anything else, his flying instructor had yelled that. Morton pulled on the yoke, more gently this time. The nose continued to come up. The bubble in the artificial horizon no longer seemed so crazily out of kilter. He checked the altimeter again. It had gone up 500 feet.

'Come on! Come on!' he screamed at the dial.

The helicopter rose another hundred feet. In the time he'd adjusted his grip on the yoke, he'd gained 200 more feet. The lights on the shore were fading. He let out a grunt of satisfaction. The chopper was once more his.

He scanned the panel. His rate of ascent was improving all the time. A thousand feet, then, in no time, another thousand. He re-entered the cloud mass. He never thought he would welcome its stygian blackness. A crabbing bolt of lightning greeted him. The thunder seemed louder than ever. But the chopper continued to climb.

What height was the Wallberg? He looked around the cockpit. The chart the pilot had been using was over in a corner. He reached for it as another stab of lightning empurpled the cockpit. He spread the map across his knees.

The pilot had marked his flightpath in red. The pencil mark took them across the Tegernsee. So he was more or less on course. He ran his finger along the line. It stopped close on the summit of the Wallberg. Against the landing point the pilot had scribbled 3.5. Was that metres or feet? Morton glanced at the altimeter. Had to be feet. The Wallberg was a mountain, not an alp. He checked the altimeter. At the moment he had 1,000 feet leeway in which to bring the chopper down in a controlled landing. He pulled his harness tighter and settled in his seat. He felt almost relaxed.

The rotors cut out.

One moment their clattering protest against the elements was insurance he was still calling the shots; the next, all he had to remind him he was still alive was the lightning scissoring through the sky accompanied by its custom-made thunder. A moment ago he'd momentarily wondered why each clap was different, thinking it was funny the way you thought of inconsequential things when you got out of trouble.

Now trouble was back with a vengeance. The fuel gauge was fine; everything on the other dials seemed fine. Except that above his head the blades were being spun by wind power. Another rip of lightning rippled in front of the windscreen. The thunderclap sounded as if it had burst inside the cockpit. As he began to juggle with the yoke, the artificial horizon once again became even more artificial. It was back to square one. Downward spiralling gauges. He was dropping at an ever-accelerating speed through the inky blackness.

Morton felt something heavy against his feet. The pilot had slid across the floor so that his head was wedged at an impossible angle against the controls. Morton kicked out savagely. His foot crunched against flesh. The body sagged into a corner. For a fleeting moment he felt sick and filled with self-disgust at having to do this to an inherently decent young man. But the moment passed, lost in the reek of burned flesh that brought on another kind of nausea. He breathed out quickly. The whistle of the useless rotors was like a banshee's siren call.

What had the instructor said? Go with the plunge. The only way to get the rotors restarted. Stay with the dive all the way to the wire. He'd dropped 3,000 feet. How close was he to the wire? The pinpricks were back all around him. Another 500 feet lost. There was something white below him. The crests on the lake.

He pushed the yoke, increasing the angle of descent. He felt himself slipping forward in his seat. The harness cut into his shoulders. Another bolt of lightning momentarily seared his eyes. He blinked to clear the sweat. There was no way he could wipe the slippery wetness from his hands on the yoke.

Away to his left he glimpsed a cluster of buildings around an elegant church spire. That had to be Rottach-Egern. The pilot's flight plan had called for him to overfly it. But at 6,000 feet, not 600.

Then, as suddenly as it had stopped, above his head came a joyous clatter. The clatter became a sustained scream as the rotors bit fully into air.

A moment ago he had been staring almost directly down into the lake. Now he was more or less parallel with it. His instructor wouldn't have given him any marks for formation flying but he would undoubtedly have appreciated the engineering skills of the chopper's designers, who had allowed this kind of manoeuvring. And the storm was easing.

Ahead was a heavily wooded slope. The greenery gave way to a snow-capped summit. The Wallberg. He had to find a way up there. He glanced again at the dials. He was low on fuel. There was no time to gain height slowly; he had to find a way up there quickly. He began to traverse the mountain's lower slope. Trees rose to meet him. He nudged the chopper just high enough to avoid the upper branches.

He spotted where the trees had been cut back and steel pylons planted on either side of the gap. They disappeared up towards the snow. The Wallberg ski-lift. He glanced one more time at the dials. The rev counter was steady, but the fuel gauge was even lower. Probably no more than two or three minutes' flying left, even at this crab-like pace. They tell you all sorts of things when you learn to fly a chopper, but the most important of all is you keep well away from wires.

Morton edged the chopper between the pylons and just above the ski-lift cables, and began to follow the gap up the side of the mountain. All the rain would make for a soft-snow landing. He tried to remember what the manual had said about that. Nothing. You're supposed to have an instinct for that kind of thing.

To his right and further up the mountain, he saw a light flashing. A portable beacon. That had to be the landing site. He pulled gently back on the yoke and crabbed towards the light. Beyond, he could just make out the lodge. Figures were emerging from its doorway and running to form a circle, turning their torches skywards as a further guide. A moment later he dropped the helicopter in their midst. The cockpit door was yanked open. Mueller stared wordlessly at Morton.

Morton forced a smile. 'I'd have preferred to use the ski-lift, only I couldn't find the ticket office.'

Morton stumbled out on to the snow and would have fallen if hands hadn't reached out to support him. He straightened and began to breathe deeply, watching the pilot being lifted out of the helicopter.

'What happened?' Mueller's voice seemed fuzzy and distant.

When he had finished explaining. Mueller shook his head. 'Let's get you inside.'

Morton realised he wasn't in the mood to argue.

An hour later Morton had drunk several cups of scalding black coffee and Mueller had explained that Gruber had rented the place for a week. He had done so before, both times at short notice. Apart from being aware he was a doctor, the lodge owner, who lived down in the valley, knew nothing about him. As usual, he had arrived by taxi from Munich Airport and picked up the keys. The taxi driver confirmed that he had dropped off Gruber at the ski-lift. The woman who ran the café at the top of the Wallberg had told the local police she had an arrangement with the owner to service the lodge; she'd sent her son with Gruber to carry his luggage and light the lodge's wood-burning stove.

The ski-lift attendant had provided a description of the other passengers he'd carried since Gruber. Most were locals. But nobody suspected a local was involved in a crime like this. Descriptions of the handful of tourists who had used the lift had been circulated throughout the area. Several had already been found and eliminated from enquiries.

After pausing to peer at the snowscape, Mueller turned from the window and sighed. 'In my next life I shall be a ski instructor, a snow-plough driver, anything. But a policeman, never again. You do it once as a punishment, and that's it. Nobody sees anything, nobody hears anything when you want them to. It's like sex. They remember all the preliminaries, never the actual moment.'

Neither the café owner nor her son had seen anyone come or go from the lodge after Gruber arrived.

'Whoever did it must have come in over the mountains,' suggested Morton.

'If so, we'll never know. By the time we got out here, the snow had covered everything. Something like this can make you quite nostalgic for the Red Army Faction or the days when the Grey Wolves left their clues everywhere,' growled Mueller.

Morton put down his cup. 'So what do we have? Gruber had been up here three days. Then this local skier slaloms by and notices the front door open. It's still open when he returns after his day on the slopes. Being a curious man, he comes and investigates.'

Mueller made a dreadful joke. 'You know what they say in England about curiosity killing the cat,' he said, shaking his head at such quaint foreign sayings.

Though the comparison was not apposite, Morton nevertheless rewarded it with a knowing smile before he continued. 'Our skier finds Gruber here, on the living-room floor. When he overcomes his shock, he goes over to the café and the good lady telephones the valley police. They come up here by helicopter, take one look, and have the good sense to call the BKA in Munich. They send their finest along in another helicopter.'

'Which blows away any clues that the first chopper failed to scatter,' said Mueller sourly.

'Quite so,' Morton agreed equably. 'Anyway, the BKA boys take one look at Gruber and remember the order that anything like this is now your province.'

'Ever since Kreuse.'

'Since Kreuse,' confirmed Morton. 'So they call you – and here we are, Hans-Dieter.'

'Except that, forensically speaking, it was hardly worth the trip. My pathologist didn't find anything – not even a pinprick. He said that given the state of the body he doubts if even a full autopsy will produce anything.'

'But he took body samples, right?'

'Back to Pullach,' confirmed Mueller. 'Where we'll all be going soon, thank God.'

The radio man in the corner of the living room, crouched over his set, endlessly tuning, looked up and laughed loudly enough for one of the fingerprint technicians dusting everything in sight to look up in surprise. Morton knew that whoever had gutted Gruber would have taken the precaution of wearing gloves.

'All the usual border checks are in force, David,' Mueller continued.

Morton nodded. Munich was close enough to be the ideal jumping-off point to almost anywhere.

'If you think of anything more, tell me please,' Mueller said.

Morton was saying all the investigation bases seemed to be covered when the door of the bedroom where Gruber's body had been taken opened, and the last member of the BND team emerged and walked over to the stove to warm his hands. Mueller introduced him to Morton.

'This is Heinz Schmeissner. He is Professor of Behavioural Studies at the University of Homburg.'

'Glad to meet you, Professor,' Morton said, remembering a report Chantal had sent him. Scheissner's knowledge of ritual behaviour was extraordinary for a man who had never once set foot in a witches' coven or so much as killed a bat for sacrifice. Schmeissner lived in and through second-hand experience. But from that he extracted things which others failed to observe, and drew conclusions they were incapable of coming to. Chantal had said he was probably the most brilliant man working in his field.

235

'The pleasure is all mine,' said Schmeissner in a cheerfully accented English. 'Your reputation precedes you.'

Schmeissner moved from the stove, a stocky figure with the hands of a pianist and a smile that Morton thought aspiring undergraduate girls must dream of in the long summer months before term began.

'Your kind of work makes me quite jealous, Mr Morton. That is not flattery: I have neither the need nor the wish to flatter. The truth is that everything I have been told about you impresses me.' Schmeissner paused, then chuckled as if they shared a secret together. 'I see you are surprised. But we have a mutual friend. How is Dr Kramer?'

'You know Yoshi?'

Schmeissner nodded. 'Probably for almost as long as you have. Every Christmas, his schedule permitting, he comes to Homburg for our carol service. What he lacks in voice perfection he more than makes up with enthusiasm!'

Morton told Schmeissner about Yoshi's forthcoming operation. It drew first a cluck of sympathy, then another chuckle. 'A new heart – a new voice. Let us hope!'

Instinctively Morton liked and trusted Schmeissner. Unlike many academics, the Professor was neither a poseur nor a snob, but someone who knew his place – and his worth. Morton guessed it would take a great deal to rouse Schmeissner, but that when he was, he would be formidable.

'Have you come to any conclusions, Professor?' Morton asked.

Schmeissner looked at Morton. Suddenly he seemed tired, not from lack of sleep or over-exertion, but from something deeper, something from within. When he spoke again, his voice was quieter. 'Are you a religious man, Mr Morton?'

'No. Not since university. Even then, not very.' Schmeissner did not seem the sort who would care about such matters.

Schmeissner chuckled again. Morton realised he used it to punctuate his conversation. 'Given what we are dealing with here, it helps me to know a person's perspective on faith.'

'What are we dealing with here?' Morton asked in a quiet voice.

Schmeissner remained silent for a moment, looking at Morton. 'The Devil. Satan. Call him what you wish, Mr Morton. That is what we have here. I am certain.'

236

Morton looked out of a window. The moon had appeared, bathing the snowscape in a soft yellow light. Such a pretty backdrop for evil. He turned to Schmeissner. 'Why do you think this is ritual-related, Professor?'

Schmeissner's voice took on a more sombre tone. 'How much do you know about such crimes, Mr Morton?'

The question had been gently put but the eyes that met Morton's were probing.

'I know the difference between paganism and the occult. And that what happened to Gruber hasn't anything to do with ouija boards, white witches or chaos magic. Let alone the alchemy of Merlin or, for that matter, the New Age,' Morton said.

Schmeissner nodded approval. He took Morton by the arm and steered him towards the bedroom, speaking rapidly in his best English. 'Gruber is the end product of a religion that is based upon a brutal philosophy. Its followers believe that life itself is a Darwinian struggle for the survival of the fittest and that they have been chosen to rule the earth.'

'Hitler tried that and didn't get very far,' remarked Morton philosophically, reminding himself as much as the others.

'In many ways these are Hitler's children. They have learned from his mistakes. That is what makes them so very dangerous. They have brought Satan out of the closet, Mr Morton.'

'It's the neo-Nazis from the East,' added Mueller. 'They're worse than our Nazis ever were. It's not just Jews now, but everybody.'

Morton remembered then that Mueller's father had been a resister against Hitler.

Schmeissner led the way into the bedroom. Mueller followed, closing the door behind them. Schmeissner took up position at the head of the table. Mueller stood across from Morton. They all looked at the body. The obscenity of what had been done to Gruber was somehow reinforced by the low-wattage light.

'One of the points I stress to my students is to take a good look at everything so that a year later, no matter what else they have seen, they will recall every detail of what I have asked them to observe.' Schmeissner looked up at the others. 'No doubt it is the same in your business?'

Morton nodded. Not only was it important to get a body

properly fixed in your mind, but you had to listen to what it wanted to tell you. He released a long, slow breath.

Gruber's chest cavity had been ripped open, and stripped bare of all his organs.

Morton's eyes returned to the crude five-pointed star carved on Gruber's chest. 'The pentagram is the classic demonic symbol,' explained Schmeissner.

'Was that done before or after the organs were removed?'

'Almost certainly after. It's like an artist leaving his signature on a painting when the canvas is dry.' Schmeissner pointed as he explained. 'For cultists four of the points represent the Four Elements of Life, while the fifth is the Great Unseen, the secret place they believe is the source of all supernatural power.'

Morton remembered again what he had seen in all the other places, each distinct, detachable, unforgettable moment. Maybe Gruber was not a part of what he was looking for. He breathed out slowly, this time into the jagged hole in Gruber's very cold neck, wrinkling his nose at the fungus-on-a-rotting-wall smell. He turned to Schmeissner. 'What's the significance of all this?' He pointed first to the hole, then to Gruber's scrotum, where his testicles had been cut out, and finally to where wax had been dripped into the sockets from which his eyes had been removed.

With an expert's ease of narrative, Schmeissner embarked upon his explanation. 'The hole was used to siphon out his blood. Drinking blood, as you probably know, is at the centre of all satanic ritualism. Taken from a dying creature, or a person who is still alive, it is supposed to increase the drinker's sexual powers.'

'Is there any proof that it actually works?' Mueller sounded more incredulous than curious.

Schmeissner smiled and frowned simultaneously. 'Hundreds of thousands believe it does. Just as they believe that smearing wax on the eyes symbolically silences a person.'

'Is this silencing always a prelude to killing?' Morton asked.

Schmeissner shook his head. 'Not always.'

'Could Gruber have been a cultist who was sacrificed? Is that why he came here – to take part in a ritual? A participant becoming the victim?'

Schmeissner gave another shake of his head. 'Cultists rarely turn on their own, Mr Morton. They know the Devil would never sanction the loss of a follower except in the most extreme of circumstances. Then there would have to be appropriate ceremonies, perhaps even a full-scale Black Mass. I have checked carefully and there is no sign of anything like that having taken place here. Besides, Gruber came here alone.'

'But you are certain that whoever followed him here was a cultist?'

There was a moment's silence before Schmeissner gave a long, indulgent chuckle. 'I think you can rule out a woman. Female cultists almost never kill – and even if they do, never without a male attendant. And then usually she will have several present at a sacrifice she has been ordered to make.'

Morton pondered this as if he had all the time in the world. 'And the testicles?' he resumed.

Schmeissner cleared his throat. 'Testes are widely regarded as luck-bringers by almost all cultists. They often carry them in little pouches around their necks. The other possibility is that in this case they were removed as part of moon worship. There's a full moon in a week, and that time of the month has always been important to cultists. That's why they have so many moon gods. And most cultists insist there is a link between the moon and human fertility – that the moon influences all the bodily fluid secretions linked with procreation.'

Morton asked his next question. 'So, assuming nobody's going to hang them around his or her neck, what happens to the testes after they've been used in moon worship?'

'They usually slice them up so everyone in the cult gets a piece.'

Mueller shook his head. 'It sounds like something they do in Chinatown.'

Schmeissner made a little reproving hand gesture. 'The Chinese only eat animal testes. You could be dealing here with one of the Caribbean cults. Or one out of Africa. Human testes are very much on their ritual menu. Just as most of them are into bleeding a victim to death, as happened here.'

'Are you saying voodooists killed Gruber?' asked Morton.

Schmeissner shrugged. 'Not specially. Nowadays, most cults borrow a piece of ritual from here, a piece from there.' He paused and looked towards the door. The radio man was standing there.

'There's a call for you, Herr Morton. I was told to say it was urgent.'

239

It was Chantal. The reception was poor, which made her voice sound somehow brisker. 'A TriStar's gone down in the Atlantic, David. We think she had a couple of your least favourite people on board. Gonzales and Suto. The plane was out of Managua. And belongs to a small charter outfit called Global Transporter.'

Morton was like a hound coming to point. 'What do we know about them?'

'Lester's still running checks. They seem solidly respectable. So much so that Elmer Crayton's mistress is on their board.'

Morton closed his eyes. The sound of the war drum in his head was suddenly louder, its tattoo keeping time with a phantas-magoria of images. Everything became clearer in a different way. Her trip to India. Elmer Crayton's death. An undreamed-of fortune. *What does she do with all her money?* Yoshi had asked. *Certainly she only pays lip-service, relatively speaking, to medical charities.* Yes, indeed. *But she likes to stay close to the profession.* Of course. How else could she achieve her special purpose? *You need doctors, nurses, all the back-up for something like this*, Anna had said. Absolutely right. *You need patients*, Anna had added. And planes to bring them. Like the one that had gone down with Suto and Gonzales. Perhaps that very one. You needed all that – and something else. You needed madness. Not the just-out-of-control madness of the psychotic, or the psychosis of the manic depressive, or the God-is-telling-me-to-do-all-this of one of the schizophrenias. You needed something far more insidious and destructive. You needed the madness of Ghengis Khan, the Inquisition, Hitler and the Holocaust, Stalin and the pogroms. You needed all that and more. You needed the madness of control, of playing God, deciding who will live and who will die. The madness of blind revenge. The madness of true madness. *An amazing woman*, Walter had enthused. Yes, indeed. Yes, indeed.

'David – are you still there? Chantal asked.

Morton opened his eyes. He couldn't prove it yet. Just as in the past he couldn't prove so many things before surmise demanded action. He had simply accepted them. Just as he had accepted that everything he would now do would be driven by this new and terrifying knowledge. He came to a decision.

'Tell Lester I want everything on Global Transporter. Where they have flown to and from in the past two years. Cargo manifests. Everything. The same for every company in which Simone Montan has any involvement. I want to know what they do, who they are linked to, every deal they have been involved with. I want them turned inside-out and then turned inside-out again. Start with the medical side. Put every one we have on it. It's round-the-clock, Chantal. If anybody needs extra help, they get it. I'll deal with Walter later. Just use what it takes.'

After hanging up, he stood for a while staring out of the lodge window at the snowscape. The moon had gone. Soon it would be dawn. But already things were not only becoming clearer but darker.

He turned to the radio man. 'I want you to check every one of your airports to see if a Global Transporter plane passed through in the last couple of days.'

As the operator bent over his equipment, Mueller entered the room with Schmeissner. Morton told them what had happened. Schmeissner's fingers played unconsciously with a bone button on his traditional Bavarian jacket, but the rest of him remained quite still. Afterwards no one spoke while they listened to the quiet voice of the radio man.

Eventually he looked up. 'One of their transporters passed through Munich yesterday evening. Munich air traffic control says the company normally uses Frankfurt, but this time it landed at Munich because it had to pick up an extra co-pilot. Despite the weather, the pilot insisted on taking off at once.'

'For Managua.' It wasn't a question.

'Yes.' The radio man confirmed. 'Munich air traffic say that was the final destination.'

Morton turned to Schmeissner and told him why, this time, he was wrong about who had killed Gruber. Schmeissner asked no questions, made not even a gesture of disagreement. Indeed, he declared in a voice of homely reminiscence: 'Dr Kramer said you are always a man to surprise people.'

'I've learned a lot from you,' Morton said softly.

The radio man looked up again. 'It's your CCO.'

Morton took the handset. 'Yes, Frank.'

'I've got Bitburg on-line. He wants you to know Sonja Crayton's dead. A heart attack. Yoshi's also had one. His happened during the night. Bitburg says there was a young woman

241

with him who called the emergency services. Bitburg wants you to know he's told the Nobel people to absolutely keep her out of things.'

'How is Yoshi?'

'One of my boys just came off talking to the hospital. The doctors say he's weak but stable. Bitburg says that in view of the circumstances he's returning to Geneva.'

Morton grunted. He had seen Walter do this before – place as much distance as he could between himself and anything he thought could embarrass him. 'Tell him before he leaves Stockholm to make absolutely certain Count Lindeman fully understands that I asked Marta Hamsum to stay with Yoshi, and that if I hear one word that besmirches her reputation, I will personally see to it that the King sets the record straight. And tell Yoshi's doctors to give him a message from me to hang in there.'

'Will do,' said the CCO cheerfully. 'One last thing. Bitburg says Madam has flown to Frankfurt. She told Lindeman she's gone to see the President of the Bundesbank.'

'Thank Walter for that,' Morton said, putting down the phone.

Outside the first hint of sun was beginning to turn the snow a faint rosy copper. Morton turned to Mueller and told him what he wanted him to do.

30

His wheelchair draped with a sterile cloth, Dr Romer moved down the corridor off which led the operating rooms. Every OR had hummed with activity since scalpels had once again sliced through unresisting skin. He was masked, gowned and capped like all the clusters of figures bent over their anaesthetised patients. Some had arrived on the same flights as their replacement organs.

The latest were those from the Bavarian harvest. Its arrival had helped to ease the shock of the news the Washington Fixer had faxed. Klinger had died in a road crash. Police said his rental car had gone out of control and the resultant fireball incinerated his body. The Fixer had taken the necessary steps to ensure the police did not unduly pursue the matter of identification.

Dr Romer manoeuvred to allow a gurney to pass. A scrub nurse was pulling and an anaesthetist pushing Pierre Savant, the powerful Marseilles gang boss, who, when he'd arrived at the clinic, had been so aggressive that Krill had almost refused to operate. Now, heavily sedated in preparation for his kidney transplant, Savant snored gently through a plastic mouthpiece.

Dr Romer waited until the gurney entered Krill's OR, then continued down the corridor. He came to a stop before a large double door. Above it a light-box flashed the words: 'Unauthorised Entry Forbidden'. The door swung silently open, then closed behind him. Instinctively he glanced up at the red lightbulb and monitor on the wall above the door. Both showed nothing.

Here the light was muted, the voices of the staff low, their footsteps deadened by the sound-absorbing composition floor and the ceiling baffling of the intensive care unit. Everything was subservient to the mechanical and electronic noises of the life-support monitors and the rise-and-fall hiss of the respirators. They were the sentries of this nether world, constantly alert and ready to sound their alarms for the nurses manning the desk in the centre of the room. Horseshoe in shape, the desk was dominated by a bank of oscilloscope screens. Each was linked to a patient, in the separate bays around the walls of the room. Each bay contained the same high bed that made it easier for the nurses to check visually. Not that they had to: the monitors told them all they needed to know.

While the other nurses continued to study the blips racing across the screens, one rose from her position and hurried over to Dr Romer.

'How are they doing, Fraulein Sachs?' he asked, glancing at her name tag: Monika Sachs. She had been one of those who had recently transferred from the Gift of Life Transplant Center.

'No problems,' she said briskly, looking at him through glasses. 'But right now it's quiet. In a few hours this place is going to be busier than the Pacific Coast freeway.'

Dr Romer nodded, wondering why Americans always needed a point of reference. 'Return to your duties,' he said formally. He began to wheel himself slowly past the bays. Beside each bed rose the usual profusion of intravenous bottles and lines. The eyes of a few of the patients revealed their fear as they returned to consciousness. But there was nothing he would allow to be done to ease their anxiety. Fear was part of the recovery process; when it diminished, a patient would know he was getting better.

He paused at the foot of a bed. Fung, still cyanosed, and festooned with tubes and electrodes, lay as immobile as a statue after his surgery. Beside him, a nurse deftly checked the IV bottles, then the tube running from his mouth to the respirator, a large square box which gave off a rhythmic hiss, the only confirmation that Fung was alive.

As Dr Romer surveyed the bottles, each providing a different life-sustaining fluid, he noticed that the liquids suddenly gave the same slight stirring, as if something had invisibly shaken them simultaneously. He glanced quickly at the nurse. She was busy writing on the chart. He looked towards the desk. No one there had noticed the movement. He looked again at the bottles. Their contents had once more settled. The earth tremor had been so slight he wondered if he had made a mistake. But he knew he hadn't – and he was relieved at what he had seen. A small tremor like that was no more than Nature releasing a safety valve.

Suddenly the red light above the door started to flash urgently. On the screen was a pulsating message: 'Code One. Recovery Room.'

Monika Sachs was already running towards the door when Dr Romer stopped her. 'Do not leave your station! There are others who can cope!'

She turned to him, stunned. 'But it's a cardiac arrest. Everybody runs!'

'Return to your duties.' He propelled himself rapidly out of the ICU. He wanted to see how the crash team were handling the medical emergency. He briefly wondered who the patient was.

'How long's O'Neill been fibrillating?' Krill was demanding as Dr Romer entered the recovery room.

'Two minutes so far. We started manual massage within twenty seconds of the monitor going blip,' called out one of the nurses around the bed.

Krill grunted. He had been in the surgeons' lounge, enjoying a coffee between operations, when the crisis light had interrupted him.

Dr Romer parked clear of the emergency area, but still close enough to follow every development. Mr O'Neill – Sam O'Neill, undisputed head of the Boston Irish Mafia – lay face up, as white as his shock of hair. In the time he had been at the clinic he had shown that behind his profane mouth was an even rougher interior. Several of the nurses had refused to go near him. In the end Dr Romer had intervened and warned O'Neill that he would refund his deposit and send him home on the next plane unless he became more amenable.

Krill glanced towards Dr Romer. 'He was doing fine. His new heart pumping nicely. And suddenly this.'

He turned back to the others, who had continued to work swiftly and calmly. 'Let's give him another shot. Set for four hundred joules this time.'

A nurse began to prime the defibrillator. Another continued to count aloud from a stopwatch in her hand.

'Two-forty,' she called out, giving the elapsed time since the emergency had started. Dr Romer knew there were perhaps three minutes left, no more than four, before O'Neill would suffer permanent brain damage. Yet, despite the time constraint, Krill was controlling the situation with the same speed and style he displayed in his OR. A string of orders continued to flow from his lips. 'Check his groin pulse!' 'Somebody draw up ten cc of 1:1000 epinephrine!'

The responses were just as swift.

'Pulse erratic and weak.'

'Two-fifty,' called out the counting nurse.

'Charged! said the nurse at the defibrillator.

'Epinephrine ready!' reported a doctor, one of several who had hurried to the scene.

'Hold everything!' Krill reached for the two paddle-shaped electrodes attached to the defibrillator and placed them on O'Neill's chest.

'Clear!' he ordered.

Everyone around the bed stepped back. Krill pressed down, touching a button on each electrode. A measured shock passed through O'Neill's new heart. Krill lifted the paddles clear. O'Neill's body continued to spasm, his spine arcing and his legs stiffening as the shock coursed through his body. He slumped lifelessly back on the bed.

'Recharge!' It would take nine seconds to do so.

'Three minutes,' called out the nurse.

'Epinephrine!' Krill demanded.

The doctor handed him the syringe with its long cardiac needle. Krill felt for and located the interspace between O'Neill's ribs. He drove the four-inch long needle into the chest cavity, all the way to the hilt, into the heart he had just transplanted. He pulled back the plunger, and when dark red blood began to bubble up the needle, he swiftly injected the stimulant into O'Neill's heart.

'Pulse?' Krill called out.

'Dropping.'

'Three-ten,' said the nurse with the stopwatch.

'Recharged!' came the cry from the nurse at the defibrillator.

Once more Krill sent O'Neill into a spasm. Once more he watched his patient sink back, limp and lifeless.

'Recharge!' ordered Krill once more. 'Add lignocaine, five hundred cc.'

A doctor drew up the stimulant and injected it into one of the IV lines still connected to O'Neill's body.

With only the remorseless counting of the nurse to mark their efforts, they continued to do everything possible to resuscitate the gang boss. O'Neill received a second dose of epinephrine and two further jolting shocks. When the counting nurse announced that six full minutes had passed, Krill stepped back from the bed.

'He's gone.'

He gently pressed closed O'Neill's eyes and looked at the others. 'Thanks, everybody.' He turned to one of the doctors. 'Get him back into theatre and see what you can harvest.'

Then, peeling off his gloves, Krill nodded at Dr Romer and walked slowly from the recovery room. Dr Romer watched him go, then he, too, left as the medical team wheeled the bed back into the OR to begin the process of removing all the salvageable organs from O'Neill's body.

Down in the staff quarters at the southern end of the island, the nightly partying had ended as usual with couples either going back to their apartments or to the villa housing the 'comfort girls', as the imported whores who were available at no charge were known. A few staff used the helicopters parked along the landing strip.

One of these was now occupied by Moshe Weill. He had brought with him the flaxen-haired Polish whore who had entertained Klinger on the flight back from New York. Having read her report, Weill had decided she would make the night pass most agreeably.

She had told him her name was Ruth, and he had smiled. She looked about as Jewish as a pork chop in a kosher butcher's. But he had taken that as a sign she wanted to please him. And she had. Now, well past midnight, he was sated and a little drunk on the bottle of tequila they had finished. A moment ago she had climbed out of the cabin to relieve herself. Now she was calling out to him.

'Moshe, Moshe, come see. Quick!'

The excitement in her voice brought him to the door of the cabin. She was pointing across the lake. 'Look, look, the sky!'

Above Mount Masaya, vapour trails were swirling in slow, elegant motions, lit by the merest of pink glows.

'Beautiful, beautiful,' Ruth said in the same voice she had used after they had made love.

He looked at her and smiled. She was like a child. A beautiful, wanton, grown-up and totally decadent kid.

'I like to see,' she said, clapping her hands in excitement. 'So beautiful.'

He stared for a moment at the display. He had seen nothing like this before. 'You really would like to go and see?'

She turned and pouted at him. 'How is possible?'

He grinned. 'Easy, in our magic flying carpet.'

She looked at him, puzzled. 'I no understand.'

He tapped the side of the fuselage. 'In this.'

She looked at him round-eyed, not quite believing. 'You can fly this, Moshe?'

'No problem. I once flew one just like it into Beirut.'

'We really go and look?'

'Sure, why not?'

Ruth glanced towards the path that led to the clinic. 'Dr Romer. Maybe he not like you . . .'

'He'll be asleep. Anyway, we can be there and back in a few minutes.'

Her eyes grew even rounder. 'You'd do this? For me?'

She climbed into the cabin and followed him up into the cockpit. He motioned for her to strap herself into the co-pilot's seat.

'I only fly once in a helicopter, when I come to island.' Ruth said.

'Maybe on the way back you do another first.' He winked, his mind already beginning to think of the renewed pleasure ahead. She reached across and began to gently massage his thigh. 'Maybe I get you a little ready, Moshe.'

He grinned at her. 'Just keep your hand there, but no more.'

'No problem,' she giggled.

He hit the engine switch and thumbed the start button. There was a dull clattering sound like coins in a washing machine, then the engine ran up to full power, sending vibrations throughout the cabin.

Ruth said something in Polish, clutching the side of her seat, her eyes firmly closed. Weill grinned. She really was a kid. He waited until the rise and fall of the engine noise had settled to a continuous roar, then lifted off. They rose swiftly.

Ahead, rushing towards them, was Mount Masaya. The vapour trails careered across the sky, criss-crossing each other to form intricate patterns, all shaded a delicate pink from the reflection from inside the volcano.

'Beautiful, beautiful,' Ruth breathed.

He had to admit it was. And though he had seen most things, he had never been this near to a volcano. 'You want to take a closer look?' he asked as they flew over the lower slopes.

'Is possible?'

'Like I've said, anything is possible when you're in my magic carpet.'

'We look,' she said decisively.

Under his command, the helicopter shot up like an express elevator until it was above the summit. Up here the glow was brighter as it rose from deep inside the crater.

Ruth leaned across for a better view. 'No see very good,' she said in a disappointed little girl's voice.

'Soon fix that.' He edged the helicopter towards the rim of the crater.

'Oh, beautiful, beautiful,' she cried out, laughing.

It really was, he thought. Like a sunrise over the Negev Desert. Only this was their very own sunrise in the middle of the night. He glanced at Ruth. She was staring wide-eyed at the phenomenon.

'Tell you what. I'll make one pass across the top and then you'll get a real look.'

She nodded, too entranced to speak.

He brought the helicopter over the edge of the crater. The sudden updraught lifted them a good fifty feet. He increased power and began to crab across the mouth of the volcano.

Beside him Ruth had her face glued to the window, staring down. 'Is like hell,' she breathed. 'Hell on earth.' Far below them the lava bubbled redly.

'Yeah. Well—'

There was something wrong. A moment ago the yoke had been free. Now it was sluggish. The rudder didn't respond. And now the rotors were slowing.

Ruth was rubbing at the glass and shouting. 'No see, no see!'

Volcano ash! It was coating everything. Weighing them down. Dragging them down.

Ruth was screaming.

'Shut up!' he yelled.

He needed more power. More lift. More everything.

The helicopter dropped below the rim.

Ruth was screaming even louder. The heat cracked the perspex. The cockpit was filled with a foul smell. Sulphur. The rudder control cables had started to melt in the heat. He could hardly breathe. Ruth was moaning softly. The sides of the cockpit were too hot to touch. The perspex melted before his eyes. The heat was unbearable. The whole world was turning bright red.

The helicoper reached the bubbling lava. For a moment it rested on its surface, as if the bubbling, boiling, molten rock would support it. Then slowly, agonisingly slowly, the helicopter sank beneath the surface.

31

Anna signalled for the waitress to bring more coffee. 'I've been there three days,' she said, 'but nobody has said or done anything you could call medically remotely suspicious.'

They'd eaten crabs and fries and watched over-fed Americans come and go from the roadside bar-restaurant north of Malibu. By unspoken consent they'd kept the conversation at the how-was-your-trip, how-was-yours level, and smiled a lot at each other's replies, but somehow managing to position their heads so that it was hard for them to read the other's expression. Only when the dessert plates were cleared away – fresh fruit salad for her, a wedge of Mom's home-made apple pie and a small alp of cream for him – had Tommy fished from a pocket a small notepad, and Anna leaned her elbows on the table and begun to talk about why they were here in her proletarian accent, which could be placed somewhere between the Fulham Road and Wandsworth Common.

'But?' Tommy prompted, not looking up from his pad.

'But,' she repeated. 'Like I said, there are these funny little rules. Like giving all the patients numbers instead of using their names. It's supposed to help their privacy. And nursing staff, when they have to address them, call them only sir or madam. In any case, patient contact is kept to the absolute minimum. Only senior doctors get to spend any real time with them. Case files are also never left in a patient's room, but kept locked away by the chief nurse on each floor. And all treatment orders are written by Dr Littlejohn.'

Tommy checked his pad. 'He's the Medical Director, right? And he hired you?'

Anna nodded. 'I nearly thought he wouldn't. It wasn't because of a problem with the paperwork Chapman prepared – that would have got me into the Mayo Clinic. But Littlejohn was most concerned to make me understand all the rules. It was quite a lecture. When I asked why it was so important to keep a proper distance from the patients, I thought he was going to go ballistic.'

Tommy smiled. 'I remember Chantal saying they have a similar patient numbering system in some of those Swiss clinics where the rich and famous go for their nose jobs and liposuction. She said in places like that security is part of the package they sell.'

'Same as this place. Guards at the gates. A perimeter fence that would impress the Chinese gulag keepers. Speed bumps on a drive that seems long enough to run a marathon. The patients see none of this, of course. The clinic's way back from the highway. Where the red carpet stops, they stop. Lots of polite signs dotted around the formal grounds warning about snakes. And like everything else, all signed by our Medical Director.'

'Littlejohn, what's he like?'

'A real martinet. Physically he's small, with a goatee beard and the sort of eyes bad novelists call calculating. He's into suede shoes and the kind of walk that went out with John Wayne. You can sense his ego even before he comes into a room. But clinically, brilliant. He worked in most of the leading transplant centres in North America before this place and it's certainly better equipped than any hospital I've worked in.'

'Where did the money come from?'

Anna shifted her elbows. 'No way of telling. The place is totally anonymous. Not even a plaque to remember a benefactor.' She broke off as the waitress arrived, apologising for the delay and explaining she'd had to brew a fresh pot.

The arrival of the coffee, by tacit agreement, broke the rhythm of a moment ago. They sat in silence, as if one expected the other to speak first about the last time they had met like this: that night in Hong Kong when she had said she was going into China alone, despite his protests. They had still been arguing when she'd caught the train to Beijing. She had almost been killed there before the Colonel managed to pull her out.

Again by common consent they both realised they were not ready yet to deal with any of that. Almost, but not quite.

Tommy looked down at his pad before he spoke. 'How do the patients arrive?'

'Private ambulance. But most come and go either by medical air ambulance or their own private planes.'

'I take it they either fly into Santa Monica or Santa Barbara then come on down by road?'

'No. The place has its own runway. It's long enough to handle a TriStar or 747.'

Tommy made another note and shook his head. 'That's a bit unusual, isn't it?'

'I thought the same. Then I checked and found there are a dozen private hospitals within a hundred miles of here with similar facilities. A lot of their patients like the idea of avoiding the hassle of a commercial airport. This is America, Tommy. The bigger the status symbol, the bigger you are in the eyes of the competition.'

He looked up and kept his eyes on her. 'Any idea where your patients come from?'

'No. Like I said, the security is very good.' She could feel his persistence and she knew this was his way of keeping the past at bay. For a moment longer she allowed the memory of what might have been between them to remain. Then the tiny gyroscopic figure inside her that always managed to stay upright took over.

'What about the staff?' he asked. His eyes were all the time on Anna's face, watching it, listening to it, questioning it.

'The nurses are Asian, mostly Filipinos or Burmese – minimum of English, maximum of efficiency. The doctors are from just about everywhere. I've managed to put together a list. Maybe you should have Lester check this out. I'll try to get some more info when I get back.'

She reached into a pocket and produced a piece of paper. 'Sorry I couldn't type it. But you should be able to read my handwriting.'

'I could always make out your handwriting,' he said with an innuendo born from tension. He took the paper, glanced at it, then smiled at her.

'What's so funny?' she asked. She had turned her palms into a prop to support her chin.

'I think we both should—'

'Look, I—' she began.

'I do—' he said at the same time.

'—meant to bring up Hong Kong before now,' she completed quietly.

'Me too,' he rejoined with his ever-ready smile.

'What happened there was my fault. I sent you the wrong signals.' She spoke directly ahead of her, from the heart, from the memory of what could never have been.

'It's OK,' Tommy said. After a pause he resumed. 'I've grown up since then. My antenna's better tuned – I hope.' He slipped the paper into his pocket.

Anna reached across the table and touched his cheek. 'I still don't need anyone in my life right now. But when I do, I hope you'll still be there.'

The answer was in his silence.

'I mean it,' she said, meaning it.

Over by the counter, the waitress was watching them.

'Back to the patients,' Tommy said, feeling quite unreasonably happy, hearing the song in his own heart, blowing out his cheeks and becoming businesslike.

She smiled. He hadn't really changed. And she was glad. 'Right now there are sixty patients. Mostly heart and kidney cases. As a junior scrub nurse, by the time they get to me they're asleep. You could have the Dalai Lama lying there and you'd never know. Once they're out of the OR, that's the last I see of them. Another rule is that theatre staff absolutely never go up to the floors.'

Anna drained her cup. 'Here's another thing. We've only done one kidney transplant since I've been there.'

'Any reason?'

'Not that I can see. Except the usual. Not enough organs to go round.'

Tommy made a note. 'So what kind of surgery goes on?'

'Triple bypasses, replacement valves. That kind of thing.'

Another note. 'It doesn't really fit with the place's name, does it?' Bit grand, calling it Gift of Life when it's really nuts and bolts.'

She allowed herself a pause. 'But the set-up is still pricey enough. The basic room rate is about twice what you'd pay at comparable places. And they don't take Blue Cross.'

'Which means patient intake is very selective.'

She paused again. 'If you've got that sort of money why go to a place like this? Why not one of the longer-established centres?

Those places must still operate a cash-and-priority service. She looked at Tommy. 'Unless, of course, there is a guarantee at my place.'

'My God,' Tommy said softly. 'You just may have hit on something.'

'I just may have,' she said. 'I just damned well may have.'

They were both silent.

'I'll call the Colonel,' Tommy said at last.

Anna slowly shook her head. 'No, not yet. I want to be absolutely certain.' She glanced at her watch. 'I've got to get back. I'm on late call. But let's meet here in a couple of days.'

'Same time?' He sounded almost skittish.

'Maybe we can stretch it to an early dinner,' Anna said carelessly.

As she stood up, Tommy asked another question. 'Is there any way I can reach you?'

'Littlejohn made it clear staff don't receive calls at the clinic.'

'What about your apartment?'

'I share it with a couple of other nurses. It wouldn't be a good idea to call there. I hardly know them.'

Tommy nodded.

She smiled once more and was gone. He waited until she was out of the door then walked over and paid the waitress. She looked at him. 'Your friend's in a hurry,' the waitress said.

'It's the work ethic. Some people have it stronger than others.'

'My rush doesn't begin for another hour,' she said. 'Want another coffee? It's on the house.'

'Thanks. But I've got to get back.'

'Where's back?'

'Santa Monica.'

'Nice place,' said the waitress.

After Tommy had pocketed his change and left, the waitress walked to a payphone at the end of the booths. She checked the number she had written down on the back of her order pad and dialled. When the call was answered she spoke rapidly, as if she was eager to please.

'You were right about her, Doctor. I couldn't hear everything. But she seemed to be spilling her guts to this reporter. A tall, slim guy. Sounded European. Lives down in Santa Monica . . .'

The waitress then repeated exactly what she had overheard. When she had finished she was thanked properly, and told someone would drop by with $500. When she had first been asked to keep a lookout for talkative staff from the fancy clinic up the road, she'd thought it would come to nothing. Now, just by keeping her ears peeled, she had earned far more in a few minutes than she made in a long week.

Twenty miles away, behind the fifteen-foot high hurricane fence which protected the perimeter of the Gift of Life Transplant Center, Dr Richard Littlejohn sat with his back to his office window, his face and body totally hidden in the high-backed leather chair. Then his hand once more reached out for the phone, plucking it from its rest with a delicate bird-like motion. When he had dialled the series of numbers he spoke briefly, in the same soft voice he used to dictate a patient's case notes. He listened for a moment, then spoke again. 'That will be absolutely fine.'

32

After Morton had asked the radio man to explain the frequencies, he sat before the set making calls while Mueller's team completed their business in the lodge. Mueller, who deserved his own reputation as a taskmaster, marvelled at Morton's driven urgency. He asked questions, issued orders, received calls back, asked more questions before giving new instructions, all with a controlled energy that seemed to be continually saying we can succeed, but we can also fail. He was like a human ultimatum, but never passing on to others the pressures he felt himself. It was, Mueller decided, a perfect example of how to get results by maintaining a furious and remorseless pace.

Morton's first call had been to the CCO on Concorde. He gave him a list of the names he wished to speak to and in what order. An on-board technician locked in the radio frequency and then boosted it so that Morton would have a totally clear and secure connection from the lodge.

He had spoken first to the Secretary-General of the United Nations in New York. There had been a short delay for the Secretary-General to usher out of his office a joint Israeli-Arab delegation which had come to discuss turning Jerusalem into an open city.

Mueller had marvelled at the way Morton addressed the Secretary-General as an equal, ending by asking him to make his own call to the President of the United States, and then waiting patiently to hear the outcome, sitting perfectly still, his eyes clamped narrow like a Chinaman's. Everybody in the lodge had heard the Secretary-General's response: 'The President has instructed Secretary Armstrong to postpone his plan.'

Morton thanked him and continued to work his way through the list. He spoke directly to the President of Costa Rica in his palace in San José, explaining that Hammer Force would like permission to conduct its annual jungle training in the north of the country, along the border with Nicaragua. The President agreed at once.

Next he called Carberry, briefed him fully, and told him to fly his entire Covert Action team to San José in Hammer Force's other aircraft, a 747 freighter. It was the only plane large enough to carry the microlites.

He then briefed Chantal and Lester and listened to their news without comment, allowing himself only a cautious smile at this further confirmation.

Finally he called Stockholm. A doctor said Yoshi was asleep.

'How is he?'

'We're planning a bypass.'

'What's the prognosis?'

'Could be better, could be worse.'

'Meaning?'

Everyone in the room heard the echoey laugh. 'It means better than worse.'

'When he wakes up make sure to tell him I called.'

'I will. He was asking if you had. The King's called twice.'

'Tell Dr Kramer I won't be able to call for a while. He'll have to make do with the King.'

The doctor laughed appreciatively.

Morton stood up, stretched and rubbed his neck, and watched impassively as two of Mueller's men carried out Gruber's body bag to the Chinook.

The sun, high above the snowscape, shone directly into the window, so that it was impossible for Mueller to read Morton's expression. But he sensed that the coiled power which for the past two hours had carefully unravelled, was turned off, at least for the moment.

33

The creeping grey, where night ends and another day begins, the moment the Indians in Nicaragua still call the first dawn, woke Danny. For a moment he remained motionless, his eyes absorbing the stealthy and deceptive speed of the sky changes, watching the subtle talcum give way to the palest of pinks, to be replaced by the full blood-red of the emerging sun. All those other dawns in northern climes and the timeless zones of jet travel had not blunted for him the impact of a tropical sunrise.

But it was something else associated with flying which now came back. During the night, from the far side of Mount Masaya, had come the sound of a helicopter. As he had sat up, the noise had stopped abruptly. He had looked across at Gates; he hadn't stirred in his sleeping bag. For a while longer Danny had remained propped on his elbow, listening for the resumption of the engine noise. It had not come. He'd lain back in his sleeping bag, reminding himself that at night, especially in the open, sound can be deceptive. Given that on the other side of the volcano was Lake Nicaragua, the chopper would have been out over water, which made it even harder to judge direction or distance.

As the colour flooded back into the forest which securely wrapped the volcano's lower slopes, he saw that the dark green foliage was covered with a heavy fall of what looked like hoarfrost. It started a little higher up and continued all the way to the summit. The sun, already warm on his skin, did nothing to melt it. The covering lay, thick and even, like cement powder. It gave off a pungent aroma he recognised. He had smelled it once when he had been in Hawaii: volcanic ash.

Danny rolled out of his sleeping bag and reached for his boots.

Close by, Gates moved then abruptly sat up. He, too, stared at the ash and sniffed at the air.

'Sonofabitch,' Gates said.

He lit a cigarette, watching Danny finish lacing up his boots while the day moved swiftly to that wondrous moment as the sun rose proud and clear. Masaya's classic shape at that moment looked a thing of beauty.

'Sleep well?' Danny asked.

'Probably better for knowing that, God willing, at least tonight it will be a proper bed. I'm getting too old for boy scouting.' Gates came out of his sleeping bag.

'Guess you didn't hear the chopper?'

'After dinner last night I wouldn't have heard a thing.' They had eaten in one of the villages back down the track, washing down the heavy spiced food with tequila and root beer. 'So what's with this chopper?'

Danny told him.

Gates filled his lungs with smoke. 'Nobody in their right mind would fly around at night in this place, especially in a chopper. Even when we were going all-out against the Sandanistas, we didn't fly any after-dark missions unless it was absolutely imperative. It was just too damned dangerous trying to set down.'

'Well, somebody was up there.' Danny continued to peer up towards the summit.

Gates inhaled. 'Maybe that pork made you dream.'

'I don't think so.' As he turned to him Danny was only mildly irritated by Gates' response.

From a long way away came the faint but unmistakable sound of rotors drowning out the babel of the undergrowth. 'Must be your chopper coming back to show you weren't dreaming,' grinned Gates, slipping into a low-tread jungle stance.

Shielding their eyes they watched the speck beyond the volcano's peak. 'Looks like he's flying a search pattern,' Danny pronounced. 'Maybe he's looking for that other chopper.'

Gates squinted into the sun. 'More likely some wealthy landowner coming home from an all-night party. They used to do that in the war, you know. Sober up by zapping anything that moved out on the lake.'

Danny continued to watch the helicopter with professional interest. 'I still think he's searching, Bill.'

'OK. So he's searching. For us? No need. Half the country probably knows the Survey gringos are in town. Has to be, the way they charged us double last night.'

Gates pulled on the boots he had bought in Managua from the same shop Klinger's shoes had come from.

They'd asked the shopkeeper to show them what looked like his entire stock while they'd tried to ascertain whether he remembered Klinger. If he had, he'd given a pretty good performance of not remembering. Afterwards they'd gone next door and rented a jeep. Since then they had done what advance men are expected to do: checked out suitable places for campsites. Last night they had reached the lower slopes of Masaya, parked the jeep off the track and camped in the open.

'Maybe today we get to try out these gizmos of yours, Danny,' Gates said, rising to his feet.

So far there had been no opportunity to use either the scanner or flying camera. And after three days in the country, they had found no sign of Dr Romer or his clinic.

'Want to bet?' Danny asked.

Every morning they had the same conversation. Each time Gates had given the same answer. 'I keep telling you, gambling's for Vegas.' The words had a soft tone that had its own aggression.

There'd been a story that Gates had gone to Vegas with his wife and after a week she'd headed out into the desert with a croupier. There were stories like that all the time in their business, Danny thought. Sometimes joshing helped. Clearly not with Bill. He decided from now on to drop it.

Gates turned and looked up to where Masaya's cone towered in the still morning. Nothing disturbed the air around the summit. From here the ash beneath the crater's throat looked like fake snow on some giant Christmas decoration.

'Sonofabitch. It's going to be a real sonofabitch climbing through this stuff.'

'What do you make of it?'

Gates considered. 'Remember what Bobby said about volcanos only looking dangerous?'

Robert Duval, the seismologist in San Francisco, had briefed them on volcanic behaviour.

Danny grinned. 'All I remember him saying is that the further you are from the last eruption, the closer you are to the next.'

'What have we got here – selective recall? Bobby also said this pile of rock has a reputation of being all show and no tell.'

'That, too, he said,' Danny agreed equably.

Gates shook his head and walked over to the jeep. It was his turn to make breakfast. He lit the portable stove, brewed coffee in a skillet and warmed up the field rations. They ate quickly, in companionable silence, locked the jeep and set off towards the summit. Both had field glasses around their necks and rucksacks on their backs containing water and provisions for the day. The pocket of each rucksack contained a handgun apiece and spare ammunition clips, together with maps of the area. They each carried a machete to hack through the undergrowth. After a while they reached the edge of the sulphur ash fall-out.

Danny stopped and pinched some of the powder between his finger and thumb. It smelled foul and felt damp. 'Must be an underground stream,' Gates said.

'Thermal springs. People would pay a fortune just to come and breathe or bathe in this stuff.'

An hour later they paused once more to survey the way upward into a moonscape. Spikes of rock rose out of the ground, and the sides of the fissures and small ravines were scarred and burned by lava flows. The reek of sulphur was strong.

'It's like being in one of those Chinese communal lavatories,' Gates grunted, leading the way once more upward.

Total silence appeared to settle over the countryside. As they climbed the ash became thicker and, as they brushed against the foliage, in a little while they were covered with grey powder that deadened their footfalls. Apart from the slash of their knives, the only sound was their hoarse breathing as the ash caught in their throats and made their eyes smart. Once more they stopped to slake their thirst from their water bottles. Gates started to sit down on the ground and immediately leaped up again. 'Holy Christ!' he cried. 'It's like sitting on a damned hotplate!'

Danny knelt and felt the earth. It was hot to his touch. He glanced up the slope. In the hard morning light, there was a strange beauty to the extravaganza of lava shapes formed over millions of years. 'Our chopper's back,' he called out.

Away to their left the helicopter thrummed into view. It passed high over where they stood. They watched it commence another sweep.

'You were right about her searching,' Gates said.

'Maybe she's keeping an eye on the volcano,' Danny said. 'That would explain why the chopper was up in the night.'

Gates grunted. 'Bobby didn't mention they do that.'

They watched the helicopter once more pass overhead and disappear. Danny trained his binoculars skywards. 'That's an Iraqi chopper.'

'Well, she's certainly a long way from home.'

'What's she doing here?'

'After the war, all sorts of stuff came on the market.' Gates reminded Danny.

They resumed climbing, picking their way across the ridges and terraces and over ravines, bridged by enormous buttresses of basalt. As they climbed higher, the forestation turned into scrub.

Suddenly, a small bundle fell from a branch and writhed on the ground, scuffling and slithering to get out of their way. Weighed down by ash, the parakeet was unable to fly. As they watched, the bird collapsed and was still.

They had climbed a little further when, from ahead, came a sudden scream and the trees were briefly and violently shaken. The troop of howler monkeys swung on down the slope. The silence seemed louder than before as they continued to work their way up towards the volcano's pumice collar. Here and there the ground was pitted with gaping funnel-shaped holes, from which emerged wisps of steam.

By now the sun was full in the sky, brightening the ash so that it looked even more like snow in a winterscape. Once more the silence was broken, this time by a deep panting. It was still a little way off, but approaching down the slope.

'Wild pig,' Gates said softly. He quickly removed his rucksack and pulled out the pistol. Danny did the same. They both took cover behind a lump of lava. They could hear the pig clearly, grunting as it trotted, dislodging small pieces of pumice in its progress.

'Wait until he commits to the charge,' Gates whispered.

The light breeze was in their faces so that, until a moment ago, the boar had not scented them. Now it burst out of the scrub, snout down, and came on at full run, short legs flying, ears drawn back, the folds of skin around its neck shuddering and wobbling with each jarring footfall.

Gates and Danny rose and fired simultaneously. The bullets glanced off the hog's hide. The boar squealed in fury, then, without breaking stride, turned and wheeled, kicking up a cloud of ash. He raced back the way he had come, still squealing.

'We'd better finish him. He's too dangerous to leave out here,' yelled Gates, setting off in pursuit.

He had covered no more than a few yards, Danny at his elbow, and gaining on the hog, when the ground appeared to disappear beneath the animal. Where one moment there had been firm rock there was now a bubbling reddish-brown mass, giving off intense heat. They watched as the boar, screaming in terror, disappeared into the morass. Then, as swiftly as the molten lava had broken through the earth's crust, it receded, sucking down earth and rock to cover its presence.

'Jesus H. Christ,' Gates said. 'I figure we should get the hell out of here.'

'Another fifty feet, and we'll have a view that'll probably save us two or three days of searching.' Danny grinned. 'Remember what Bobby said about volcanos only looking dangerous.'

'Sometimes you take people too literally, my friend.'

They continued upwards, the sun hot on their skin. They did not speak, conserving their energy for the ascent. They reached an outcrop of rock just beneath the rim of the crater. After they had drunk from their water bottles, they looked across the intervening moulder of jungle to the vast expanse of Lake Nicaragua. Barely visible through the heat haze was the Solentiname Archipelago. They began to quarter with their glasses the ground along the lake shore, looking for any building large enough to house a clinic. But apart from the ruins of a fort or two, legacies of the days when the British, Spanish and French had all briefly held sway here, there was nothing large enough. As they began to widen their search, the helicopter reappeared. They followed its flight across the water, as it passed over several of the islands. Finally it disappeared.

They kept their glasses trained on the area where they had last seen it. The chopper did not reappear. They were about to turn away when Gates stopped. 'Oh, boy,' he breathed. 'Oh boy, oh boy.'

From where the helicopter had vanished from their view had emerged a small jet aircraft. It flew low and straight across the water.

'A Lear!' cried Danny happily. 'Now, who would have a Lear in a place like this?'

Gates gave his pirate's smile.

'Only someone with very important passengers to carry.'

'Or maybe just one passenger?'

'Our Dr Romer?'

'Oh boy, oh boy,' Gates said again.

They watched the jet scream across the lake and on over the jungle.

Gates reached in his rucksack for a map of the lake, spread it on the ground and frowned. 'According to this, there's no island where she came from.'

'Maybe the map's out of date.'

'It's the latest Agency issue.'

'Let me check mine.' Danny produced a map. 'Here, this looks big enough to have a suitable airstrip.' He jabbed at an island at the eastern end of the archipelago.

Gates gave another frown. 'How old's your map?'

'Four years. It's one that Intourist, of all people, put out.'

'Just before the Russians stopped coming here.' Gates looked thoughtful. 'And about the time Romer's plane crashed in Ecuador.'

'That's quite a leap, Bill.'

'I know it. But that's what comes of hanging around with Morton.'

Danny stared out across the lake through his glasses. Beside him Gates went on: 'Clear away the smoke and you find more smoke. That's how the Stasi always worked.'

'It's not somewhere you'd start a clinic, Bill.'

'Or go looking for one.' A rejuvenating smile had settled on Gates' face.

'Do we go looking?' Danny asked.

Gates looked at his map. 'Easier said than done. I don't know about yours, but mine says that whole area is a military zone. At minimum they'll have patrol boats. And even on a dark night I wouldn't chance the Nicaraguan Navy wouldn't hit you.'

Danny nudged him. 'It's either our first chopper, or one like it.'

From where they had last seen the helicopter disappear, one had appeared. It began to systematically quarter the lake.

'Whatever they've lost, they sure want it back badly,' Gates murmured.

Suddenly the clatter of rotors was joined by a strange humming and vibrating sound that seemed to be coming from under their feet. Jets of vapour rose above the crater's rim and then fell back.

Danny and Gates scrambled up the scree. Several hundred feet below, the floor of the crater was bubbling and boiling. As they watched, another bituminous jet rose into the air and fell back in a lazy stream into the cauldron. Almost at once a new column rose slowly towards them, holding something in suspension. As the column drew level with the rim of the crater they could see the unmistakable shape of a helicopter rotor. Then, with infinite grace, the rotor fell back into the volcano.

'Jesus H. Christ,' Gates said. 'Let's get the hell out of here.'

Gathering up their maps, they hurried down the slope, the sulphur making their eyes smart and stinging the backs of their throats.

34

Dieter Vogel's home was in a leafy Frankfurt suburb, about as far from the financial turmoil of the Bundesbank as he could reasonably live. Englestrasse was one of those streets created in the post-Second World War building boom. Now, almost half a century later, it was a mature avenue, with small but well-kept front gardens and maids' quarters at the rear. The security systems were discreetly hidden behind Gothic wrought-iron gates and the lower windows looking onto the street were mullioned, the result of using bottle-glass.

Even without the list provided by Mueller, which Morton had stuck to the dashboard of the unmarked BND car, he would have had little difficulty in recognising who lived where on Englestrasse.

Number 2, with its clipped privet hedge and clematis trained up a wall, was, for sure, where the retired commander-in-Chief of NATO lived. Only a general would have everything so perfectly ordered. Opposite was a turreted splendour, home of an industrialist. Only a tycoon at risk of kidnapping would have such an aerial on the roof. Number 7 was hidden by sufficient shrubbery for the hum of the barges on the nearby Rhine not to penetrate. That would be the home of Frau Saltzman, who had helped found the Green Party.

He drove past the steep-roofed mansion of the owner of the national chain of supermarkets and, next door, standing in identical respectability, the home of the founder of an even larger chain of sex shops. Morton passed a dozen more houses before he reached number 24. Like those on either side, it was half hidden from the street by stands of elms and conifers. There was no outward sign of life in the Vogel mansion.

Shortly before he had driven into Englestrasse, a BND operative, parked out on the trunk road that led to the airport, had used his carphone to call Frau Sauermann at the Bundesbank. Posing as the finance director of the Moscow Central Bank, he had apologised for the short notice, but sought an immediate interview with the President. Frau Sauermann had replied that Herr Vogel's schedule made such a meeting impossible. Then, perhaps sensing her caller's disappointment, she added that in any event, the President was not expected in the office until later that morning. It was a further confirmation.

In Englestrasse itself, the first activity of the day had begun. Outside number 27 – belonging to Herr Bauer, the Chief Manager of Frankfurt's largest department store – a chauffeur waited beside a car. At number 31, home to a retired German ambassador, a delivery truck driver was unloading boxes of wine. Elsewhere, other vans and trucks had began to arrive, deliver and depart.

Hans-Dieter had said this activity would last for ninety minutes, no more. Then Englestrasse would return to its morning peace, with only the sound of bird calls to show life existed along the length of this gently curving street, bordered on one side by a small park and, on the other, by Kaiser Allee.

In spite of its name, Mueller had explained that on Kaiser Allee people kept their birds in comparatively modest cages, not in the splendid aviaries the residents of Englestrasse favoured. It was this which had given Morton the idea. He had asked how the aviaries were serviced. From the answer all else had flowed.

Passing number 43 – a stockbroker and his family – Morton saw that the time on the dashboard clock was 7.15. A moment later the car radio confirmed that the surveillance teams were all in position.

He drove into Kaiser Allee and passed the telephone company repair van carrying a BND listening team. They already had removed a manhole cover and were down in the tunnel, checking wires.

Two hours ago, when Madam's 747 landed at Frankfurt-Main from Stockholm, a BND vehicle had followed her to the Frankfurt-Hof. Meanwhile it had taken ingenuity on the part of another operative to tap into the hotel's switchboard before she entered the penthouse suite. Her subsequent brief call to Vogel's home confirming their breakfast meeting had been overheard by Morton and everyone else on the surveillance network.

Afterwards, on his check pad, Mueller had made another tick, marvelling again at how well Morton continued to read the situation. And it was true: in a dozen different ways he had asked the same question – will this help? – of those he had continued to call, first from the Chinook which lifted them off the Wallberg to Munich Airport and then during the flight to Frankfurt, from Concorde.

On that leg had come news from Lester that his programmers had finally succeeded in writing the software needed to establish links between the victims' organ thefts; even now the first tentative connections were being made. Lester had also managed to rework Meditale to find his way past the blocker on Thrung's disc. Beyond the blocker was a further series of numbers. In an inspired moment, Lester had gone back through Thrung's weightlifting records and discovered that the numbers represented the poundage Thrung hoisted at the Olympics before he was disbarred. What Lester had called only routine checks and balances had done the rest. The numbers had finally been matched against a list of names which turned out to be gang leaders in a score of countries who had received organ transplants.

Similar checks and balances had also enabled Lester to unravel the mystery of the letters which had looked like airline tag numbers. They *were* numbers. From there on, it had been, again to paraphrase Lester, plain sailing. It had taken a dozen of his best hackers the rest of the night to discover that the numbers corresponded with the files of patients at the Gift of Life Transplant Center.

Somewhere north of Wuerzburg, Chantal had come on to say she could stand up in any court and swear that the substantial sum of money in a deposit account for Otto Proel, pilot, deceased; place of death, Ecuador, had been transferred from a bank in Liechtenstein, wholly owned by another in the Cayman Islands, in which Simone Montan was the principal stockholder. The same bank had, two years before, transferred $409 million to the account of Gift of Life Inc. at the Malibu branch of the Bank of California. Drug Rehab also kept its account here. Again, all legally verifiable. They had both known it would never come to that.

Right up until touchdown at Frankfurt Morton had gone on

having times checked, distances measured and decisions made. One had been not to tap into Vogel's telephone at home. It had a security system, Hans-Dieter said, which, ironically, had been installed by the BND; the best estimate from his people was that it would need a day to find a way around it. Morton had said it wasn't essential to do so.

He drove out of Kaiser Allee towards the ring road which led back to the city. A mile along he saw the van pulled off the highway. He parked in front.

The van's sides were sprayed with pictures of exotic-looking birds. The BND paint shop had worked into the small hours to replicate the distinctive logo of the Frankfurt specialist firm that sold rare caged birds. The operative in the van's passenger seat walked over to the car. He took Morton's place behind the wheel and drove to join one of the surveillance teams.

The van driver wore a green coverall and looked like any other deliveryman who had pulled over for breakfast between calls. He was a BND shooter; his Uzi was clipped beneath the dashboard. He nodded and went on eating as Morton opened a sliding panel behind the driver's seat and went into the back of the van.

There were half-a-dozen men in the confined space, standing or squatting before the ranks of equipment covering both walls. With them was Mueller, dressed like the others in green coveralls. They were all listening attentively to Johnny Quirke.

During the night he had flown from Geneva with several of Danny's pocket-sized scanners and flying cameras. He held a life-sized model parrot in one hand. A moment ago he had removed it from one of birdcages suspended from the van's roof. Quirke nodded at Morton and continued with his briefing.

'All you have to remember is that the camera operates on the same principle as flying a model aircraft. It'll do pretty well anything you want: perch on a tree branch, land on a window ledge, sit on top of a chimney. Its eyes are the lenses. Each camera has a life of thirty minutes. Then you need to call it back for recharging.'

Quirke picked up a small control box. 'The scanner is programmed to receive the sound that comes with your pictures.' He picked up a bucket. 'It fits in the bottom. It'll look as if you're carrying bird litter.'

A technician in the back of the van who was squatting over a small switchboard looked up. 'Unit three reports she's just left the hotel. It's the same Mercedes.'

Mueller looked at a large-scale map pinned to one side of the van. 'We've got twenty minutes, no more.'

'Perfect.' Morton smiled. No one had seen him do that since he'd arrived in Frankfurt.

35

After she settled into the upholstered comfort of the back seat of the Mercedes, Madam opened the slim attaché case and removed the two documents she had received over the suite's fax machine. Both had been prepared by Theodore, Muldrake and Company, the long-established City of London chartered accountants who had acted for Elmer and, upon his death, helped her form the Organisation. Subsequently, she had persuaded the firm to divest itself of all its other prestigious clients and concentrate solely upon the affairs of the Organisation.

A glance told her the documents were the work of Archibald Theodore, the senior partner. No one else had such fine copper-plate handwriting. That he had used it indicated that he was fully aware of the sensitivity of what he had written. She began to read the first document.

Prefaced with the caveat – 'Best Estimate' – it detailed Sonja Crayton's investment portfolio, which had formed the basis of her separation agreement with Elmer. Theodore had calculated that the present value of her stockholdings was a little below $4 billion.

Madam ran her eyes down the list. She had thought the amount would be larger. Elmer's widow had handled her financial affairs no better than the rest of her life. She put aside the document, lost in thought for a moment, remembering the chill which had gone through her when Elmer had shown the agreement to her; far too generous, she had told herself at the time.

Yet it was not the financial settlement which had finally decided her to have Sonja killed. She had never ordered anyone to be killed purely for financial gain. Elmer's widow had become an embarrassment. While she remained out of the public eye, it had just been possible to tolerate her behaviour. But gradually, as she had returned to the world where Madam knew she herself was regarded as a role model for any society hostess, Sonja's behaviour had become openly spoken about. There had been that incident when she had propositioned a junior presidential aide at a White House reception. That other time when she had threatened to stage a scene at a Buckingham Palace garden party because she felt slighted at being placed in the wrong receiving line. 'I am Mrs Elmer Crayton,' she had stormed at a Royal equerry. 'If my husband were here, we would be standing close to Her Majesty.' There had been numerous other occasions when she had behaved equally foolishly, sometimes even stupidly. And recently she had begun to behave like, Elmer would have said, a trollop, as if she had learned nothing in her years with him about judging people. Instead there were all those boring little men she had insisted on bedding, thinking nobody knew. Sonja never understood that you didn't do certain things, not when you were Elmer's widow. That you behaved with proper decorum and showed proper respect to the memory of the most wonderful man who had walked this earth. Instead, she seemed neither to realise nor care that her bouts of drunkenness and casual affairs were increasingly besmirching the very name she clung to – Elmer's. And Elmer had said that there was always a bottom step to everything, over which one crossed at one's peril. And finally Sonja had managed to do that. The only solution had been to make sure she would never do so again. That her organs had not been harvested was a pity; they could have gone some way to making up for all her mistakes.

Madam reached for the telephone in the arm rest and dialled her secretary on board the 747, still parked at Frankfurt-Main, its crew awaiting her further instructions. The call was answered instantly.

'Karen, please send a wreath to Mrs Crayton's funeral.'

'Any particular kind of flowers, Madam?'

'Roses.' Elmer had once said Sonja hated them.

'And the message, Madam?'

'No message. Just "Madam".'

She replaced the phone and picked up the second document. it was headed 'Sovocorp'.

Reading it through quickly for the first time, she thought how right she was to entrust all such matters to Archibald Theodore.

273

Only he could have reduced the complexities of Sovocorp to a couple of pages. His opening paragraph synthesised everything. She began to read a second time, this time slowly and carefully.

'Sovocorp was created for the sole intention of developing and exploiting the post-Communist void in the Soviet republics. Offices have been established in Moscow and all the principal cities. The short-term intention is for Sovocorp to become the pre-eminent source of private financing for the former Soviet Union. The long-term intention is for Sovocorp to replace all other sources of investment, which presently include the US and a number of European governments, the World Bank and the Bundesbank. Sovocorp will then become the only conduit through which all other corporations will in future be able to trade with the Soviet republics.'

There followed a breakdown of Sovocorp's present investments in the republics, some US $35 billion, and its networking with all the principal banks, both internal and external. She paid particular attention to the paragraph concerning the Bundesbank. Satisfied she had understood the role the bank had cast for itself, she replaced both documents in the attaché case and sat back to run through her mind how she would conduct the meeting with Dieter Vogel.

The van drove the length of Kaiser Allee and parked at the bottom end of Englestrasse. Several of the operatives emerged carrying birdcages, sacks of seed and buckets of cage litter. They did what workmen everywhere do at the start of a new day, made a show of being busy while doing nothing useful. One of the men put down his bucket and cage with its two parrots. Others gathered round so that anyone watching from the upper windows could not see. They spoke volubly, sounding like workers looking for any excuse not to start what they were being paid for. The operative removed a parrot and pressed a button beneath its tail feathers to activate the camera and sound system. He handed the bird-shaped camera to a colleague, and repeated the process with the second bird, handing it to another colleague, then dipping a hand in the bucket and flicking a switch. Both bird-shapes immediately stretched their wings and flew to a nearby tree. The workmen began a show of trying to recover the parrots, running towards the tree, offering birdseed from their buckets.

In the van Morton and Mueller stood behind Quirke, watching the screens. Both cameras provided clear views of the street as well as the excited voices of the operatives.

'We're in business,' pronounced Morton.

He left the van, followed by Mueller. Both wore the peaked caps of crew chiefs the world over. There was a certain amount of foreman's consulting and pointing and nodding before they each went to front doors and ponderously explained that the regular aviary cleaning service had been involved in a breakdown and they had taken its place.

To each housekeeper Morton spoke loudly, the way a deaf person often does, and tilted his head slightly to one side, so as to hear better through his old-fashioned hearing aid. Faces nodded and hands closed the doors; no one seemed to remember this was the wrong day for the aviary service to call. No one asked why the cleaning service would be carrying birds that they had so stupidly allowed to escape.

'We're getting a perfect picture,' Quirke reported in Morton's earpiece.

'How about sound?' he murmured through his throat-mike.

'Ten-ten.'

Morton began to lumber up the street like a foreman, urging his men to catch those damned birds.

'Your shapes are now at number thirty-four. One's landed on a window sill. We're getting a good view of the bedroom. The maid's looking directly into the camera,' Quirke reported happily.

An operative once more dipped his hand into his litter bucket and the parrot flew into the next garden.

The van began to move slowly up Englestrasse. From the upper windows of several of the mansions, maids were watching the scene. One jumped back as a parrot landed on a window sill. She gave a cry of delight and opened the window to try to catch the bird.

Morton heard Quirke's urgent voice in his earpiece telling the operative to get that camera out of there – *now*. A moment later the maid's squeal of disappointment was loud in his ear. On both sides of the street operatives were releasing more camera-shapes.

Outside number 24 a Mercedes was parking.

Madam emerged and spoke into the security intercom. Waiting

for the gate to electronically open, she glanced down the street. A number of workmen in green coveralls were carrying empty birdcages back to a van. Others were dipping into their buckets and tossing handfuls of birdseed on the ground. Their foreman seemed to be angry with them, waving his hands. He pulled his cap peak lower over his face and strode back into the van. She walked up the pathway, her attaché case tucked under her arm like a purse.

'Everything OK?' Morton asked, entering the van, closing the door behind him. With the immediacy of action, his manner had become a settled and determined swiftness, as if the last of the introspections had lifted and the final gnawing doubt had gone.

'Some of the people are trying to call the regular service to raise hell,' grunted Mueller.

The technician crouched over the switchboard sounded majestically unruffled. 'No chance. The boys in Kaiser Allee have just reported they've put all the phones in the area temporarily out of order.'

Mueller joined Morton to watch Quirke making constant adjustments on his master control panel. He wore a headset and lip-mike. He didn't take his eyes from the screens as he explained. 'We now have eight camera-shapes around number twenty-four. The one on the chimney is simply to pick up sound. Same with the one at the mullioned window beside the front door. But the rest are just about in perfect position.'

A screen displayed a view of the living room. Quirke pointed to an adjoining screen. 'Vogel's study. The angle's a little high because the camera's perched on a branch.' Other screens displayed shots of the kitchen, the dining room and one of the upstairs bedrooms. All the rooms were empty. Through a speaker came a man's voice.

'Some breakfast, perhaps?'

'No, thank you. Just coffee, Herr Vogel.'

'Madam,' murmured Morton.

'And there they are,' said Quirke. They watched Vogel lead the way into the study and motion Madam to an armchair. Behind came a maid with a tray of cups and a coffee pot. They all heard Vogel curtly dismiss the maid, and saw him walk over and close the door behind her.

Quirke spoke quickly into his lip-mike. 'Whoever's working

the camera by the front door, move it to the back patio.' He turned to Morton. 'That way we'll get two views of the study, and better sound quality.'

Morton's quick nod of confirmation was the only response among the silent watchers of what was happening on the screen. The sound of coffee being poured by Vogel was loud.

Madam was sat in one of the deep leather chairs, enjoying the quality of the room. Apart from the antique desk, the study was furnished with the finest of hand-painted Bavarian furniture. Three of the walls were shelved from floor to ceiling with leather-bound books. The carpet was one of the very best Isfahan had produced.

She watched Vogel turn from the tray, two coffee cups in his hands. He put one down on a side table and handed her the other, giving him a further chance to appraise her.

He had read everything provided by the Bundesbank's formidable intelligence-gathering resources. Madam held directorships in over a hundred companies, several leaders in their fields. Her charity-giving was well documented, as was her interest in medical foundations. But she herself remained as enigmatic as she appeared now. Dressed in an unrelieved black two-piece suit and blouse, she remained in composed silence, sipping and looking at him expressionlessly as he sat in a chair opposite her.

'I'm sorry I missed your party in Malibu,' he said at last. 'But you must have heard what happened to me.'

'I did.'

'There will be other occasions, I am sure, when I will be glad to accept your invitations.'

'I'm glad.' It was like playing opposite a bad actor. The sheer badness of his performance decided her to do what Elmer always did. Cut to the chase. 'Well, shall we begin?' she asked.

He nodded gratefully. 'You said this was something important to me, personally.'

'It concerns your transplant,' Madam said calmly.

In the van they could all see that in the silence in the study, Vogel seemed frightened of himself. After a while he spoke. 'Very well. I shall not enquire how you learned of my condition. But it is correct. I need a new heart. How can you help me?'

She opened her attaché case, but did not remove anything. He smiled tightly at the negotiating ploy.

'First I want to talk to you about Sovocorp, Herr Vogel.'

He put down his cup with studied deliberation. He couldn't remember the company being listed as one where she was a director.

'May I ask what, exactly, your connection is with Sovocorp?'

'I own it. But that is not relevant.' It was best to get such matters out of the way at once. She looked at him dispassionately. 'How much do you know about Sovocorp, Herr Vogel?' For the briefest of moments those in the van saw his eyes go to the open attaché case.

'Enough to know it is not in the organ transplant business,' they heard Vogel say.

'As such, no. But in your case there is a connection.'

'What does that mean, Madam?'

'Before I explain, please answer my question, Herr Vogel. Sovocorp. How much do you know about it?'

A year ago the bank's analysts had prepared a position paper on Sovocorp. The company had been described as a financial predator. A small, malevolent smile crossed his lips. 'Only that the Bundesbank does not regard Sovocorp as a threat. It if becomes one, we shall deal with it.'

'And how will you do that, Herr Vogel?'

The smile was still there. 'You don't really expect me to tell you that? Is that why you have come here? On the pretext of my medical condition to find out our attitude to Sovocorp?'

In the study she continued to stare at him. She had not expected him to be this stupid. But then, brilliant men often were. She had learned that from observing Elmer's dealings. She sighed. 'Upon it will depend whether I will help you with a transplant.'

There was a stunned silence.

'What did you say?' asked Vogel eventually.

She repeated what she had said.

Vogel abruptly stood up. 'I think this meeting is over.'

She took a harsher tone. 'Please sit down, Herr Vogel, and stop being so childish. I have not come all this way for you not to hear me out. There is another matter. Of some negatives.' Once more she saw his eyes flick to the attaché case.

In the van everyone saw Vogel subside into his chair.

'*Mensch*,' murmured Mueller. 'The woman is a real killer.'

'In more ways than one, Hans-Dieter. In more ways than one,' Morton agreed.

Madam sipped her coffee in the lengthening silence. She deliberately ignored Vogel, her eyes glancing out of the door leading to the patio and the garden beyond. Someone had a good eye for landscaping. There was a parrot on the patio. And another on a branch of a conifer a little further away. They must be the birds those men were trying to catch.

'What negatives?' Vogel's voice was strained.

In the van they watched her produce an envelope from the attaché case and hand it to Vogel.

'She's playing a blinder,' Morton murmured. 'Knowing just when to vote with her actions.'

'These are only prints,' she explained. 'The negatives, as you will understand, are in a safe place.'

He removed the photographs from the envelope. They were the same as the ones he had been shown in the Stasi office in East Berlin. He shoved them quickly back in the envelope and looked at her. 'Where did you get these?' His voice was so low that she barely caught the words.

'Again, that is not important, Herr Vogel. Be glad that I have them and not somebody who would have taken them at once to the media or the authorities.'

'Match point,' Morton whispered.

'I can guarantee to return the negatives to you, Herr Vogel,' Madam said.

'Game, set and match,' said Morton. It wasn't hard to imagine what was on those negatives, only whether Vogel's preference was for boys or girls.

'What do you want?' Once more Vogel's voice was so low that the listeners in the van had to strain.

'I would like more coffee for a start, Herr Vogel,' Madam said, icily calm.

He walked to the desk and returned with the pot. She noticed the effort he was making to control the slight tremble in his hand. She waited until he returned to his chair before resuming. 'Herr Vogel, let me come to the point. Your private morals are of absolutely no interest to me. But I will use them, if needs be, to convince you to do what I want. Is that clear?'

No one in the van could be absolutely certain Vogel had nodded.

'Very well. What I require from you is for the Bundesbank and Sovocorp to co-operate fully together in the redevelopment of the old Soviet empire.'

There was silence.

'A perfect negotiating style,' Morton said to no one in particular. 'Step by step she's leading him to the point where everything she asks for will seem perfectly reasonable.'

'What do you want the bank to do?' Vogel asked at last.

She shifted slightly in her seat. 'Essentially, it is very simple. The Bundesbank has, under your guidance, already established itself as the leading financier to the former Soviet republics. From now on, the bank will work through Sovocorp. If you wish, this can be presented as a joint venture. As you will know from the position paper you received a year ago, Sovocorp is firmly established in all the republics. It will therefore be perfectly logical for the bank to enter into such an arrangement.'

'How did you know about the position paper?' he whispered. Who was her spy in the bank?

She gave a little shake of her head, the first sign of her impatience. 'Please, Herr Vogel. Let us not waste time on such trifling matters. You would hardly expect me to come here and not be fully briefed. What I am proposing is, as you well know, feasible. And the advantage to both the bank and Sovocorp is obvious. The details can be worked out later between your people and mine. But the basis will be that Sovocorp will receive fifty-one per cent of all net profits accruing from such an arrangement, plus service fees that will not be less than five billion DM annually.'

'You're not serious?' No one had ever dared to propose such outrageous terms.

'I'm very serious about everything I suggest, Herr Vogel,' she said with extraordinary calm.

Vogel watched her, not able to speak, not trusting himself to do so.

'*Mensch*,' said Mueller again.

'Now for the commercial,' Morton murmured.

When Madam spoke, her voice was different, lighter and somehow reassuring. 'See the positive side, Herr Vogel. Sovocorp can bring much to the table. And on the wider front, it will help the bank achieve order in the present void and chaos in the republics. That will place your country, if you will allow me to use the term, in pole position. The deal is a good one for the bank and Sovocorp. Again, if it will help you, I am perfectly willing to present the arrangement as being your creation. The important thing now is that you accept it – and do so in the right spirit.'

In the van they watched Vogel look around his study as if he could somehow escape.

'Well, Herr Vogel, do you accept?'

'And if I don't?'

'Almost certainly, you'll die. I can guarantee that no heart will become available to you. But if you co-operate, I can promise you a transplant.'

His eyes fixed on the bird on the patio. It must have escaped from one of the neighbouring aviaries. He rose from his chair and walked towards the door.

'Where are you going?' she asked sharply.

'To catch that bird,' he said, pointing. He needed time to think.

'Move the patio camera-shape, quick!' Quirke said into his lip-mike. The on-screen picture from the patio disappeared.

'It's flown into that tree,' they heard Madam say. 'Leave it, Herr Vogel. It'll make its way back to its cage when it's feeding time.'

Vogel returned to his seat, once more feeling the sheer power of her personality.

In the van they avidly continued to follow the play which Madam had written and directed as well as casting herself in a starring role.

'I need your response, Herr Vogel.'

'It seems I have little alternative,' he said in his bad actor's voice.

'Is that an acceptance?'

'Yes.'

'I am pleased to hear that, Dieter. If I may call you that, now that we are going to be close associates.'

This time Vogel had the good sense to say nothing.

'Now to your transplant. I am happy to tell you that a heart is available for you. But to receive it requires your return to California. There is a private hospital there where you will undergo all the preliminary tests. Then you will be flown to another place for the actual operation.'

'Why the two venues?'

'Dieter, please! You must try not to question everything. There are perfectly good medical reasons for this which you need not trouble yourself with. All you should be concerned with is that, ten days or so after your operation, you will be back here, a new man. Naturally you will need a period of convalescence, but during it you will be able to do light work. By then, I hope, the alliance between the bank and Sovocorp will be formally established.'

They heard his half-hearted protest. 'But for me to leave here, when there is so much planning to do—'

'You can delegate. Just leave orders for others to follow.'

They watched her once more forcing him to hold her gaze, and heard her voice continue to relentlessly drive forward. 'As I understand it, your medical condition is urgent. Therefore I have arranged for you to fly to California on my own plane. It has all the comforts you will need. I shall also arrange for a full medical team to be on board. And I shall accompany you.'

They saw her glance at her watch. 'I would like us to leave in a couple of hours. That should still allow you sufficient time to arrange matters at the bank.'

'My staff. What do I tell them?'

'They know about your heart condition. You need tell them nothing further. To do so would anyway be out of character for you, Dieter.'

They saw her offer him another smile. 'Your deputy is perfectly capable of running matters in the time you will be away. And your secretary can keep everyone at bay until you return.'

The defeat in his voice was plain to see on-screen even before his words reinforced it. 'You have thought of everything.'

'It is my job to do so, Dieter.'

'And the negatives?'

'You will receive them after your operation. I promise you that.'

'This clinic – where is it?'

They heard her sigh, almost good-humouredly. 'Dieter, please . . .'

In the van Morton gave a sideways glance at Mueller. 'She's really very, very good at what she does.' But it wasn't praise.

36

Through the window the sky was filled with dark and mountainous cloud. Dr Romer knew as he stared into the crowded conference room that soon the afternoon storm would come and once more bring relief to his body.

The pain was greater than usual, and had grown since Friedrich had awoken him at dawn with news of the disappearance of Weill and the helicopter, together with one of the whores. He had ordered the island thoroughly searched and a boat had checked the sea immediately around. His immediate fear had been that Weill had been kidnapped by his old paymasters – Mossad was certainly capable of that. Next he had considered whether the disappearance was somehow related to Morton. There was not a shred of evidence to support either possibility.

While the search had swiftly widened, Friedrich offered a convincing preliminary picture of what could have happened. On a drunken impulse, Weill had flown the whore to some idyllic place for a tryst; then, realising he was in trouble – that they both were – he had dumped the chopper and was probably halfway out of the country by now. Given the nature of the ground, Friedrich had added, there were a thousand places where he could have hidden the helicopter. A possibility, certainly. But he had to *know*. Friedrich, no one, would understand this need. It was an integral part of him, the well-spring of his inner driving force.

Now, hours later, only the dangerous spots of colour in his cheeks were evidence of its presence. Every member of staff not on duty had been summoned here. Latecomers stood two and three deep around the walls, or squatted on the floor before the podium. The only other person on the dais was Friedrich. He stood slightly to one side of Dr Romer's wheelchair.

Since its parking brakes had hissed softly, no sound had broken the oppressive silence. For a moment longer Dr Romer continued to search the faces, continued to listen for the slightest clue with the sharpness of the blind.

He could see surprise, concern and, in a few cases, almost shock. This confirmed his own conviction that none of the staff were implicated in what had happened.

Before coming here he had read Weill's file. There was nothing to suggest that behind those grave brown eyes of Weill's there lived a fool. And Weill would have known there could be only one consequence of his action. It was not only the unauthorised taking of the helicopter which made the matter serious; it was the fatal character flaw it revealed in Weill. The realisation had produced a small explosion of internal fury in Dr Romer. Until now he had trusted Weill. To lose him would be a great pity, but there was no way Weill could simply be dismissed. He would have to be killed. He felt his throat seize up with indignation: why did people behave so stupidly?

Now, when he finally spoke, the harshness in his voice was more pronounced than usual. 'Despite all efforts no trace has been found of the helicopter. So far no reason has emerged as to why Weill would have taken it, or a comfort—' he quickly corrected himself –'or a female member of staff.'

The whores always produced an ambivalent feeling in him. He recognised the necessity for them, but their presence reminded him of his own weakness; each time he used one to satisfy his sexual needs he was afterwards filled with self-loathing at having been reduced to that.

'This morning I flew to Managua to enlist the support of the authorities. They launched an immediate search and quickly established that the helicopter had not crossed any border. So it is still out there – somewhere.'

The first rain squall punctuated the silence. Instinctively he turned his head towards the window, watching the water stream-ing down the glass and already beginning to feel the pain ease in his body. Before coming here he had been told those fools in Managua were calling off the search. On one matter the Prime Minister was emphatic: no suspicious strangers had entered the country. Indeed, the only recent arrivals were a couple of American seismologists who were the advance members of the team due shortly to inspect the earthquake fault lines and the activity on Mount Masaya. The Prime Minister had laughed softly: the gringos had spent the night camping on the mountain's slopes, but they had not called in to say they had heard anything. So no point in looking there, Señor Medico.

The full force of the rainstorm began to lash the windows. 'Somebody must have heard the helicopter take off . . .'

He deliberately left the sentence incomplete, gazing into the room, his long head to one side, looking like a child studying insects in a jamjar.

At the back of the room a man stood up. He was small, pale-faced and with a slight paunch.

'Identify yourself,' Dr Romer ordered.

'Bergmann. Laboratory technician.'

'What can you tell me, Bergmann?'

'I had been working late on some blood cultures and was returning to the staff quarters when I heard the helicopter take off. It was about two in the morning. It flew towards the volcano, from where there was some activity. A glow in the sky and some vapour trails. The helicopter was quite visible for a while against the glow. Then it flew to the other side of the mountain. Shortly afterwards the engine stopped. I thought perhaps it had landed.'

'Why didn't you report this before?' Dr Romer stared at him intently.

'I didn't realise the helicopter was still missing.' Bergmann was fiddling with a button on his lab coat.

A shower of rain crashed against the window. 'Did it not strike you as unusual to hear a helicopter flying at night?' he asked with deadly patience.

'No, doctor, in all truth it did not. I often work late, so I assume others do the same.'

'A commendable attitude, Bergmann.' After the technician sat down, Dr Romer once more studied the faces before him. 'Did anyone else hear it take off?'

No one moved.

'I suppose you were all . . . asleep?' He turned to Friedrich. 'Have all the staff been interviewed?'

'Yes, Dr Romer.'

If anyone had heard, they were not going to admit it. Small truths could be as hard to establish as big ones. 'Very well,' Dr Romer said. 'So no one apart from Bergmann heard the helicopter take off.' He began to pace out his next words. 'What we have is that it took off, flew towards the volcano and disappeared.'

Once more a long and uneasy silence was the only response.

Dr Romer turned to a small group of men in flying coveralls, the clinic's pilots. 'Who checked the volcano?' he asked.

'I did.' The speaker was a tall, thin-faced man.

'Identify yourself,' Dr Romer snapped, raising his voice above the rain battering against the window.

'Sorry. Daley. Chopper pilot.' The Texas drawl was pronounced. It had been Weill's idea to recruit Americans who had run drugs across the Mexican border. But Dr Romer had never become used to their casual ways. He nodded for Daley to continue.

'As Bergmann says, there was some activity in the crater. But nothing serious enough to have given Weill a problem – even if he was stupid enough to fly directly over the crater. Anyway, he should have been able to get clear. When I checked the crater, everything seemed pretty docile. Just the usual vapours.'

'Did you see anybody on the slopes?'

Daley considered. 'Yeah . . . a couple of guys near the top. There was a jeep parked someways down the slope.'

Dr Romer felt a sudden tension. He experienced it flying sometimes, waiting for a crash that didn't happen. Why hadn't the American seismologists heard the helicopter?

'What were they doing?'

'Nothing, really.'

'What do you mean, *nothing*? Be precise, can't you?'

'Sorry, doctor. They were just, well, just standing there. Near the summit.'

'Did they have any equipment with them?'

'Not that I noticed. Just binoculars. I could see them looking at me. But that didn't strike me as unusual. They could have seen I was flying a search pattern and it probably made them curious.'

286

The tension was easing. 'Would Weill's helicopter have made more noise in the dark, Daley?'

Daley frowned. 'More noise? I'm not sure I follow.'

'At night doesn't everything sound louder?' Dr Romer asked patiently.

'I suppose so. But I've never really thought about it.'

He couldn't be certain if the tension was still there or not. 'You have something else to tell me?'

'Nope. That's about it.' Daley sat down.

Dr Romer patrolled every word he had heard as the rain lashed against the window; the storm was fiercer than usual. It seemed hardly credible that Weill would have risked flying over the crater, even if he had wanted to impress the whore. But why hadn't those seismologists reported hearing the helicopter? Perhaps they were heavy sleepers? Or they just didn't want to get involved? Something like this could detain them here for days; those fools in Managua made up for their ineptness with bureaucracy. He looked towards the pilots. 'Who was in charge of the search on the lake?'

A short, red-haired man stood up, still chewing on a matchstick. 'Austin. Chief Pilot. I ran a full grid search—'

'Can you stop chewing on that matchstick?'

Austin looked at Dr Romer almost in surprise, then removed the matchstick and stared at it for a moment before dropping it on the floor.

'Now, this grid search?' Dr Romer resumed, turning his head squarely towards Austin.

'It's designed to miss nothing. One leg I flew a north-south axis, the other east-west. Nowhere is the water deep. Our on-board echo-finder would have spotted something as big as a chopper.'

When Austin finished, Dr Romer sat in silence, once again seeing in his mind's eye the painstaking search pattern. Austin was right. Weill had not crashed into the lake. He turned to Friedrich. 'I want you to organise a search of the slopes of the volcano. The helicopter could have fallen into one of those ravines up there.'

Friedrich looked out of the window. 'We'll have to wait until morning. By the time we get up there now, it will be dark.'

Dr Romer nodded.

Friedrich stepped to the front of the podium and instructed all

287

available personnel to report to the airstrip at first light for the airlift to Mount Masaya.

Scrambling down the slopes of Mount Masaya, Danny and Gates had not spoken, concentrating only on keeping their footing. Plunging back into the jungle proper, they once more found themselves half-choked and covered with lava ash which, in the half-light, gave them a ghostly appearance. After they'd wiped the powdered sulphur from their faces and got into the jeep, Gates turned to Danny.

'That damned rotor spooks me. It probably belonged to that chopper you heard. But whatever he was doing flying over the crater in the dead of night, I don't want to hang around to find out. If there's enough active energy inside this mountain to bring down a chopper, it means it could blow any time.' He had needed to raise his voice above the rain that had started to hammer on the roof and the side of the jeep.

Danny turned to a briefcase on the floor. 'I still need to call Chantal and tell her about the island.'

The briefcase contained a Bosstars, a battery-powered solid-state transmitter/receiver which worked on the same principle as a normal satellite telephone, but with total in-built security as it operated through Hammer Force's own satellite.

'OK. But make it quick, otherwise we'll have to swim out of here.'

Water had started to drip between the seams in the roof as Danny ran up the aerial and slipped on a headset. He began to dial. The hammering on the roof increased. The Bosstars gave a line-busy signal. He redialled, this time the main Hammer Force switchboard. Static. The satellite had failed to connect. They both felt the jeep's wheels begin to slither under the force of the water sweeping down the mountainside.

'I'll get the engine started,' Gates yelled, clambering into the driving seat.

Danny redialled Chantal's number. This time she answered. 'Danny? Where are you?'

In as few words as possible he told her about the island being the possible location of the clinic.

Gates had the engine running and had begun to slowly drive the jeep down the track.

In Geneva Chantal was telling Danny: 'Stay on the line and I'll try to patch you into David. He's somewhere between Frankfurt and the airport in a BND van.'

Something crashed against the side of the jeep. Gates cursed as he saw a piece of lava the size of a cannonball bouncing on down the slope. A moment later the jeep slithered sideways, caught in a flow of mud. Gates expertly applied the brakes and spun the steering wheel. It was like driving on hot chocolate. Steaming mud continued to bubble up from the earth. Gates manoeuvred the jeep on to firmer ground, and once more felt the lugged tyres gain a full grip. Another piece of pumice glanced off the bodywork. He increased speed so that he was bouncing up and down in his seat.

Behind him Danny braced himself against the side of the jeep, cradling the Bosstars.

'Danny – this is David.' Morton's voice could hardly be heard above the full fury of the storm now lashing the jeep. 'How close can you get to the island?'

'I don't know yet.' The jeep's movement slammed the words out of Danny. The reception was breaking up.

'You're not wrong,' Morton assured him. 'I know it in my gut. Let me tell you what's been happening this end.'

The transmission beccame worse. 'Da . . . José . . . Sean Car . . . ommy . . . oon . . .' The rest was completely lost.

As Danny pulled off the headphones a piece of lava skeetered over the roof.

'Jesus H. Christ!' The wheel was spinning uselessly in Gates' hands. The jeep was being swept along, its tyres clear of the ground. The drag of the water was overpowering. He pushed open the door; already the flow was lapping against the hubcaps.

Danny hurled himself sideways as the trunk of an uprooted tree tore through the tailgate flap. Its additional weight forced the wheels back on to the ground. Gates slammed the gears into low ratio. Dragging the tree behind it, the jeep had travelled only a short distance when a jet-stream of muddy water spurted from a gap in the rock. It caught the jeep side-on with such force that he was hurled across the cab and out through the opposite side into the torrent. Winded and dazed, Gates was swept along with the now out-of-control jeep.

Danny managed to get to his feet, clamber past the trunk and

289

into the driving seat. He slammed the clutch into top gear. The jeep began to race like a speedboat through the water, the tree creating a coffee-coloured wake. He switched on the headlights. The beams provided only a restricted view because the nose of the jeep was tilted even more steeply forward as the angle of descent down the slope increased. There was no sign of Bill.

A moment ago, Gates had seen the jeep bearing down on him. Now its wheels were creating waves which were forcing him once again away from the vehicle. In seconds the gap had widened to yards. When he tried to stand and wade towards the jeep, the water was up to his thighs and threatening to sweep his legs away from under him. Rain lashed his body. He could dimly see Danny wrestling with the wheel. Then the jeep was moving even further away, towing the tree. It was now or never. Taking a deep breath, Gates plunged into the torrent and struck out with all his remaining energy. Above his head hurtled another piece of lava. He heard it crash on the roof of the jeep. Trying not to swallow the foul-smelling water, he swam on.

Danny glanced over his shoulder. A huge black boulder now rested in the back of the jeep, reducing the vehicle's momentum. With the loss of speed steam began to emerge through the vents in the side of the bonnet as the water reached the hot metal of the block and continued to rise up through the engine compartment.

Thank God, Danny thought: if this had been a petrol engine it would have stalled by now. But the powerful diesel continued to work even though water had reached the doorposts. His feet on the pedals were already submerged, and the weight in the back had become even more pronounced. He had a vision of the rock splitting open the floor and dropping through the chassis, wrecking the drive shaft. He continued to look and call for Bill.

Half blinded by the mud, Gates plunged towards the tree trailing behind the jeep. His hands encountered leaves. They slipped through his grasp and his body sank back into the water. He again hurled himself forward, feeling the mud sucking him back, pulling him down. His hand grasped a branch. He could see it bowing like an angler's rod under the strain. He hung on, too exhausted to do anything but allow himself to he pulled through the water. He began to slowly work his way up the trunk. He could feel his strength ebbing and his arms threatened to come out of their sockets. Water streamed from his clothes and boots as he inched himself towards the tailgate. He flopped into the back of the jeep, finding further progress blocked by the chunk of lava. He sprawled against the stone, too tired to call out. After a while he managed to crawl forward into the front.

'I'm too old for this,' he gasped, falling into the passenger seat. Danny glanced at him in relief.

The water was now around their calves. Suddenly they felt the wheels touch bottom again. They had been swept on to a ridge. The weight in the back tilted the jeep's nose skywards so that its headlights were like two searchlights. Water began to pour out of the cabin. The sound of the engine grew stronger. The wheels found a grip, and like some badly mauled animal, the jeep lurched forward, its engine bellowing defiantly as it moved off the ridge and headed down the slope. To their left the flash flood poured into a ravine.

Shortly afterwards the rain ceased. An hour later, without further incident, they reached the metalled road at the base of the volcano.

'Holy Christ,' Gates whispered, after Danny had pulled into the verge.

They sat in silence, saying nothing more for a while. Then Danny walked to the back of the jeep to inspect the damage. The Bosstars was crushed beyond repair. Pieces of pumice had shredded their rucksacks. But their weapons remained intact. There was no sign of their binoculars. However, the suitcases with their spare clothes had somehow survived.

'Bill,' he called out, lugging the case into the open. 'You'd better get changed before you catch pneumonia.'

Only when he had stripped and put on fresh clothes did Gates speak. 'Holy Christ,' he said again. 'I never want to do that again.'

For the next hour they worked in silence to clear away the tree and manhandle the rock out of the jeep. By the time they had finished it was pitch-black. It would be another hour before the moon rose behind the crater.

Gates lit a cigarette and squatted on the ground. They both looked back up the mountain. There was no sign of life. Not even a pinprick of a glow came from the summit.

'Sonofabitch,' Gates said, climbing behind the wheel.

They drove in weary silence towards Managua.

37

Standing in the window of the safe house across the street from the beach at Santa Monica, Tommy cradled the phone against his shoulder, watching the ocean and waiting for Lester Finel to return. A moment ago, in Geneva, Lester had broken off to take another call. The green waves were flecked with spume, a surfer's dream. At this early-evening hour there were only a couple of kids riding their boards, stick figures against the setting sun.

His view was slightly distorted. The Housekeepers – the Hammer Force division responsible for all safe houses – had coated the window with a clear varnish to protect against any bugging device.

Lester was speaking to someone about Suto and Gonzales. Tommy could tell he was not pleased because he was being overly polite, saying 'sir' a lot to the man he was talking to. 'I need those files of yours now, sir, otherwise I'm going to have to request them through the Secretary-General's office,' Lester was saying.

Tommy turned back into the apartment's living room. As with all safe houses, the furniture seemed to have come from a garage sale: nothing matched. A few cheaply framed prints hung on the walls. On the dining table was a computer and terminal screen, a shredder and a fax machine.

Lester was saying, 'Thank you, sir. That's very good of you. I'll make sure the right people know about your help, sir . . .'

A couple of hours ago he'd faxed Lester the list of doctors' names Anna had given him. Afterwards he'd gone to the deli down the block, and spent an hour jogging off the cholesterol and thinking about her. He knew women found him attractive. The combination of his boyishness and aloofness seemed to intrigue them. Except he hadn't been aloof with Anna. Perhaps, he decided, he had been just too boyish.

Lester's words brought him back to the present. 'Sorry about that, Tommy. This new breed of bureaucrats have to be schmooshed even more than the last lot.' He cleared his throat. 'Your list. Problem. Every name. They're all dead.' It was Lester's strength to not bother with middle gears.

Tommy broke the dead silence. 'What do you mean – dead?'

'What's with today? Don't I make myself clear? Dead, Tommy. As in stopped breathing. Cardiac arrest. Heart failure. Brain dead. Natural causes dead. Just dead.'

'I don't want to sound stupid, Lester, but are you telling me that all the doctors on that list have died?' Tommy asked incredulously.

'Buried. Cremated. Gone.'

'How is that possible?'

Lester swallowed his impatience. 'No problem, Tommy. Mostly they died out on the east coast. New York, Boston, Philadelphia. A couple in Florida. One in the mid-West. Another in Alaska. All a long way from California.'

'And these people in the clinic assumed their identities?'

'You have it,' said Lester, all enthusiasm again.

'But how? Aren't there checks, records? Computers to keep an eye on that sort of thing?'

'Don't blame computers, Tommy. It's the human element. Nobody in California bothered to check.'

Tommy walked back to the window. The kids were riding the crest of another wave.

'When doctors die, isn't it the same as when they are struck off? Their affiliations get cancelled? And everybody gets to know? Isn't that how it works?'

Lester was unperturbed. 'In theory, yes. In these cases, no. They went into the local dead files and that was it.'

'But don't the names on those files get sent to some central register? In Washington, maybe? Or wherever?' Tommy demanded.

Lester was talking before Tommy had quite finished. 'That's the point. My computers discovered not. Don't know why. And probably never will. Some of the names go back years. Today, some of those doctors would be in their seventies, even eighties.

293

Ever heard of someone that old working at the cutting edge of medicine?'

Tommy said he hadn't. 'So who are these people?'

Lester sounded enthusiastically appalled. 'Mean you haven't worked it out? Simple enough. Your doctors have been struck off, or blacklisted for some other reason. No matter.'

'And given false IDs,' Tommy completed.

'On the button,' Lester agreed.

There was silence. In his mind's eye Tommy could see Lester making that weird hand movement.

'I'll let everyone know,' Lester said, hanging up.

Tommy's phone rang almost at once.

'So there you are,' the CCO said brusquely. 'The Colonel wants Anna out of that clinic – pronto. Then you're both to get down to San José to join Johnny Quirke and his boys.'

'San José as in where?'

'As in Costa Rica. It's the jump-off point. Things are moving, Tommy.'

Tommy put down the phone. The surfers were coming off the beach. He wondered if Anna surfed. Then he wondered how he could get a message to her. She had said not to phone. But to drive up there would take too long. He dialled information and asked for the Gift of Life number, then dialled again.

A pleasant woman's voice announced in his ear: 'Gift of Life. How can I help you?'

'I'd like to speak to Miss Anna Cruef.'

'Is she a patient, sir?'

'No. A member of staff. A nurse.'

'Staff are not permitted to receive calls.'

'This is an emergency. Her father has been killed.'

'One moment, please.'

There was a click on the line. 'Director's office.'

'I'd like to speak to Anna Cruef. It's her brother calling. It's a family emergency. Our father has been killed in an auto accident.'

'I'm sorry, but Nurse Cruef can't be reached right now. But I will see she receives your message as soon as possible. Is there a number where she can reach you?'

'No, not really. I'm just leaving to fly to the scene of the accident.'

'Where was your father killed, Mr Cruef?'

'Costa Rica. He'd just driven out of San José airport.'

'I'm sorry to hear that, Mr Cruef. I'll make sure your sister gets the message.'

'Tell her it's important she joins me in Costa Rica as soon as possible.'

'I'll tell her.' The voice was gone.

Tommy put down the telephone. A death in the family was always the most urgent signal to withdraw. He called the airport information to check the next flight to San José and booked two seats. There was enough time for Anna to make the flight.

In the Director's outer office, the secretary pressed the intercom. 'He's called, Dr Littlejohn.' She told him what Tommy had said.

'Thank you, Peggy.'

The VDU screen on his desk showed Madam's flight from Frankfurt was forty minutes ahead of schedule. The hour needed to refuel would be sufficient time to run a medical slide rule over Dieter Vogel. Then he would be on his way to Managua – unaware of the problem which had arisen over his transplant. A while ago a message had come from Dr Romer that the heart held in reserve for Vogel had been transplanted into another patient: was there one available at Gift of Life? If so could it be put on the plane?

Dr Littlejohn turned to the keyboard and began to type swiftly on to the screen. 'Your request for an organ. Will send you live donor.'

After pressing the transmission button he turned back to the staff file he had been reading. When he finished he picked up the phone and dialled an internal number, speaking in the soft, sibilant voice patients found so reassuring.

Anna completed laying out a full complement of surgical instruments for the next day. The final operation had taken Dr Lasswell longer than everyone had anticipated; the surgeon had experienced difficulty in controlling the bleeding points after the heart bypass. Then, towards the end of the closing procedure, he had been summoned to take a telephone call. When he'd returned, Anna had noticed he seemed more tense than usual. Once their work was completed, other members of the team had quickly followed him from the OR, leaving her to clear away and lay up. She didn't mind; it fitted in with her plan.

Now, an hour later, she left the OR and walked quickly down the corridor, which at this hour was deserted. At the far end was the door which led down to the basement where she'd discovered the room where staff records were kept. She had decided to return there now and search for further clues for Tommy to follow up. She pushed open the door and closed it behind her, standing for a moment to allow her eyes to adjust to the surroundings.

The stairs were made of metal and painted the same dark blue as the cinder-block walls. There was an emergency light bulb on each landing which made the intervening shadows seem that much deeper. Grasping the handrail firmly she began to descend.

There were five flights down to the basement and the further she went, the more the walls seemed to crowd in upon her. She shook her head, irritated with herself that an old childhood fear had found its way to the surface. As a teenager she had not liked to go down to the cellar at home for one of the boxes in which her father kept his old papers. Sensing her unease, he would come and stand in the doorway leading down to the cellar. Then, as now, she had constantly glanced up to be reassured by his presence before continuing down the steep staircase she remembered being as poorly lit as this stairwell.

Once more she leaned over the handrail to peer down. The spiralling stairs were lost in collapsing perspective. She turned and glanced upwards. And froze.

The door at the top of the stairwell had suddenly opened and closed. Somebody was coming down, moving with infinite caution. Each deliberate footstep gave a metallic echo. A man's shoes. She forced herself to look up again. Three flights above her she had a glimpse of white OR clogs, and dark blue scrub-suit trousers. As the figure passed directly beneath a landing light bulb she could make out the bold red stripe painted on the sides of the clogs. Only Dr Lasswell marked his shoes like that.

She looked around for a means of escape. On each landing was an emergency exit. The landing below was only a few steps away. Above her Dr Lasswell's footsteps drew closer. She knew she would be unable to explain to him what she was doing here. Moving as quickly as she dared she reached the landing. She tried the emergency door handle. It turned but did not open. She remembered the area on the other side was Administration; at this hour the offices would be empty and there would be no need to keep the door unlocked.

Dr Lasswell's footsteps had stopped. She forced herself back against the wall, trying to decide whether she would throw caution to the wind and run on down to the basement. From there she could take a service elevator and escape before he could catch up. The chances were he would not recognise her in the gloom.

There was a sudden shaft of light from above, then the sound of the door opening on the landing above. Darkness again as it closed. She waited, holding her breath, listening. Nothing disturbed the silence of the stairwell. She slowly let out her breath, relaxing. One of the nurses had said Dr Lasswell was a keep-fit fanatic. He'd probably been working late in his office and instead of taking the elevator had used the stairwell to reach one of the patients' floors. She continued her descent.

After the stairwell the basement corridor was brightly lit from neon strips suspended beneath the tangle of ceiling pipes. An arrow on a wall had a word painted above it: Autopsy. The records room was next door. She followed the arrow, the sound of her footsteps lost in the gurgle from the pipes. She turned a corner; the corridor, like the stairwell, seemed to go on endlessly.

The room containing the records was halfway along. From her previous visits she had discovered that a spare door key was kept above the jamb. Reaching up she retrieved the key and inserted it in the lock. She glanced both ways along the corridor. Only the pipes disturbed the silence. She turned the key and opened the door.

Inside the room stood Dr Lasswell. Without a change of expression he pointed the bulbous-nosed barrel of the gun in his hand towards her and pulled the trigger.

38

A little before midnight Dr Steven Krill parked his jeep at the edge of a clearing overlooking Lake Nicaragua. Dressed in a sweatshirt, shorts and a pair of scuffed loafers, he sat for a moment, listening. Twice on the drive here he had thought he had heard another vehicle behind him. Now only the familiar sounds of the jungle filled his ears. He must be more jumpy than he realised.

He caught his reflection in the driving mirror and did not much like what he saw. His eye sockets were sunken and the skin, taut as a drum, gave his face a skeletal appearance. Performing three transplants in fourteen hours would have taken its toll on even a younger man, and even without losing O'Neill.

As such, the gang leader was no loss; none of his patients were. He had no illusions that they were any more than the scum of the earth. But these past six months he had deposited in his Swiss bank account more money than he could ever have hoped to earn in London in five years. Another year and he would be out of here, free to do what he wanted. To go where he chose, into all the bars in the world, to drink when he liked, to order his life as he wanted. In another year he would have discharged his commitments, paid in full and down to the last suture. Then no one could touch him with their silent, accusatory stares. He knew his staff suspected what lay behind the extra little effort it took him to hold a knife, tie off a bleeding point, do all those things that nowadays took a fraction longer while he waited for his hand to steady. But soon he would not have to bother any more to tense his wrist muscles, force his brain to concentrate. Soon he would be free.

For a start that would mean not having to drive out here in the dead of night to get a drink. It was both humiliating and degrading having to do so. But one of the terms of his contract forbade him alcohol. Such a restriction was something no man should have to endure, and shortly after arriving on the island he had made an agreement with Weill to supply him with whisky. The security chief obtained it in Managua. The stuff tasted watered, and he paid many times more than for a vintage malt in London, but it was better than drinking lab alcohol mixed with fruit juice.

It was Weill who had first brought him here and shown him where he'd buried the old water cooler to store the bottles. Tonight, more than ever, he needed a drink. That business with O'Neill had been bad. He should have spotted there was something wrong while O'Neill had been in the OR.

Was that why Romer had sat there like a bird of prey? That was when he appeared at his most threatening and ominous, as if time no longer existed, as if he had become an all-seeing eye, aware of everything, missing nothing, only waiting to see if you had reached the pure, perfect concentration you always needed when trying to save life. One of the problems with Romer was that he had never been a surgeon, never had to make a life-or-death decision. Had never known the fear of failure.

From that fear, nurtured like a well-spring during those minutes fighting for O'Neill's life, had come the other fear which still gripped him. This fear was all to do with having his need for alcohol once more bring him down. Perversely, only the whisky kept it at bay. Until he had his first drink it would continue to attack his will and his nervous system like a ravenous cancer. It was there now, alive in him and silently saying he could not overcome it alone, that only alcohol would banish the fear. And it told him he had not quite run away from feeling. Krill got out of the jeep and stood for a moment looking out across the lake. The moon was rising behind the volcano, its summit hidden by the wreath of cloud that seemed to sit there permanently at night. Thank God he wouldn't be one of those in the morning who would have to search its slopes. Romer had become obsessive about Weill and that bloody helicopter. What the hell did its disappearance matter? Romer could buy a whole fleet of helicopters with the fees he charged.

And it was more than a bloody chopper that had gone up the spout. It was his whole deal with Weill. How was he going to get his gargle now? Maybe one of the pilots would like to earn a little extra? All he'd have to do would be to drop a few bottles into his flight bag each time he went to Managua. Austin, maybe? Or Daley? Either looked the type who would like to put one over on Romer just for the hell of it.

You could get awfully tired of the doctor. No sense of humour was another of his problems. If you fitted a pair of jackboots to those stumps he'd be a doppelgänger for an old SS recruiting poster. Yet there'd been fleeting moments when he'd glimpsed something else in Romer's eyes, the hint of a beacon fire on a dark, treacherous shore, calling him home, home. Then it had been just as quickly extinguished, leaving only that look which could send a chill rattling along your backbone.

Krill walked across the clearing and knelt before a tree stump. He spread his hands, palms down, moving them slowly over the ground as if they were mine detectors. It had become a game, something to heighten the anticipation. When his right hand felt something hard beneath the earth, he brushed away the leafmould to expose the top of the cooler and lifted the lid. The moon had disappeared into the volcano's wreath, plunging everything into darkness. He felt around inside the container. His hand encountered only the jar of breath-freshener tablets. The moon began to climb above the cloud. He stared into the cooler. There should have been two bottles.

He felt the strength draining from his body. In the undergrowth life was pulsing normally. Yet here, within his carapace, everything had stopped except for his fear. He shut his eyes, trying to force himself to be calm, trying to keep in a distant corner of his mind what had happened. The reality burst into his consciousness.

Cursing softly, he stood up and looked around him. The jungle stared back, strangely alien now. He waited for his breathing to settle, rotating his neck to free up the tension. He knew he was only barely functioning. He froze. From behind him, on the far side of the clearing, had come the soft but unmistakable sound of a footfall. Even as he moved to lower the lid on the cooler, a voice stopped him.

'Good evening, Dr Krill.' Friedrich stepped into the clearing. 'I believe these are yours.' In each hand he held a bottle.

The words burst the carapace. The fear gave way to blind anger.

Krill dropped his deltoids like a boxer flexing his shoulders before coming out of his corner, his mind already searching for a knock-out blow. He stepped towards Friedrich. 'How dare you spy on me! When Dr Romer hears—'

Friedrich gave a short laugh. 'Please, Dr Krill. Threatening me will do you no good. And I don't think you will wish to discuss the matter with the Doktor. You see, I am aware of your employment contract. And, of course, also of your arrangement with the lately departed and, for me, unlamented Weill. Unhappily for you, being the tidy man he was, he left a full record of that arrangement.'

Krill could suddenly see possibilities in the face before him. 'What is it you want?'

When he had followed Krill here, there had been no clear plan in Friedrich's mind. Now, staring into this gaunt face, with its permanent purple smudges beneath eyes which glittered like anthracite, everything fell into place. Friedrich spoke softly, his professional voice. 'Would you like to discuss a new arrangement, Dr Krill?'

Krill could feel his anger showing through; it was like glimpsing the blazing thing behind the mask of sanity. He forced himself to become calmer, introducing in his voice the coldness of a final diagnosis. 'Are you trying to blackmail me, Friedrich?'

Friedrich stepped closer. He could sense the wheels going round in Krill's head as he tried to assess the situation. 'Blackmail? Such a hard word, Dr Krill.'

'Don't bait me, Friedrich. Remember who I am.'

'And you remember I'm not one of your staff,' Friedrich snapped, momentarily losing his façade of tolerant calm. He had never felt at ease with Krill.

Krill tried to look away from Friedrich. His voice had been too high; he should have said nothing. Instead he felt compelled to plunge recklessly on. 'Would you please come to the point? I somehow don't feel you actually intend to report the matter to Dr Romer.'

Friedrich smiled, a quick, perfunctory smile. 'Very well, Dr Krill. According to Weill's records, you have paid him fifteen thousand American dollars. I will require four times that amount. And all to be paid in cash, in the same currency. Let us call that a continuation fee.'

For the moment Krill had the feeling that both Friedrich's eyes were controlled by one optic muscle. 'That's sixty thousand dollars,' he protested. He knew his resistance was partly a weak-willed thing, like the tremble in his hands.

'That is also precisely half of what you are paid for one week's work. Which still leaves you fifty-one weeks' income to bank in Geneva. So let us not haggle.' He looked hard at Krill. 'Are you, by any chance a Jew, Dr Krill?'

'What?' Krill shook his head. 'No. Why do you ask?' What the hell was Friedrich driving at now? But the blades inside his head had altered their pitch, mashing his brain in a different direction. And this bloody tremble was like a rictus.

'Your name is unusual for an Englishman.' He spoke as if he knew all about unusual names.

'What's your game, Friedrich?' This was like trying again and again to score directly in front of the posts, and failing. They kept piling into you and you had the feeling you'd never hold on to the ball, never put the winning points on the board.

'I don't like Jews,' Friedrich said softly.

'Fascist, are you?'

'Jews deceive people,' Friedrich said, sounding like a man who dealt only in things he had experienced.

A month before flying out for the last time from East Berlin, he had killed a Jew, an informer for Mossad. He had taken him to one of the interrogation cellars after others had decided he would reveal no more. There he had gone to work. He'd whipped the Jew until he collapsed, until the flesh on his back was flayed to the bone. Then he had handcuffed him to a hook in the ceiling, so that he hung like a side of beef. Afterwards he had heated the knife in the gas burner each cellar had for the purpose, and sliced open the Jew's guts, spilling his entrails on the floor. Sometimes he still dreamed of those days.

'Not my problem, Friedrich.'

'Not your problem, no.' He spoke in a tone suggesting centuries of hatred had been compressed.

'Weill betrayed his own people,' he continued in that same soft voice.

Krill could feel his eyes burning, his throat dry, his skin greasy. He needed that drink more than ever. He forced his voice to sound polite.

'My father was Dutch. The Krills are an old Protestant family, Friedrich.'

Friedrich allowed himself a moment's pause. 'I'm glad to hear that, Dr Krill.' He made it sound as if he was prepared to introduce a ceasefire in their relationship. Krill was still listening. But Friedrich was not in the least insisting or rushing matters. No one understood better than him what it was like to possess the impatience of a Krill to find out what was going to happen. A laboured manner would only add to Krill's anxiety, making him all the more ready to accept the proposition.

'Now to the other part of our arrangement. The new charge will be two hundred dollars for each bottle.'

'That's outrageous! Absolute bloody daylight robbery!' He was no longer angry.

'Spoken like a true Englishman, Dr Krill. But if you think about it, the price is reasonable. You have a new situation now. If I may say so, it is rather like surgery. Every time a patient goes into your operating room, it is more expensive.'

Friedrich nodded towards the water cooler. 'In matters of delivery, I think we can continue as before.'

He stepped closer to Krill and politely extended the bottles. 'You may have these as you have already paid for them. But I will expect our financial arrangement to be completed within twenty-four hours. Within twelve hours of that, your supply will continue as before. I understand you had a weekly order of seven bottles?'

Krill nodded.

Friedrich bore in a little harder, using the same slow way of speaking. 'That's two thousand eight hundred dollars. Let's round it up to three thousand. That'll cover incidentals. Transport, that sort of thing. Agreed?'

He paused, but Krill did not speak and he took his silence for tacit agreement. 'I will leave you, then, to enjoy your drink in peace. Good night, Dr Krill. I've enjoyed doing business with you.' Friedrich turned and walked from the clearing; a little later came the sound of his jeep driving away.

Only then did Krill take the first long swallow that warmed his gullet and belly. Afterwards he closed his eyes, digging his knuckles into the sockets and kneading them slowly. Now, more than ever, he needed to get drunk. He opened his eyes and swallowed another mouthful; the raw spirit burned in his stomach like a torturer's poker. This time the alcohol had not immediately eased the fear or banished the realisation that he had handled things badly. He should have exerted his authority over Friedrich – browbeaten him, the way he did his own staff. Instead he had let the miserable Kraut dominate him. The more he thought about it the more his fury increased.

He sat on the ground, swallowing, not bothering to wipe away the whisky that dribbled down his chin. But at last the fear was going. There was now nothing, save a dull empty feeling as the alcohol shut down his senses.

The bottle was almost empty when he noticed, far across the lake, lights moving across the sky. It took him a while to recognise them: aircraft navigation lights. He wondered blearily who would be flying at this time of night.

Then, much closer, he saw a glow appear in the side of the volcano, just below the summit. As he watched the glow detached itself, and began to travel much faster than the navigation lights, out over the lake in a noiseless, graceful arc before plunging into the water. He stared at the volcano, not quite believing what he had seen or heard.

He stood up and walked to the edge of the lake. The water, which a moment ago had been as flat as a millpond, seemed to have been stirred. A wave lapped against the shore and he had to step quickly back to avoid getting his feet wet. In all the times he had come here, he had never known the water do this.

There was a pungent smell of lava. To have created a wave and a stench like this, what had shot out from the volcano must have been huge. So what the hell? Nothing to worry about, Romer kept saying that. The hell with Romer. The hell with everybody except Friedrich. The Kraut would keep him supplied with all that mattered.

He finished up the bottle, then, as with all the others he had drunk, tossed it into the lake. A moment later another surge of water came towards him, faster and more powerful. It broke against the shore, then rushed into the clearing, carrying with it several bottles he had previously dumped.

He looked at them, stupefied. Then he began to pick up the empties and toss them into the lake, watching them sink beneath the surface. This time they did not reappear. And the water's surface had returned to its flat, unbroken appearance.

Suddenly he was too damned tired – and a little drunk – to care what was going on. Time to stop; thank God he could still do that. Time to sober up.

He went to the lake's edge and lay down on his stomach. The smell of lava was stronger. He took a deep breath and plunged his head under the water. He held it there as long as he could. Withdrawing, he gasped, then sucked in another lungful of air and repeated the process several times. If not exactly sober, he was not as drunk as he had been.

From the cooler Krill removed the jar of tablets, shook a few into his palm and began to chew them. The strong liquorice taste would disguise the smell of alcohol. He replaced the unopened whisky bottle, covered the cooler with moulder, then walked back to the jeep.

Across the water he could see the aircraft navigation lights on the far side of the volcano.

39

From the co-pilot's seat in the Lear Morton had estimated the fireball was about a mile away on the port side and travelling in eerie silence at twice their speed as it sliced through the night sky, before plunging into the lake. The pilot called the tower at Las Mercedes, Managua's international airport, to report what they'd seen, and a sleepy voice replied that there was nothing on his radar, adding they were clear to land. The jet was one of two Hammer Force maintained on the west coast. Their pilots were former US Air Force combat veterans who had flown in and out of Sarajevo or on combat missions in the Gulf War.

'What the hell was it?' the pilot asked.

'Lava. Let's take a look on the way in.'

'I thought a volcano is supposed to sound like the end of the world when it pops.'

'Not always. Sometimes the energy force is released so suddenly there isn't time for the usual sound-effect to form.'

'That's more dangerous?'

'Can be.'

'And you still want us to get close?'

'Now that some of the energy is released there shouldn't be a problem.'

'I'll take your word for it.'

The Lear approached Mount Masaya from the west. In the moonlight the jungle was ghostly white as far as they could see. There was no sign from where the fireball had emerged.

'It looks like it snowed down there,' the pilot said.

'Lava ash,' Morton explained. Among much else since leaving Frankfurt, he had immersed himself in the information on volcanic behaviour one of Hammer Force's librarians had sent by data transfer to him aboard Concorde.

'Look at that.' The pilot pointed to a gauge. 'The outside air temperature's shot up thirty degrees since we've been here.'

They watched the needle continue to climb. Then, as the volcano fell behind them, the gauge returned to a normal reading.

The pilot shook his head. 'It must be like a pressure-cooker down there. Somebody had better put out an advisory.'

'No point. That'll just bring people flooding.' The last thing he wanted was to be overrun by rubbernecks.

Five minutes later, the Lear touched down at Las Mercedes. Morton settled back while the pilot went through the landing procedures. In the distance, the lights of the terminal building glowed weakly. Here everything was on low wattage. During the flight he'd read everything he needed to know about Nicaragua: the place was like a dark pit in which the worst of Nature combined with bloody revolution and wholescale corruption to drag down a people into the most abject poverty and hardship. He had paid special attention to the material he had asked for on climatic conditions, noting how, unfailingly every afternoon, rainstorms swept down from the volcanic peaks of Costa Rica on to Lake Nicaragua. There was enough electricity in those storms to knock out even a sophisticated electronic defence system.

When Lester discovered that the only detailed map of the Solentiname Archipelago had been made by a priest going from island to island preaching liberation theology until the Pope finally had him silenced, he'd called a monsignor in the Vatican's Secretariat of State who had faxed him a copy. Lester had sent it on to Concorde. The map described thirty-seven of the islands. The priest had been forbidden to visit the thirty-eighth. On the map it was marked as part of a *zona militaire*.

Morton had called the Secretary-General of the United Nations in New York. In their short conversation he had come as near as he ever did to saying that as far as anything could be certain, he was. And the Secretary-General, being the man he was, had declared his understanding by asking no questions. Since then, during the flight, Morton had been kept fully informed on what was happening.

Technicians on board Concorde, on the ground at Los Angeles, had monitored the 747 bringing Madam and Vogel to California. From the plane she had spoken to someone called Pierre in Malibu; telling him and someone she referred to as another darling boy, Dirk, to be ready to join the flight when it arrived.

Lester's programmers had discovered that in the past twelve months the aircraft had twice landed at the airstrip ajoining the Gift of Life Transplant Center, and that Global Transporter's TriStars regularly flew patients in and out. Each time the TriStars made refuelling stops in Managua.

As the Lear turned off the runway on to a taxiway, the pilot asked the tower for parking instructions. The same sleepy voice said they could park where they liked at this hour. Morton wondered how much this casual indifference played its part in making sure everyone here on the ground looked the other way while those patients were off-loaded. Then he began to run through his mind again everything else that had happened.

First, the Secretary-General had called the German Chancellor and informed him of Vogel's destination, why he was going there and what he had promised Simone Montan. At Morton's suggestion, the Secretary-General had added that the BND would provide all the necessary taped evidence. When the Chancellor overcame his shock he had reacted like the shrewd politician he was: *Natürlich*, Germany would co-operate fully. But there must be no publicity and absolutely no prosecution of Vogel or any Bundesbank staff found to be implicated in dealings with Sovocorp. Such a public disclosure could have the most damaging political repercussions. The Chancellor had not said so, but he had meant for himself. Instead, Vogel would sign a full admission, which would be a guarantee of his own silence, and retire from business life. The government spin doctors would create a suitable reason for his departure. *Natürlich*, there would be no mention of his transplant or where it had been obtained. *Natürlich*.

The Secretary-General had then called the other leaders of the big seven industrial nations. With the German Chancellor's undertaking already in place, together with a substantial number of Deutschmarks pledged, he explained what he required. It was a mark of the great respect he commanded, unlike his recent predecessors, that he obtained immediate agreement.

Matters had continued to move swiftly. The Secretary-General had called the president of each Soviet republic and briefed them one by one. All had agreed to call an immediate halt to all Sovocorp activities. Each call concluded with the same promise: the big seven would not only underwrite the losses arising from that halting, but would inject further substantial sums into the local economies.

A similar undertaking of financial support had been given to the President of Costa Rica, where the Hammer Force 747 had arrived.

His last call had been to the President of the United States. As well as providing America's portion of the required finance, the President agreed to instruct his new Director of the FBI to post sufficient agents around the Malibu mansion, Drug Rehab and and the Gift of Life Transplant Center. They would make no further move until Morton gave the word

Meanwhile, Secretary of State Wallace had first telephoned the United States Vice-consul in Managua and instructed him to cooperate fully – a short call – and then made a far longer call to the President of Nicaragua. Secretary Wallace explained what he had just learned and how the matter was going to be dealt with. He had used his best crisis-management voice to give the President two choices. He could either become the Saddam Hussein of Central America, a pariah among all civilised nations, or he could receive a substantial American aid package. And, of course, all the credit going for acting so decisively. He would become a leader respected far outside his own controlled media. The icing on an already rich cake had been the offer of a state visit to Washington. When? the President had asked. As soon as this was over, the Secretary had promised. The President of Nicaragua had said he was glad to be of service.

The pilot brought Morton back to the present. 'Another incoming for you.'

Morton once more flicked the button on his headset and the voice of Sean Carberry was in his headphnes.

'Tommy's just arrived. But without Anna. He waited until the last moment, then called the hospital one more time. Someone said she'd got his message, but she was still in theatre. They seem to be working her pretty hard. There's another flight due from LA around daybreak. Tommy's going to meet it.'

'Any reason to worry?' Morton asked.

'None as far as Tommy can see.'

'Fine. But I want him and everyone else up on the border by mid-morning. We only have a thirty-minute window with that weather.'

'No problem,' Carberry said carefully. 'Gives us plenty of time to check the microlites.'

As Morton broke the connection, the engine whine faded. He could see Danny and Gates walking towards the Lear. With them was a mournful figure in a dark suit. Teeling had the look of someone who couldn't still quite believe he was caught up in something like this. Morton turned to the pilot. 'I'll be gone a couple of hours.'

'You want me to off-load those boxes?'

'No. But just make sure anyone who asks knows what's in them.' Morton left the cockpit and edged his way past the boxes stacked in the cabin. Each bore the distinctive logo of the US Geological Survey and labels stating that, 'for Customs purposes,' the contents were seismic detection equipment. He opened the passenger door, waited for the in-built steps to unfold, then stepped down into the humid night air.

Introductions made, Teeling pointed to a car parked nearby. 'We can go to my office. There's a secure link patched in directly to your Concorde and the Secretary's office in the State Department, with a feeder to the White House and, of course, to the Secretary-General's office in New York. It's all tested out A-OK.'

Morton looked properly impressed. A-OK. He hadn't heard that expression since he couldn't remember when.

As Teeling led the way to the car, Morton turned to Danny and Gates. Both were dressed in crisp drill shirts and trousers. 'You two don't look like you've been up a volcano.'

'It took an hour in the shower to wash that ash out. In the meantime Mr Teeling did a little rummaging in his wardrobe,' Gates explained.

'They needed a few tucks here and there,' Danny continued. 'But Mr Teeling's a dab hand with a needle and thread.'

'Actually a sewing machine,' said the Vice-consul.

'No Mrs Teeling?' Morton asked politely.

'Never got round to it,' replied the Vice-consul.

The others smiled as if they understood these things, and to show that for a moment they allowed Teeling to share an affinity with them. It ended when they reached the car and the three of them crammed into the back, as if this was the nearest they wanted to come to telling Teeling that he was now really not a part of this, and that, whatever he imagined his role had been, it would soon be over.

At this hour the traffic mostly consisted of trucks loaded with earth or building-site debris. Teeling kept up his tour-guide commentary.

'. . . In the city centre most of the old buildings are deserted. But government still operates from there. The shanty towns are coming closer to the centre and the whole place is a planner's nightmare. The cathedral has been left like it was on the night it was firebombed during the revolution. And the Bank of Managua is now a refugee hostel . . .'

They smiled and nodded and tuned him out, talking in low voices about what lay ahead. Teeling was still maintaining his commentary when the Lincoln reached the embassy compound. 'I . . . I always say this country is a miracle of survival, something that Washington doesn't seem to always understand. In that sense it's rather like Beirut.'

'Have you ever been to Beirut, Mr Teeling?' Morton asked, the smile on his lips almost in absentia.

'Well . . . no. But I can imagine this place is very similar.'

Morton made a show of pondering this before bringing to a close the mating ceremony Teeling had tried to promote. 'Just take us to your office, Mr Teeling. Then you can leave us. I'll call you when we're ready to return to the airport.'

Emerging from the car they stood for a moment in silence, the others studying the building, Teeling looking at Morton. 'Are you sure I can't be of further help?' he asked.

'No, really not. You've done wonders already. More than enough, Mr Teeling.'

'I really would like, you know . . .'

But Morton chose not to hear him, following Gates and Danny into the building. After a moment, Teeling followed them, his moment of glory ended by this man who until a few hours ago he had never heard of and whose expression seemed impossible to fathom. Morton. It probably wasn't even his real name.

Through her blurred vision Anna could see light. It was grey and opaque and seemed to be coming from a long way away. Like the noise. It was like the sound of the ocean. She tried to move. But something was pinning her down. Her mouth felt thick and clotted. She closed her eyes again, trying to concentrate. The noise was louder. It wasn't the ocean, yet as familiar. And now there was this other sound, like leaves stirring in the breeze. If only she could free herself from what was holding her down. She opened her mouth. But nothing emerged. But the other sound, whispering, had stopped. Only the first noise continued to fill the aching hollow in her head. A steady throbbing that seemed to come from all around her. But she could see nothing beyond the bright light shining directly into her eyes. She felt a finger lift one eyelid, then the other. Then something cold and wet was pressed against her lips and she was trying not to choke.

'Stop struggling and drink.' The commanding voice was also familiar.

She swallowed and once more closed her eyes. The black chaos in her mind was sorting itself out. But, with dawning realisation, the pain became worse, as sharp as a knife stab. The throbbing noise was louder. She recognised it now: the powerful engines of a large aircraft. But who had brought her on board? Where was she going? And why couldn't she move? She tried again to do so, but the effort was too much. She felt dizzy and sick and the pain seemed to be spreading by the moment.

'Leave her. She'll be all right.' A woman's voice, cold and peremptory, and one she didn't recognise.

'In another hour the shot will have completely worn off.'

'Call me immediately it has. I want to question her myself, Dr Littlejohn.'

There was the sound of a door opening and closing. Anna opened her eyes again. She turned her head. An oval window was on her left. Beyond, she could see sunlight through cloud. Once more she tried to move. But she was lying stretched out and securely held in place. She managed to raise her head sufficiently to see the straps pulled tight across her body, pinioning her arms and legs, the way a trauma victim would be pinioned on a gurney. She was still in her scrub suit and her body felt hot and clammy.

She forced herself to keep her eyes open, to try to take in her surrounds. She was in a small cabin. Apart from the gurney, there was no other furniture. The cabin door was in the bulkhead in front of her. Even through her fogged vision, she could see that the door was expensively veneered, and the handle gold-plated. Only someone for whom money was no problem could afford such a finish. Madam. This had to be her plane. Slowly, the black liquid in her head was clearing and another familiar feeling surfaced: a compulsion to brush her teeth and try and to remove this awful taste in her mouth that she also remembered from the past. The time she had last felt like this, totally, completely and absolutely defenceless, she had been a few days short of her nineteenth birthday and lying in a hospital emergency room with peritonitis, in a cubicle no bigger than this cabin. A doctor had given her an injection. She had remembered no more. But when she awoke from surgery, there had been the same taste in her mouth, the taste of anaesthetic.

Lasswell. Her last clear memory was of him standing in the staff records room pointing that weapon at her. It must have been a tranquilliser gun, filled with an anaesthetic powerful enough to have knocked her out cold.

She looked around the cabin for a clock. There was no way of telling how long she had been unconscious. Except it had been dark when she had gone to the basement and now it was day. The sun was above the cloud and, wherever the plane was going to, it was flying south.

Anna lay back on the gurney, feeling a terrible exhaustion: mentally, physically and emotionally it seemed to envelop her. That would be the after-effect of the anaesthetic and the knowledge made her feel a little better. She worked her tongue over her parched lips. She desperately needed a drink. She closed her eyes, enjoying the warmth of the sun on her skin. She did not know how long she had lain like this before the door opened and Dr Littlejohn entered. In his hand he carried a tumbler half-filled with a milky substance. He closed the door behind him and walked over to the gurney.

'Here, drink this.'

She shook her head. 'Another one of your little concoctions, Littlejohn?'

'There's no need for bravado, Nurse Cruef. This is just something for your headache. It will help get rid of all that anaesthetic in your body. I fear that Dr Lasswell, in his eagerness, used a rather bigger dose than usual. Luckily it has done you no harm.'

'How considerate of you.'

He ignored her sarcasm and placed the glass against her lips. She clenched her teeth. 'Don't be so childish, Nurse Cruef. It's only a solution of glucose and distilled water mixed with a little aspirin.'

She tasted a little of the mixture on her tongue and recognised the concoction. She quickly swallowed the remainder of the liquid. 'Can I have something else to drink?' she asked.

He shook his head. 'No. It would only make you sick. Let this work through your system first. In the meantime there is somebody waiting to ask you some questions.'

'Madam?'

'He could not quite conceal his surprise. 'At least you know how to address her correctly.'

'Why am I strapped down like this?'

'Well, for a start, you were asleep during take-off. And in the circumstances I don't want you wandering around. You've been quite enough trouble as it is.'

Anna watched the cabin door open and a woman dressed completely in black stood there, her eyes hidden by sunglasses. 'Leave us, Dr Littlejohn.'

'Yes, of course, Madam.'

She stepped aside to let him pass, and carefully closed the door behind her. Then she looked at Anna for a long moment before walking over to the gurney. She tested one of the restraining straps. Satisfied it was secured, she sat on the edge of the gurney, studying Anna. When she spoke her voice was curious.

'Who do you work for?'

'You know perfectly well I work for Dr Littlejohn.'

'I meant who do you really work for?'

Anna did not fail to notice the undertone. She wasn't certain. She was fishing. The confirmation came in her next words.

'It was very foolish of you to talk to that reporter. Not that he will publish anything.'

'Wait and see.'

Madam reached foward and slapped Anna sharply on the cheek, as she might have struck her own child who had given a cheeky reply. 'You disappoint me, Anna. That is not the answer I would have expected from you.'

Anna closed her eyes and winced as if from the blow to hide her relief. She doesn't know. She damn well doesn't know!

'Who does this reporter work for?'

Anna opened her eyes. No bluff is ever the same, the Colonel had once said, but one element is always essential for a successful one and that is the ability to deceive by detail. And to deliver it at the right speed.

'He's a freelance. He'll sell the story everywhere. Once he does, you'll all be finished.'

Anna forced herself to stare into those watchful eyes.

'And what exactly is this fantasy he will try to publish?'

'It's not a fantasy. It's a horror story.'

'I see.' Madam nodded her head, as if marvelling at Anna. 'And how were you able to come to such a definitive judgement after such a short time in the Center? Or did somebody tell you what to look for?'

'Yes. The reporter.' Almost as an afterthought she added: 'He arranged for me to talk to several transplant surgeons.'

'And who were they?'

'I'm not going to tell you.'

Madam's voice became a shade regretful. 'I am sure they would be very proud to hear you say that, Anna. But even if I believed anything you have said, it doesn't really matter. And there is very little you could have learned in any case. Your duties were very limited and you were being carefully watched all the time.'

'Not enough for me not to have told the reporter about those staff records.'

Anna saw something come and go in Madam's eyes.

'I see. That's very interesing. And what exactly did you discover? As you've told this reporter, perhaps you would like to share it with me.'

'That you're in a dirty, dirty business!'

Once more Madam shifted on the gurney. 'Is that what your reporter friend said?'

'Yes. And that's what he's going to publish.'

Madam sighed. 'How very simplistic. But then, I suppose the nature of his work is never to look at the situation in all its shadings. If you had done that, you would surely have seen matters differently, and not even spied for this reporter.'

Anna could feel her relief growing. Madam had accepted the reporter's existence. Now the bluff called for attack.

'You mean you should be allowed to play God? To decide who will die so that others can live? You're no different from Mengele, and all the others who followed him. What you're doing is destroying the basic value system which makes medicine different from everything else. Which makes everyone who works in medicine different. People trust doctors. What you are doing is the most vicious abuse of that trust. Where's the informed consent? What you're doing is a violation of every ethic, every human decency. You're all as dirty as each other.'

Madam laughed inappropriately, or so it seemed to Anna. 'How little you seem to grasp the reality. We should not be talking of ethics, but tragedy, Anna. The tragedy is the failure of society to provide enough suitable organs for those who – yes – who *do* deserve them. Instead, so many people are kept alive who serve no useful purpose.'

'Is that how you see all those people who have been butchered for their organs? As useless people? Many were young, with their lives ahead of them!'

Madam spoke with total composure. 'But again, you have not thought the matter through. Those people may or may not have made a contribution to society at a later stage. On the other hand, those who received their organs have already proven themselves. To give them the right to go on living is to ensure they will go on doing so.'

'Who are these people?'

Madam shook her head. 'I fear you would not approve of them, Anna. But then, such matters are always relative.'

'I'm not going to debate ethics with you.'

Madam sighed once more. 'That is a pity. It would have been interesting to hear your views, however infantile they might sound. No doubt they reflect the nonsense this reporter is going to write.'

Anna managed to continue the flare in her voice. 'The one thing we both know is that you're only in it for the money. And that makes you even more despicable!'

Madam looked out of the cabin window. On a bright morning like this, all those years ago, she had returned from India to bury Elmer. What did this child know about love and passion? What did she know about anything? Or this reporter? They were the watchdogs of a society that had never understood its priorities. She turned back to Anna.

'The money,' Madam said in her gentle voice, 'is only a small part of the reason.'

'You're not asking me to believe the reason is mostly altruistic?' Anna said incredulously.

'I'm not asking you to believe anything, you stupid child!' Madam's voice was suddenly harsh. 'I had hoped the intelligence that allowed you to discover a little of what we are doing would at least have made you realise that you have been given a privileged glimpse into a new world. One in which all the previous developments in medicine will pale in comparison. Because of what my doctors have achieved, soon we will be able to control any degenerative disease, even cancer, by simply removing the afflicted organ. One day, I am certain, we will be able to give worthy recipients not only a new heart or eyes, or a liver or pair of lungs, but also a brain!'

'A brain? That's impossible!'

'Right now, yes. But in twenty years' time, who knows? All the pointers show that anything is possible. The tragedy is that people like you and your meddling reporter have never understood the future. He would have exposed grave-robbers, and yet without them we would never have understood the mysteries that dissection revealed. It has always been the same with pioneers, particularly in the medical field. So, to answer your question, yes, one day it will be possible to transplant a brain.'

As she spoke Madam's voice had risen.

'You're mad, absolutely mad,' Anna said, as calmly as she could.

Madam slapped her, harder this time. 'Never call me that, you stupid child. Ever.'

Anna stared defiantly at Madam.

'Dr Littlejohn told me you were unusually bright, not that I have seen much evidence so far. But that's what made him suspicious in the first place. He doesn't get too many applications from people

317

of your intelligence to be scrub nurses. That, of course, is why you were chosen by him – by us both.'

There was silence in the cabin.

'Chosen? For what?' Anna asked eventually.

Madam stood up. 'You surprise me. I would have thought that with your intelligence you would have guessed. A situation has arisen where we need a live donor. Dr Littlejohn says that you are a suitable subject to provide a new heart. Naturally that will put an end to your present life. Despite some of your very stupid remarks, I am sure you are a person who is an individualist. So I am very pleased to tell you that you heart will continue to live on in the body of a great and respected individualist. In that sense, of course, you yourself will also live on.'

She paused, looking at Anna. It must take great strength and will to show no reaction. In different circumstances Anna could have made a genuine contribution to the Organisation.

'This person . . . who is he?' Anna managed to whisper.

'Herr Vogel, head of the Bundesbank. He is in an adjoining cabin, resting in preparation for his surgery, otherwise I would have introduced you. I wanted you to know, Anna, in the hope that you will come to understand what we are trying to achieve.'

Madam gave another small and unexpected laugh. Then she turned and walked from the cabin.

40

Shortly after daybreak, the two helicopters clattered over the slopes of Mount Masaya and settled in a clearing just below the tree-line. The search parties had arrived to look for Moshe Weill, the comfort girl and the missing helicopter. As the clinic staff emerged into the open they looked around curiously. None of them had been this close to the volcano and they were awed by its forbidding presence.

Friedrich and Engel, the two Kommando One operatives, were to lead the searchers. Among them was Monika Sachs. Like her companions, Monika wore stout climbing boots and lightweight clothes. Even so, as she stood on the lava scree, the heat from the ground penetrated the soles of her footwear. Monika looked towards the summit. The cloud which had been visible from the island had dispersed and nothing disturbed the air around the volcano's throat. But the stench of lava was strong enough to make Monika turn to Joseph West, the clinic's protein chemist, and wrinkle her nose.

'I lost my sense of smell years ago,' he apologised.

'But don't you feel the heat?' she asked.

'Yeah. But it makes a change from my lab. A lot of the work I do is at sub-zero temperatures,' he explained, pulling his baseball cap lower over his forehead.

Everyone stood clear as the helicopters lifted off; their pilots would return at the end of the day. Then Friedrich divided the thirty staff into two groups and briefed them.

'We will search the mountain in opposite directions. If anyone sees anything, tell Engel or me. We'll be in constant touch by walkie-talkie.' Each man had a handset clipped to his belt.

Monika and West were in Engel's group. They would travel eastwards across the volcano's slopes. Friedrich and his party would search in the other direction. The plan was for the two groups to meet on the opposite side of the mountain overlooking the lake. The search parties separated into the jungle. Here the powder had coated the ground to a depth of several inches, and Monika told West it was like walking through snow, except that she'd never known snow which smelled like this. Every few minutes Friedrich or Engel reported each other's progress. It was Friedrich who brought the first excitement.

'We have something.' Engel's group gathered around him to listen to Friedrich's words over the walkie-talkie. 'We've just come across a dozen dead pigs who seem to have been flayed alive.'

Those around Engel could hear other voices on in the background. Then Friedrich was back. 'We've found a woman's body. It looks as if she was scalded to death. What flesh is left is hanging from the bone.'

'The whore?' Engel asked.

'No. A mulatto. There's nothing to show what she was doing up here,' Friedrich replied. 'We're moving on.'

Once more Monika glanced towards the summit. The sun was beginning to show behind the peak, tinting the rock a reddish-brown. By the time they had walked for another hour the sky was a pale blue. The further east they went, the more the cindery ash turned to a grey-brown sludge that gave off a still more sickening stench. People began to slip and slide against each other. Several times they came across dead birds and howler monkeys which had become trapped in the mire and were rapidly decomposing in the heat. In the distance Lake Nicaragua had never looked more inviting to Monika.

Engel's voice had begun to fade as Friedrich's party moved slowly westwards. Here the ground was scarred with scoriae, small boulders and sharply pointed pieces of rock. Once more Friedrich stopped to take a bearing. He estimated they had now come halfway around the mountain. There was still no clue to what had happened to Weill's helicopter; nothing to show if it had crash-landed and torn a path through the overgrowth or plunged into any of the ravines they had peered down. He switched on the walkie-talkie to report his position to Engel. There was no response. The ridge they had just traversed was probably blocking out the transmission. He turned to the others.

'You continue on while I go up there and try to raise Engel.' He pointed to a pile of massive boulders a hundred feet or so above where they stood. While the others trudged on through the moonscape, he began to follow the path of an ancient lava flow which led up to the boulders. At the halfway point he paused to catch his breath. Below, the jungle stretched unbroken as far as he could see. He placed the transmitting end of the walkie-talkie to his mouth and began to intone.

'Hello, Engel. Do you receive me? Hello, Engel. Come in if you receive me. Over.'

Still only static. His party had disappeared behind one of the volcanic outcrops formed by lava flows probably tens of thousands of years before. Friedrich turned and continued to climb, reaching the first of the boulders.

A dull rumbling came from somewhere deep beneath his feet, as if an express train was thundering through a tunnel. Then, no more than a hundred feet further down the slope, the ground cracked open with explosive force. As he dived for cover behind a boulder, molten rocks spewed from the fissure and careered down the mountainside. Behind the fusillade came the lava, smoky and glowing and racing over the ground.

One fiery tongue dropped into a gorge. Another caught up with Friedrich's search party. He watched the molten rock pour down upon them as they emerged from behind the outcrop. Those not instantly killed screamed in blind terror as the red-hot flow swept them into another ravine. In a moment there was nothing to see but the residue of lava congealing as it cooled in the air. From behind the boulder Friedrich screamed frantically into his handset. 'Engel! Something terrible has happened! Engel, can you hear me? For God's sake, answer!'

After a few moments he stopped. The only response had once more been the hiss of static. He shoved the handset into his belt and set off to locate Engel's party.

A mile away they all had heard the rumbling. Then a total silence once more settled over the landscape. Without knowing why, Monika feared the eerie silence more than the noise. But years of self-dependency had taught her to stay calm no matter what the situation. Monika smiled reassuringly at West. She could see that he and many of the others were scared. 'It's probably just a landslide,' she said.

A moment later a flicker of orange-brown flame forked out of the mouth of the crater before being sucked back inside.

'You'd better call up the helicopters!' cried West. 'This place is about to erupt!'

Another tongue of flame shot above the rim and receded while Engel began to speak urgently into his walkie-talkie. He turned to the others, the sudden fear in his voice plain.

'We're on the wrong side of the mountain. I can't raise them.'

'They'll see what's happening and be here in no time,' Monika said firmly. 'But I think we should try to reach the others. Then we can all be lifted off at once.'

As she turned to retrace her steps, the ground suddenly began to tremble. People started to scream. Their cries turned to shrieks as the rock beneath their feet started to liquefy and hundreds of funnel-shaped holes caused by previous eruptions were suddenly unplugged. From deep within the earth surfaced jets of super-heated steam, so powerful that a number of people were horren-dously scalded. Monika saw one of the clinic cooks have his eyes gouged out by a jet. Before anybody could stop him, the half-crazed man staggered blindly down the slope. He gave one last despairing scream as he plunged over the side of the gorge.

Monika grabbed West's hand and, slipping and slithering, led them towards an outcrop. More jets appeared, making it almost impossible to see or breathe. Boiling mud began to spurt from the holes, and in moments the ground was awash with the hot, thick, cloying, evil-smelling substance. One moment the mud was around Monika's ankles, the next she could feel it against her calves and rising all the time.

'I can't make it,' gasped West.

'Yes you can!' Monika yanked harder at his arm. Those a little further down the slope who were trying to follow her to the outcrop were already struggling waist-high in the filth. The more they desperately tried to break free, the deeper they sank. Engel was the first to go. With a choking cry he disappeared beneath the surface.

The outcrop was only yards away. Monika glanced over her

shoulder. With his free hand West was clawing frantically at the mud, now around his chest. She threw herself forward. She could feel his grip loosening. She looked over her shoulder again, to encourage him. The mud was up to his neck. His eyes bulged in terror. She felt dizzy from the mud's fumes. It was like being in a great cesspool. She turned back towards the rock, ignoring the shrieks from behind her. The grip on her hand suddenly loosened. West's pitiful cries were no more.

Behind Monika others disappeared beneath the surface as she floundered on. A few feet from the outcrop the ground once more shook. The mud was rising even faster but the rock was closer now. She could *feel* it coming closer. But she could no longer see. A fountain of mud had spurted in her eyes. She couldn't see anything and her fear was total. She stretched out her hands in front of her. She could feel the mud up to her armpits, burning her skin. She waved her hands weakly towards where she had last seen the rock, to ward off the mud. She could hear the sucking as the outcrop finally freed itself from the earth which had bound it for aeons. Then she heard the terrifying sound of the rock beginning to move and gain momentum. She screamed in her blind terror.

Monika was still screaming when the outcrop crushed her, and continued to roll down the mountainside, gathering mud and bodies to its stony embrace. The flow spread like a thick glue, from which stuck arms and legs and, in West's case, his severed head, with its baseball cap still ridiculously in place.

That was the first thing Friedrich saw when he reached the scene. He sank to his knees, disoriented and unable to comprehend. He shut his eyelids and the sound of his breathing was loud in his ears. He forced himself to look once more. The severed head and limbs were still there. As reality continued to impose itself upon him, the panic which he had managed to keep at bay during his scramble to reach here finally could no longer be contained. He stood up, his eyes never leaving the remains of those he had known as flesh and blood, and he screamed uncontrollably, so much so that he almost lost his balance. Struggling to avoid falling into the mud, he threw out his hands. His walkie-talkie slipped from his grasp and sank beneath the dark bituminous surface that continued to puff and gurgle.

Friedrich began to scramble back the way he had come, ignoring the fresh cuts and lacerations each time he fell on the scree. He was oblivious to everything except the need to flee this charnel-house. He had gone a short distance when he heard a new roar. He glanced fearfully towards the summit. There was nothing to see. Yet the noise continued. Then he began to wave frantically as he recognised the sound of an aero engine. It took him a moment longer to realise that it was not the comforting clatter of a helicopter but the deeper sound of a jet aircraft engine. And it was fading.

From the Lear's co-pilot's seat Morton watched Mount Masaya disappearing behind the starboard wing. Even the sun gilding the summit had not diminished the angry red glow rising from deep within the crater. As the plane crossed the shore of Lake Nicaragua, they flew low over the water. Away on their port side the outward islands of the Solentiname Archipelago were visible.

In the cabin Danny looked up from a copy of the map the priest had made, and called through the cockpit door. 'According to this we should be coming up to that *zona militaire.*'

Morton said he could see the warning buoys dotted across the lake's surface, and then the pilot announced that the island was on his radar. Danny and Gates came foward and crowded into the cockpit doorway. They could all now see the island as the Lear rushed towards it.

'Goddamn place looks perfect,' Gates growled.

They were close enough now to make out the dense dark greenery which rose directly out of the water. To the north, hills stood out above the jungle. Behind towered the volcanic peaks of Costa Rica. Teeling had said that on a clear morning you could count twenty; after a good lunch the figure often rose to twenty-five. They had all smiled rather longer than his joke deserved.

'The map estimates the island's five miles long and a couple of miles wide,' Danny said. 'From here, I'd say that's pretty accurate, considering that priest never set foot on the place.'

They'd spent most of the time in Teeling's office going over the information about the island which had emerged after a Nicaraguan government minister had arrived. While his voice had as little volume as his body, he'd possessed the memory of the born guerrilla who had once waged his own war from the island against

324

the Contras led by 'la Cia'. Gates had shown no more than a quick reflex reaction to the mention of the Agency. When the minister finished he'd departed with the same discreet smile.

'There's the runway,' said the pilot. 'Looks well kept.'

The strip extended almost from the water's edge back into the jungle. On either side the vegetation had been cut back just sufficiently for safety. From the air the runway would have been hard to spot.

To the left of the runway two helicopters were parked in front of a cluster of buildings.

'Staff quarters,' Morton said. He pointed in the opposite direction. 'The clinic's over there, about a mile away. The *finca* is just beyond.'

He climbed out of his seat.

Danny and Gates were already scrambling into their white coveralls, each with the bold red logo of the US Geological Survey on the back. In the cabin Morton picked up a knapsack and, squeezing his way past the boxes labelled as seismic detection equipment, made his way to the toilet at the rear.

The knapsack contained a couple of Danny's flying cameras and sound-scanners. Both would feed into the battery-operated viewer in the knapsack. Built into its frame was a miniature satellite dish capable of transmitting audio and images to the receiver in the Lear's cockpit. This had the capacity to boost the sound and pictures on to Concorde. From there the CCO could relay them to all who needed to know.

In a separate pocket of the knapsack was a Heckler and Kock MP5K 9mm sub-machine-gun and clips of ammunition, while a small but powerful field radio was fitted in the base.

The pilot announced over the intercom that they were about to land. A moment later the Lear dropped on to the runway. Through the toilet's porthole window the jungle seemed close enough to touch the wingtips. The pilot would be concentrating, judging when to throttle back. Morton grasped the toilet flush handle to produce an effect the manufacturers had not intended, but which Hammer Force technicians had devised for the very purpose he now needed: a means to leave the aircraft undetected. He turned the handle anti-clockwise and a section of the bulkhead beside the toilet swung open against the side of the aircraft. Below was the runway.

The Lear had reached the far end of the strip and was turning to taxi back. At this point the jungle was no more than twenty feet away. Morton grabbed the knapsack and jumped. He hit the runway with a force that punched his breath away, but he kept rolling and reached the enclosing shadows of the foliage before the plane completed its turn. Behind him the bulkhead had already been closed by the automatic timer in the handle.

Squatting on the ground, Morton opened the knapsack and removed the viewer – a three-inch-square screen – and one of the bird-shaped cameras. This one was disguised as a parakeet. He activated then launched it, guiding the shape so that it flew down one side of the runway, providing a clear picture of the taxiing Lear. On the screen a tiny figure appeared from one of the buildings. He was signalling where the Lear was to park. Morton made an adjustment to the scanner and the camera flew across the runway to land in a tree. The figure was wearing a baseball cap and a loose sports shirt. Morton watched the image on the screen that was being received in the cockpit.

Inside the Lear Danny called to the pilot. 'How's the reception?'

'Ten-ten. 'The CCO's reporting the same. And the welcome committee's just arrived. He doesn't look too friendly.'

As the Lear's engines died, the pilot watched the man walking slowly arond the aircraft, inspecting it. By the time he came around the other side and reached the cabin door, Danny and Gates were already standing on the tarmac.

'Hello, there,' said Danny cheerfully. 'I'm Ronnie Hyde of the United States Geological Survey.' He nodded to Gates. 'And this is Bob Matthews. We're part of the team running a seismic rule over the whole country for the government. And you are. . . ?'

Kessler stared at them. Less than an hour ago he had taken the call from Managua. The Minister had been apologetic, but the President had said every island was to be checked without exception. With Friedrich out at the volcano, Kessler had decided to display the kind of initiative Dr Romer always commended. He would handle the matter personally.

'Kessler,' he said at last.

'Glad to meet you, Mr Kessler,' Danny smiled, the wrinkles deepening around his eyes. Beneath Kessler's shirt he had spotted the shape of a shoulder holster.

'Likewise,' Gates added. He looked towards the buildings. 'They seem very well built for this part of the world. What's their purpose?'

'Houses,' Kessler said shortly.

'Many folk live out here?' Danny asked pleasantly.

'A few.'

Gates turned back to him. 'Foreigners like you, Mr Kessler?'

'Yes.' He hesitated; how far should he go? 'We are employed on a research project.'

'What kind of research do you do in a place like this?' Danny enquired politely.

'Marine biology.' One of the nurses had told him she'd always wanted to be a marine biologist.

Danny and Gates nodded at each other, as if Kessler's words were the most natural explanation.

'What is it you want to do? The Minister did not explain,' Kessler asked.

Danny gave another wrinkly-eyed smile. 'It's simple, really. All we have to do is position a few sensors. They're fully automated, so we don't have to hang around waiting for them to send back a signal to our base. Once the signal shows any seismic changes we call the government and, I guess, they call you.' He smiled again. 'It's not perfect, but it's better than getting no warning.'

Morton tweaked the scanner to improve the sound quality. Already the CCO would have passed on Kessler's name for Lester's computers to trace. That accent of Kessler's should help. There'd been a number of Prussians in Kommando One.

'How long will this take?' Kessler demanded.

'Not long,' assured Danny.

'Where will you position these devices?'

Gates looked about him, as if deciding. 'Well, here for a start. This runway's a good sounding-board for any pre-tremors. Concrete always is. Wood, not. Have you many wooden buildings on the island, Mr Kessler?'

'No.'

'That's good. Wood's very bad in a situation like this. They found that out in San Francisco in 1906,' continued Gates.

Danny frowned. 'As I recall it, most of the damage there was done by fire, Bob.'

Gates smiled at Kessler. 'Mr Hyde's from San Francisco. Folks there always like to blame the '06 quake on the fire, Mr Kessler. Fact is, it was a wood-built town that just tumbled down.'

Gates gave Kessler another smile as if they both understood such loyalties. And Danny seemed to understand them too, for he smiled as well, as if a deal had been struck and they were all in business together.

'Be as quick as you can,' said Kessler, his impatience beginning to surface.

Danny glanced towards Mount Masaya. 'Have you experienced any unusual activity recently from up there?'

'A little. But the volcano is a long way away. It has caused no real problems here.'

'Well, that's good to hear,' said Gates. 'Now, the quicker we get started, the sooner we're out of your hair, Mr Kessler, and can let you get back to that marine biology.'

'Sounds really interesting work,' Danny added.

Half a mile away, Morton recalled the parakeet, bringing it flying back above the runway to alight almost beside him. As he placed the bird-shape and viewer back in the knapsack, he could see Danny and Gates beginning to bring out the boxes from the Lear. Inside each sensor was a dime-sized transponder Danny had added to the standard seismic equipment.

Morton removed and assembled the sub-machine-gun, inserted a clip and stuffed a couple more clips into his pockets. Finally he covered the exposed parts of his skin with insect repellent, using up the entire tube. He slipped the knapsack over his shoulders and, taking a bearing from the sun, headed northwards into the jungle, gun in hand, moving at light-infantry speed.

The dense mass of green was dark and heavy while the sudden cries of howler monkeys and the constant low buzz of insects added to the feeling of menace, as if the jungle was a living thing, the eerie light making every leaf seem different. The further he went, the more the ground sank beneath his feet until, in places, it was like walking in a quagmire that sucked at his ankles. Only the repellent kept the insect swarms at bay. He walked steadily, the only sign of tension that around his jaw as he listened for any variance in the sounds of the monkeys or the beating of bird wings.

After a while he noticed that the ground began to slope gently upwards and become firmer. But the insects continued to attack and, despite the cream, they found their way into his nostrils and mouth. There was nothing he could do except regularly pinch his nose and spit.

Suddenly, from ahead and to his left, he heard voices. Moving with incredible speed and silence through the shadows, hardly pausing to bend back snagging boughs, he was in time to see the two women in white uniform pass by on the track below him. They were speaking in German, complaining about having to do extra duty. The nurses turned a bend and were out of sight.

From the knapsack came a soft bleeping sound. He unzipped the base holding the field telephone, and slipped on the attached headset with its one earpiece and throat-pad microphone. He keyed a switch on the telephone.

'We're all done up here,' the pilot said. 'Danny's just saying his goodbyes to Kessler. No problems that end. I've also just had a check call from Carberry. He's reached the launch point and they're picking up the signals from the sensors loud and clear.'

Reception could be different when Sean came to launch; there had been no time to test the sensors under tropical rainfall conditions. Morton signed off, repacked, and resumed moving through the jungle, staying parallel to the track. No one else appeared.

Ahead, he could see that the undergrowth had been cut back, and about a quarter of a mile from where he stood was a collection of buildings which blended perfectly with the landscape. He watched the nurses go into the largest of them. The main clinic. The remaining structures would be the labs and the other back-up a place like this would need. To one side was a group of three buildings without windows. One was a bunker shape and half buried in the ground. Near the buildings was a pond. The Minister hadn't mentioned the pond.

Beyond, barely visible through the trees, was another building with a deep verandah. The *finca*. A group of white-coated figures was coming from that direction. Almost certainly doctors. In moments the group was lost to sight.

Morton lay on the ground, the smell of moulder strong, and once more opened the knapsack. He felt immensely happy. He removed the viewer, then both bird-shapes and sound-scanners

329

and activated them. He despatched one camera towards the clinic and the other towards the *finca*.

Suddenly the earth beneath him rippled. The sensation was so slight and so swift that, if he had not been expecting it, the movement would have passed undetected. The volcano must have twitched at its base several miles below ground and sent to the surface a shock-wave which had already spread over thousands of square miles in the time it took him to adjust the flightpath of the cameras.

They both had some distance to cover when a door in one of the windowless buildings opened and two white-coated men emerged carrying a stretcher. Whoever was on it was completely covered with a sheet.

Morton manoeuvred one of the cameras towards the pond. On the viewer-screen the surface of the water was stirring. He made another slight adjustment to a scanner and the stretcher party came into closer focus. The bearers had reached the pond and were removing the sheet. Beneath was a man's naked body, with its chest cavity exposed. Another adjustment and the man's face filled the screen. Even without his eyes, there was no mistaking that face. He'd seen O'Neill in Armagh on a Noraid-sponsored junket.

The bearers tipped the corpse into the water. The surface immediately boiled from the feeding frenzy. Only piranha fed like that.

The stretcher party returned to the building, closing the door behind them.

A moment later the second camera reavealed a movement on the *finca*'s verandah. The figure was still in shadow at the back of the broad deck.

Morton reached into the side pocket of the knapsack and removed the powerful telescope sight specially designed by Johnny Quirke to fit the sub-machine-gun. He clipped the sight on to the barrel and then spreadeagled himself in the firing position. At that moment the figure propelled his wheelchair to the edge of the verandah, his long, narrow head turned towards the volcano. Morton peered through the scope at the ravaged face of Dr Romer.

41

Dr Romer stared out towards the volcano, thinking it was strange that something so inanimate could produce such concern in Madam. Since leaving California she had called from her plane to enquire if there had been any significant change in the crater's behaviour. He had assured her there had not. He had been tempted to remind her that before choosing the island he had studied the volcano's behaviour.

Though the white ash had clearly spread further down the mountain during the night, he regarded this as no more important than the column of smoke which, a moment ago, had begun to billow from the cone. Several thousand feet above the crater the smoke spread to form a blanket through which the sun could barely penetrate. That the unmistakable aroma of sulphur had increased was also to be expected. But there was absolutely no cause for concern, he had reassured Madam, politeness itself.

He had adopted a different tone when Krill complained about the smell during the briefing for Mr Vogel's forthcoming transplant. He had asked Krill, with just the right injection of malice, if that was why he was chewing those dreadful breath-fresheners. Krill had flushed but said nothing. Neither had he raised any objection to how the heart for Mr Vogel's transplant would be obtained. In matters of ethics, with Krill you received back what you paid.

He had no doubt that Krill had scheduled the operation for mid-afternoon to give him more time to recover from his drinking bout. When Friedrich returned, he would have him conduct a thorough search to discover where Krill hid his drink. Then he would have to decide what action to take for such a flagrant breach of contract.

But for the moment there was something deeply exciting and satisfying about knowing what was going to happen. The plan to use a live donor opened up another avenue. Instead of the unexpected risks which sometimes attended a harvesting – Klinger's choice of donor in Washington was a good example – live donors could be brought here. There was plenty of room to build a properly secure compound. Then, when an organ was required, it would be only a matter of wheeling a donor into an OR. He would discuss the idea with Madam when she arrived. He looked at his watch. Her 747 would be landing in Managua shortly.

From the direction of the airstrip he saw a plane appear above the treetops. The Lear would be on its way to collect Madam's party. Yet instead of heading across the lake to Managua, the plane was banking towards the Costa Rica shoreline. Frowning, Dr Romer went inside the *finca* and dialled the security office. 'Kessler – that plane. Where is it going to?'

He listened intently, his frown deepening, as Kessler explained about the call from the Minister and the visit of the American seismologists. 'Kessler, you have exceeded your authority. I will wish to see you later.'

Dr Romer broke the connections and then redialled the direct number of the President of Nicaragua in Managua. The line was dead. He dialled several alternative numbers he had for the President. The result was the same. He tried to make calls to other government numbers. Again the ringing tone failed to materialise. At the best of times the country's telephone system was unpredictable. On the satellite communications screen, the fully functioning signal pulsed steadily. But no one in Managua possessed a receiver. The nearest one was on board Madam's 747.

He sat for a while, thinking. There was probably nothing to worry about over the visit of the Americans. But when he spoke to the President, he needed to be firm, reminding him that no one, in any circumstances, was allowed on to the island without his personal approval. When the Organisation paid the kind of bribe money the President demanded it could make its own demands.

From the airstrip came the renewed sound of jet engines running up to power. A moment later he saw the clinic's Lear heading towards Managua.

Dr Romer turned back into the room, clapping his hands. At

once a maid appeared, carrying his artificial legs. With practised skill, she fitted the limbs to his stumps and carefully arranged his shoes in their customary position. Checking that the right amount of cuff showed at each sleeve of his favourite dark blue suit, the woman left the room, still not having said a word. Dr Romer was ready to receive Madam.

Morton saw that both cameras had ceased transmitting. With their batteries exhausted, they would remain inert on their perches. One parakeet roosted on a branch at the rear of the *finca*. The other perched on a sill of one of the clinic windows. From there it had relayed a near-perfect image of an elderly, wizened Chinese in a bed surrounded by all the paraphernalia of a life-support system. Morton had once more made a positive identification. It was Fung, the undisputed godfather of all the Hong Kong Triads.

Both cameras had provided Morton with other invaluable glimpses inside the *finca* and the clinic. Apart from Romer, the only other person in the house appeared to be the woman. After she'd dressed him, he'd watched as Romer propelled himself over to a bank of screens. They must be part of the security system the Minister had mentioned. Afterwards Romer had returned to the verandah, where he remained in shadow.

The other camera had given a view of a surgical team in the midst of their OR preparations. Gowned and masked, they were uniformly anonymous. Just as he had been about to reposition the camera, one of the nurses had dropped a tray of instruments. A man's voice had shouted angrily at her and she had apologised profusely. Sorry, Dr Krill. Another piece had fallen into place. But he had to get closer.

He estimated the nearest building was about 200 yards away. The ground in between was devoid of any cover. It looked like there was no alternative but to cross it and hope everyone would be too busy to notice him. He began to use the scope to search the ground for trip wires. He had checked about half the area when he paused.

At this point the ground looked different, as if a trench had been dug. He adjusted the focus on the sight. Beneath the thin layer of soil he could make out concrete. A pipe. He began to follow its course. The pipe started beside the windowless building from

333

which he'd seen the stretcher party emerge and disappeared into the jungle about fifty yards to his left.

Morton tucked the scope into a pocket, slipped on the knapsack, picked up the sub-machine-gun and began to run across the deadfall-littered ground towards the spot. The pipe turned out to be about three feet in diameter and, at this point, above the ground but half buried beneath the welter of undergrowth. He knelt and sniffed its surface. There was no smell of sewage. He began to follow the pipe back into the jungle, where it finally stopped beside a stream which ran on down towards the lake.

He lay on his stomach and placed his face to the opening. A dank, chill smell came from within the pipe. A drain. With the amount of rain which fell every afternoon, there needed to be an efficient drainage system from the clinic.

Removing his knapsack he shoved it into the mouth of the pipe and slung the sub-machine-gun across his back. He pulled out the scope and pressed a button to activate the image-intensifier. It would serve as a torch inside the pipe. Holding the scope he entered the pipe face-first and, pushing the knapsack ahead, he began to crawl.

Soon the dim light from the mouth of the tunnel faded, leaving him in total darkness. He peered through the scope. The pipe stretched endlessly. He resumed crawling, ignoring the strain on his thigh and calf muscles, counting under his breath how many feet he estimated he was covering in a minute. The sub-machine-gun grating against the top of the pipe was loud in his ears. When he calculated he had reached the edge of the clearing, he moved the gun so that it was against his hip to reduce the noise.

He paused to look up for signs of cracking and crumbling. Satisfied that no earth had begun to seep through, he scrabbled forward again. The floor and sides of the pipe felt increasingly slimy and here and there the rainwater had remained in tiny pools. His legs not only ached, but felt sodden and cold. He continued to count. Soon he estimated he was halfway under the clearing.

There was a rustling sound in front.

He brought the scope to his eyes and stopped. Ahead, no more than ten feet away, a large snake was uncoiling. Its fangs glowed in the image-intensifier. The reptile began to slide towards him.

Morton reached for the sub-machine-gun and switched to single

334

shot. He turned his head to one side and pulled the trigger. In the resulting flash he saw the snake disintegrate. Yet even in this confined space the sound of the shot was muted and there were no cordite fumes. Johnny Quirke's boffins had created an ammunition designed to eliminate such effects.

Waiting until his eyes once more adjusted to the darkness, he moved forward, not breaking his counting as he passed over the remains of the reptile.

From far ahead came another sound he could not immediately identify. Then he recognised the hum of machinery. He must be getting close to those windowless buildings. He crawled on.

Propped up in bed, Fung stared at the parakeet perched on the sill outside the window. Since being returned from the intensive care unit to his own room, he had dozed on and off. Each time he opened his eyes the bird had not moved.

Birdwatching had long been his hobby, and he knew that birds rarely remained still, even when they were roosting or incubating their eggs. Yet the parakeet continued to stare unblinkingly, not making the smallest ruffling of its feathers. He had never known any bird remain still for so long.

He pressed a bell-push on the wall. As he did so he felt an uncomfortable fullness in his bladder and remembered the nurse had told him his catheter and its plastic bag would remain in place for another day.

She came into the room, the pale blue eyes the only visible part of her face. A surgical cap covered her hair, and her nose and mouth were hidden behind a sterile mask. She had explained that her precautions were necessary to help eliminate the risk of cross-infection.

'What's the problem, Mr Fung? Want me to change your bag?'

'No. It's the bird.' He nodded towards the window.

She smiled. 'We've got lots of birds here. He's probably just enjoying your company.'

'He hasn't moved for the last hour.'

'A whole hour? Oh, I doubt that, Mr Fung. When you come around from a big operation, time always seems longer than it really is.'

Fung stared into the masked face. 'I think the bird is dead.'

She laughed. 'I don't know about elsewhere, but round here when birds die, they just fall over.'

'Then why doesn't it fly away?'

The nurse nodded. Indulging patients was part of her job. 'OK, you want it to fly away – no problem.'

She walked over to the window and rapped the glass. The parakeet did not move. She rapped harder. The bird still remained motionless.

'That's odd,' the nurse said. 'Maybe he's sick or something.'

She glanced towards the volcano. Maybe the bird had flown over there and become poisoned from all that ash. Even from here the smell of sulphur was strong.

'Bring me the bird,' Fung ordered.

She turned from the window, still smiling. 'I can't do that, Mr Fung. That parakeet is probably full of disease.'

They looked at each other in silence for a moment.

'I don't think so,' he said finally. 'I don't think it is a real bird.'

The nurse studied Fung carefully. You couldn't always tell whether an anaesthetic had fully worn off; patients often said the strangest things in that twilight period. 'It looks like any other parakeet to me, Mr Fung. Why don't you let me draw the curtain so you can get a little more sleep? Then, when you wake up, the bird will have gone.'

'Don't treat me like a child, *waibin*. Open the window and bring me the parakeet.'

Fung's sharp tone made the nurse's smile vanish. 'I'll open the window, Mr Fung. But I can't let you handle the bird.'

When she opened the window, the smell of sulphur made her eyes burn. She reached out a hand towards the bird. The parakeet stared unblinkingly at her, making no effort to fly as she grabbed it. She closed the window, holding the bird from him.

'He's dead, Mr Fung, right enough. I'll get rid of it right away.'

As she began to close the window he stopped her. 'Leave it open. Sulphur smell is good for yin and yang. They help me get better.'

'I'll leave it half open,' she said, turning back into the room. 'And these wing and wang – who are they?'

'Yin and yang,' he corrected. 'You *waibin* understand nothing. Bring me the parakeet.'

336

She shook her head firmly, beginning to establish her authority. 'He's going straight into the incinerator, Mr Fung. That's the only place for him.'

She hurried out of the room before Fung could reply.

In the corridor Professor Surikov emerged from a room, fishing for the last morsels of popcorn in his coat pocket. He looked at the nurse in surprise and pointed at the bird.

'What's that doing here?' he asked.

'It was outside Fung's window. He thinks it's not a real bird. I'm going to dump it before he asks for an autopsy!'

He reached for the bird, squeezing its body with his fingers. There was no give in the body. Maybe it was suitable for stuffing. One of his technicians was something of a taxidermist. He extended a wing and let it return to rest. Next he prised open the beak. From inside the parakeet came a faint whirring sound as if a spring had finally run down.

The nurse stared in disbelief.

'Give this to me,' Surikov said. 'The *Chefarzt* had better see this.'

Clutching the parakeet in one hand, he hurried down the corridor.

Suddenly a ripple coursed through the floor and, for a fleeting moment, the walls and ceiling seemed to tremble. The sensation passed so swiftly he could not have been sure he had felt the tremor until the nurse called after him. 'Nothing to worry about, Professor. If you'd lived in California you'd say that was no more than a twitch of a horse's tail!'

He smiled at her and continued on his way. A twitch of a horse's tail. He must remember that.

The tiny shock-wave raced through the pipe as Morton sensed the blackness lifting. Light, faint, but growing stronger with every yard he crawled, was spilling into the pipe. He remained perfectly still, waiting for the next tremor. It did not come. But the sound of humming machinery was louder as he resumed crawling.

He stopped beneath an iron grille set in the top of the pipe. Running into the opening were gulleys from various directions. He rolled over on his back so that he was staring directly up at a patch of sky; in the time he'd been in the pipe the sky had turned from dark blue to this milky colour: the afternoon storm was gathering. He reached with both hands and pushed against the grille. It did not budge. He ran a finger around its edge. It was bedded in cement. Placing his boots against the grille he shoved steadily upwards. The grille remained firmly in place. He re-positioned himself and, drawing a deep breath, spread his boots to exert equal pressure and again shoved upwards. A sliver of concrete fell on his face. He felt the muscles in his legs tighten as he pushed harder. The grille suddenly broke free and rose into the air. He shoved it to one side. Reaching for the sub-machine-gun and knapsack, he raised his head through the opening.

He had emerged between two of the windowless buildings. The bunker was a little further away. The pond was beyond that. The humming was coming from the building to his right. Scrambling out of the opening, he quickly replaced the grille and ran to the door of the building on his left, from which he had seen the stretcher-bearers emerge with O'Neill's body.

Glancing over his shoulder to make sure no one had seen him, Morton quietly opened the door, stepped inside and closed it behind him.

Even without the pungent smell of chemicals in the brightly lit white-tiled room, he had stood at enough post-mortems to recognise the purpose of the steel table with its lip to catch bodily fluids and, suspended above it, weighing scales with their stainless-steel basins to hold organs. Necropsy tables were the same the world over. To one side was a standard surgical trolley containing an assortment of pathologist's scalpels and bone-cutters. The single largest instrument was a small electric saw, still connected by its flex to one of the many power outlets in the walls.

Of more immediate interest to Morton were the white scrub suits and long doctors' coats hanging from a row of pegs in an alcove. On a shelf beside them was a stack of sterile caps and masks. He inspected the garments, selected those he needed and pulled them over his own clothes, finally covering his hair with a cap and fastening a mask across the lower half of his face. He slung the sub-machine-gun over his shoulder and buttoned up the white coat to conceal the weapon. He took a pair of scrub trousers and used them to clean his boots before tossing the garment into a soil bin. Next to it was a stack of empty containers. Each bore a bold

338

stencilled warning that the contents were a dangerous pathogen sample, to be opened only in a contagion laboratory at the Center for Disease Control in Atlanta.

He fitted the knapsack into a container, then, carrying it, he left the autopsy suite. He strode purposefully over to the building from which came the steady humming sound. Beneath him the ground gave another delicate shudder. For the briefest of moments it had felt as if he were walking on an air cushion. Instinctively he looked towards Mount Masaya. It still showed no renewed sign of life.

In the *finca*, Dr Romer stared fixedly at the dismembered parakeet on the table. Surikov had completed its dissection to reveal the bird's electronic innards: the power pack and the micro-computer which had controlled its flight and operated the camera lens in each eye.

'It's a spying gadget,' Surikov pronounced, licking his lips, wondering if he was going to be somehow held responsible. The *Chefarzt* could be very unpredictable.

'I can see that,' Dr Romer said from across the table. Had those Americans brought this here? But why? Or was this somehow connected with Weill? This was the sort of gadget Mossad would use. Had he made an even bigger mistake over Weill?

The parts, along with the table, and everything else in the room, moved fractionally sideways before, quicker than an eye-blink, everything returned to its normal position. Surikov looked uneasily towards the window.

Dr Romer glanced at the monitors. The tremor had been so slight it had not disturbed the security cameras around the island. 'Stop worrying,' he said, picking up a telephone and dialling. He barked into the phone, 'Report here at once,' and turned back to the table. 'In your time with the KGB did you ever see anything like this?'

'No, *Chefarzt*, never,' Surikov said emphatically. He dug deep into his pocket, his hands encountering only traces of popcorn. That look in the *Chefarzt*'s eyes increasingly made him wish he had not brought this thing here. 'It could be a Chinese invention,' he suggested.

Dr Romer studied him dispassionately, 'Why would the Chinese want to spy on Mr Fung?'

'Maybe it is the Japanese, *Chefarzt*. I have heard there is no love lost between their gang lords and the Triads.'

'Stop guessing, Surikov.'

In the lengthening silence they heard the jeep arrive and park. Moments later there was a knock on the door. Kessler waited respectfully until Dr Romer motioned him forward and pointed to the workings on the table. 'Is this device familiar to you, Kessler?'

After carefully inspecting the components, Kessler shook his head. 'Those Americans. Describe them to me, Kessler. Everything about them. Everything you said, everything they said to you. Everything.'

He listened intently while Kessler completed his first description. 'Wait!' Dr Romer wheeled himself over to the communications screen. He pressed keys on the keyboard to feed the description into the computer. In silence they waited while the screen began to fill with details from a Stasi file. It was headed: 'Nagier, Daniel Martin'.

At the end of the biography came the injunction: 'Care should be taken to allow for the physical description furnished not being a definite match, but the best one available on file.'

Dr Romer turned back to Kessler. 'Describe the second man.'

When the operative finished the screen produced a second Stasi file, on 'Gates, William Gerald.' It carried the same caution over the physical description.

There was no file for the pilot.

Dr Romer's face was sculptured marble. So Morton had sent his people. They had come and gone like thieves in the night. But had it been only an inspired guess – something Morton was renowned for? And how much had they learned? They had been on the island only for a short while. And they had not come near the clinic. Kessler had been positive of that. Nor had they asked any suspicious questions. It could be pure chance they had come here. Was he, for once, unduly concerned? He turned to Kessler, his voice filled with all its old authority. 'Bring me one of those sensors they left behind.'

The jeep drove away. When Kessler returned he was carrying a small steel box painted matt black. A stubby aerial stuck out of one side.

'Break the box open,' commanded Dr Romer.

Surikov did so. Dr Romer peered inside at the tangle of vari-coloured wires connected to a pair of electrodes on a control board. Beneath was a tiny coil, no bigger than a dime.

'Do either of you understand anything about this contraption?' Dr Romer asked.

They shook their heads. At that moment another tiny tremor raced through the room. The electrodes instantly came together and separated.

'It seems to work, Herr Doktor,' Kessler said.

'Yes. But what is this for?' Dr Romer pointed at the coil. 'It could be a listening bug.' He turned to Kessler. 'I want Friedrich brought back here at once.' Friedrich had been Kommando One's surveillance specialist. 'And in the meantime I want you to collect all the other sensors and bring them here.'

When Kessler hesitated, Dr Romer looked at him piercingly. 'Is there a problem?'

'While the Americans were planting the sensors, they worked separately. I could only be with one of them. I did not see where the other man placed his boxes.'

Dr Romer stared at him. Not only had Kessler exceeded his authority by not immediately reporting the presence of the Americans, but he had behaved extremely stupidly in allowing them to separate like that. Friedrich would have to deal with Kessler. But for the moment there was still work for the fool.

'I want every operative to search for the sensors as well as to look out for any bird that does not fly away when approached. And all operatives are to go to the armoury and collect their weapons.'

He waved for both men to leave, then turned back to the screen. He used the keyboard to connect with Madam's 747. The insert in the corner of the screen informed him that the plane was in Managua. Moments later a fair-haired young man's face appeared on screen.

'Who are you?' Dr Romer demanded abruptly.

'My name is Dirk, Dr Romer. I'm one of Madam's social secretaries,' Dirk said politely.

'Where is she?'

'Madam took off from here a few minutes ago in that dinky little Lear you sent. I fear it was a little cramped for space which

341

is why only Pierre, her other secretary, could travel. But what can I do for you, Dr Romer?'

'Nothing.' He cleared the screen, his mind already beginning to plan what he would say to her.

When Morton entered the building he discovered the source of the humming. Inside the door was a refrigeration unit, large enough to cool a place several times this size. A strange light was coming through the translucent wall and door immediately in front of him. Stencilled on the door was the red-painted warning: 'Do Not Enter Without Eye Protectors'. Set in the floor was a broad red plastic strip and, beside it, a table on which were several pairs of goggles.

He took off his cap and mask, put on a pair of glasses and approached the door. It had no handle, but as his feet touched the strip, the door opened automatically. He stepped inside, the container in one hand, and the door silently closed behind him.

He was in a room about thirty by twenty feet and lit by a low-level flux of ultraviolet light. The walls, floor and ceiling were uniformly tiled in a pale green.

The floor space was occupied by surgical trolleys. There seemed to be dozens of them, parked in neat rows, each with a glass dome. The light came from the bulbs hanging above each dome. He was reminded of a hatchery. From the dome ran lines and cables to monitoring equipment on the lower shelf of each trolley.

On one wall were two large dials, labelled Temperature and Humidity. The temperature gauge gave a reading of 94.5 Fahrenheit; the 100-mark on the dial was painted in red. The humidity gauge registered 83 per cent. He could now understand the need for a refrigeration unit that size: anything smaller would not have been able to maintain an atmosphere which precisely replicated the warmth of a human body.

On the floor beneath the gauges were several black plastic drums. Each bore the same label: 'Organ Preservative'. This must be the solution Anna had mentioned the Russians had developed.

Suspended from the ceiling between the rows of trolleys were signboards. Printed, once more in red, on each laminated surface was a bold, single word. HEARTS. LIVERS. KIDNEYS. LUNGS. EYES. TESTES.

This was Romer's organ bank. As he put down his container, something caught in his throat and his eyes closed for a second. Then he walked over to one of the trolleys. Extending from its dome was a pipe with a tap to drain the organ preservative into the large sterile-steel bowl beneath the glass. In the solution was a pair of human lungs, inhaling and exhaling the oxygen and blood pumped to them by the heart-lung machine on the bottom shelf of the trolley. He lifted the dome. The rhythmic sound of breathing sounded like that of someone at rest. He watched the lungs continue to inflate and deflate for a moment longer, then opened the drain pipe. Liquid began to pour on to the floor. Next he yanked the cables from the heart-lung machine. The wetly gleaming lungs collapsed and began to lose their healthy pinkish-grey colour. In minutes they would be no longer transplantable.

Walking from trolley to trolley, Morton drained their bowls and ripped out the pipework which provided life-sustaining support for the human organs. Each time he left the dome raised. When he finished he used the trolley holding the now shrivelled lungs to wedge open the door before walking back to the refrigeration unit. He began to adjust the settings to lower the output. Almost at once the unit's temperature gauge began to rise. He strode back to the door. The dial on the wall had started to move towards the 100-mark and the floor was awash with preservative. In a short while the exposed organs would be hosts to untold billions of bacteria.

He picked up his container and was almost at the door when he froze. Outside came the pounding of footsteps, coming closer. He backed towards the organ bank. Then the footsteps were passing the door, a voice shouting in German for them to hurry.

Moments later he heard a door sliding back on its rollers. That would be the bunker-like building. Next came the unmistakable snicks of gun bolts being checked and slid home, and voices confirming this had been done. The bunker had to be the clinic's armoury. And those footsteps almost certainly belonged to Klinger's pals. From the voices, he judged there were at least twenty. That would have been Kommando One's full comple-ment. Romer had thought of everything. Or had it been her idea to recruit the Stasi killer squad?

The main voice was shouting fresh orders. Any intruders they came across searching for the black boxes were to be arrested. Call in at once if they came across any suspicious-looking birds. There was a lot of *Ja*, Kessler, understood, and then the footsteps were receding, heading, as far as he could judge, across the open ground.

Morton edged once more towards the door, holding the container in one hand, the other about to turn the handle. Any minute now this place would become a bacterial nightmare and he didn't want to be around when that happened. As he reached for the door, the handle turned.

Long ago he'd learned all there was to know about instinctive reactions. Like Jackie Kennedy throwing herself across her assassinated President. Or a father sacrificing himself in a fire for his child. And in movies it was the hero who managed the lightning reflex which was always the perfect response to a situation, usually by diving through a window or jumping from a roof. Only this wasn't *Dallas* or a film set. But the unwritten rule about dealing with a slowly turning door handle was clear.

Morton remained perfectly still as the door opened.

Kessler stood there, dressed in a black coverall.

Emerging from the armoury he had noticed the change in the sound of the organ bank's refrigeration unit. He'd briefly wondered if he should call Maintenance, then remembered that almost all its staff had gone to search for Weill. Telling the others he'd catch them up, he'd decided to check the unit himself. He'd used one hand to push open the door; in the other he held his Glock automatic pistol. The weapon dangled at his side, close to the knife tucked into his belt. Not expecting to meet anybody, he had stepped across the door's threshold before he saw Morton.

Kessler's jaw dropped. The pistol was still pointing to the floor when Morton hurled the container into his face. Instinctively his gun hand came up to ward off the blow. Even as Kessler realised his mistake, that he should have ducked or used the other hand, Morton was on to him, slamming into his body with such force that Kessler was driven against the refrigeration unit. The pistol flew from his grasp as Morton kicked the door shut, seeking the advantage the goggles would give him in the ultraviolet light.

As the door slammed shut, Kessler spun sideways, grasping for his knife. He slashed as Morton dived forward. The blade severed the strap of his goggles. They skidded across the floor. Kessler

344

slashed again, slicing a long tear in Morton's doctor's coat, exposing his sub-machine-gun. He punched Kessler in the throat. There was a satisfying grunt. Kessler stepped back a pace then raised his knife above his head, slashing downwards in a vicious curve. Morton ducked inside the sweep and rammed the top of his head under Kessler's jaw. There was the sound of splintering bone and a gurgling scream as Kessler fell back against the unit. Several of his teeth were embedded in his lower lip. But once more he found the strength to slash, driving Morton back across the room. Morton kicked out, catching Kessler in the crotch, sending him gasping across the floor. Kessler scrambled for his pistol. Morton yanked the sub-machine-gun up under his arm and pulled the trigger. The bullet completed the destruction of Kessler's face.

When he'd recovered sufficiently, Morton walked over to the body. He stripped off Kessler's coverall, then removed his own doctor's coat and scrub suit and put on the coverall. It was a little tight in places, but it would have to do. In one of the pockets he found a bunch of keys. He looked at the name tags stitched over the coverall's breast pocket. Kessler. He dragged Kessler's body into the organ bank and left it lying in the organ preservative. The temperature gauge had reached the 100-mark. This place was already a microbiologist's paradise. He shoved the trolley with the pair of ruined lungs back into the room and allowed the door to close. Removing the knapsack from the container, he unzipped the compartment with the field telephone and slipped on the headset. He clicked a button on the lip-mike. When there was an answering click in his earpiece he spoke softly, describing where he was and what had happened.

'Understood.' It was Tommy's voice. Sean had made him the radio man over at the launch point in Costa Rica. Tommy said that a short while ago Danny had turned up, while Bill had taken the Lear back to Managua airport. From there he would co-ordinate the evacuation when the operation was over.

'There's just one last point. Anna never showed,' Tommy said.

Morton spoke even more quietly. 'There's no one better than Anna when it comes to taking care of herself. She showed that in China.' He paused; there was really nothing more he could say. 'Tell Bill I want the FBI to go in and start taking apart the Gift of Life Transplant Center. Also the Malibu mansion and Drug Rehab.'

345

He didn't expect to find Anna in any of those places. But it was time to wrap up the periphery. He looked at his watch. Noon. Three more hours before the rainstorm.

He left the organ bank and walked across to the bunker. Stencilled on the locked steel door was the red-painted warning: 'No Entry'. He fished out Kessler's keys and found one which fitted the lock. He rolled back the door just enough for him to step inside. Closing the door, he turned on the light.

The bunker was well enough equipped to start a small war. Rifles, shotguns and grenade-launchers were neatly racked, together with crates of ammunition. On one shelf was a collection of curious-looking hand guns and small tin boxes. He inspected a gun, sniffing at the slightly bulbous nose of the stubby barrel. There was a faint sweet odour. He broke open the breech. Beside the firing pin was a small plastic cylinder, about half the size of the fuel container in a disposable cigarette lighter. He pinched the cylinder between thumb and forefinger. There was a hiss of escaping gas. He understood now how the pistol worked. He opened one of the boxes. It was filled with small circular pellets. He held one under his nose; the pellet gave off the same slightly sweet smell. He inserted the pellet in the gun breech, closed it and aimed at the light switch. When he pulled the trigger there was a hiss of gas being expelled under force. He walked over to the switch. The fléchette's lethal sugar concentrate was oozing down the plastic face of the switch.

He had solved the mystery of the weapon used to kill Stamp. To kill all the others.

Morton shoved the gun and box of pellets into the coverall pocket for Johnny Quirke and his boffins to examine in detail. Then he settled down in a corner to wait. In the distance, he could hear the clatter of helicopter rotors.

346

42

High up on the collar of Mount Masaya, Friedrich began to wave frantically. He had chosen to climb towards the summit to make it easier to be spotted. The ascent had been difficult because in places the ash was the depth of a snowdrift, a choking evil-smelling carpet spreading as far as he could see. A moment ago he had heard but barely seen the helicopters – his eyes were swollen by grit which also clogged his nostrils and left his throat raw, making it impossible for him to shout. Then he realised the pilots would have difficulty in picking him out as he was covered from head to foot in warm ash, which had cascaded from the crater a short while ago.

The clatter of rotors was louder and the pitch had changed. The choppers were descending. He gave another despairing croak. The choppers were several hundred feet below, crabbing along just above the tree-line where they had dropped the search parties. He waved even more frantically. Then he realised the pilots would be looking down the slope where they expected the searchers to be, not up here. Even as he watched, the helicopters separated and began to fly in opposite directions. In moments they were gone from sight. Friedrich slumped to the ground, too exhausted to do anything except listen to the fading engine sound.

From deep inside the crater came another of the rumbles which had punctuated his climb. The dust-cloud high above the volcano turned a shade redder under the reflection from the crater's throat. He dared not go any higher. He looked back down the slope that had cost him so much energy to climb. He tried to think, calculate, decide. It would take the helicopters at least five minutes to circumnavigate the mountain. There might just be time for him to reach the tree-line. Surely then they would see him?

He lurched to his feet and, half blinded, staggered back down the mountainside. Each time he fell he somehow dragged himself to his feet and plunged on. He could hear the rotors! From his right, rounding a massive outcrop of lava, came a helicopter. It was no more than a hundred feet away and almost level with him, its blades kicking up a small ash storm. Once more he waved frantically. The helicopter was obscured by the rising clouds of ash. The engine pitch was changing. The helicopter was pulling away. He screamed, but the words choked in his throat. The pitch had altered again. The helicopter was hovering! The dust storm was settling. He could see the pilot. He was waving with one hand.

Friedrich sank to the ground, this time in relief.

Over his radio Daley called to his fellow pilot. Austin, 'I've got him. He's up here on the east side and half buried in the ash. It's Friedrich, right enough. And he looks about done in.'

On the other side of the mountain, Austin chewed on a piece of matchstick. 'No sign of anybody on this side. They must have made their way down. Looking at this crater I don't think we should hang around here any longer than we have to.'

Moments later Austin's helicopter appeared and took up station close to Daley's. Both pilots assessed the situation.

'We can't land down there,' Austin said. 'I've got the winch, so I'll haul him up. You use the bullhorn to direct him.'

Austin manoeuvred the helicopter so that it hovered directly above Friedrich. Daley pulled away to one side to give him a clear view of the rescue area. He pressed a button on his control stick and his voice boomed out from the loudspeaker beneath the helicopter's nose. 'We're going to lift you off, Friedrich. Just stay perfectly still. When the harness reaches you, place it first under your armpits and then between your legs. The winch will do the rest. Wave if you understand.'

Friedrich stood up and waved. About fifty feet above his head he saw a trap open in the helicopter's underbelly and a yellow harness emerged on the end of a steel cable, which began to descend towards him. He reached up both hands ready to grab. From above, the amplified voice uttered more instructions.

'Take your time to make sure the harness is properly secured. You're going to be carried back to the island in it because there is no way to swing you on board. But there's nothing to worry about. This is a cargo-carrying winch, and it's designed to hold a truck. All you've got to do is double-check each clip is pushed home. When you've done that, wave. Understand?'

Friedrich waved both hands. The harness was a few feet above his head. It remained there.

'The damned winch mechanism's stuck,' Austin growled over the radio to Daley. 'I'm going to have to drop lower. Just tell him not to panic.'

Daley pressed the bullhorn button. 'Friedrich, we're going to have to drop a little lower, so there's going to be a little more ash blowing around you. You'll have to put up with that. Understand?'

Friedrich waved. They could bury him in the stuff as long as they pulled him free in the end. The helicopter was slowly descending, whipping up the ash around him, but he forced his eyes to remain fixed on the harness. He reached up and grabbed the webbing, gathering it to him. He thrust the harness under his armpits and locked the chest straps in place. He began to work the webbing between his legs. To do so he had to lift one leg off the ground, to bring the harness under his foot and up inside his leg. He put his foot back on the ground.

He couldn't move! A fissure had opened, and in that same millisecond he had slipped into the crevice up to his waist, and would have fallen further if the rock had not once more closed about his lower body, crushing it. He screamed. No sound came from his lips.

'Holy Mother of God,' Daley yelled over the radio.

'What's happened?' Austin asked. 'There's a hell of a pressure on the winch. What's he doing, pulling at the cable? For Chrissakes, tell him to leave it to me!'

Daley told him what he could see.

'I'll try to pull him free,' Austin said.

As his helicopter rose in the air, there was the high-pitched whine of cable tension. Abruptly the noise stopped.

'Holy Mother of God,' Daley said again.

Beneath Austin's helicopter he could see the torso. It was swaying and spraying blood and pieces of bone over the ground, mixing with the spume of gore rising from the ground where Friedrich's lower body remained trapped. Then the swirling ash obscured everything.

Dr Littlejohn looked out of the cockpit window as the Lear began its descent towards the island. He turned to Madam, seated across the aisle in another leather armchair, and smiled in relief. 'It looks idyllic down there,' he said.

As they had passed the volcano, the lake's surface had been covered with a film of white ash; now the water was clear and sparkling.

'I'm glad you like it,' Madam said.

She turned away, looking out of the window through her wraparound sunglasses. It was idyllic. But she remembered her feeling of unease when she had visited the island before. Yet then her fears had turned out to be groundless. There had been only the minor irritations of the howler monkeys and the daily mid-afternoon downpour. She smiled. If the volcano was in any way a threat, Gustav would have told her. He was very concerned about any threat to the project. It was reassuring to have such dedication.

'Something amusing down there, Madam?' Dr Littlejohn asked politely.

She turned to him, still smiling. 'I was just thinking how much we have achieved in such a short time.'

'It must have been quite an operation, getting everything out here.'

She nodded, pleased that he had recognised the huge effort it had taken. 'The Organisation had the resources. Everything on the island is state-of-the-art. You'll see for yourself, Dr Littlejohn. The best equipment, the best surgeons. And, of course, Dr Romer.'

Dr Littlejohn had to smile. They were the very same words she had used when she had first approached him. 'I look forward to meeting him, Madam. We've only spoken on the telephone. It'll be interesting to hear his view on how far matters can go medically.'

'Dr Romer says there are no limits. One day we will be able to replace every bodily organ and part. The facilities on the island are fully equipped to deal with that eventuality.'

The intercom clicked and the pilot announced they would be landing in a minute.

Dr Littlejohn turned in his chair and looked past Dr Lasswell, seated across from Pierre, to the nurse perched on the fold-up seat at the rear of the cabin.

'How are our patients?' he asked.

The nurse glanced professionally down at the two stretchers on the floor. On one lay Anna, on the other Dieter Vogel. Anna remained securely strapped. Vogel looked expressionlessly at the nurse. Anna stirred, but her eyes remained closed. Before she had been transferred from the 747 to the Lear, Dr Littlejohn had given her a mild sedative to prevent her from calling for help as she was carried across the tarmac at Managua airport.

'Everything's just fine back here,' reported the nurse.

As the Lear dropped on to the runway Madam glimpsed the white-coated group waiting around an ambulance and a jeep. A little apart from the others was Dr Romer in his wheelchair. As the plane made its turn ready to taxi back, she spotted several black-coveralled figures moving through the jungle along the edge of the runway. They appeared to be searching. She frowned. From the very beginning she had said security was to remain invisible.

Moments later the cabin door opened and a white-coated man entered, carrying a metal tray covered with sterile green cloth. 'Good morning, everybody,' Surikov said. 'Before patients disembark, I need to take some blood. It will take only a flick of a horse's tail.' He beamed, pleased at remembering the nurse's figure of speech.

Krill would need to know the blood cross-match so as to ensure that the donor heart was not rejected. After everyone had filed out of the cabin Surikov walked down to the stretchers, looked at Anna, then turned to Vogel. 'Good trip?' he asked pleasantly, setting down the tray between the stretchers and removing the cloth.

'Thank you, yes.' During the long flight he had been given a relaxant and had slept for most of the journey.

'This won't hurt,' Surikov said. He placed a tourniquet around Vogel's wrist and pulled it tight. He tore open the packets containing the needle and the alcohol sponge. Vogel's eyes followed the preparations with indifference. As Surikov expertly tightened the tourniquet, the veins on the back of Vogel's hand stood out. Surikov wiped the skin with the sponge and inserted a needle. He connected it to a syringe and drew off blood. He unscrewed the self-sealing syringe and connected a new one to the needle. In all he filled four full vials of blood. He placed them in the tray rack marked 'Recipient'. He stuck a sterile patch over the pinprick and turned to Anna.

She was staring at him. Something about this white-coated figure was distantly familiar. But her mind was still too clouded to remember. When she tried to move her hand as he slipped on the tourniquet, he spoke sharply to her in Russian – 'Be still.'

Surikov. She had come across his photograph in the medical literature while reading up on organ transplants. She looked defiantly at him. 'You've sunk a long way, Professor Surikov,' she said.

'How do you know my name?' Surikov asked in a surprised tone.

'We know all about you, Surikov. And Madam and Romer, too.'

He tightened the tourniquet and said no more as he drew off blood. But his mind was in turmoil. How did she know his name? And Madam's and the *Chefarzt*'s? Was it through the people who had left the camera and the sensors? Who were those people? The *Chefarzt* had not said. But he had been concerned.

Anna watched him stiffen and turn pale. 'You'll never get away with this, none of you, Surikov.'

Surikov straightened and, carrying the tray, walked back down the cabin. What did it matter what she knew? In a few hours she would be fish-bait. And to tell the *Chefarzt* what she had said could rebound. The *Chefarzt* had always taken care that staff only knew no more than what they needed to know to do their work. To report what the woman had said would lead to probing questions, something the *Chefarzt* was very skilled at. Long ago, in all the research centres in Russia and East Germany, he had learned the art of keeping silent. It was a policy which had served him well. He would continue to live by it, he decided as he left the plane.

Anna turned to look at Vogel. But Vogel had turned away to avoid the look in her eyes.

Out on the tarmac Madam watched the ambulance crew move forward to bring out the stretchers. Dr Littlejohn, Dr Lasswell and the nurse hurried forward to assist them. Since they had been introduced, Dr Romer had not said a word to any of them. He had not even bothered to respond to Pierre's greeting. As the discomfited youth walked over to wait by the jeep, Madam turned to Dr Romer. 'Is there something troubling you, Gustav?'

'Troubling me? No, of course not.'

'I thought it was perhaps something to do with those guards I saw. What are they searching for?'

'They're checking on the seismic sensors I have installed.'

'Why did you do that?'

'It reassures the staff to know we have taken such a precaution.'

He had never lied to her before; he was surprised how easy it was. He felt a small sense of shock that he had done so now. But he had thought carefully about the alternative. To tell Madam about the Americans could only lead to endless questions. That was one of her few failings. She had to pursue everything long after the topic was exhausted. And what was there to tell? The more he'd thought about it, the more certain he had become that it was pure chance that Morton's people had come here. If they'd learned anything, by now they would have been back in force.

They watched in silence Vogel's stretcher being carried across to the ambulance.

'He is very important to our plans, Gustav,' Madam said quietly.

Romer's eyes remained on the stretcher party as they loaded Vogel into the ambulance. 'The operation will be routine. Krill is very excited at the idea of having a donor actually to hand. It makes it so much easier to transplant.'

'Good.'

'I am considering expanding the idea of bringing the donors here until we need them. It will be like having our own living organ bank,' he said.

'We can speak of that later, Gustav.'

Anna's stretcher was being manoeuvred out of the Lear. As Dr Littlejohn approached, Madam waved him away. 'He can be very wearying at times,' she murmured. She glanced towards where she had seen the guards searching. They were no longer there. 'Have you solved the problem with the security system?' she suddenly asked.

'To do that we would have to take out the whole system and install a new one. It seems hardly worth it for the short time the storm lasts.'

He glanced towards the peaks of Costa Rica. Already the clouds were forming.

She smiled. 'Probably not.' One of his many qualities was a proper appreciation of the need to take a proper profit. The other was hers alone to enjoy. No one, not even Gustav, knew of her consuming need to avenge Elmer's death. She turned and pointed to where, across the lake, the helicopters were approaching.

'There's something hanging beneath one of them.'

Dr Romer used a hand to shield his eyes against the glare. The helicopter was still too far away to make out what it was. But even from here he could see it looked too small to be Friedrich.

A moment before Daley had used his radio to call up Austin. 'What are you going to do with the body? You can't just dump it into Romer's lap.'

'I'll take it to the pond.'

Daley laughed. 'Perfect.'

While he continued to fly towards the landing strip, Austin's helicopter headed northwards before crossing the shoreline. Making sure Friedrich's torso remained just above the trees, he flew inland.

Inside the bunker Morton heard the rotor pitch changing and the dull monotonous roar turning to an insistent whine. He judged the helicopter was descending out over the open space. But when he'd scanned the area for trip wires he hadn't spotted any landing tracks on the ground. And the space was too far from the main clinic building to be a helipad for patients.

He levered himself up then walked towards the door, stopping by a shelf of walkie-talkies. They were the type the Stasi had used. He took one and opened the door. The engine noise was steadier. The chopper was hovering a couple of hundred yards away above the pond. Morton blinked. The surface of the water was beginning to thresh from the blood and bone from the severed body. The last time he'd seen anything as gruesome as this had been on the Great Barrier Reef that day they'd brought up the remains of a tourist whose cage had been insufficient protection against a killer shark.

As he watched, the chopper began to settle downwards slowly, swaying from side to side. The water was foaming. The torso, still secured in the harness, sank beneath the surface. After a few minutes the helicopter climbed sufficiently to expose the harness. Pieces of flesh still hung to the webbing. The pilot descended once more. He waited another few minutes. When the chain next emerged from the water, the webbing itself had been devoured by the piranha.

'All done,' came a voice over the walkie-talkie.

'Anybody see you, Austin?'

'Only one of the Kraut guards. He popped his head out of the armoury, but didn't seem interested. Those boys are dumping bodies in here all the time. Anyway, I can't see him now, Daley. How are things your end?'

'All clear for you to come in. Everybody's on the way back to the clinic.'

'I'll be with you in a minute. Just watch out for my chain.'

'You'll be OK now you've dumped Friedrich.'

'And made a lot of fish very happy.'

'For sure,' murmured Morton from the lee of the bunker. Austin and Daley. The Americans were two more names to add to the list. Friedrich, too. It seemed Romer had set up his own United Nations down here.

As the helicopter disappeared across the treetops, there was a new engine sound, this time from the track leading out of the jungle to the clinic. Into sight came a jeep, followed by an ambulance. Seated beside the jeep driver was Madam. She had the same cold, calculating look Morton had seen on her face at the reception in Stockholm for the Nobel laureates. A little distance behind the ambulance, gliding effortlessly over the ground, came Dr Romer in his wheelchair.

From inside the bunker he heard the urgent bleep of his field telephone.

Steven Krill once more looked around the OR with a feeling of professional pride. Despite the absence of West and one or two other members of his surgical team, who were still up on the damned mountain, he and the rest of the staff had worked wonders. Even that idiot nurse who earlier had dropped the tray of instruments had since pulled her weight. Everything had been prepared with a precision even his old colleagues at Harefield would surely have admired.

The two operating tables were positioned side by side, but with sufficient room for him and the other surgeons to move between them. Each table was surrounded by the heart-lung machines and the trolleys of specialist equipment which, for the moment, were covered with green sterile cloths. Monitors were grouped around the tables. Only the soft whirl of the ventilators in the skylights disturbed the silence.

Satisfied that everything was in place, Krill closed the door of the OR behind him and went to the surgeon's lounge. He looked at his watch: it was a little after one o'clock in the afternoon. Another two hours before he would make his first incision. But elsewhere, he knew the preparations would already be underway. They would concentrate on the recipient. The donor's role was more functional. A provider, no more. It had been ever so.

Morton was listening to Tommy, who had just told him that Anna had been on the Lear which had flown out of Managua shortly after Bill had arrived at the airport. Bill had been certain the other stretcher case fitted Vogel's description. Both must have been in the ambulance which had disappeared around the far side of the clinic.

'Is Sean or your father near you?' Morton asked.

'Dad's not far away. Sean's out by the microlites.'

'Fetch your father.'

Moments later Danny's voice was in Morton's earpiece. 'I just heard. Is there anything we can do about Anna?'

'We'll move up the launch time, Danny. I'd like to go now if possible.'

'What about the weather? We need the rain cover, David.'

'Hold it a second.'

Morton went to the door of the bunker and peered out. Thunderheads were building above the peaks of Costa Rica. The sky was already darker. And things were being helped by the volcano. A column of reddish-black smoke had started to emerge from its throat. He could taste the ash in the air. He went back to the field telephone.

'It's a go,' said Morton. 'When you get here you'll get me on the old Stasi frequency. I'm using one of their walkie-talkies.'

'Understood.'

Morton removed the remaining ammunition clips from the knapsack and stuffed them in every available pocket. Then he smashed the field telephone with his gun butt. It had served its purpose. Next he went up and down the racks, looking for what he needed. He piled the boxes of shotgun cartridges in the centre of the floor, keeping one box back, then stacked as many of the weapons as he could around the ammunition. He emptied the shells in the box and broke open their casings. In minutes he had a small heap of black powder. He trailed it out to the door. He stepped outside and, using a single shot from his sub-machine-gun, ignited the powder. It flared and began to race towards the piled weapons. He closed the steel door and ran.

At that moment Mount Masaya finally spoke. A single thunderous explosion came from deep within its crater. Seconds later the bunker erupted with an altogether less impressive sound.

'God's on my side,' murmured Morton. 'For sure.'

He raced towards the clinic building.

43

In the *finca*'s living room, Madam and Dr Romer both rushed to the window. The rim of the volcano was glowing, as if the rocks were being heated by some vast inner force. The glow deepened. From the crater, a fiery column was emerging. It appeared semi-solid as it rose into the air, accompanied by a piercing noise, like a gigantic bellows fanning a bed of coals. When the great molten phalanx was perhaps a hundred feet above the rim, its accompanying shriek stopped and, as if no longer able to sustain itself, the column fell back into the crater with a sound like a full-scale artillery barrage. In the ensuing silence, a dark pall began to spread above the volcano.

'My God, Gustav!' What's happened?' Madam whispered, turning to him.

Something in her voice caught his ear. It was still there in her face. It was something he had thought never to see or hear in her: fear. Slowly, with what was almost an affection he had never thought he would feel for anybody, he reached out his right arm and touched hers. 'It's all right, Madam. There is no risk. There is nothing to be frightened of.' He spoke precisely – a seasoned observer offering his diagnosis.

She could feel the strength in his voice and for a moment she almost imagined it was Elmer standing there beside her.

'Would you like a cigarillo? Or a drink?' he enquired politely. 'I have your favourite brandy. And the cigarillos are Cuban.'

She looked quickly at him. How did he know about her preferences? Why was he looking at her like this? Surely to God, he didn't think . . .

But he did.

'I have something to say to you,' he began, keeping his voice low. 'It is something I have long wanted to say, Madam. I admire you so much, more than I have admired any woman. There are qualities in you that I have seen in no one else except, if I may say so, myself. We both know exactly what we want. And, in your case, what you want, and have achieved, has been done without exploiting your most powerful weapon, if I may again say so – your femininity. Yet a moment ago I sensed what, if I may put it, is the accompanying drawback to that quality. Vulnerability. You are more vulnerable than you probably realise. You need, in the best sense of the word, somebody to protect you. To take care of your emotional needs.'

From far away he heard his voice continuing to enumerate the advantages of what he was offering. 'I know that you respect me – and respect is the basis of any worthwhile relationship. From it could grow so much else. And it would be allowed to develop naturally, without restrictions. You could come and go as you do now, but knowing I would be there for you – always.'

She closed her eyes. When she opened them Elmer was no longer standing there. 'Please remove your hand, Gustav. Don't ever touch me again.'

She stepped to one side as he did as ordered. She looked at him and spoke with chilling finality. 'Gustav, whatever fantasies you have entertained, do not include me in them. Our relationship is purely a business one. You are an employee of mine. Never forget that. An important employee, but still an employee. Because of your importance, I shall overlook the gross impertinence of what you have said. But let me make this very clear: I am not interested in any relationship whatsoever with you, other than the one which exists. If that is now not acceptable to you, then let us end our business relationship here and now. Well?'

Never before had he made such a serious miscalculation. How could he have been so wrong, allowed such a hope to even begin to nurture? Instead, a moment ago, a part of him had died for all time. When he finally spoke it was with a mortal flatness of tone. 'Please accept my apologies, Madam. I shall never refer to the matter again.'

Beyond the window the pall was spreading and the glass was smearing with ash.

'Thank you, Gustav.'

In the continuing silence the sound of running footsteps on the verandah was unnaturally loud. Then Pierre burst into the room. He was covered in cindery powder and trembling slightly. 'Madam, I think we should leave at once,' he blurted out. 'This volcano's the most dangerous damned thing I've ever seen.'

Dr Romer turned from the window and looked at him icily. 'Are you an expert on volcanos, *Junge?*'

'You don't have to be an expert to see what's happening out there.'

Madam spoke as to a spoiled child – indulgently, but with a hint of warning. 'Pierre. Remember whom you are talking to.'

Dr Romer inclined his head, acknowledging her rebuke to this pouty-lipped cherub, knowing it was her way of returning a little of the pride she had stolen from him.

'Sorry,' Pierre said.

'That's all right, darling boy.'

She turned to Dr Romer. 'I must say I had not expected the mountain to behave like this, Gustav.'

He continued to stare out of the window, ignoring them, even when Pierre came and stood in his customary position behind Madam. The sky had grown darker, yet when he finally spoke his voice was calm and authoritative. 'What has happened is good. The pressures inside the crater have been released by the expulsion of sufficient lava. That column contained many hundreds of thousands of tons. Thankfully, before it could break up, it fell intact back into the crater, sealing it once more.'

'I didn't know you were an expert on volcanos,' Pierre said, not quite politely.

But the calm remained with Dr Romer, reinforced by the deadness he felt, and between them they restored in him the very supremacy he had almost been ready to share with her. He continued to deliberately ignore Madam, his eyes only on Pierre. 'Geography has always been an interest of mine, *Junge*. What we have witnessed here is a combination of two kinds of eruption. One is the classic vulcanian. The other is what is called the sulfaturic type.'

'Sulfatura – sounds Italian,' Pierre said.

'Sulfatura is a small town in Italy. The crater there last erupted in the twelfth century. Since then it has constantly threatened to do so, but has never lived up to its threat. This volcano is the same kind.'

Pierre seemed increasingly confused by the whole explanation. 'Aren't volcanos all really – ?'

'Pierre, stop asking your tiresome questions, there's a darling boy.' Madam had once more spoken indulgently, not the way she now acknowledged Dr Romer, in a voice that suggested he was more contained than she had known him, and yet somehow less at ease with her. 'You said the crater is sealed – but for how long?' she asked.

Dr Romer walked over to the drinks cabinet and selected another of the bottles of expensive wine Wolfgang Kreuse had given him. He uncorked it with a small flourish, then bunched one hand and inserted the cork between his thumb and forefinger.

Pierre had lapsed into an aggressive sulkiness. Madam watched with a detached interest.

'The column of lava,' Dr Romer said. He withdrew the cork and drove it back into the neck of the bottle, needing some force to do so, then turned to them. 'When I released the cork it had expanded. The same with the lava, so that when it fell back into the crater, it fitted even more tightly.'

He waited briefly for questions. When none came he continued in that same certain voice. 'Just as the cork can continue to ensure the perfection of this fine wine for many more years, so that lava will cork the volcano for even longer. So you see, there is really nothing to worry about.'

He smiled for the first time at Pierre. 'Let us, as they say in your country, *Junge*, drink to that.' But there was no affection in his smile.

'Whatever you say, Doctor.'

'Then fetch the glasses, darling boy. Make yourself useful,' Madam said sharply.

As Pierre brought the glasses from the drinks cabinet, there were new footsteps on the verandah, and a coveralled figure appeared in the doorway. His skin, like his coverall, was covered in ash. Ignoring the others he spoke rapidly in German to Dr Romer. 'Doktor! There has been an explosion. The armoury is destroyed!'

'What are you saying, Pressman?'

Dr Romer's face suffused with colour and the hand holding the bottle shot out towards Pressman in disbelief. 'How can there have been an explosion? How? *Tell me how!*'

He had shouted loud enough for the mulatto in the kitchen to look up from her preparations. In the living room the whole matted knot of Dr Romer's fury, against both male and female, coalesced into one screamed question. *'Is the organ bank safe?'*

Pressman could only manage a nervous shake of his head.

'What else?' The moment of terrible fury had passed. In comparison, the question was asked in a voice a little above a whisper.

'The autopsy room, Doktor.'

Pierre stared opened-mouthed at Dr Romer.

'Close your mouth, darling boy. It's not an attractive sight,' Madam ordered. She turned to Dr Romer. 'What has happened, Gustav?'

He told her. She had one other question: how had it happened? He turned back to Pressman and continued to question him in German, in his voice the harshness of cross-examination.

'This ash must have found a way into the armoury, Doktor.'

'That is not possible, Pressman. Unless somebody left the door open. Where's Kessler?'

'I don't know, Doktor.'

'Find him. Then send him here.'

Pressman ran from the room.

Madam stared after him, then turned to Dr Romer. 'What else did he say?'

'Nothing of importance. We'll know more shortly. I've sent for his superior.'

She had the sense to know he would not be drawn further.

Under Mike's watchful eye, the shooters emerged from the Costa Rican army trucks which had brought them to the small plateau high above the country's pan-American highway. In the distance, a dull black expanse under the lowering sky, was Lake Nicaragua, the border at this point between the two countries.

Each shooter was dressed in a black coverall and ceramic helmet, fitted with a radio earpiece and a transmitter/receiver. Each man wore body armour and a trauma pad under his clothing.

Some carried a Heckler and Kock sub-machine-gun, others a Steyr or Ruger rifle, or a Remington pump-action shotgun. In addition all had a Smith and Wesson .38 as a sidearm. Mike also carried a Webley grenade-launcher strapped across his back.

After inspecting the shooters he pointed towards the barely visible cone of Mount Masaya. 'For those of you who haven't flown into an ash storm, it's no different than flying through a sandstorm. As long as you don't get hit by a piece of lava, you'll be OK. If you do, you won't know anything about it.'

There was a collective chuckle from the shooters. Earlier they had all seen the spectacular display the volcano had produced.

Danny stepped forward from where he had been standing with Sean Carberry and Tommy. They were also in full combat gear. In addition Tommy carried a radio backpack. Danny addressed the shooters, his voice brisk and businesslike. 'The Colonel's working on the old Stasi walkie-talkie frequency. Once you hit the ground, set your receivers to that. And make sure you identify him and Anna before you fire. Otherwise anybody who gets in the way is a legitimate target.'

He turned to the microlites parked in a row behind him. 'Your homing devices are preset for the sensors we've sown on the ground over there. Just follow the signal. Hopefully, we're not expected. If you are – well, it won't be the first time.'

Once more there was a general chuckle.

Sub-machine-gun strapped to his back, Danny went to the first microlite in the line-up. Like the others its entire framework had been stealth-painted. The carefully baffled engine would give him precisely forty minutes' powered flying time. That provided a five-minute margin to land on the island or ditch in the water.

Danny lay on the padded body-rest and strapped himself down so that his shoulders and chest were almost parallel to the narrow fuselage. He gripped the microlite's handlebars and pressed the start button. The engine fired at once. He taxied to the edge of the plateau, the microlite's thick rubber tyres cushioning his progress over the ground. As he turned into the wind, the second machine was already starting up.

The moment Danny opened the throttle there was a thumping sensation in his back as the engine went to full power. Seconds later he was in the air. From the control box between the handlebars came the bleep of a homing device from somewhere on the island.

Fung continued to watch the sky darken until a nurse came in. She was petite and Asian and silk-skinned, not at all like the nurse who had removed the strange parakeet. 'Have there been more birds that don't fly?' he asked.

'Please, I do not understand,' she said in her sing-song Burmese accent.

'It no matter.' He sighed. 'It no matter at all.'

She closed the window and drew the curtains before switching on the room lights. Turning to Fung, she laughed. Ash covered his face and scrawny arms and had formed a circle around his eyes, so that he looked like a mangy panda in a mediaeval·Chinese play. 'Okey-dokey, I'm going to have to clean you up, Mr Fung,' she said cheerfully, turning to the room's washbashin and running a tap.

A dark brown trickle emerged from both faucets. The liquid smelled strongly of sulphur. She closed the tap and went over to the bedside phone to dial Maintenance.

A harassed voice eventually answered. When she began to explain the voice cut her off. 'The supply pipe under the lake from the mainland has broken. So's the phone line. We'll be switching to the back-up water supply up in the hills just as soon as I figure out the connections. But you'll just have to be patient.'

After she hung up the nurse turned to Mr Fung. 'Okey-dokey, guess I'm going to have to wipe you off the best I can.'

As she reached for a towel he stopped her. 'Leave ash. Very good for body. Full of yin and yang.'

She smiled. She knew all about the power of the twin pillars of Chinese traditional medicine.

'Okey-dokey,' she said again, hurrying from the room.

Throughout the clinic, windows were being closed and curtains drawn as if it were night. On those facing south, the reflection from the fire at the armoury and the adjoining building began to fade as the clinic's firefighting crew brought the flames under control.

The armoury itself had been razed to the ground; nothing

remained except fragments of metal. As clues to how the fire had started they were useless. When the firefighters used their hoses to battle their way into the organ bank, they found a body among the charred and twisted trolleys. It was so badly burned it was impossible to identify. A couple of firemen wrapped the remains in a blanket and dumped them in the pond. As they hurried back to join the others, dousing the last of the flames in the autopsy suite, the water supply to the hoses suddenly stopped.

The spectacular explosion from the crater had sent Krill running from the surgeon's lounge to the OR. He stood in the doorway, stupefied. The entire theatre was covered in a film of ash which had seeped through the ventilators, completely contaminating the OR.

He went to the intercom on the wall, flicked the switch and spoke urgently. 'This is Dr Krill. All OR staff report immediately to OR One. I repeat. Immediately.'

He began to shove the nearest trolley out of the room. The OR would have to be emptied completely and hosed down before it could be reset for the transplant operation.

Close to the OR, in adjoining windowless bathrooms, Anna and Vogel were immersed in baths, the first stage of their preparation for surgery. The pleasantly warm solution was designed to give their bodies a thorough surface cleansing. Afterwards they would each be dressed in a sterile scrub suit and taken to nearby cubicles to await the arrival of the anaesthetist.

Dr Lasswell had started to add a little more of the preparation to Vogel's bath when he heard a sudden commotion next door.

The nurse who had accompanied Anna on the flight had been about to pour a wooden scoop filled with the liquid over Anna's head when she stood up and made a grab for the handle. Still groggy from the sedative, Anna had missed her footing and fallen back into the water. The furious nurse held her down as long as she dared before releasing Anna's head, leaving her gasping. 'Dr Lasswell. The bitch tried to escape,' the nurse yelled. 'I need an extra hand in here.'

'Press the emergency button. It's that red one between the taps.'

Krill's urgent voice over the ceiling loudspeaker in each bathroom overrode further conversation. From the corridor came the sound of running feet. The nurse called out for assistance. But no one stopped. Krill's command took priority over all else.

Danny's microlite engine cut out; the powered part of his flight was over. But on the control box the signal from the homing beacon remained steady. The microlite flew itself so that it was like riding through the sky on a surfboard. The sky seemed even darker now that the glare from the volcano had faded.

After drifting over the lake for a while, he could see the faint line where the water met the darker mass of the island. The homing signal was still steady as he came in low over the trees. A moment later he spotted the airstrip, away to his right. His rate of descent grew steeper. Then, with leaves brushing against the wheels, the microlite swooped with a last gentle whoosh into a clearing. As the wheels touched, Danny kicked hard on the rudder bar-brake and the microlite stopped obediently in its own length. He released his safety straps and rolled on to the ground, listening.

From the direction of the runway he could hear voices, but they were too far away for him to make out what they were saying.

Morton entered the clinic through a door which led to the kitchen supply area. Storerooms led off the corridor. At the far end were double doors with glass portholes. Sub-machine in one hand, the walkie-talkie clipped to his coverall belt, volume turned down, Morton moved quickly to the portholes. Beyond was the main kitchen. The handful of staff who had begun the evening meal preparations were standing by a window staring towards the volcano and talking volubly among themselves.

As quietly as possible, Morton opened the door and closed it just as carefully behind him. No one at the window turned. He ran on tiptoe across the kitchen to a corresponding set of doors on the far side.

Beyond was a corridor painted in neutral cream. There was no one in sight. The doors on either side bore no markings. He put an ear to the nearest one. No sound came from within. He tried the knob; the door was unlocked. He pushed it open. The room was where the kitchen staff changed; hanging from pegs were their work skivvies. He closed the door and checked the others in the corridor. More storerooms.

366

He reached the end of the corridor where it divided. He chose the left fork, sensing it would lead him further into the clinic; at various intervals loudspeakers were set into the ceiling. He had gone a little distance when the corridor veered sharply to the right. At the bend a TV monitor camera was mounted on a wall and pointed directly at a door a little further along. He could make out the sign painted on the door: Records. The camera's transmission light blinked unerringly, silently blocking his further progress. To shoot out the camera would alert everyone. To retreat would take him back to the kitchen area.

He began to walk boldly down the corridor, holding the walkie-talkie to his ear as if listening to instructions, and taking care to keep his head averted from the camera lens. He had passed the guarded door when from the loudspeakers a woman's voice began to intone. 'Security Officer Kessler report to Dr Romer at once in the *finca*.'

Morton didn't check his stride as he worked a finger under the stitching around the tag and removed Kessler's name from the coverall. He shoved the tag in a pocket.

Rounding a corner, he found himself in a carpeted corridor where the doors had numbers. He cracked open the nearest one. The patient was asleep and almost hidden by the monitoring equipment around the bed. As he closed the door, further down the corridor a nurse emerged from another room and headed in the opposite direction, disappearing down an intersecting corridor. He waited a moment then walked rapidly after her.

The woman on the speaker was continuing to call.

Morton had entered the intersecting corridor when a man's voice stopped him. 'What are you doing here?'

He turned to face the frowning, white-coated figure standing a few yards away. He must have come out of one of the rooms. He had his hands in both pockets.

'I'm looking for Kessler. Have you seen him?' Morton asked politely.

'No, I haven't,' said Surikov, frowning. 'Anyway, you're not allowed in this area, especially with a gun. What do you think our patients would say?'

Morton gave an apologetic smile. 'I'm sorry. But Kessler's supposed to be guarding the woman – the prisoner. Do you know where she is?'

Surikov popped a handful of popcorn into his mouth and chewed noisily. 'Down in the OR area. Kessler wouldn't be allowed in there. Krill would have a fit if he saw him. That nurse and doctor from California are minding her.'

Morton shook his head. 'I've still got to check. Romer wants Kessler urgently.'

'What's he done?'

Morton shrugged. 'God knows. But the sooner I find Kessler the better for me.' He looked around him. 'I'm sorry – this is my first time in this area. Which is the way to the OR area?'

Surikov shoved more popcorn into his mouth. 'Down this corridor. First right, then right again. Then follow the corridor all the way to the end. You'll see the sign. If the red light's on, stay out. Otherwise Krill's likely to throw something at you.'

'Thanks,' said Morton.

As he hurried down the corridor, the woman was once more ordering Kessler to report to the *finca*.

Pressman rushed into the *finca*'s living room carrying a lifeless parakeet.

Dr Romer was alone. After they had emptied the wine bottle, Madam had suddenly asked if she and the *Junge* could use the guest suite. After he had left them, he heard the suite's door being locked.

'Where did you find it?' he asked Pressman.

'Out at the back of your kitchen, Doktor.'

After Pressman had broken open the bird-shape Dr Romer stared at the components for a considerable while. Then he wheeled himself over to the security monitors and began to switch from camera to camera. In the gathering gloom it was hard to make out anything. But once or twice he thought he caught glimpses of movement. He reassured himself they would be the guards. Then, suddenly and unaccountably, he began to shiver, the way he had when he had watched the hunter's moon rising behind the volcano and he had thought about Morton.

'Are you all right, Doktor?' asked Pressman.

'Yes, yes, of course. Continue to look for Kessler. And find out what's happened to Friedrich and the others. They should be back by now.'

Pressman did not move.

'What are you waiting for?' demanded Dr Romer.

'Friedrich is dead, Doktor. One of the pilots has just reported the matter to the security office.'

Dr Romer stared at him as if he could not believe what he had been told. 'Dead? How? Where?'

Pressman told him what Daley had said.

'And the others?'

'They have not come back, Doktor.'

Dr Romer spun in his chair to face the window. He knew, instinctively, that the searchers would not be returning from the volcano. His shivering increased. Behind him he could hear Pressman walking quietly from the room. And, behind him, Pressman was certain he heard Dr Romer say, 'impossible'. But perhaps it was 'no – possible.'

Morton stopped before a pair of swing doors. Above was a light-box which warned: 'No Admittance When Surgery is in Progress'. The box was unlit. He eased open the door and slipped in quickly. The soft lighting of the corridor was replaced by hard fluorescent bulbs which cast no shadows on the tiled walls and ceiling and the white vinyl floor.

He paused to get his bearings. The area he was now in was still in the non-sterile part of the OR complex which would include staff changing rooms, a lounge for the surgeons to relax between operations, and the induction rooms. The sterile areas would begin with the ORs. Beyond them would be the instrument sterilising rooms, the immediate post-operative recovery area and the intensive care unit.

Around him were several unoccupied gurneys. Patients arriving for surgery would be transferred on to them before being wheeled to the anaesthetic induction rooms. Those must be beyond the heavy-duty plastic flaps across from where he stood.

He slipped the sub-machine-gun's strap over his shoulder and pulled out the fléchette gun and the box of pellets. He shook several into his hand, replaced the lid and put the box back in his pocket. He loaded a pellet into the gun and, keeping the others in his clenched palm, walked past the gurneys to the door flaps.

Against a wall were surgical trolleys, their green drapes covered with ash that gave off a faintly bad smell. From the far end of the corridor, beyond yet another set of double doors, came the sudden spray of a pressure hose being played on tiles.

Moving quickly Morton peered into the first doorless room. It contained a row of lockers and a pile of cotton fabric dresses on a table beside a canvas hamper. The nurses' changing room was deserted.

The next opening was a storage space for IV stands. He checked the room opposite. Another changing area – for surgeons or male staff, judging from the pile of scrub suits on the table and the size of the clogs standing before each locker. He passed two more changing rooms. From the numbers of lockers he had counted, there were facilities for up to fifty OR staff.

The hosepipe had stopped and he could hear the soft sucking sound of galoshes on the wet tiles. From a ceiling loudspeaker a voice broke the silence. 'OR One ready for resetting.'

Morton peered into another room. It contained an anaesthetics trolley. The next three rooms held identical equipment. From the cubicle beyond came the sound of relaxed breathing. The curtain across the opening was drawn. He pulled it gently aside.

On a gurney, dressed in the white scrub suit, in chemically induced drowsiness, lay Dieter Vogel. The President of the Bundesbank did not stir as Morton closed the curtain. He trod lightly to the next cubicle. Its curtain was also drawn. Once more he carefully pulled it aside.

In the centre of the floor, strapped to a gurney, was Anna.

Standing with their backs to him were a white-coated man and a nurse. She was holding a kidney-shaped bowl from which he had taken a syringe, still in its sterile cover, and an ampoule.

Dr Lasswell was about to remove the needle cover when he turned, astonished.

'Both of you step away from the bed,' Morton said softly.

The nurse was the first to react. She hurled the bowl at Morton. He took the blow on the forearm of the hand holding the pellets at the time instant as the index finger of his other hand pulled the trigger of the fléchette gun.

The pellet hit the nurse in her left eye. She collapsed against the wall, blood running from the ruptured retina as the sugar concentrate made its way along the optic nerves to her brain. She was already losing consciousness as Morton reloaded. But in the seconds it took him to insert a new pellet, Dr Lasswell made his move.

He whipped off the needle cover and lunged forward with the syringe, coming in low. Morton raised his knee and rammed it against Dr Lasswell's nose with such force that the bone was driven deep into his nasal cavity. Dr Lasswell fell forward, his head resting against Morton's leg, the syringe falling to the floor. Morton stepped aside and crushed it underfoot as Dr Lasswell's head thumped once against the floor.

'You OK, Anna?' Morton asked as he unfastened the straps. Apart from being white-faced, she seemed in remarkably good condition.

'Better for seeing you,' she said fervently, sliding off the gurney.

Dr Lasswell was groaning. Anna bent down and lifted his head, then let it drop. She did it twice more in rapid succession. The groaning stopped.

'I owe him that. The bastard was getting me ready to have my heart transplanted into Vogel.'

'Maybe they'll use his heart now instead,' said Morton softly as he looked out into the corridor.

Beyond the double-door flaps of the OR came the sound of activity. He turned and led the way back up the corridor, Anna walking barefoot beside him. As they passed a locker room she grabbed a pair of clogs. Then he handed her the fléchette gun and quickly explained how it worked. Holding the machine-gun in one hand he pushed open the door flaps leading back into the patient receiving area.

Over by the far door, slightly to one side of Surikov, stood Pressman.

Pressman's journey here had begun a few moments before as he was coming from the *finca*. Surikov had stopped him to report his encounter in the corridor. There was something puzzling about the man, Surikov had said. His coverall had seemed ill-fitting and it had no name tag. And everyone knew the *Chefarzt* was a stickler that all security staff had to be smartly dressed and wear their ID. And though the man spoke German, it was not with the Prussian accent of the other guards. Pressman had asked what the guard looked like. Blond, Surikov had said. The only fair-haired operative had been Klinger. The last vestige of doubt evaporated in Pressman's mind when Surikov said the man had told him Kessler was supposed to be minding the woman.

Now here she was – with this stranger in a Kommando One coverall that could have fitted Kessler. All this Pressman saw in the same instant as he shoved Surikov to one side and raised his machine-pistol. He moved quickly. But he might have been a deep-sea diver weighted down at the bottom of the ocean.

In one smooth, unbroken movement, Morton switched the catch to rapid fire and hurled himself straight forward as he pulled the trigger, firing with his arms at full stretch, as if he need to further reduce the distance between the barrel and its target. The first shot caught Pressman squarely in the forehead, but his entire face seemed to break open.

The impact spun him round towards Surikov, so that Pressman appeared to be appealing for help, the way his hands began to flap, unaware that the nerves in his shattered brain had already cut off all contact with them. And Surikov could not help. The same short, sustained burst caught him in the chest, ruining his white coat. His own hands emerged from its pockets, scattering popcorn over the floor in a strangely unco-ordinated manner.

For the briefest of moments, though already clinically dead, Pressman and Surikov stood and faced each other, their mouths, like their hands, now working as if they were each talking simultaneously. Morton stepped forward and kicked their feet from under them. They collapsed on top of each other on the vinyl.

Still running forward, Morton opened the door leading out of the OR complex. In the corridor the loudspeaker was once more intoning for security officer Kessler to report at once to Dr Romer in the *finca*.

Then a very English voice overrode the woman's. 'This is Dr Krill. We have shooting in the OR area.'

His voice pursued them down the corridor until it was lost in the insistent ringing of bells from all parts of the clinic.

44

In the clearing Danny picked up a lightweight scanner and began to slowly rotate like a diviner seeking a borehole, holding the instrument in both hands at waist height. Shadows began to appear on the fluorescent screen.

'A small vehicle and two men,' he murmured. 'A couple of hundred yards away and stationary.'

'It's probably those guards in that jeep,' whispered Mike. Gliding in over the treetops he had spotted the jeep racing along the runway.

Behind them Carberry listened to Tommy, crouched over the radio, softly calling out the rendezvous co-ordinates to the last of the shooters after they had drifted down on the island. Twenty of them had already reached the clearing after hiding their microlites in the undergrowth.

'Try the Colonel again,' murmured Danny. Between directing the shooters Tommy had been calling Morton on the old Stasi frequency without success. He tried once more. There was still no response.

Carberry turned to Mike. 'I want that jeep.'

Mike and two shooters disappeared into the jungle. Ten minutes later the others heard the sound of an engine, then the jeep bounced into the clearing.

With Carberry behind the wheel and Danny and Mike squeezed in beside him, Tommy and four of the shooters squatted in the back. The others ran behind as the jeep set off towards the track leading to the clinic.

The sound of the bells ringing in the clinic stopped Madam as she was about to mount Pierre one more time. This afternoon there had been a coldness to their lovemaking he had not experienced before; the more he tried to please her, the more impossible it had been to do so.

She pushed him aside and went to the window of the *finca*'s guest suite. Apart from the bells, there was nothing unusual to see down at the clinic. The flames in the organ bank and mortuary were no more than a glow to silhouette the firefighters. The pall seemed to have sunk lower over the crater's summit. But from there came no sign of life.

Somewhere in the *finca* a phone was ringing. It stopped. A moment later, there was a loud hammering on the door. Dr Romer was shouting in German. '*Schnell*! *Schnell*, Madam!'

Pierre couldn't understand the rest. But as she turned her naked body from the window, there was true madness in Madam's eyes. There was no mistaking what Dr Romer had just said. 'Morton *ist hier*!'

At a crouching run, sub-machine-gun held high across his body, Morton led Anna out of the clinic. The jungle was only yards away. They reached it undetected and Morton switched off the walkie-talkie to reduce the risk of detection; a moment ago he'd heard an urgent German voice ordering all guards to report to the OR. They began to move swiftly through the undergrowth; only the soft sound of mulch under their feet marked their progress. The sound of the alarm bells began to fade.

They passed a stream, scrambled up a slope and worked their way around a rock mass. They had passed a fallen tree when Anna felt a wire tighten under her foot, then go slack. She pointed to the ground. Morton nodded. Somewhere another alarm would be sounding. The only thing to do was to place as much distance as they could between the wire and themselves. In the distance came the squeal of a jeep racing over a track and braking. They began to move towards the sound. Ahead through the undergrowth lights were visible. The *finca*. Morton suddenly paused and sank to the ground. Behind him Anna did the same.

He could sense the man from here – his deep-brain nerve cells were releasing body odour. Fear and tension were always the hardest to mask. A moment later came the soft click of a bolt being jemmied. Morton signalled for Anna to remain still. Then, crouching double, he moved with extraordinary silence and speed to where the guard had been. He'd gone.

Morton picked up a piece of deadwood and lobbed it to his right. From his left came the sound of a footfall. A voice called out in German, asking who was there. Another nervous footstep. Morton eased the walkie-talkie from his belt and placed it on the ground. He turned up the volume; there was a faint hiss of squelch as if someone was breathing noisily through his mouth. As the footfalls resumed, moving more quickly now, lured by the sound, Morton rolled to his right, the ground foliage hardly moving under his weight. From the walkie-talkie came a voice in German: Security Office to all guards who have not gone to the clinic. Report at once to the *finca*. Pilots to warm up the Lear.

The footfalls stopped again. The guard was crouching over the walkie-talkie. He picked it up and brought it to his mouth. Morton jack-knifed off the ground and kicked the machine-pistol from the man's hand before ramming the barrel of his own weapon against the man's windpipe, crushing it. The guard was dead before he hit the ground. Morton picked up the walkie-talkie, shoving it in his belt as Anna appeared. They continued through the undergrowth, drawn now by the insistent ringing of the telephone in the *finca*.

The sound had stopped when they reached the edge of the jungle. They were standing opposite one side of the *finca*. Out front was a jeep, probably the dead guard's. Though lights were on in several of the rooms, there was no sign of life inside the house.

'Kitchen door,' Morton breathed in Anna's ear, pointing to a door to the left, remembering the geography lesson the flying camera had provided. Together they ran across the open space to the door. Morton pressed his ear against a panel. Silence. He squinted through the keyhole. Nothing moved across his field of vision. He turned the handle and eased open the door. Anna closed it behind her.

The kitchen was larger than the camera had indicated; maybe Romer did a lot of entertaining. That could explain the size of the slicing machine on a butcher's block in the centre of the kitchen. Two internal doors led from the kitchen. Morton remembered that the one on the left accessed the main part of the *finca*, while the other led to the pantries.

As Morton went towards the door on the left, the other door opened and the housekeeper stood there. As she opened her mouth to scream, Anna shot her. The fléchette pellet passed over the woman's tongue and down her throat. She coughed and would have collapsed if Morton had not caught her and lowered her to the floor. He closed the woman's eyes; the light was fading from them. There was nothing else Anna could have done.

She was loading a fresh pellet when the voice from the external door gave its first order. It was Semper, a guard.

'Drop your guns,' Semper ordered. He shifted his machine-pistol to cover them both, an unnecessary precaution given that the two guards beside him each had a weapon trained on Morton and Anna.

They dropped their guns on the floor.

'Kick them towards me,' ordered Semper. 'Nice and slowly. Do it now.'

They did as ordered.

Semper nodded to one of the others. 'Find something to tie them with.'

The guard ran across to the door leading to the pantries. He returned with a ball of heavy twine. Semper pointed his machine-pistol at Morton, then moved it a fraction to indicate a kitchen chair. 'You. Over there.'

Morton walked over to the chair.

'Sit.'

He sat.

In moments the operative had securely bound him to the chair and repeated the process with Anna.

'So. Who are you?' Semper asked.

'Now, that's for you to decide,' said Morton politely.

Semper hit him in the chest with the butt of the pistol, using sufficient force to rick the chair off its back legs. Anna tried not to wince.

'Next time it will be her turn,' Semper said with a smile people like him often managed at a time like this. But there were also priorities to follow.

'Fetch the Doktor,' he said to one of the others.

Moments later Dr Romer and Madam appeared in the kitchen. They looked briefly at where the mulatto's body lay, then turned to Morton and Anna. Madam spoke in that slightly chilled voice he remembered from the salon in Stockholm. 'Colonel Morton. What does one say at a time like this?' She laughed the good-humoured laugh of the not quite sane.

'These things happen, Miss Montan.'

'Indeed they do, Colonel.'

She turned to Dr Romer and explained when she had last met Morton, then walked over to the chairs and inspected the bindings, in the same expert way she had checked the straps on Anna's gurney on the plane. She turned to Semper and the two other guards. 'You may leave now. And very well done. There will be others, of course. Go and join your colleagues to find them.'

She waited until the guards left before turning back to Morton. 'I suppose you don't want to tell me how you found your way here?'

'I'd prefer not to.'

She sighed. 'Not that it really matters.'

'It's over, Miss Montan. For you and your Dr Frankenstein. For Krill, Littlejohn and all of your other Frankensteins.'

Dr Romer glared and was about to speak when Madam cut him off. 'You remember what you were saying earlier, Gustav, about the need for living donors? I think that's an excellent idea.' She stared at Morton and Anna. 'Yes, an excellent idea.'

Her laugh was now replaced by a not quite sane smile; she continued, this time addressing Morton. 'As I have already told Anna, she will have a chance to become, medically speaking, a pioneer. I am now happy to extend the same privilege to you, Colonel.'

'You're ill, Miss Montan. I'm sure even Dr Romer can recognise that.'

Her not quite sane smile remained fixed upon him. 'Please, Colonel Morton, don't be so banal. Even if Anna cannot, then surely you can understand that we are no longer living in a time of gradual and marginal change? We are not looking at the transplant world as even ten years ago. Neither, I am glad to say, are we living with outdated concepts of morality. There is a new dawn, Colonel. And with it has come a new liberation. No longer do we have to fear the kind of fear we once looked upon God with. We are now living in a world where we can *be* God. Do you understand that, Colonel?'

He looked at her for a long enough time and then shook his head. 'You're wrong, Montan. You're as wrong as all the others who thought they could play God.'

'You disappoint me, Colonel. You really do.'

Madam turned to Dr Romer. 'Come, Gustav. You have preparations to organise.'

Without another look at Anna or Morton, they left the kitchen.

They had tried everything: manoeuvring the chairs back to back; trying to use their fingers to unpick each other's twine; trying to move themselves towards a cupboard in search of a knife. But they remained securely trussed.

'Let's try for my gun,' said Morton. 'It's on single-shot. Maybe there's a way of using it to blow the cord apart.'

Once more they began to wiggle their chairs across the floor. Suddenly the kitchen began to move with them: pots on the cooker, plates and bowls on the work table, then the tables and cooker. The butcher's block with its slicer was dancing all by itself. Then pans, cutlery and crockery began to rain on to the floor as cupboards and drawers flew open under the full force of the tremor. There was a louder crash as the block upended and the slicer crashed to the floor near Morton's chair. The lights flickered and went out.

From beyond the door leading to the *finca* came the sound of furniture falling and a scream cut off in mid-yell.

The shock-wave toppled Morton and Anna, as if the ground had quietly slipped from under their feet. Plaster showered down from the ceiling and from the roof came a sound like nails being wrenched from rafters. Then the sickening sliding was over. Somewhere a generator had started. A moment later the lights flickered, then steadied.

The slicer was immediately beside Morton's head, its start button close to his face. Using his nose, he depressed the button. The slicer blade spun to life. In seconds he had cut himself free, then Anna.

They reached the door leading to the main part of the *finca*. It was jammed. Using all his strength, he forced it open. Beyond, a heavy dresser had tipped over. Under it he could see a young man's naked body; only his partly crushed head protruded and the once blond hair was covered with blood. His eyes had that surprised look of unexpected death.

Apart from the thump of the generator and the sound of creaking wood, the silence was unbroken.

Then, from the front of the villa, came a high-pitched whine, not unlike that a hovercraft makes as it runs up to power, only not quite as loud. A second or two later it was lost in the more recognisable noise of the jeep starting up and driving away at speed.

Morton ran to a window. It faced the wrong way. He went to the door. It, too, was jammed. By the time he had shouldered it open, the engine noise had faded. And with it, Madam and Romer had disappeared.

Built to conform to the California Uniform Building Code for earthquake-proofing buildings, the clinic's structural damage had mostly been confined to broken window glass, buckled doors and plaster cracks.

The occupants did not escape so lightly.

In OR One the newly prepared instrument trolleys had been tipped over, scattering monitoring equipment and operating tables. Then, in the manner of those freakish incidents which often occur in these situations, the tremor had claimed its first human victim.

Krill had been coming through the doors of the OR to make a final check when he was thrown off his feet and sent skeetering across the floor at what was probably the very moment a trolley spilled a selection of scalpels Krill would need to use during the operation. One of the knives penetrated the carotid artery on the left side of his neck. A nurse had found him, already close to death, and oblivious of the ash which had again started to drift down through the shattered skylights. She ran from the OR, the sticky warm smell of blood mixing with that of her own vomit.

Vogel was the tremor's second victim. His gurney had been propelled out of the cubicle with such force that when it collided with the opposite corridor wall he was hurled to the ground. Unable, because of his pre-medication, to take any steps to protect himself, his head had hit the floor with sufficient force to cause multiple fractures of his skull. He would never regain consciousness in the short time he had left to live.

In his room, Fung had lain in bed, gripping the mattress while the frame leaped up and down in those few terrifying seconds. In that time everything else in the room also moved. Monitoring equipment crashed into furniture. An armchair waltzed in crazy tempo with a night table.

A floor below, in the intensive care unit, Al-Daba of the Bekaa Valley and Cohn of Chicago, perhaps in keeping with the new relationship between Jew and Arab, found themselves flung together in unexpected embrace. Their beds, free from the moorings of their life-support systems, carried them across to the horseshoe-shaped nurses' station with such force that the gang leaders were tipped on to the monitor screens.

There were many similar incidents involving other patients, staff in the kitchen, technicians in the laboratories, nurses and doctors in all parts of the clinic.

But when the tremor stopped, people picked themselves up, looked at each other and told one another that the worst was over. If only the bells would stop this insane ringing.

In that first split-second when the tremor had sped on its way to God knew where eventually, the commandeered jeep had risen into the air, exposing its chassis, then fallen back on its side, spilling Danny and the others into the undergrowth. The shooters running behind the jeep had felt the earth undulate and when they fell to the ground, they felt they were being held down by some gigantic unseen vacuum.

From his position in the midst of a tangle of undergrowth, Tommy could see trees all around him caught up in a jig of their own, swaying first one way, then the other, as if whipped by some silent hurricane. But there was no wind and the only sound was of wood snapping like matchwood. Then that, too, stopped.

Carberry shouted it was an earthquake, which must have been unnecessary, as he struggled to his feet. He had been in Los Angeles the last time the city was rocked by tremors. This one seemed small in comparison. 'It's OK, everyone. The show's over. Let's get moving,' he said in his best Angeleno way.

'Take a look at that.' Danny was pointing to the crater. Some way below the summit, the rocks had started to glow. A moment ago the area had seemed no larger than a football pitch; now it was the size of a dozen stadia. As the glow spread, it deepened, and at its centre it was blood-red. Elsewhere the sky was the colour of deep night, a winter's night beginning to fill with hot swirling snowflakes. Through the ash they could see the glow spreading.

Shaking themselves down, the Task Force checked their weapons and equipment. Spread out in loose formation, they began to move through the jungle.

They had gone a short distance when behind them they heard the noise of an engine, and then a second one.

Mike started to run back to the track, clutching his grenade-launcher. He had still a little way to go when the jeep roared past. Its only occupant was the driver, crouched low behind the wheel so that it was impossible to be sure if it was a man or woman, or even a child. Immediately behind came a wheelchair travelling at almost the same speed. It appeared to be skimming the ground and the passenger looked like a dwarf.

'It's Romer!' Danny yelled behind Mike.

Mike fired the launcher. The shot fell wide of both vehicles. By the time he had reloaded, they had both disappeared around a bend in the track.

Over the radio Tommy at last heard a familiar voice on the Stasi frequency. 'I've got the Colonel,' he said, 'and he's got Anna!'

As Morton began to give orders, a burst of gunfire rent the darkness.

'The Colonel says he's spotted a couple of jeeps with heavy machine-guns,' reported Tommy. He called out the co-ordinates Morton had just given him.

Another chain of bullets began to flay the area where the Task Force had been a moment before. In a dip in the ground, Tommy crouched with his radio, listening to the noise of battle. From ahead came the familiar sound of automatic weapons as the shooters ranged in on the jeeps. The first fireball was quickly followed by a second as the vehicles exploded. The firing stopped.

Morton was back on the radio. 'All units to head for the airstrip and secure the Lear and the helicopters.'

The first shadowy figures of the returning shooters began to run past Tommy. He hefted his radio on to his back and followed them. A moment later Morton and Anna were beside him. She smiled at Tommy.

'Glad to see you,' Tommy said. 'Really glad.' His look was respectful, even tender.

'Me too,' she murmured, before Morton spoke to Tommy in a low, fast voice.

'Tell Bill that Madam and Romer have bolted. Almost certainly they are going to try to use the Lear to get out of here. We're going to try to stop them. I want Bill to tune up the evac. choppers and have the local cavalry standing by.'

Part of the deal was that the Nicaraguan Army would have the glory from arresting everyone in the clinic.

As Tommy began to relay the orders, Morton and Anna pulled ahead. Several of the shooters had righted the jeep. Morton motioned for Anna to get in the back. When Tommy arrived, he joined her, along with Carberry and as many shooters as the jeep could carry. Morton sat up front between Mike and Danny, who was behind the wheel. The barrel of Mike's grenade-launcher pointed over the jeep's windscreen.

'Let's go—'

Morton's words were lost in a rending, roaring sound that came from the fiery area high up on the side of Mount Masaya. Then slowly, almost lazily, part of the mountain detached itself and started to move down the slope.

As they bumped down the track, they could just make out the sound of aero engines being run up to full power from somewhere ahead in the swirling ash.

Between them, Austin and Daley had lifted Dr Romer out of his wheelchair and into the Lear's cabin. They placed him in the nearest armchair and secured his seat belt. He said nothing; for all the expression in his eyes, he might have been dead. Madam was already in her seat.

Leaving Austin to close the cabin door, Daley made his way up the narrow walkway between the seats to the flight deck.

Madam stopped him. 'Fly directly to Medallin,' she ordered.

'What about your 747? You'd be more comfortable—'

'Don't argue,' she snapped.

'Whatever you say.' He shrugged and went into the cockpit to start up the engines.

She settled back in her chair, deliberately ignoring Dr Romer. The Organisation had several safe houses in the jungle around Medallin. From one of them she could begin to replan – and decide what she would do with Gustav.

After leaving the kitchen, he had, at last, told her everything about the Americans. About Nagier, who had pretended he was one, and Gates, who most definitely was one hundred per cent Boston. Gustav told her about the sensors and the parakeets that weren't birds. He'd told her everything in a voice which had been so over-controlled that his tension had seemed even greater. At times he had flinched as if he thought she was going to hit him; at other times he had contrived not to look at her. She had not interrupted him once and asked no questions. When he had finally finished, she had thanked him for telling her and added that he must know what it meant. Yet she had not made up her mind what it did mean for Gustav when the tremor had struck.

She listened to the start-up sounds from the cockpit and fastened her seat belt. She began to think. They were finished here, of that she had no doubt. But the clinic was only a building which could be replaced. *It is the concept that matters*, Elmer had always said. *As long as you don't lose that, you don't have a problem.* She could build elsewhere. And, for herself, plastic surgery could make her disappear from the face of the earth. All the Mortons in the world would not be able to recognise her. It would take time and energy; it would mean certain sacrifices. She would have to forgo her position as a society hostess; she would have to give up her seat on all those medical foundations and charities. But these would be small sacrifices to achieve what she had promised Elmer – revenge for the world's failure to keep him alive, to have had him beside her, to have borne his child.

Gustav would undoubtedly be difficult to replace. But not impossible. *Nothing is impossible*, Elmer had said, *just as long as you remember the bottom line.*

She could almost feel Elmer here now, seated beside her. He was so close she could almost sense his fingers touching the side of her face, see his eyes looking into hers, his strong voice urging her that she must continue with everything for his sake. And do it without Gustav.

'Elmer says it's over, Gustav,' she called out to Dr Romer.

'*Bitte?*'

She unfastened her seat belt and walked back to his seat. Without saying a word she lifted out Dr Romer and dragged him back to the cabin door. Austin was beginning to close the door.

'What are you doing?' Dr Romer shouted in sudden fear.

'Wait,' shouted Madam at Austin. 'Help me with Dr Romer.'

'Help. . . ?'

'Help me to throw him out.'

Dr Romer began to struggle violently as Austin grabbed him by the leg stumps. Together they tossed him out of the door. A moment later his wheelchair followed.

'Close the door, Austin,' she said, smiling her most definitely not quite sane smile.

'Yes, Madam.'

She walked back to her seat and strapped herself in. Through the window she could see the crumpled body and wheelchair.

Austin was striding up the walkway, a faint sheen of sweat on his forehead. 'The side's just blown out of the volcano, Madam.'

'But you don't have to fly out over the lake. Elmer would have told you that.'

'Elmer?'

'Never mind,' she said sweetly. 'Head for Bluefields.' The area was on the opposite side of the island, on Nicaragua's Atlantic coast. From there they could fly directly down to Columbia over the sea.

'We've still got to go out over the lake,' Austin said patiently. 'We need to fly into the wind to take off. It's a basic law of flying.'

She glanced at him. 'I know. Elmer told me all about them.'

In the cockpit Daley had brought the engines to full power. Not that he could tell by their noise: he could hear nothing above the roar from across the lake.

'She's crazy as a coot,' grunted Austin. He told Daley about Dr Romer as he settled in the co-pilot's seat. 'Now she's going on about some guy called Elmer.'

'Another of her toyboys, probably.'

Daley nicked the left-hand throttle and the Lear began to taxi back along the runway. The wipers could barely keep ash from forming on the windscreen.

The lava mass rolling down the side of the volcano was gathering speed, accompanied by an even more deafening roar which sent lightning-like scintillations high into the dark sky.

The jeep bounced off the track on to the runway. There was no sign of the Lear through the swirling ash, only the sound of its engines coming from somewhere in the murk that obscured the upper end of the runway. It was barely possible to make out the two helicopters parked on the far side.

'Everybody on board – fast.' Morton had to shout above the noise from the mountain. 'I'll fly one. Tommy, you take the other.'

Danny gunned the jeep across the strip. The shooters on foot followed, running backwards, guns at the ready. Since the brief firefight they had encountered no opposition. They did not do so now.

Jumping from the jeep, Mike ran back to the centre of the runway and knelt. He fired a succession of grenades up the runway into the murk. The explosions were too small to indicate a hit. He ran to the nearest helicopter.

Morton was first into the air; Tommy's helicopter followed in seconds. They had climbed no more than a hundred feet when the great mass of lava, accompanied by its sustained, stupendous roar and gathering momentum all the time, bounced across the lower slopes of Mount Masaya and into Lake Nicaragua.

'Thank God that's over,' Tommy yelled over the radio.

Daley lined-up the Lear for take-off. A moment ago there had been explosions further down the runway. But they had looked like pinpricks compared to the fireball which had now disappeared, along with the deafening roar. In the sudden silence he could make out the clatter of rotors.

'They're probably waiting out over the lake for us to fly between them so that they can take pot-shots. We'll keep low and by the time they realise it we'll be on the way to Bluefields,' Daley said.

The Lear began to roll, the ash swirling against the windscreen. 'We need to get up above this crud as quickly as possible,' Austin said.

Daley grunted and pushed the throttles open a little more.

Morton glanced out of the cockpit window. A couple of hundred feet away on his port, slightly below where he hovered, Tommy held his helicopter in a similar position. Morton could just make out Mike crouching in the open cabin doorway of Tommy's chopper, cradling the grenade-launcher. Mike would probably only have time for one shot before the Lear was past and gone. Sean, who was crouching in the cabin doorway behind him holding a machine-gun, would have a slightly better chance; he might even fire off a full mag in the seconds he would have between sighting the Lear and it disappearing.

Three o'clock.

The hour that Krill had fixed for the operation that would now never begin. When Fung should have had his surgical dressing changed and now never would. Time for a hundred and one things in the clinic to happen which now would not. And, of course, the time when the afternoon rainstorm usually began.

A few seconds past three. No one in the helicopters could be certain who heard it first. A dozen voices cried out more or less simultaneously to claim they had been the first to hear the change of engine pitch as the Lear's nose wheel came off the ground.

'He's going to be below us,' yelled Tommy into his lip-mike. 'I'm going down!'

'Hold your position!' Those words of Morton's undoubtedly made him the first to have seen what was happening out on the lake.

A second ago the water had been dark and flat. Now, where the fireball had entered the lake, warm air at the water's surface was being forced upward, cooling rapidly and producing a giant shroud of mist that hid the full reality of what was happening for a few more seconds.

But it could not do so for longer. Under the massive pressure of the displaced water, the wave continued to grow in a monstrous surge of water, fifty feet high and travelling at over a hundred miles an hour and constantly fuelled by a lake that was really a small sea.

The black-faced horror swept on, whipping aside the last of its shroud, baring its full fury in a roaring avalanche.

On it came, faster and faster, now no longer a broad front, but assuming a blunt spearhead shape, ready to crush anything in its path, and all held together by a surface tension at its edges, making a sound like all the steel bands on earth. A sound like nothing on earth.

The tidal wave continued to grow and gather speed.

A few more seconds past three. Austin and Daley saw the first droplets of water hit the screen and felt relieved. The afternoon rainstorm would wash off the ash from the fuselage and wings which had begun to create drag problems.

Behind their cabin Madam was saying something. Austin half turned in his seat to hear better. Daley's strangled scream stopped him. Austin turned back in time to see the towering, trembling concave wall, foaming at the crest, rising towards them. And then it was above them!

From the cabin came an unearthly scream.

The Lear was still climbing when the tidal wave engulfed it, snapping off both wings at once and crushing the fuselage.

In the helicopter, now several hundred feet above the foaming crest, Morton thought, but could not be certain, he saw bodies being swept inland as the monstrous wave hurtled down on the island. First the runway disappeared, then the clinic staff quarters. The buildings disintegrated with the same swiftness as trees were uprooted. The wave surged on. The very ground it was submerging seemed to give it strength and momentum, so that it seemed to grow even taller and more powerful. Morton followed it, knowing where it was going, what it was about to do, and feeling glad. She had said we could all be God. She had been wrong then, too. Only God could be God.

Seconds after reaching the shore, untold billions of tons of water descended on the clinic and *finca*. For a brief while the buildings remained visible under the foaming surface. Then, as if the great surge was washing the sky clean, wiping everything clean, the light improved sufficiently for Morton to see the wreckage. Beds, tables, equipment began to sink beneath the surface. The bodies took a little longer to do so. But soon they too had disappeared. Then there was nothing to see.

For a while the two helicopters circled to make absolutely certain. When they heard the sound of more helicopters approaching from the mainland, Morton ordered them to break away.

'I guess that's it,' Tommy said over the radio.

There would be clearing up to do: bodies to be recovered and finally identified. The Organisation dismembered, just as the Lear had been broken. But all that was for the future.

For the moment there was one other matter. He used the radio to call Concorde. When the CCO acknowledged, Morton asked for a Stockholm number. When it was answered, he asked for an extension. A moment later he heard a familiar voice.

'How are you, Yoshi?'

'David? Where the hell have you been?'

'Busy. And you?'

'Sore. Otherwise fine. It's like joining a new club. They all know you by your scar tissue.'

They both laughed softly.

'What happened your end?'

'They drowned in their own cesspool, trying to play God.'

There was a short pause before Yoshi spoke again.

'The one thing I've learned from this is that nobody can do that.'

'For sure.' Morton had never been more certain. But for good measure he said it one more time. 'For sure.'

Afterword

This novel is rooted in fact. Consider the following news report which appeared in the *Daily Telegraph* on 12 August 1993.

> Brazilian police arrested eight alleged baby traffickers at Rio de Janeiro airport yesterday. They are suspected of links with a gruesome international organ transplant racket. They were about to hand over a fifteen-day-old baby to an Israeli couple who were allegedly to take the child to Germany on false papers. Police said they suspect the gang, led by a Brazilian man, has for two years been selling South American babies to European transplant clinics where their kidneys, hearts and even genitals are removed before they are left to die.

Two months earlier, the same newspaper, one of many, had reported – on 21 June 1993 – of a scheme by British doctors to preserve the organs of accident victims without the permission of relatives. Under the scheme bodies would be kept cool by chilled preservation fluid, pumped into the kidneys through a catheter. Dr Maurice Slapak, the surgeon in charge of the transplant unit at St Mary's Hospital, said that the bodies would be ' "biblically dead" as well as brain dead.' The report continued:

> Dr Slapak said kidney preservation could become standard practice in accident and emergency units in Britain. Car rear seat belt laws and an ageing and more frail donor population are thought to be the cause of fall-off in transplants, which has occurred in continental Europe and the United States. An aggravating factor in Britain is that managers of intensive care units are reluctant to keep brain-dead patients

alive on life-support systems while preparations are made to 'harvest' organs – the medical jargon – because they are not reimbursed.

In October 1993, the National Health Service reported that there were currently 4,300 people waiting for kidneys, 300 for hearts, 200 for heart-lungs and 100 for livers. The figures were not expected to significantly change. Similar waiting lists, per head of population, exist in most countries in Europe and the United States.

In the course of researching the subject, I gathered a cross-section of views which reflects what I have tried to convey in this novel. Within a few months I had acquired a substantial file of well-documented reports of the steps wealthy patients take to try to bypass the ever-lengthening lists of those waiting for transplants. With their money they are trying to buy extensions of life. The moral issue seemed often to come down to whether they were accessories to the murders sometimes committed to provide these organs.

Time and again I received reports of 'fattening houses' in Latin America, where undernourished street children and young adults are nursed back to health so that their organs are healthy enough to be removed for transplanting. There were reports about private clinics in India, Thailand and the Philippines, as well as Central America, where such transplants are performed. There were accounts of mercenary pilots in the Pacific Rim and Central America who ferry organs from one site to another.

But perhaps the most shocking disclosure of all is that the oldest and most sacred of all oaths – the Oath of Hippocrates – is being ignored by a growing number of doctors. Sworn to do no harm to their patients, they do so by illegally removing their organs for that basest of motives: to profit from misery.

My research took me into a world few people know exists. It is peopled by men like William Cantarino. Once a New York City detective he is a character no dramatist would dare to create. He is a human organ-hunter. What he does is totally legal. For him, and others like him, sudden death means business. He has put it like this:

'I must try to convince relatives, parents or children, or spouses, in the depths of grief, to donate organs from the deceased. I need to be a diplomat, psychologist, social worker and undertaker, all rolled into one. In each case I deal with, the brain is dead, but the body remains in medical limbo. Sustained by drugs and machines, it will never be able to be resurrected as a living person. In theory it can be kept "alive" forever. No one wants that. It is too expensive. It is pointless. I try to convince those relatives to donate the organs of their loved ones to give hope for others. I always tell them that a kidney transplant saved my life. I received an organ from a murder victim. I was a cop at the time. My sister donated a second kidney.'

Today there is not a major city in the world that does not have its organ-hunter. They are men of low profile, well versed in the customs and rituals of death – but who always see it as an opportunity to extend life. They understand the nuances of fear, sorrow, despair; the basics of grief. They understand, but they do not, for a moment, allow those responses to emotionally influence them.

Yet I received repeated evidence from responsible sources that time and again people would not wait for organs to come from such a legal source.

In Mexico City the Chief of Police told the story of a child who had been kidnapped and killed. When his men recovered the body they found it bore the marks of expert surgical intervention. Only a doctor could have done that, said the police chief. In Asunción, Paraguay, Judge Angel Campus had this story to recount:

'Our police raided a house in this city recently and discovered seven Brazilian baby boys. They were aged between three and six months. I have good evidence that the babies were going to be sold to private clinics for $5,500 each. It is easy to understand the market forces. The son of a millionaire gets kidney problems. The father is not going to spare money to pay to make his child healthy again. So the babies we rescued were undoubtedly destined for such a fate.'

One of the many questions that Judge Campus raised, but to which he could offer no definitive answer, was the legal position of someone who knowingly accepts such an organ. Knowing it has come from a donor who has been murdered, is he or she an accessory to murder?

The criteria for a legal transplant are clear enough. The seriousness of a patient's condition: will he/she live for a significant length of time after the transplant? Is he/she a 'worthwhile member' of society? How long will it take for a suitable organ to be located? How long for the transplant team to gear up? Time is always a crucial factor. And money. Time and again I was told that the first procedure many transplant centres will perform on a potential recipient is known as 'the wallet biopsy'. Can he/she pay?

In the United States, the majority of transplant centres will not implant a new organ in anyone over the age of fifty-five. Homosexuals and the mentally handicapped are often excluded. A spokesman for the American Council of Transplants informed me: 'Supply and demand dictates no less. There are too many high-fliers, the power people, needing replacement organs to have any to spare for the less fortunate. We live in the age of reality.'

Bruja Goldman, a research fellow at the Campus of Friends World College in San José, Costa Rica, went on the record as follows.

'Children of the Third World as young as four months are either being kidnapped or killed and dismembered for their organs. Only doctors have the skill to do that. The children have been bought for as little as $20 and their organs can fetch $100,000 – and often more. There are no consent forms involved. There are no legal niceties.'

Dr George Abouna, formerly of the University of Kuwait Hospital, was, in 1992, a respected figure in world transplant circles, sitting on important steering committes and advisory bodies. He believes:

'The illegal traffic of organs is growing. More and more wealthy patients from North America, Britain, Europe and the Middle East are travelling to India, the Philippines and Thailand to obtain transplants. Hundreds of these operations take place every year in India. Facilities are often insanitary and hospitals eager to discharge patients after operations. In many cases hospitals do not adequately screen donors. Some recipients have contracted hepatitis and AIDS. Many of the organs come from street children.'

Susan Davidson, was, for eight years the Director of the widely renowned Adam Walsh Child Research Center in Orange County, California. In October 1993 she confirmed to me what she has said many times previously:

'I get persistent reports of children being taken by ambulance-men to private clinics and hospitals in South American cities like São Paulo. The men receive a kickback for every child they bring in. The doctors place the children on life-support systems until brain death is clinically confirmed. They then remove all the healthy saleable organs. These are transplanted into the bodies of those able to pay. A perfectly healthy child can have the market value of $200,000. On just five children the return can be $1 million.

'What is happening is beyond the ken of the average cop. He is used to homicide, not this kind of stuff. It is so fantastic that he does not know where to begin. Further, where *does* he begin? He has not the resources to travel to South America, to places like Nicaragua. And he has little chance against the network that operates this transplant racket. The Mafia, the French syndicates, the Triads and the Japanese are all involved. Shipping stolen organs around is not a problem. Packed in proper preservative they can be flown across borders. Men who traffic in drugs won't have a problem with doing that.'

Increasingly, as the lists of those waiting for transplants grow, the desperation of those with money to buy an extension of life becomes all too clear.

In 1993, US victims of renal failure persuaded the National Kidney Foundation of America to launch a survey to establish 'public reaction to a plan which will make the bereaved families of organ donors eligible for financial compensation'. The schemes being proposed included a payment of a flat fee to donors' families, reimbursement of medical expenses and even a form of life insurance for those who allow their loved ones' kidneys to be removed.

The idea of involving cash, rather than just conscience, as the incentive for donating organs led to an ethical debate within the medical establishment that showed a surprising number of doctors ready to encourage cash payments for kidneys.

There was talk of a need to amend the US Transplant Act of 1984 – which makes it a felony to buy or sell organs – so that, in the words of one transplant surgeon, 'the ethical considerations can fit into the reality of the nineties'.

While that debate continues, organ-stealing has gathered apace. In 1993 there were over 500 reports of attempts to obtain them illegally.

In Karachi, Pakistan, the Chief of Police announced in October 1993 that he had 'strong circumstantial evidence that a sophisticated network exists to move people from Asia to at least one transplant clinic in the former Soviet Union'.

This image of a well-run secret network is not new. Such networks have extensively operated for years, under the control of gangs smuggling women and children around the world for the purpose of prostitution.

Jean Fernand-Laurent, a former United Nations investigator into slavery, has documented for that organisation the activities of those networks, stating in his report to the Secretary-General of the United Nations that they are:

> ... growing daily. There are a number of inter-related networks involved in the traffic: one flowing from Latin America to Puerto Rico and beyond, to southern Europe and to the Middle East; one flowing from south-east Asia to the Middle East and central and northern Europe; a regional market in the Arab countries; one supplying North America. The traffic is often carried out under the cover of what purport to be marriage bureaux or advertisements for jobs in touring stage shows. There is evidence of procuring networks supplying Geneva from Paris; Switzerland and West Germany from Bangkok; Singapore from Malaysia and the Philippines; Spain from France. South American prostitutes are shipped from Argentina to Melbourne, young Hawaiian and Californian women to Japan and Swedish women to the Middle and Far East. The networks frequently interlink. Much as airlines interline baggage, so the separate slave networks hand on their human cargos, one to another. The networks are well disguised and almost all involve the secret traffic of poor women and children towards rich men in all directions. It is only now that we are even beginning to see its ramifications.

*

Those police officers in the Third World who are only now beginning to realise the ramifications of what they face admit that, with such networks in place, it would be simplicity itself to move live transplant donors around the globe. The *Arab News*, published in Riyadh, took the highly unusual decision – given the friendly relations between Saudi Arabia and India – of reporting in some detail that children in the Indian subcontinent were being killed for commercial transplantation or shipped elsewhere for the purpose.

Commenting on the report in the *Sunday Telegraph*, London, Dr James Le Fanu, a respected medical observer, noted that 'a kidney bazaar has developed [in India] with an estimated turnover of £10 million a year ... India is rapidly becoming the international centre for transplantation of live organs'.

In November 1993, Argentina's Health Minister, Julio Cesar Arazoz, following an investigation into 'irregular activities' in numerous hospitals in Buenos Aires, took the unprecedented step of publicly announcing: 'We have found clear evidence of a wide network of illegal organ traffic. There are cases in which people have had their corneas and kidneys removed illegally.'

In one Argentinian hospital, in the northern city of Cordoba, Roberto Rueda, the judge leading the judicial investigation, said the medical files of some 200 patients showed 'clear evidence' they had been allowed to die prematurely to remove their organs.

The country's Health Ministry confirmed 'a substantial number of those organs will have been sold abroad. In Argentina, where some 6,000 patients every year require a transplant, and only a very few receive one or more replacement organs, there is no register that keeps track of organs removed for that purpose'.

Meanwhile, in a separate investigation, an Interpol alert remained in force, at the time of writing, for the arrest of Dr Florencia Sanchez, the Director of a mental hospital near Buenos Aires. The warrant states that he is 'accused of selling corneas and kidneys from patients, together with very large quantities of their blood'.

Judge Hector Heredia, leading the investigation, stated that the evidence 'shows that in the past ten years over 1,400 patients have disappeared from the hospital. We fear the great majority did so after being subjected to the mass removal of their organs'.

On the other side of the world, in Hong Kong, came the news that wealthy Chinese continued to travel to the mainland to receive human organs taken from executed criminals. The practice is carried out without the permission of the prisoners or their families, contravening an international convention against torture and other cruel, inhuman or degrading acts which China signed in 1986. The International League for Human Rights has repeatedly called for China to eliminate the practice. The appeals have, so far, been ignored.

In the latest available figures – for the year 1992 – China admits to having executed some 700 people, but Amnesty International believes the figure to be considerably higher. Most of those put to death were convicted criminals. But Asiawatch, the New York-based human rights organisation, has recorded the executions of forty-one people who participated in the pro-democracy demonstrations that led to the Tiananmen Square massacre of 1989.

The Chinese authorities have established a well-tried system in which the police inform hospitals in advance of any executions. Transplant patients are then alerted by telephone or fax that an organ will be available so that they can reach the transplant centres in time. Almost all of these are in the province of Guandong. The organs are removed according to a well-established ritual. The usual form of Chinese execution is a gunshot in the base of the skull. But human rights observers say executions are so planned that if, for instance, eyes are needed, prisoners are shot in the heart. The authorities also ensure that prisoners scheduled to have their organs removed are not tortured and are fed special diets. Immediately after execution, the prisoner's corpse is transferred to an adjoining OR where the organs are removed by a surgeon. The body is then disposed of and the organs taken to a transplant centre.

At the time of writing, the Nangfang hospital in Canton was the leading hospital for such transplant surgery. In 1993 it had performed, according to Asiawatch, over fifty such operations, mostly on overseas Chinese, from the United States and Britain. The hospital has a special medical wing for foreigners and advertises its unique service in the Chinese-language media.

A hospital spokesman told the *Sunday Times* of London, which revealed its activities, that there was nothing 'unethical' about the practice. 'These are criminals. What do you want their consent for when you are going to execute them? They might as well do something for other people with their organs.'

Dr Krishna Reddy, a leading tranplant surgeon in Madras, India expressed the following opinion: 'The rich are getting more desperate. More and more, medicine and greed have become unholy partners. There is, it must be said, an unholy alliance between Hippocrates and the underworld – and the underworld is winning.'

Can it be stopped? Or has fiction already become fact?

The question came into sharper focus in the closing days of December 1993, as this book was going to press. A television documentary, 'The Body Parts Business', produced by the distinguished Canadian film-maker, Judy Jackson, and narrated by Bruce Harris, the Latin-American director for Covenant House, the international child-care agency, was broadcast by the BBC. The contents were judged to be so disturbing that the film was shown outside peak viewing time. It documented the most impressive evidence so far of a global traffic in illegal human organs. It centred on Argentina, Honduras and Russia.

In many ways, the activities of the Organisation I created, were mirrored by the true-life activities of the organ hunters featured in the film. There were detailed case studies that could have come from the files of the Organisation: a fourteen-year-old paraplegic disappeared from an Argentinian psychiatric institute and his mutilated body was found minus its organs; an eight-year-old boy who had escaped from his captors in Tegucigalpa, the Honduran capital, described their dealing in human organs; in Moscow a forensic detective reported seeing in a city morgue unidentified bodies with their organs removed prior to death.

The doctors in the film report sounded every bit as terrifying as Dr Romer. And behind them all were shadowy figures who, in terms of their power and evil, more than equalled Madam. In so many ways the film was a rare example of fact imitating fiction.

Time magazine reinforced the horror depicted in the film in its 6 December 1993 issue, by revealing how a Moscow company – again reminiscent of the Organisation of these pages – had 'sold more than 18,000 thymus glands, 1,172 pairs of eyes and 3,000 pairs of testicular membranes since the collapse of the Soviet empire'. The organs were sold to Western outlets, supposedly for 'medical research' or for use in the cosmetic industry. The magazine concluded that it was 'time for the world to be outraged'.

In the interval between writing these words and their publication I have no doubt that further revelations concerning the traffic in human organs will prompt a similar outcry. But will it be heard? Acted upon? How many of you will say – here and now, after reading this book – that this exploitation must stop? On that answer, *your* answer, depends literally the lives of all those who continue to be victims of the organ hunters.